Akitada and the Way of Justice

THE AKITADA STORIES

I. J. Parker

I·J·P

Copyright 2011 by I. J. Parker

This book is a work of fiction. Names, characters, places, and incidents are the product of the author's imagination or used fictitiously. All rights reserved. No part of this publication may be reproduced or transmitted in any form or by any means, electronic or mechanical, without permission of the author or publisher.

Published 2013 by I.J.Parker and I·J·P Books,
428 Cedar Lane, Virginia Beach, VA. 23452.
http://www.ijparker.com

First published electronically 2011.

Cover design by I. J. Parker;
Cover images by Kawase Hasui;

AKITADA AND THE WAY OF JUSTICE/ I. J. Parker - 2nd Ed.
ISBN 978-1492890508

Praise for I. J. Parker and the Akitada series

"Akitada is as rich a character as Robert Van Gulik's intriguing detective, Judge Dee." *The Dallas Morning News*

"Readers will be enchanted by Akitada." *Publishers Weekly* Starred Review

"A brisk and well-plotted mystery with a cast of regulars who become more fully developed with every episode." *Kirkus*

"Parker's research is extensive and she makes great use of the complex manners and relationships of feudal Japan." *Globe and Mail*

"The fast-moving, surprising plot and colorful writing will enthrall even those unfamiliar with the exotic setting." *Publishers Weekly,* Starred Review

". . .the author possesses both intimate knowledge of the time period and a fertile imagination as well. Combine that with an intriguing mystery and a fast-moving plot, and you've got a historical crime novel that anyone can love." *Chicago Sun-Times*

"Parker's series deserves a wide readership."
Historical Novel Society

In Memory of Cathleen Jordan
who was the first to publish
the Akitada stories.

Contents

Foreword

"Akitada's First Case"   1

"The Incense Murders"   39

"Rain at Rashomon"   71

"Instruments of Murder"   99

"The Curio Dealer's Wife"   131

"The Master of Go"   147

"The New Year's Gift"   177

"The O-bon Cat"   211

"Moon Cakes"   251

"The Tanabata Magpie"   291

"Welcoming the Paddy God"   335

Foreword

The stories in this book were written over a number of years and in no particular order. By the time the first of them appeared in print in 1997, three of the Akitada novels were complete, and I had come to know Akitada very well. Though I keep the novels pretty much in sequence, I did not write the stories with any sort of order or chronology in mind. They were my chance to see Akitada at different times of his life, as the aging senior official, as the naïve youth, and also as the burdened man of middle age. "Akitada's First Case" thus was not really my first acquaintance with him. It wasn't even my first short story about him. Perhaps because it is a "coming-of-age" story, it brought me the Shamus award in 2000.

But readers like to have things properly sequenced and I like to watch him change over the years, and so I have arranged the stories chronologically in this collection. Akitada is barely twenty in "Akitada's First Case," and fifty in the last story, "Welcoming the Paddy God." In between lies a difficult and often troubled life that leaves its marks and shapes the man he is to become. I am not done with him. There are still great blanks in his life that must be filled, and I want to see him in his old age, looking back at his past and weighing the true importance of human experience.

As a detective (a job that did not exist in eleventh century Japan) he does not fit modern categories. "Akitada's First Case" was eligible for the Private Eye Writers Shamus award because, in this instance, he accepts payment for finding a missing girl. But he is just as likely to work from his position in the government, either in the Ministry of Justice or as a provincial governor or in some other official function. He also takes cases *pro bono* because they happen to come his way and his sense of justice or pity for the victims compels him. However, because of his legal training and his consistent personal interest in criminal affairs, he is never an "amateur detective."

A short story leaves little room for character development, so his private life—which plays an important role in the novels, is here often only touched upon. Similarly, his close associates, Tora and Seimei, and his wife Tamako, only make brief appearances. And the historical setting is more specific and narrow here: all the stories take place in eleventh century Kyoto and its immediate surroundings. The customs of the period usually focus on a seasonal and religious celebration, such as the New Year or the Festival of the Dead.

And now to the stories!

I. J. Parker,
November 5, 2011

AKITADA'S FIRST CASE

The events in the first story take place when Akitada is twenty. He is poor, very unsure of himself, plagued by a demanding mother, and bullied by his co-workers and his superior at the Ministry of Justice. Because he succeeds beyond his expectations in solving the disappearance of a young woman and bringing justice to her grieving father, he will pursue criminal investigation for the rest of his life. (This story won the Shamus award in 2000.)

Heian Kyo (Kyoto): 1008; during the Poem-Composing Month (August).

The sun had only been up a few hours, but the archives of the ministry were already stifling in the summer heat. A murky, oppressive air hung about the shelves of document boxes and settled across the low desks. These were normally occupied by scribes and junior clerks, but at the moment they were empty.

Akitada, having celebrated his twentieth birthday with friends the night before—an occasion which involved emptying a cup of wine each time one failed to compose an acceptable poem—had overslept and crept in the back way. Now he knelt at his desk, feeling sick and staring blindly at a dossier he was supposed to be copying. He winced when two of his fellow clerks, Hirosawa and Sanekana walked in, chattering loudly.

"Sugawara!" Hirosawa stopped in surprise. "Where did you come from? The minister's been asking for you. I wouldn't give much for your chances of keeping your position this time."

Sanekana, a pimply fat fellow, sniggered. "You should have seen his face," he announced gleefully. "He was positively gloating at the thought of getting rid of you. Better go to him quick!"

AKITADA AND THE WAY OF JUSTICE

Akitada blanched. He could not afford to lose his clerkship in the Ministry of Justice. It had been the only position offered to him when he graduated from the university. If only the minister had not formed such an instant dislike for him. Inexplicably, His Excellency, Soga Ietada, had found fault with everything Akitada had done until he had become too nervous to answer the simplest questions. As a result, the minister had banished him to the archives to do copy work alongside the scribes.

To make matters worse, his fellow clerks had recognized Akitada as a marked man and quickly disassociated themselves from him.

Akitada eyed Sanekana and Hirosawa dubiously. "I don't suppose you would cover for me?" he asked. "I might have stepped outside when you looked for me."

They burst into laughter.

With a sigh, Akitada rose.

His heart was beating wildly and his palms were sweating when he was shown into the great man's office with the painted screens of waterfowl, the lacquered document boxes, and the broad desk of polished cryptomeria wood. On the desk stood the porcelain planter with a perfect miniature maple tree, the bronze brazier with its enameled wine flask, and the ministerial seal carved from pale jade—all of them witnesses to Akitada's prior humiliations.

The minister was not alone. A thin elderly man in a neat, dark grey silk robe was kneeling on the cushion before the great man's table. "It is a matter of honor, Excellency, no, of life and death to me," he said, his voice uneven with suppressed emotion. "I have, as I explained, exhausted all other possibilities. Your Excellency is my last hope."

"Nonsense!" barked Soga Ietada. Being stout, he was sitting cross-legged at his ease, tapping impatient fingers on the polished surface of his desk. "You take it too seriously. Young women run away all the time. She'll show up one of these days, presenting you with a grandchild, no doubt."

The old man's back stiffened. He did not glance at Akitada, who hovered, greatly embarrassed, near the door. "You are mistaken," the man said. "My daughter left my home to enter the household of a nobleman. She would never engage in a fleeting, clandestine affair."

Soga raised his eyes to heaven, caught a glimpse of Akitada and glared, saying coldly to his guest, "As you say. I can only repeat that it is not in my power to assist you. I suggest you seek out this, er, nobleman. Now you must excuse me. My clerk is waiting to consult me on an urgent case."

Akitada's heart skipped a beat. Maybe it was not another reprimand after all. A case? Would he finally be given a case?

The older man bowed and rose. He left quickly, with only a passing glance at Akitada.

When the door closed, the minister's expression changed to one of cold fury. "And where were you this morning?" he barked.

Akitada fell to his knees and touched his forehead to the floor. "I . . . I was feeling ill," he stuttered. Well, that was the truth at least. His stomach was heaving and he swallowed hard, waiting for the storm to break over his head.

"No matter!" snapped the minister. "Your work has been unsatisfactory from the start. As you know, you came here on probation. Since you have proved inept at all but copying work and are now far behind in that, you cannot afford the luxury of ill health."

"Yes, your Excellency. I shall make up the time."

"No."

Akitada looked up and caught a smirk of satisfaction on Soga's face. "I assure your Excellency . . ." he began earnestly.

"I said 'no'!" thundered the minister. "Your time has run out. You may get your property and leave the ministry this instant." He slapped a pudgy hand on the document before him. "I have already drawn up the papers of dismissal. They spell out your gross inadequacies in detail."

"But . . ." Akitada sought frantically for some promise, some explanation which might sway the minister's mind, at least postpone his dismissal. "Your Excellency," he pleaded, "you may recall that I earned my position by placing first in the university examinations. Perhaps if I had been given some legal work, I might have proved satis . . ."

"How dare you criticize my decisions?" cried the minister. "It is a typical example of your poor judgment. I shall add a further adverse comment to my evaluation of your performance."

Akitada bowed wordlessly and left the room. He went straight to his desk, ignoring the curious eyes and whispers of Sanekana and Hirosawa, and gathered his things. These consisted of some writing implements and a few law books and were easily wrapped into a square of cloth, knotted, and tossed over one shoulder. Then he left the ministry.

Suffering under the humiliation of his dismissal, he did not pause to consider the full disaster—the fact that he would no longer draw the small salary which had kept rice in the family bowls and one servant in the house to look after his widowed mother and two younger sisters—until he had passed out of the gate of the Imperial City.

Then the thought of facing his mother with the news made his knees turn to water, and he stopped outside the gate. Lady Sugawara was forever reminding him of a son's duty to his family and complaining about his inadequate salary and low rank. What would she say now?

Before him Suzaku Avenue stretched into the distance. Long, wide, and willow-lined, it bisected the capital to become the great southern highway to Kyushu—and the world beyond.

He longed to keep walking, away from his present life, with his bundle of books and brushes. Somewhere someone must be in need of a young man filled with the knowledge of the law and a thirst for justice.

But he knew it was impossible. All appointments were in the hands of the central government, and besides he could not desert his family. A son's first duty was to his parents. He despaired of finding a clerkship in another bureau. If only there were someone, some man of rank, who would put in a good word for him, but Akitada was without helpful relatives or patrons of that sort.

He sat down on the steps of the gate, and put his head into his hands.

"Young man? Are you ill?"

Akitada glanced up. An elderly gentleman in a formal robe and hat regarded him with kindly interest. Belatedly recognition came. This was the man who had just been turned away by Soga, a fellow sufferer. Akitada rose and bowed.

"Are you not the young fellow who came in while I was with the minister?" the man asked.

"Yes." Akitada recalled the embarrassing subject under discussion and blushed. "I am very sorry, but I had been sent for."

"I know. But I thought you had an urgent case to talk over with the minister?"

Akitada blushed again. "I have been dismissed," he said.

"Oh."

A brief silence fell. Then the older man said sympathetically, "Well, it looks like we've both been dismissed. You look pretty low." He paused, studying Akitada thoughtfully, then added, "Maybe we can be of assistance to each other."

"How so?" Akitada asked dubiously.

The gentleman gestured for him to sit, then gathered the skirt of his gown and lowered himself to the step next to him. "I have lost a daughter and need someone to help me find her, someone who knows the law and can quote it to those who keep showing me the door. And you, I bet, could use the experience, not to mention a weekly salary and a generous reward?"

Akitada looked at the gentleman as the answer to a prayer. "I am completely at your service, sir," he said with fervent gratitude. "Sugawara Akitada is my name, by the way."

"Good. I am Okamoto Toson."

"Not the master of the imperial wrestling office?"

The modest man in the grey robe smiled ruefully. "The same. Let's go to my house."

Okamoto Toson lived in a small house which lay, surrounded by a garden, in a quiet residential street not far from the palace. He was a widower with two daughters. It was the younger who had disappeared so mysteriously.

Okamoto took him to a room which was, like the rest of the house, small, pleasant, and unpretentious. Yet Okamoto was known to be wealthy and he was well respected by nobility and commoners alike. He was a man of the people who had been drawn into the world of the great due to his knowledge of wrestling and his managerial ability.

The walls were covered with scrolls showing the rankings of wrestling champions, but one scroll was a painting of a court match with the nobles seated around the circle where two massive fighters in loincloths strove against one another. The emperor himself had attended and was enthroned under a special tent. Over toward one side of the picture, the artist had depicted the small figure of Okamoto himself.

Akitada wondered why the minister had dismissed such a man without giving him the slightest encouragement.

Okamoto's story was brief but strange. Recently widowed, he had been left with two young daughters. The older had taken over the running of the household, but the younger, Tomoe, was a dreamer who spent her time reading romantic tales and talking of noble suitors. Being apparently something of a beauty according to her father, whose face softened every time he spoke of her, she had attracted the eyes of a certain nobleman and permitted his secret visits—no doubt after the pattern of the novels she had read—and the man had convinced her to leave with him.

All this had taken place without the father's knowledge, and Okamoto was apologetic. Akitada gathered that the death of his wife had caused him to withdraw from all but court duties, and since his older daughter Otomi had run the household efficiently, he had seen no cause to worry.

It was, in fact, the older daughter who had reported her sister's elopement with a nameless nobleman.

At this point in the story, Okamoto excused himself to get his daughter Otomi. Akitada stared after him in dismay. Either the girl had been incredibly foolish or someone had played a very nasty trick on her. No member of the aristocracy would take a young woman as his official wife or concubine without her father's knowledge.

Okamoto returned with a pale, plain young woman in a house dress. He said, "This is my elder daughter, Otomi. Please ask her anything."

Akitada and the young woman bowed to each other. She went to kneel behind her father's cushion, her eyes downcast and her work-reddened hands folded modestly in her lap.

Akitada was unused to speaking to strange young women, but he tried. "Did you know that your sister had a . . . er . . . met someone?"

The young woman shook her head and said, "My sister did not confide in me. She is a foolish girl. She is always reading stories, and sometimes she makes them up. I did not think anything when she said she had fallen in love with a nobleman."

"You did not share a room?" Akitada asked, puzzled how a lover could have visited Tomoe without her sister's knowledge.

To his dismay, Otomi began to weep in harsh, racking sobs. Akitada shot a helpless look at Okamoto.

The older man smiled a little sadly. "Hush, Otomi!" he said, explaining, "The girls did not get along. Tomoe said her sister snored, and Otomi wanted her to stop reading by candlelight."

Otomi sniffled. "I think she just said those things because she wanted to be alone to receive this person. How could she go away with him like that in the middle of the night without a word to anyone! But my father has always allowed her to do whatever she wished."

Okamoto shook his head. "No, Otomi. You exaggerate." Turning to Akitada, he said, "This is really not like Tomoe. No good-by! Not so much as a letter! I am afraid the poor child has been abducted by a man who had no intention of treating her honorably. That is why we must find her." His short, stubby hands became fists. "This person of rank knew we are only ordinary people without learning and he thought it would be easy to fool us. You, being a young gentleman yourself, will understand much better than I the person who took my child. What do you think we should do? Please speak frankly. I shall not take offense. My child's life is precious to me."

Akitada hesitated. It crossed his mind that Tomoe had run off with some commoner, perhaps even a rich man's servant. He said awkwardly, "I do not want to worry you more, but I am wondering why the minister dismissed you. You are a highly respected man, and have had the honor of addressing His Majesty."

The older man looked uncomfortable. "I was a little surprised myself. Still, I am nobody. It is only my association with wrestling which brings me in contact with the 'good people.'"

Akitada turned back to the young woman. "I assume you never saw your sister's visitor. But perhaps she described him when she talked about him. Anything, the smallest detail, may help me to find him."

She nodded. "Tomoe said he looked exactly like Prince Genji. And that, like Prince Genji, he wore the most ethereal perfumes in his robes. Is there such a man among the great nobles?"

The question struck Akitada as incredibly naïve. He blurted out, "Prince Genji is a character in a novel."

"I thought so." Otomi's expression was almost triumphant. She reached into her sleeve and produced a crumpled bit of paper. "There," she said, extending it to Akitada. "She left this behind."

It was a poem, or rather a fragment: "By the pond the frogs sing in the branches of the fallen pine; / Let the two of us, like a pair of ducks, join their . . . " Either the author had been interrupted or had discarded a draft. But the brush strokes were elegant; both the calligraphy and style were those of a courtier. Apparently that much of Tomoe's story had been true.

Folding the paper, Akitada tucked it into his sleeve and said, "This may be some help." Okamoto's anxious eyes met his, and he felt great pity for the distraught father. "It is possible that the man was sincere in his feelings for your daughter," he said gently.

Okamoto regarded him fixedly. "He took Tomoe without my permission." When Akitada nodded, he laughed bitterly. "The poem is just a bit of verse, that's all. The fine gentleman dashed it off at a moment's notice to turn a poor girl's head."

Akitada said helplessly, "Well, I'll make inquiries. Can you describe your daughter to me?"

Okamoto tried, but tears rose to his eyes, and Otomi spoke for him.

"Tomoe is in her sixteenth year," she said, "but well grown and tall for her age. She has an oval face, her skin is very white, and her eyes are large. Tomoe's hair reaches to her ankles and is very thick. I brush it for her every day." Otomi compressed her lips before continuing, "In front of her left ear she has a small brown mark which looks like a little bug. She hates it and always wears her hair loose so it covers her ears." She gave Akitada a fierce look. "My sister is very beautiful. She looks nothing like me at all."

Okamoto shivered and wiped the moisture from his eyes. Immediately Otomi rose to get another robe and draped it around his shoulders solicitously. "You are tired, Father," she said. "I shall fetch a brazier of hot coals and some wine."

Embarrassed, Akitada rose, saying, "I am very sorry for your trouble and shall try to help."

Okamoto rose also, leaning on his daughter's arm. "Allow me," he said and pulled a slender, neatly wrapped package from his sleeve. "This is a token of my gratitude for your interest and will defray any immediate expenses."

Akitada accepted with a bow and took his departure, wondering why the girl Otomi looked so complacent, almost happy, as she stood beside her father.

His first visit was to the headquarters of the municipal police to see if there had been an accident involving a young woman. He was shown to an office where an harassed looking sergeant was bent over paperwork. Akitada sat down and waited.

"Of all the things to happen!" the sergeant muttered to himself. "And the coroner is sick! Heaven only knows if I got this right. No names, he says. How is a man to file a report without names, I ask you."

Akitada leaned forward. "A troublesome case?" he asked.

The sergeant looked up. "Oh. Sorry, sir. Didn't realize you were there." A puzzled frown, then a tentative smile. "Haven't I seen you in the Ministry of Justice?"

Akitada bowed slightly. "Sugawara Akitada," he introduced himself. "Junior clerk."

"Right! Yes, we've got a nameless suicide. And the report was brought in by a nameless citizen." He looked over his shoulder, then leaned forward to whisper, "It's all very hush-hush. Your boss talking to my boss. Actually it was the captain of the palace guard."

"Ah!" nodded Akitada. He asked in a whisper, "Masahira or Morikawa?" There was a right guard and a left guard of the palace.

"Masahira," mouthed the sergeant. He continued in a normal tone, "I've been told to file a report without names; just the 'unfortunate female victim' and the 'person who made the discovery.' On top of that we don't have a coroner's report. All I know is the girl was dead when we pulled her from the water."

A girl! Akitada became alert. "Perhaps," he offered, "I could be of assistance. I am not a coroner, but I learned a little forensic medicine when I was a student at the university."

The sergeant was relieved. "If you wouldn't mind taking a look," he said, getting to his feet. "Just a bit of the jargon and I can finish my report. We've got her in the back room."

The back room was a barren space, dim with the shutters closed, and contained nothing but a covered body on a mat. A faint smell of rotted vegetation hung in the air. The sergeant threw open the shutters, then pulled back the straw mat which covered the corpse.

Akitada held his breath. He saw the face first, and felt an almost physical pain that someone so young and beautiful should be forever lost to the world. Slender brows arched over eyes shaded by thick lashes, now wet against the pale cheeks. The small nose and softly rounded lips were almost childlike in their freshness and innocence. She looked asleep, and like a sleeping child, she touched a hidden desire to cherish and protect.

Too late! The long hair, matted with mud and rank vegetation, stuck to her skin, was tangled in the clammy folds of her fine silk clothes (lovely rose colors shading all the way to the palest blushing skin tone), and reached to her small, slender hands and feet. There was so much hair, so many layers of wet silk that she seemed to be wrapped in them as in a strange pink and black cocoon.

Akitada knelt beside her, feeling strangely reverent, his eyes on her face. He saw no marks on her except for a thin red line high on her neck beneath the jaw. It disappeared under her hair. He extended a hand, almost apologetically, and brushed aside a strand that covered her right ear.

There it was, a dainty dark brown mark, no bigger than an orange seed. According to her sister, it had worried her, but Akitada thought it most beautiful, this small imperfection in the otherwise perfect face of the girl Tomoe.

"Oh," he murmured, overcome with pity and regret. The puzzle had turned into something far more real that touched him deeply.

The thin red line widened and deepened just below the ear but did not continue around her neck. It was recent. Whatever had caused it had not been strangulation, though something might have been put around her neck and then jerked backward.

"What is it?" asked the sergeant. "Anything out of the ordinary?"

She was everything out of the ordinary to Akitada's mind, but he asked, "Did she have anything around her neck?"

"No. Well, was it suicide or what?"

"What makes you think it was suicide?"

"My boss told me it was. He said she left a letter or something before drowning herself."

Akitada sighed. It was too likely that Tomoe had written a tragic love letter. If Masahira was the lover, he was beyond her reach. He looked at the lovely silent face before him. A young romantic girl would have found the noble captain irresistible. Masahira was in his late thirties and one of the most handsome men at court. All the empress's ladies in waiting were said to be in love with him. For all that, Masahira had had an excellent reputation up to now. Married to a daughter of the chancellor, he had never been rumored to have affairs or even flirtations. If he was indeed the man, Tomoe must have seen him at one of the wrestling contests held in the palace. He would be in attendance, riding at the head of the imperial guard, resplendent in golden armor shining in the sunlight and seated on a prancing steed.

"Well?" urged the sergeant. "Shouldn't you take off her clothes?"

Akitada recoiled from the suggestion. Instead he gently opened her lips and felt inside. He pulled out a fragment of a water plant and some wet dirt. "She drowned," he told the sergeant. "The fact that she swallowed water mixed with vegetation and pond mud proves that she was alive when she fell in."

"Ah," nodded the sergeant. "I shall put it in my report."

Akitada turned her head and felt the skull, moving the wet hair aside from the skin. On her left temple he found a bruise, slightly swollen and discolored. Her hair had become glued to the scalp and as he pulled it loose the tips of his fingers came away red.

The sergeant peered. "Must've banged her head when she went in."

Akitada looked up. "Not if she committed suicide. She would have walked into the water. Unless she jumped from a high place and hit some obstruction. Where was she found?"

"She didn't jump. It was just a murky garden pond full of frogs."

Frogs! Akitada was momentarily distracted by the memory of the poem. He asked, "Was the water deep?"

"No. It only came to my hips."

Akitada looked at the sergeant. "Would you drown yourself in that? Where was this place?"

"Small villa in the western part. You know how things are over there. It's pretty much deserted. She was staying there by herself. Not even a servant. If you ask me, it was your typical love nest."

"Whose house?"

The sergeant cast up his eyes and grinned. "Ah! Your guess is as good as mine. The chief says it's immaterial. She committed suicide. Case closed."

"But what about her family?"

"We'll post a notice! If anybody missed her, they can claim the body." The sergeant looked worried suddenly. "It *is* suicide, isn't it? Or . . . an accident?"

"You mean, could she have run into something with her head and fallen in the water? I don't know. You will have to show me the place."

The sergeant frowned. "Aren't you first going to look at the rest of her?"

Reluctantly Akitada checked the small hands, the dainty feet in their white silk socks. Both were unmarked except by muddy water. Then he straightened her clothes gingerly. The dampness made the silk cling to her skin, outlining high, small breasts, a narrow waist, and delicately rounded hips and thighs. In spite of himself, Akitada felt the blood rise warmly to his face and looked away in self-disgust. Turning the body on its side, he found a long tear in the back of the outer gown. A sharp, thorny branch was caught in the hem, and the silk showed streaks of dirt and many small rips.

"Did you or the constables drag the body along the ground?" he asked the sergeant.

"No. Two of us scooped her out of the water and laid her on the mat she's on now. She weighed very little, even with all the water."

Akitada gently laid Tomoe on her back again, plucking at the layers of silk until she looked more decently covered. Then he rose.

"I am afraid, Sergeant, that this young person was murdered."

The sergeant turned first red than white. "No!" he said. "I can't put that in my report. I don't care what you think you saw, it can't be murder. The chief said *suicide.*"

Akitada shook his head. "It's murder," he said stubbornly. "She was knocked unconscious and then dragged to the water and drowned. Now let us go to this villa and see what we can find out."

The sergeant looked panic-stricken. "Are you mad? You shouldn't even be here. Come on." Taking Akitada's arm, he pulled him out of the room and locked the door after them.

"Now," he said as they were standing outside, "you'd better go home and forget all about this."

Akitada gave him a long look, then said, "As you wish," and walked away.

The sergeant stood and watched him turn the corner, wondering belatedly what Akitada's business had been.

Lord Masahira occupied his family mansion on the corner of Kitsuji and Nishidoin avenues. It was a large, generously staffed establishment, and Akitada had considerable difficulty being admitted. The man he was about to meet was a favorite with the emperor and related by marriage to the chancellor. That gave him the sort of power which would make even Soga grovel. No wonder the minister had dismissed Okamoto without the slightest encouragement. No wonder he had used his influence to keep Masahira's name out of the investigation. They were covering up a murder.

Akitada saw again the still face of the dead girl and the pain in her father's eyes, and a hot anger against Masahira filled his heart. He had known at the police station that he could not tell Okamoto of his daughter's murder without at least identifying her killer first. And Masahira was the most likely choice.

The handsome captain of the imperial guard was in a small garden enclosed by the walls of several buildings. He was sitting on the edge of the wooden veranda and had Akitada's visiting card in his hand. Glancing up, he said, "You are Sugawara from the Ministry of Justice?"

Akitada bowed deeply. He knew he was in the presence of one of the first nobles of the land but was much too angry to prostrate himself. Considering the collusion between this man and the minister, he also did not feel obligated to go into long explanations of his status.

When he raised his head, he saw to his surprise that the man before him had red-rimmed eyes and looked as if he had not slept. Beside him, on the polished boards, stood an untouched tray of food.

"Well? What does Soga want?" Masahira asked curtly.

If the minister found out about this visit, he would see to it that Akitada never worked again in any imperial office. On the other hand, Masahira's question proved that he had recently consulted Soga about Tomoe's murder. Righteous disgust gave Akitada the strength to continue.

"I am here on behalf of Okamoto Tosan," he corrected Masahira. "He has asked for my unofficial assistance in locating his daughter Tomoe. Perhaps I should explain first that I have just come from police headquarters where I have seen the body of his unfortunate child."

A slight flush appeared on Masahira's pale face. "I see," he said tonelessly. "Well? I was under the impression that the matter was being handled by Soga. Is it money the old man wants? How much? Come on! Let's get it over with."

Akitada stiffened, remembering the grief and worry of Okamoto. "It is not a matter of money, and the young woman's father is not yet aware that she is dead," he said coldly.

"Oh?" Masahira waited.

Heavens, did the man think this was a blackmail attempt? Akitada flushed with fresh anger. "I shall, of course, report to him," he said quickly, "but I came to you first because I hoped that you might wish to see him yourself to explain what happened."

Masahira turned away. "No. You may tell Okamoto that I am responsible for what happened and that my life means nothing to me now. I am at his disposal if he desires to discuss the affair or avenge his honor."

Akitada was thunder-struck. He had expected fury, denial, bluster, but certainly not this quick admission of guilt. He looked at the man's back and wavered in his estimation. The broad shoulders sagged and his neck, bent, looked vulnerable for all its strong muscles and neatly brushed glossy black hair. But he could not afford to feel sympathy. Masahira was, at the very least, a sly seducer of innocent young women, at worst a heartless killer.

"I am afraid, it is not going to be that simple," he said, "not in a case of murder."

Masahira spun around. "What? Murder? She drowned herself. Because she thought I had deserted her."

"No. Someone knocked her unconscious, dragged her to the pond, and drowned her." Akitada outlined his observations of the evidence.

Masahira ran his hands through his hair. "It cannot be. Here! He fished a piece of paper from inside his robe. Read for yourself!"

The letter was still warm from lying next to Masahira's skin. Akitada unfolded it and read the childlike characters. "I cannot bear this lonely place any longer. I think you do not want me and will leave me to die alone. How could I ever have believed you? My sleeves are wet with tears. Soon they will be wetter still."

"Tomoe wrote this?" Akitada asked, returning it.

Masahira nodded. "I blame myself entirely. I should not have left her alone there. She told me she was frightened and begged me to stay. When I refused . . ." He turned away.

"You could have taken her back to her father," Akitada offered, his anger melting rapidly along with his suspicions.

"You don't understand." Masahira's voice broke. "I loved her." He put both hands over his face. "I could not bear to give her up."

"Then why did you not bring her here and legitimize the relationship," Akitada asked. "A man in your position is expected to have secondary wives."

Masahira turned and looked at him bleakly from moist eyes. "I meant to. In fact, I was preparing my household to receive her when it happened," he said stiffly.

Akitada digested this information and decided to accept it. "Regardless of the letter, which is ambiguous at best, someone killed her," he said at last.

Before Masahira could respond, the door opened and a tall, handsome woman entered. Her robes were costly, and her glossy black hair swept the floor behind her, but her features were thin and pinched. Lady Chujo, Masahira's wife and the chancellor's oldest daughter. When she saw Akitada, she gave him a sharp, appraising look before addressing her husband.

"I apologize if I am interrupting, husband," she said in the soft, nasal tones of the upper classes. "I wished to know if there is any news."

"My wife," introduced Masahira. "My dear, this is Sugawara Akitada. He has come from Okamoto Toson about Tomoe." To Akitada he said, "My wife is aware of the tragedy, but not, of course, of the fact that murder is suspected."

"Murder?" Lady Chujo's eyes flicked over Akitada without interest. "Impossible! My husband found the letter the unfortunate young woman wrote before walking into the pond. I suppose her father must be distraught. It is only natural. But you must convince him that he is wrong about this and that it is absolutely essential the unpleasantness be handled discreetly. Naturally you will also give him our condolences."

Akitada took an instant dislike to the woman. An unpleasantness, was it? To be resolved by a message of condolence? Aloud he said, "Madam, Tomoe's father is not yet aware of her death nor of her connection with your husband. I came here because explanations had better come from Lord Masahira."

The proud head came up and the lady stared Akitada in the eye. "Impossible," she said again. "A man in my husband's position cannot be expected to deal with such low-bred notions. The girl was a foolish child frightened by hobgoblins and fox spirits. I am certain the proper authorities will rule her death a suicide."

Masahira interrupted at this point. "Did you say Okamoto did not know she went with me? But Tomoe wrote him a letter before she left with me."

A letter? Here was another puzzle. Of course there was only her sister's word for the fact that Tomoe had left without notice. What if Otomi had known all along where Tomoe was?

Aloud he said, "He did not . . . does not know. He only suspects that Tomoe was lured away by a man of high rank. It was the sergeant at the police building who told me that you had reported her death."

Lady Chujo said irritably, "They should make certain such people can be trusted not to blab confidential matters to every curiosity seeker!" She glared at Akitada who was once again reminded of his own precarious position. A word from Lady Chujo to her father, and Akitada could find himself banished to the island of exiles in the far north.

He bowed and said apologetically, "Forgive me, but I was merely carrying out Mr. Okamoto's instructions." With brilliant inspiration, he added, "He is very distraught. No doubt the tragedy, when it becomes generally known, will win him much sympathy from his many friends and supporters."

Lady Chujo looked thoughtful, and her husband said quickly, "Yes, of course. I had better go and explain. Though I still don't understand how he could have been so completely in the dark. I made no secret of my intentions to Tomoe. It is unfortunate that the empty villa frightened her, but I thought that the young women would arrange for someone to stay with her."

The young women? So Otomi had known!

"Indeed," cried Lady Chujo. "My husband was making even more generous arrangements for her, when she panicked. He was bringing her here. But, being a most superstitious person—one of those who are forever muttering spells and buying silly amulets against Heaven knows what—she simply went mad with fright." Lady Chujo was warming to her subject. "If she did not drown herself, then she ran into the water out of fear. It was an accident. It is really no one's fault, but the silly girl's."

Masahira said unhappily, "Don't! Tomoe was not silly. She was very sweet and very young. I should have looked after her better."

Lady Chujo bit her lip. She was clearly tired of the subject. Her eyes fell on the tray of food. "You have not eaten," she said. "Let me get some hot food. This dreadful incident will make you ill, and you know you are on duty tomorrow for the emperor's birthday."

"I am not hungry," Masahira said with a grimace, but she went to pick up the tray anyway. She left the room, scented robes and long hair trailing, without so much as a nod to Akitada.

"I do not wish to trouble you any longer, sir," Akitada said nervously, "but could you direct me to your villa?"

Masahira sighed and rose. "Come! I will take you myself. If you are right about its being murder, it would be a terrible thing, but at least I would not feel that Tomoe killed herself because of me."

Akitada had not expected the offer or the sentiment from such a powerful man and was surprised again.

They rode—Masahira had superb horses—and crossed the city quickly. In the western district, they entered an almost rural setting. There were few villas and some, now abandoned, had become overgrown with vegetation. Empty lots were covered with tall meadow grass which was alive with rabbits and deer. They passed a few small temples, their steep pagodas rising above the trees, but the streets were mere dirt tracks and the bridges, which crossed small rivers and canals, were dilapidated.

Yet here and there, in the midst of the desolation, a few secluded mansions and villas survived, their rustic fencing in good repair, and the thatched roofs mended. Masahira stopped at one of these, dismounted, and unlatched the gate.

At that moment, a curious figure detached itself from the shadows of the large willow tree at the street corner and walked toward them.

At first glance, the scrawny man appeared to be a monk. He was dressed in a stained and worn saffron robe, his head was shaven, and the wooden begging bowl, dangling from the hemp rope about his skinny middle, bounced with every shuffling step he took. When he reached them, he stopped and stared slack-jawed and with vacant eyes. Akitada saw that he wore several small wooden tablets with crude inscriptions around his neck.

"He's just a mendicant," said Masahira. "They live in small temples around here." He tossed a few copper coins to the man, while Akitada rode into the courtyard. Dismounting, he glanced over his shoulder at the beggar, who had not picked up the money, but was still standing, staring foolishly after them until Masahira closed the gate.

They were in a small courtyard of a charming house in the old style, all darkened wood and sweeping thatched roof.

Akitada looked curiously about him. A stone path led to the front door and then continued around the side of the house to what must be the garden. The cicadas were singing their high-pitched song in the trees.

Inside there was only one large room, but this had been furnished luxuriously with screens, thick mats, silk bedding, and lacquered clothes chests. There was also an assortment of amusements suitable for an aristocratic young lady. A zither lay next to a beautiful set of writing implements, games rested beside several novels and picture books, and a set of cosmetics and combs accompanied an elegant silver mirror. Three tall wooden racks were draped with gowns of silk and brocade in the most elegant shades and detailing, and Akitada counted no less than five fans scattered about. In the short time since she had left her father's house, Tomoe had been spoiled by her noble lover. He looked around for evidence of the sister's having been here, but found nothing.

Masahira wandered dazedly about the room, touching things. He brushed a hand over one of the gowns, then picked up a fan, looked at it, and let it drop again. "Well?" he asked.

"I understand that you could not spend much time with Tomoe," said Akitada, "but I have been wondering why she did not have at least a servant for companion?"

"There was a need for secrecy at first. I wished to keep the affair from my household. Tomoe herself insisted that she needed no one. But, as I said, I thought surely her sister . . ." he passed a hand over his face, "at any event, she became fearful. The foxes make strange sounds at night. She was not used to it. She developed a fear that I might meet with an accident and never return. She had dreadful dreams. One day I found her nearly incoherent. That was when I decided to bring her into my home." He sighed deeply. "Too late."

Akitada looked around the room distractedly. This had been the second reference Masahira had made to the sister. Had Otomi known of this place? If so, why had she lied? In his mind's eye, he saw again the complacent look on the plain girl's face as she stood beside her father and said, "My sister is very beautiful."

He became aware of the fact that Masahira was looking at him and asked, "May I see the pond now? And perhaps you could tell me how you came to find her body."

Masahira nodded. He led the way into the garden. They followed the stepping stones through dense shrubbery, but trees and weeds had grown up around the path and brushed and tore at their clothes. All around them the cicadas sang, pausing as they passed and resuming again a moment later.

"I had gone home to speak to my wife about Tomoe," said Masahira, holding a branch aside for Akitada. "To my surprise, she was immediately receptive to the idea. You must understand that I have no other women, and my wife is childless. She confessed that she looked forward to raising my children by Tomoe, and to having her companionship. Overjoyed, I returned the next day to tell Tomoe." He fell abruptly silent.

The stepping stones only went as far as a stone lantern. Here Masahira turned right. "The pond is this way," he said. His voice shook a little. In a distance, Akitada could hear frogs croaking. There was no sign of foxes, but the dense shrubbery rustled with animal life.

They emerged from the trees. The pond lay before them, basking in the hot sun.

"When I got to the house, it was empty," Masahira said, staring at the still water with a shiver. "I was puzzled, for I knew Tomoe was afraid of the garden, but eventually I went to search for her there. I almost turned around when I got to the pond without seeing her."

The pond was shaped like a gourd, and they stood near its widest end. Up ahead, where it narrowed, a small bridge arched across a dense growth of water lilies and lotus. Clouds of small gnats hung low over the water, and dragonflies skimmed the surface. The sound of the cicadas was less strident here, but the atmosphere of the pond, stagnant in the summer heat and choked with vegetation, embraced them like a suffocating shroud.

Masahira pointed to a thorny shrub near the path. "I saw a small piece of silk there and knew she had come this way. That was when I went to look in the water." He walked forward to the muddy edge and stared down. "She was here."

AKITADA AND THE WAY OF JUSTICE

Akitada joined him. The water was brown but not deep. He could see the muddy bottom, pitted here and there by the feet of the sergeant and his constable. A huge silver carp appeared, rose briefly to look at them and sank again. Other fish, fat, their colors dull grey and copper in the muddy water, shifted lazily across the mud, and a large frog, suddenly conscious of their presence, jumped in with a splash and swam away. In this neglected garden, human beings were the intruders.

Masahira said, "She could have slipped and fallen. But I cannot imagine what would have brought her out here."

Akitada glanced across to where a fallen pine projected over the water. "There are the foxes," he said.

Two young cubs had climbed up and looked at them curiously. Masahira cursed, clapping his hands sharply. The cubs yelped and ran. A moment later their mother appeared, a handsome vixen with a long bushy tail, her ears pointed and her sharp nose twitching to catch their scent.

Masahira clapped again, but the fox stood her ground. "They behave as if they owned this place," he complained. "I shall have workmen clean up this wilderness and drain the pond." He turned abruptly and walked back.

Akitada stayed another moment, looking at the fox. Then he also turned to go.

What had happened here? He no longer suspected Masahira. It was clear that he had loved the girl and had made arrangements to bring her into his family. Who then? The envious sister? A jealous lover? Or a stranger, some vagrant coming across the lonely girl? The image of the scarecrow monk flashed into his mind, and he hurried after Masahira.

He caught up with him in the house and asked, "That beggar outside the gate, do you know him?"

Masahira was surprised. "Yes. He is one of the monks in a small temple a short distance away. Why do you ask?"

Akitada, with the certainty of conviction, said, "He looked deranged. I think he got in and attacked Tomoe." Masahira shook his head, but Akitada added quickly, "Perhaps she caught him stealing. He could have picked up something and knocked her out." Looking around the room, he pounced on an iron candlestick, examined it and put it back disappointedly. Next he picked up the heavy silver mirror. "Yes," he cried. "I see a dent here and . . ." He dashed out into the sunlight with it, squinting at the rim. "There!" he shouted triumphantly. "Do you see it? That is a drop of blood and a long hair is stuck to it. This was used to knock her out. Now do you believe me?"

Masahira came to look and nodded. "Yes," he said sadly. "You must be right, but the man has always been quite gentle. He has never hurt a living thing. He is not very bright and sells talismans that the other monks inscribe with spells against demons."

"Of course," said Akitada. "Fox magic. He knocked at the door, and when Tomoe opened, he offered her one of his charms. I suppose they are those wooden tablets he had around his neck. Then he saw all these fine things and no one to watch them but a young, delicate lady. He helped himself and, when Tomoe protested, they struggled, and he hit her with the mirror. He thought she was dead and decided to hide the body in the pond."

Masahira frowned. "Could not someone else . . .?"

"No, no. It all fits," cried Akitada, rushing out. "Let us go back and tell the police.

When they reached the police building, the sergeant was talking to Okamoto Toson, who had finally come to report his daughter missing, and had ended up identifying Tomoe's body.

An uncomfortable scene ensued.

Okamoto's eyes went from Akitada to Lord Masahira. He recognized him instantly and prostrated himself. Masahira went to help him up, whispering something in his ear. Okamoto stiffened, then nodded.

Masahira turned back to Akitada, saying in a tight voice, "Perhaps it will be best if you leave things to me now."

Akitada looked at Okamoto.

The old man was very pale, but he nodded. "Lord Masahira is right. You have done your part and quickly, too. If you will excuse me now and allow me some time to mourn and bury my child, I shall reward your efforts in a day or two."

Akitada flushed with embarrassment. He stammered that nothing was owed, that he was sorry to have brought no better news, and left as quickly as he could.

He slept poorly that night. Something kept nagging at him. When he finally fell asleep, he dreamt of foxes. At one point, the vixen appeared on the fallen pine.

She raised herself on her hind legs and paraded back and forth, dragging her tail behind like the skirts of a long robe, making a strange snickering noise. Then the fox's black eyes and pointed muzzle changed into the sharp features of Lady Chujo, who laughed, baring her fangs. He sat bolt upright, staring at the stripes made by the sunlight falling through the closed shutters of his room.

Stripes . . . lines . . . the thin, red line on Tomoe's neck . . . the monk selling amulets . . . charms against fox spirits. Of course. The frightened Tomoe had bought one and she had worn it before her death. Someone, the murderer, had torn it off her and had caused the red line on her neck.

Amulets! Lady Chujo had mentioned Tomoe's belief in amulets. How had she known?

Akitada threw on his clothes and ran to police headquarters. A yawning sergeant was just sitting down when Akitada burst into the office.

"That monk," cried Akitada. "Did you arrest him?"

The sergeant's mouth fell open again. He nodded.

"What did he say? Did he visit the girl?"

The sergeant nodded again.

"Well?"

The sergeant closed his mouth and sighed. "It's too early," he said reprovingly, "for so many questions, sir. However, the man absolutely denies killing the girl. He sold her a charm, that's all, he says. Of course, we can still beat him and get a confession that way, but Lord Masahira has asked us not to."

Thank God for Masahira, thought Akitada. He, Akitada, had made a terrible mistake. He asked, "Did he say when he sold her the charm?"

"Yes. The day before we found her." The sergeant shook his head. "It didn't do her much good."

"The monk is innocent. You must let him go."

The sergeant raised his brows. "On whose say-so?"

Akitada's spirits sank. He knew now who the killer was, but he would never prove it. No doubt the poor monk would be beaten into some form of confession and then condemned to forced labor at some distant frontier. And all of it was Akitada's fault. He had been wrong about the identity of the murderer three times. He had lost his job, failed Okamoto and Tomoe, and added the burden of guilt to his other miseries.

He went to see Lord Masahira.

Recalling too late that it was the emperor's birthday, Akitada fully expected to be turned away. Instead he was admitted instantly to face who knew what additional disaster.

He found the captain, dressed in the grey robe of mourning, standing on the veranda of his study. He held something in his hand and was staring at it fixedly.

The face he turned towards Akitada was drawn and white. Today Masahira looked old beyond his years, and Akitada was about to intrude into the man's grief with a dangerous knowledge. Reminding himself of the vacant-eyed monk in police custody, Akitada stammered, "Forgive the interruption, sir, but I have reconsidered the facts and I now know the monk is innocent.

He merely sold one of his charms to Tomoe. It was the day before her body was found. I . . . believe someone else . . ." He broke off fearfully.

"Yes." Masahira's voice was flat, his eyes weary. "So you know what really happened?"

Hanging his head, Akitada murmured, "I believe so. Your lady . . ." He broke off. "I am very sorry, sir."

Masahira sighed heavily. "No sorrier than I. I am responsible, even though I did not kill Tomoe. It was my foolishness that caused the tragedy. A double tragedy. I thought my wife was too accommodating when I asked her if I could bring Tomoe here. I should have suspected." Masahira's voice was bitter. "I found this in my wife's writing box!"

Akitada glanced up. Masahira dangled a small wooden tablet with an inscription. The hemp string was broken.

The amulet.

"Lady Chujo must have gone to the villa after you told her," said Akitada. "She mentioned the amulet, but Tomoe had just bought it from the monk, and not even you could have known that."

Masahira said, "I did not." He added heavily, "My wife will not be arrested. But she has agreed to renounce the world and spend the rest of her life in a remote nunnery. The monk will be released, of course, but I must ask your discretion. I already have Okamoto's."

Akitada thought again of the dangerous ground he had trodden. Deeply grateful, he bowed. "Of course, my Lord. I only regret having brought such misfortune to you and your family."

Masahira waved this aside. "Okamoto is a most admirable character." He paused to look at Akitada. "I think," he said, "that, whatever your motives were originally, you acted from concern for him and pity for . . ." his voice shook, but he went on, "his daughter. You were quite right in your feelings about both." He broke off abruptly and turned away, weeping.

Akitada was backing from the room, when Masahira spoke again. His voice had regained the tone of authority. "About your position at the ministry. I have had a word with Soga. You are to return to work immediately."

The Incense Murder

Akitada's relationship with his mother deteriorates rapidly until he comes to regard her with bitter resentment and suspicion even while he struggles to obey and serve her—a state of affairs which will darken his life until her death a decade later. This story introduces Kobe, a captain in the Imperial Police, who will reappear in many of Akitada's cases.

Heian-Kyo (Kyoto): 1010; during the Clothes-Lining Month (March).

On a gray spring morning in a week of cold, drizzling rains, Akitada was summoned by his mother. Their relationship was strained at the best of times, but on this occasion she would get him involved in a case that was not only deeply disturbing but nearly ended his career and perhaps his life. He would forever after fear dealings with his parent.

But that morning, unsuspecting, he walked along the covered gallery and saw that the roof had sprung another leak. He expected to be told to fix it and sighed. They had no money to spend on workmen and no servants able to carry out the heavy work.

Lady Sugawara was at her morning devotions, kneeling and bowing before the small Buddha statue on a shelf in her room. Akitada sat down to wait and looked around. At least the roof was solid here. The house might be falling down around their ears, but his mother's quarters would remain as comfortable as ever. She would not have it any other way.

She made her final bow and turned. "Ah! Akitada, I want you to go to your Cousin Koremori."

Otomo Koremori was a cousin on Akitada's mother's side and no connection to the Sugawaras, a fact for which Akitada was grateful. Koremori was past fifty now, a wealthy man who had married well, and a recent widower. Since he had lost his only son Akemori in a duel a few years before and was now childless, Akitada's mother had initiated more cordial relations. She expected Koremori to leave his property to her or to her children when he died. Koremori knew it and behaved accordingly. Akitada could not abide Koremori.

He said, "I cannot go immediately, Mother. I am due at the Ministry."

His mother raised her brows. "Nonsense. Why should you not make time for a close family member? Please remember who you are."

AKITADA AND THE WAY OF JUSTICE

What he was was a junior clerk in the Ministry of Justice and in enough trouble already. "I could go after work, Mother," he said reluctantly.

She frowned. "Very well, but don't forget again like last time. I want you to take him this fan. He admired it the last time he was here. Tell him it's a small present to cheer him up. Oh, and write a suitable card for it."

The fan was his mother's favorite and dated back to better times. That she was willing to part with it meant she was embarking on a new campaign to influence Koremori's final arrangements.

Akitada took the fan, bowed to his mother, and retreated.

That evening Akitada arrived at the Otomo residence, feeling resentful. The weather had worsened. Wet, cold, and tired from an unprofitable day in the archives, he did not look forward to this visit and hoped to make it a short one.

Koremori sat behind a large desk in an elegantly furnished study. Handsome shades were lowered to keep the room cozy, and silk cushions awaited guests. Above him hung a scroll with the admonition: "Remember your duty to past and future generations." When the servant admitted Akitada, he looked up and stared at Akitada with his usual unpleasant expression.

As a child, Akitada had thought of him as a fat toad because of his bulbous eyes and broad face. Today he looked more than usually toad like.

"Oh, it's you," Koremori said ungraciously and gestured toward a cushion.

Akitada sat down and sniffed the air. The room reeked. The smell was not unpleasant, just powerful. Some of the redolence came from his cousin's perfumed robe. Sandalwood and cloves. But other scents mingled, and Akitada saw that a table held preparations for an incense guessing game.

This game was an aristocratic pursuit in which the participants submitted their own concoctions anonymously, then guessed the ingredients, and chose a winner for the best fragrance. Akitada disapproved of such waste of money, time, and intelligence.

He bowed and said stiffly, "My mother sent me, Cousin. She recalled that you admired this trifling object on your last visit and asked me to present it to you." He took the fan from his sleeve and passed it to Koremori.

Koremori's wide mouth twitched. He glanced briefly at the words Akitada had written on his visiting card and attached to the gift, then laid fan and note aside.

"Tell your mother I am obliged for her thoughtful present." He stared at Akitada. "So. Still a clerk in the Ministry, are you?"

"Yes, Cousin. I hope I see you well?"

"Never better." Koremori's lip twitched again. "Be sure to tell your mother. She takes a great interest in my health."

Akitada felt himself flush. Koremori never missed an opportunity to make him feel small and his mother mercenary.

Koremori added, "Apart from her ill-advised marriage, she has always shown proper family feeling."

AKITADA AND THE WAY OF JUSTICE

Akitada did not consider himself related to Koremori. He was a Sugawara. Though innocent, his most famous forebear had been found guilty of treason and had died in political exile to the subsequent ruin of his descendants. Akitada reminded himself, as always, that he had nothing in common with Koremori, either in their values or appearance. Akitada, tall and as slender as a whip, regarded Koremori's short, fat body as just punishment for over-eating and indolence. His cousin's luxurious lifestyle was, to Akitada's youthful idealism, immoral and indecent. But remembering his mother, he suppressed his anger and said nothing.

Instead he averted his eyes from the offensive Koremori to look around the room and he noticed the incense table again.

A man given to excess in everything from family pride to fine food, Otomo Koremori was a connoisseur and passionate practitioner of the incense cult. He spared no expense in this pursuit and was counted among the most knowledgeable experts on exotic ingredients.

The paraphernalia on the table included packets of incense in neatly labeled envelopes or twists of expensive papers. The lacquer ware utensils were dusted with gold and silver and inlaid with mother-of-pearl. Small ladles of silver and gold lay beside burners of gilded bronze.

Koremori suddenly clapped his hands and shouted, "Out, vile creature!"

Akitada jumped, but his cousin was not addressing him. Flushed with anger, he rose to throw his ink stone at a small black and white kitten. The stone brushed the little animal, which squealed and scurried under the desk. Koremori scanned the room.

Akitada said quickly, "It's only a kitten."

"I hate cats. Is it gone?"

"It's gone," Akitada lied. From the corner of his eye, he saw the kitten emerge and stretch a tentative paw for his red paper card that dangled from the edge of Koremori's desk.

Koremori sat down again. He clearly wanted Akitada gone as much as Akitada wanted to leave. Both tried to find the appropriate words. Koremori said, "I am quite busy at the moment with preparations for another incense party, and the cat could spoil everything if it disturbed the samples."

The kitten snagged the card and withdrew with it under the desk.

Akitada said politely, "Your expertise in that field is well known, Cousin. Under the circumstances, I won't take up more of your time . . ."

But Koremori had heard the rustling of paper and peered under the desk. He roared, "Kenzo!"

A young boy ran in. His black hair was tied into two fat brushes over each ear, and his bright eyes took in Akitada in a single measuring glance before he told Koremori, "Kenzo's busy, Master. Will I do?"

"Why is this cursed cat running loose in my room?" Koremori pointed under the desk. Take it back to its mistress this instant! If I ever find it here again, I'll have you whipped."

AKITADA AND THE WAY OF JUSTICE

The boy got to his knees and scooped out the kitten, detaching Akitada's card from its teeth and putting it back on the desk. "Come, little tiger," he crooned, "let's go into the garden and watch the goldfish."

Koremori glowered after them. "Did you see that? Not so much as a bow!"

Akitada got to his feet. "I shall give Mother your message, Cousin," he said.

Koremori nodded. "I wish I had more time to chat," he said grudgingly. "My household has been standing on its head all day."

As if on cue, the door flew open again, and a very beautiful young woman swept into the room, silk gowns fluttering and long hair trailing on the floor behind her. Her clothes were luxurious, the short sleeves of her embroidered Chinese coat revealing many layers of exquisitely hued robes of the thinnest silk.

"Oh, darling," she cried, "have you seen my kitten?" She stopped abruptly and looked in consternation at Akitada.

Koremori had turned a deep red. He cleared his throat. "Forgive the interruption, Akitada. This is Yoshiko. Yoshiko, my dear, do not worry. No harm is done. Akitada is only a cousin, and he is leaving."

Akitada bowed to the young woman. He wondered what his mother would make of the news that Koremori had a mistress.

The pretty Yoshiko blushed, fluttered her lashes at him, then sank gracefully on a cushion. "Cousin Akitada," she murmured. "How very pleasant to meet you."

"He is leaving," snapped Koremori.

Akitada bowed again, to both this time, and departed.

When he made his report to his mother, she sat bolt upright. "Who is she?" she demanded.

"I don't know, Mother. Just a pretty young woman. I thought she might be his mistress."

Lady Sugawara hissed. "Mistress. Or concubine? And you say this so calmly? What if she gives him a child? What then?"

Akitada did not care, but he said, "He is no longer young and not at all handsome."

"Fool! What difference does that make? He is wealthy and she is beautiful. You did say she was beautiful?"

Lady Yoshiko was indubitably beautiful. Akitada nodded.

"Hmm. This is not good." Lady Sugawara stared through her son, deep in thought. "Of course it may not last," she finally said, "but meanwhile you must double your efforts to ingratiate yourself. Make yourself indispensable. Remind him that blood ties outweigh all other bonds in importance. Show a loving concern for his health by mentioning the risk of exertion at his age."

Akitada sighed inwardly. "I'll try, Mother."

The following morning the weather had cleared a little and Seimei, who had been his late father's secretary and now served as general factotum in the Sugawara house-

AKITADA AND THE WAY OF JUSTICE

hold, brought in Akitada's rice gruel and another urgent summons from his mother. Akitada gulped down his food and hurried to his mother's room.

She looked excited. "Quick!" she said when she saw him, "Run over to Cousin Koremori's right away. He needs your help."

Akitada shook his head. "I am due at the ministry, Mother."

"It cannot wait," she snapped. "Someone is trying to kill him."

Surprised by his mother's concern, which was so exactly contrary to her hopes, Akitada asked, "Should we interfere?"

Lady Sugawara stared at him. "What do you mean?"

"Sorry. I meant, how do you know?"

"Never mind. Hurry up and go over there. He will explain. And remember what we talked about. Here is your opportunity to demonstrate your devotion."

"Yes, Mother."

Akitada bowed and went to work as usual.

When he arrived at his cousin's house that evening, he found the police there and wondered if Koremori's fears had been real after all. The servant who met him reassured him. It was not his cousin who had died, but an elderly maid.

As they passed Koremori's ancestral shrine, the door opened and a constable stepped out. He recognized Akitada, who had spent too much time at court hearings and murder investigations—thereby irritating the police captain, Kobe, and his superior, the minister of justice.

The constable grinned. "Is it you again, sir? It must be murder for sure then."

Akitada grinned back and stopped. "Not guilty this time. I'm just paying a visit to a family member. What happened?"

"Lord Koremori sent for us. He found his wife's nurse dead on the floor in here." The constable gestured at the shrine.

Akitada peered past him. The tiny room was exquisitely furnished. On its walls were paintings of famous incidents involving Otomo forebears, and on the altar table a finely carved and gilded statue of the Buddha presided over the name tablets of the deceased, prominently among them that of Koremori's son.

In front of the altar, an old woman lay on the floor, her body twisted, her hands clutching at her throat, and her tongue protruding from a blue-tinged face. The footed bowls with offerings of food and money, the incense burners, and the candlesticks that had stood on the altar lay scattered across the floor. Oranges, coins, ashes, and a number of dead flies and moths were among the utensils on the polished boards. It looked as if the poor woman had done the damage before dying in painful convulsions. Her fingers had left fumbling traces in the ashes from the incense burners. A heavy, acrid smell hung in the air.

"Was it murder?" Akitada asked, stepping inside and bending over the corpse. There were no obvious signs of an attack.

AKITADA AND THE WAY OF JUSTICE

The constable shook his head. "I doubt it. No wounds. No contusions. No signs of strangulation. She was an old woman with a weak heart. The captain didn't see anything wrong either, but Lord Koremori kept insisting that she was poisoned by the incense and that the poison had been meant for him. The smell's still pretty strong, but I ask you, who would die from sniffing incense? His lordship got quite rude when we didn't agree with him." He gave Akitada another grin. "Maybe you can get this straightened out, sir."

Akitada had a sinking feeling that he should not have come at all. Kobe would find out that he had been here and complain to the minister again. He shook his head at the constable's suggestion and followed the servant to his cousin's study.

Today Koremori looked ill. He sat behind his desk chewing his fingernails. "Where have you been?" he demanded. "I sent for you this morning."

"I was working at the Ministry," Akitada said.

"You might have considered that my problem outweighed whatever it is you law clerks do all day long," Koremori said angrily. "You are great disappointment to your mother and me. At your age, my son Akemori was already a captain in the emperor's personal guard."

He was probably right about his work, but Akitada was not about to agree. Koremori had always thought his late son excelled in all areas while Akitada was a dismal failure. He had this in common with Akitada's mother.

"I wanted you to be here to make sure the police don't gloss over this matter," he continued when

Akitada said nothing. "My assassin must be found. Frankly, this Kobe fellow struck me as a lazy official."

"Kobe is a hard-working and conscientious officer. You can safely leave the matter in his hands." It was the truth, even though the captain had never missed an opportunity to be ungracious to Akitada.

Koremori seemed to swell. "Are you refusing to help me?"

Akitada bit his lip and said, "What makes you think someone is trying to kill you?"

His cousin settled down. "That's better. Well, as you know, I am preparing for another incense party. I believe the old crone helped herself to some of the incense from that table over there. With the judging to be tomorrow! And now I have a death in the house, and the whole affair will have to be called off. It is outrageous."

A house where there had been a death was taboo because contact with the dead made people ritually impure. But clearly this had not prevented Koremori from sending for Akitada, who said somewhat curtly, "Tell me about the dead woman."

Koremori scowled. "She was my late wife's nurse and then my son's. I should not have kept her. She was clearly past her duties. She only took care of the ancestral altar, replacing the food offerings and burning incense to the spirits of the dead every morning. When the servants found her dead, they called me." He paused and gazed into the distance—perhaps picturing the scene in his mind. "'Dead as dust and cold as copper coins,' you might say."

In addition to organizing incense parties, Koremori was also devoted to poetry contests and practiced whenever an opportunity arose.

"Dust and copper coins?" Akitada did not control his sarcasm.

"Don't be dense. It's what she was lying on. Ashes from the over-turned incense burner and a little pile of coins from one of the offerings to the dead. The verse symbolizes the futility of human desires rather neatly, don't you think?"

"Very appropriate." Akitada felt slightly sick.

"You may jot it down for future reference," Koremori said generously.

"What about the incense? How did she get it?"

Koremori rose. "Come and see for yourself."

On the table near the door, the tray now held only one small packet wrapped in paper, tied with silk, and labeled with an elegantly brushed phrase. One end of the paper twist had been opened and re-folded carelessly. Akitada bent and sniffed. The remnant of ground incense inside seemed to have the same odor as the ancestral shrine.

He had heard stories about people becoming ill after experimenting with exotic combinations of incense ingredients but, like the constable, he had never encountered a case where the victim had been killed. The opened package was labeled "Transcending Life."

"How do you know this was poison?" Akitada asked. "Apparently the police think the nurse died from natural causes."

"Hah! That shows you what they know. There was a very unpleasant smell in the shrine. When we found the dead woman, my major-domo mentioned that she had complained earlier about running out of incense, but she had clearly found some. Then I came in here and I saw that this sample had been opened. It arrived late yesterday. I decided to test it. But after getting a pinch started, I was called out of the room. When I returned, there was the same strong stench in the room and Yoshiko's cat lay on the floor, dead. I held my breath and ran to open all the shutters to air out the room but nearly fainted anyway. There's your proof that someone wants to murder me."

Akitada regarded his cousin. Koremori looked ill but Akitada did not like the note of triumph in his voice. Still, poisonous incense would explain the dead flies in the shrine. There was something vaguely troubling about the scenario, something that had nothing to do with Koremori's fears. "Whose incense sample is this?" he asked, nudging the opened paper with his fingernail.

"I don't know. The samples are anonymous. We identify each sample by its title." Koremori detached the label and gave it to Akitada before returning to his desk.

Akitada followed, frowning at the label. "But why would the nurse help herself to a contest sample?" he asked.

"How should I know? She was a very unpleasant and disobedient servant and was probably too lazy to get fresh incense from the household stores. Really, it served her right." He paused, then added, "It was lucky in a way. If she had not helped herself, I would not have discovered the plot and would be dead by now."

Akitada thought the luck depended on your point of view. His dislike for Koremori increased. He laid the label on the desk. "Whom do you suspect?"

"No idea. That's where you come in, my dear Akitada. Your success in criminal investigations is well known. You will work it out quickly, I'm sure."

"If this is a murder case, I'm afraid I cannot get involved. The minister has strictly forbidden it."

"Soga?" Koremori waved a dismissive hand. "Never mind. I will speak to him."

"I doubt he will permit it. He has been very clear on that point in the past. I regret that I cannot be of assistance, Cousin, but Captain Kobe is very efficient."

Koremori opened his mouth to protest when the door opened and a teary-eyed and agitated Lady Yoshiko rushed in. "Oh, Koremori," she cried wringing her hands, "it is too dreadful! What shall be done about poor Oigimi? I'm too distraught to manage." She saw Akitada and blushed. "Cousin Akitada," she murmured, raising her sleeve to dab at her eyes.

Koremori looked away.

"Perhaps," offered Akitada, "I may be of assistance, Lady Yoshiko. If you are worried about funeral arrangements for, er, Oigimi, I could stop at a temple and ask the monks to come and read the services."

She looked at him with a tremulous smile. "You are the kindest man, Akitada," she murmured. "Do you think they would come?"

"Don't be an idiot, Akitada," snapped Koremori. "Oigimi was her *cat*."

"Oh," said Akitada.

The young woman looked reproachful. "She was a very beautiful cat, black with four white paws, and so sweet. She never left my side. I am sure some divine creature's soul inhabited her body."

"Never mind, my dear." Koremori was irritated but he restrained himself. "We are very busy just now. Please speak to one of the servants about the cat."

"You never liked Oigimi," Lady Yoshiko accused him with a charming pout. She turned to Akitada. "He always thought the poor little sweet thing would disturb his papers." Her eyes fell on the desk, and she saw the incense tag with the words "Transcendent Life." "Oh," she said, "I shall ask Sakanoue," and left.

An uncomfortable silence fell, then Akitada asked, "Who is Sakanoue?"

"A friend. A distant relation who amuses Yoshiko. But to get back to my problem. What will you do? Remember, the killer may try again."

"Is there someone in your household who would want to kill you?"

Koremori threw up his hands. "How should I know. I treat my servants well."

"What about your friends? Specifically the participants in the incense party?"

"Quite impossible! And don't ask for their names. They are far too important to be troubled with questions."

Akitada raised his brows. "You are not making this easy. Who would benefit from your death?"

Koremori's mouth twitched. "Apart from some small bequests for the servants, my property will go to your mother."

Akitada felt trapped. "Very well. If you can get permission from the minister, I'll look into it." He picked up the tag. "The handwriting is elegant. Do you recognize it?"

"It's vaguely familiar, but I can't say."

Since further conversation seemed unprofitable, Akitada rose to leave.

As he had suspected, his mother took an avid interest in the news about Koremori's will. "Very proper," she concluded. "I daresay Koremori exaggerates his danger but it is good to know that his affairs are in order. There is still the young woman. Of course the affair may not last, but meanwhile you must spare no effort to ingratiate yourself. Make yourself indispensable. Exaggerate the danger. Convince him that but for you he might die. In short, act like his son Akemori would have acted under the circumstances."

The thought was revolting, but Akitada said, "Yes, Mother."

A messenger arrived early the next morning with a note from Koremori: "I have spoken to Soga. Come."

Reluctantly—it was amazing that even a dull day in the archives seemed preferable—Akitada returned to his cousin's house to question Koremori's major-domo.

He found Kenzo—a small, thin, middle-aged man of neat appearance—in the ancestral shrine, instructing the youngster who had removed the kitten from Koremori's room in the proper polishing of the floor.

"A terrible thing," Kenzo said. He shook his neatly coiffed head. Every strand of his hair had been pulled back sharply, wound about with a black silk cord, and tied at the precise apex into a smooth loop. As a result of this extreme hairstyle, his thin eyebrows were permanently raised, as if in astonishment at the oddities of life. "Tomoe—she was the dead woman—asked me for incense that morning. I went immediately to the store house, but the supply was gone. I think the maids must have helped themselves. I suggested she skip the incense just once, but she refused quite rudely. She should never have taken the master's incense but she always thought of herself as belonging to her dead mistress and her son." He shook his head again and adjusted the black sash that held the stiffly starched blue cotton robe at his neat waist.

"It's surely unusual for an experienced servant to disobey in this manner," Akitada suggested.

Kenzo agreed. "Tomoe has always been difficult. She came here as her late ladyship's nurse and took orders from no one but her mistress. It was very frustrating. All the other servants disliked her."

"Why was that?"

Echoing Koremori, Kenzo said evasively, "She was an unpleasant person." When Akitada raised his brows, he added, "It's true. Even the master had trouble with her. Only the day before she died, I heard them shouting at each other in the master's study. Imagine a servant shouting at the master of the house! A very unpleasant woman."

At this point, the boy looked up from his chore and said, "Tomoe took money and things from people. I told the maid not to give the old demon her best sash, but she slapped my face and said to keep my mouth shut."

"And very good advice, too," said Kenzo. "Nobody asked you." He apologized to Akitada. "He's only a silly boy and not very bright, as you can see, sir."

"Not at all," said Akitada, smiling at the boy. "I am sure he is quite clever."

The boy nodded. "I watch everything and I remember. You were visiting the master yesterday and the day before that. Go ahead, ask me about the master and Tomoe."

"Enough, Jiro!" snapped Kenzo.

But Jiro had something to prove. "I heard them. The master was going to send Tomoe away, but she talked about her mistress and Master Akemori, and the master got really quiet, and when she came out, she looked very pleased."

Kenzo lost his temper. "Leave the room this instance, Jiro. You're as foolish as a monkey."

Jiro gave Akitada an impudent grin, dropped his oily rag, and scampered off.

Akitada did not agree with Kenzo's estimate of Jiro, but he said nothing. Instead he asked, "Were any of Lord Koremori's guests regular visitors in this house?"

"Ah, you mean the incense party. Only Lord Sakanoue. He's related to the young lady, I believe, and visits her quite often. The other gentlemen only attend for the incense guessing."

Koremori had refused to give Akitada the names of the contestants, but Kenzo had no such reservations. When Akitada asked, he listed them. "In addition to Lord Sakanoue, there was the senior secretary of the imperial household office, the captain of the inner palace guards, the recorder in the ministry of popular affairs, the abbot of the Ninna Temple, and Professor Tachibana from the university."

It was as he had thought. They were men above and beyond reproach and incapable of concocting poisonous substances in order to do away with Koremori. Akitada thanked Kenzo for this very precise and useful information and asked to speak to some of the other servants.

This effort also produced little that was new. They had not liked Tomoe and had hoped the master would dismiss her. They denied taking or hiding the incense stores. They refused—quite properly—to comment on the new mistress or her relative, though Akitada caught a smirk or two from the maids. The general feeling was that Tomoe had died from old age and poor health and that they were not particularly sorry.

Akitada thanked them and went to find his cousin.

"Well," Koremori greeted him, "have you learned anything yet?"

"Yes," Akitada said grimly. "You were not the intended victim."

AKITADA AND THE WAY OF JUSTICE

Koremori's jaw dropped. "But . . ."

"The nurse was meant to die."

Koremori sneered at that. "Don't be ridiculous. Who would go to such lengths to get rid of an old woman?"

"She was blackmailing the people in this household. I think she blackmailed you."

His cousin glared. "How dare you suggest such a thing!"

"What did you and Tomoe quarrel about the day before she died?"

"Who says we quarreled?"

"Kenzo. He overheard you. My guess is that you tried to dismiss her and she threatened you. What did she know that would make you tolerate her in your house?"

Koremori flushed and looked away. His pudgy fingers drummed on the desk. After a moment, he heaved a deep sigh. "I suppose it had to come out. You see before you a broken man. I'm ashamed of my foolishness. Look at me, Akitada. I'm old and ugly. Yoshiko only wanted me for my wealth. I knew about those visits from the handsome Sakanoue, but she claimed they were related and merely good friends. I accepted it. I've been very lonely since my wife died. I did not want to lose Yoshiko. It was hopeless, of course. I surprised them caressing each other. The nurse, who should have been there, left them alone together – a serious dereliction of her duty, but no doubt Sakanoue paid her off. I was very angry with the woman and called her to my study to dismiss her. She became rude and threatened to tell people about the affair. That is what Kenzo overheard." Koremori shuddered and buried his face in his hands.

Akitada felt an unaccustomed surge of pity for his cousin.

Koremori dropped his hands. "It must have been Sakanoue who tried to poison me. Yes, I'm sure it is *his* handwriting on the tag. Yoshiko recognized it, too-- do you remember? Dear heaven, perhaps she even helped him. Oh, what a fool I've been!"

Akitada did not like any part of this theory and stiffened his resolve. "Are you accusing your mistress and Sakanoue of plotting to kill you? What would be their motive?"

Koremori made a face. "Isn't it obvious? They are lovers."

"That is ludicrous. The poisoned incense could have killed everyone at the party, and Sakanoue was to be a participant."

"You forget that I test all samples first. He knew that and expected me to be dead before the judging. I don't think I like your attitude, Akitada. What is the matter with you? You're my cousin. We are family."

Akitada snapped, "By marriage only, I'm thankful to say."

"What?" Koremori's face reddened. "You would do well to think before you insult me."

"I *have* thought. You killed the old woman because she blackmailed you, and now you are trying to punish Yoshiko and Sakanoue by accusing them."

Koremori's eyes bulged. "Have you gone mad?"

AKITADA AND THE WAY OF JUSTICE

"Sakanoue and Yoshiko have no need to kill you. Yoshiko can leave you any time. But your pride cannot tolerate scandal. I expect the nurse knew that."

"That is an outrageous lie. Get out of my house, now!"

"I'm not done, cousin. There is still the little matter of murder. As an expert in the preparation of incense, you are familiar with poisonous substances, and you knew the nurse was fanatical about her shrine ritual. You made sure there would be none of the usual incense in the house. Then you prepared the poisoned incense and left it where she would find it. You murdered her, Koremori."

Koremori stared at him. "I never knew you, Akitada. Your mother was right about you all along."

Even coming from Koremori that hurt. Akitada rose and looked down at his cousin. "You don't know me at all, Koremori. I never liked you, but I didn't think you capable of murder. You actually gloated over the old woman's death and made verses about it. Then you tried to use me to pin the crime on your rival. You made sure that I had all the clues: the tag written by Sakanoue and his relationship with Yoshiko. And, while you were about it, you got rid of Yoshiko's kitten. It irritated you, and you used it to test your poison."

Koremori gave him a twisted smile. "You think you're clever, but you are only a fool after all. Even if you were right, you could do nothing. There is no proof."

"That remains to be seen. I will lay charges against you, and the police will question your friends, your servants, *and* Lady Yoshiko. They will find I am right. Even if by some miracle you escape prosecution, the scandal of the investigation will put an end to your social life." Seeing Koremori's fury, he added, "What would your son have thought of such a father . . . or did the old nurse perhaps reveal something of his true parentage?"

Koremori turned perfectly white. "You would not dare drag Akemori's name into this. His memory is sacred." He looked up at the scroll about a man's duty to his past and future generations. "Have you no family feeling?" he asked with a shaking voice. "We are related, Akitada. What about your mother? What about your sisters? Will you ruin them, too?"

Akitada had hit on the true motive for the murder. Akemori had not been his cousin's son. He cared nothing whatsoever about Koremori's reputation or his family pride, and he did not want his money, but he knew his mother. In her world, the life of an aged servant was negligible when compared to the honor of an aristocratic house.

His cousin was a broken man. The aging lover had been betrayed by his mistress. The doting father had learned that his beloved son was not his own. Koremori seemed sad and pathetic rather than evil.

Koremori saw Akitada's determination waver and pleaded. "Don't do this. I'm an old man and have nothing left but my name. Yes, I wanted to punish the old woman for her lies, but I didn't know she would die. I just wanted to make her ill. It was an unfortunate accident."

AKITADA AND THE WAY OF JUSTICE

"I am sorry for you, Cousin," Akitada said uneasily, "but you know that I must tell the police."

Koremori's head sank. "I understand," he muttered. "You want my life. Very well. Give me until morning to put my affairs in order. My will. I want to make provisions for the old woman's family and for my servants."

"You will only get exile." said Akitada.

"I want to die. I have nothing left. Akitada, would you let me die by my own hand? Please Akitada? A death for a death. Isn't that enough? Let me keep my honor and my good name."

Suicide was not what Akitada wanted; it made him both judge and executioner. It was also improper to suppress his knowledge of a crime. But he knew that to his cousin death was preferable to the public shame which would accomplish little for the victim.

They stared at each other. "Please!" Koremori said again, and Akitada nodded.

The next morning Akitada sat in his room in the black depression that had seized him during a sleepless night. He had regretted his promise almost immediately. Soon he would be told of Koremori's death. Nothing had been gained by it, except some money for the dead woman's family. The fact that he was spared his mother's wrath only made him feel worse.

When Captain Kobe was announced, Akitada was gloomy but not apprehensive. "Please sit down, Captain. What brings you?"

Kobe sat and looked at him fixedly. "There has been a tragedy at the Kiyowara mansion. Koremori was your cousin, I understand?"

Akitada nodded and sighed. "On my mother's side. Thank you for bringing the news, Captain."

"You don't seem surprised."

"No."

"Then you already knew that we would find two bodies this morning?"

Akitada's head jerked up. "*Two* bodies?" he gasped.

"Yes. Your cousin and his mistress are both dead. Any idea what killed them?"

Akitada tried to grasp what had happened. Yoshiko dead? Perhaps there had been an accident, but the icy fear of what he had caused twisted inside him already. Dazedly, he asked, "Poison?"

Kobe's voice was cold. "I know you have a reputation for solving crimes that the police are too stupid for but, pray, enlighten me in this instance: How could you know?"

Akitada sensed anger and knew he deserved it. "I guessed. Was it incense? Koremori dabbled in the stuff."

Kobe let a long silence fall, watching Akitada's growing agitation. "You paid several visits to your cousin recently," Kobe finally said. "What was the occasion?"

Akitada bit his lip. He would have to explain his part in Koremori's suicide. "I delivered a greeting from my mother. A mere courtesy visit."

"Three times? Did you take him a present each time?"

AKITADA AND THE WAY OF JUSTICE

"No. Only the first time. Why?"

Kobe ignored the question. He drew a red card from his sleeve and held it up. "Is this yours?"

Akitada nodded. "Yes, I wrote it and attached it to the fan."

"Really? We found it attached to a package containing poisoned sweets."

"What?"

"Apparently your cousin shared your present with his mistress. They died together. But you already knew that."

Akitada held his head. "No. How can this be? Koremori I can understand. But why Yoshiko? And why my card—oh!" He shuddered when he realized the magnitude of his error and the horror of what Koremori had done.

"I really regret this," Kobe said after a long pause. "But you of all men will understand that I have my duty. I came myself to spare you and your family as much indignity as possible."

Akitada woke from his stupor. "What? You're arresting me? No, you've got it wrong, Kobe. My cousin committed suicide. Well, murder and suicide. This is Koremori's revenge." Akitada took a deep breath. "I'm afraid I made my cousin a foolish and very improper promise last night. I let him take his own life instead of facing a murder charge. You see, Koremori poisoned the incense that killed his late wife's nurse. She blackmailed him. He admitted it to me. His new mistress was having an affair with a younger man, and the nurse knew. After killing the woman, Koremori planned to use me to pin this murder on the lovers."

Kobe raised his brows. "Nonsense. You cannot kill people with incense. The old woman had a heart attack."

"Perhaps, but it was brought on by poisoned incense. She got hold of some that Koremori had prepared. He knew she would use it in that tiny closed room. Once she was out of the way, he claimed the poison had been intended for him by Sakanoue and Yoshiko, and that the maid got hold of it by accident." The story sounded crazy even to Akitada.

Kobe snapped, "You cannot expect me to believe such nonsense. Granted you have on occasion guessed correctly, but that doesn't mean you you'll get away with murder now."

A man like Kobe would not understand Koremori's convoluted reasoning, but Akitada tried again, more despairingly.

"Captain, you don't know my cousin's mind. His reputation was everything to him. When I confronted him, he admitted what he had done. He begged to be allowed to commit suicide, and I agreed. But he wanted revenge. He decided to take Yoshiko's life and make it look as though I had murdered both of them." Akitada grimaced. "I should have expected this trick. It's the way Koremori's mind worked."

Kobe said coldly, "No. It's the way *your* mind works. It's absurd. Nobody but you could think up such a tale on the spur of the moment."

AKITADA AND THE WAY OF JUSTICE

Akitada swallowed. "Captain, you cannot seriously suspect me of such a heinous crime. You know me. I've always been on the side of justice. Besides what would be my motive?" But even as he said it, he already knew and despaired.

"According to Koremori's will, you were his favorite cousin. He left you his fortune, which is considerable. I believe, his precise words were, 'in the hope that it may repay him for his kindness to me.'"

Akitada stared at Kobe. "I won't touch it. Give it to the families of the dead women."

Kobe shook his head. He looked unhappy but determined.

"I bet Koremori wrote the new will before he killed himself." Akitada felt the perspiration turn icy on his back and face. "It is his revenge, Kobe. Because I knew what he had done and might yet expose him."

"This is not getting us anywhere." Kobe rose. "Let's go," he said wearily.

Akitada looked around the room. What would become of them all? His sisters were mere children. What would his mother do? "Wait," he said. "My mother selected the fan I took to Koremori. She will tell you so." He already quailed at the thought of that interview.

Kobe shook his head. "Not worthy of you. We know about the fan. I think you brought the sweets on your third and last visit. Come, it's time."

How quickly a man's fortune changed! By not going to the police, Akitada had caused Yoshiko's death and his own arrest. *Your actions will return to you*, said the proverb. He had erred out of weakness, and now he was lost.

As he stumbled to his feet, his eyes fell on the red card and he saw again a young boy holding a black and white kitten and removing the red card from its teeth. He snatched it up.

"The card," he said, holding it out to Kobe. "Look at it. It's proof that I am innocent. Do you see the marks? Yoshiko's kitten made those. When I went back the second time, that kitten was already dead. Poisoned." He took a shuddering breath. "I have a witness. If you don't believe me, ask for Jiro, one of the servants. He is only a boy but very bright and observant. He came to catch the kitten while I was with Koremori on my first visit. The kitten was playing with this card."

Kobe took the card and looked at it. Akitada saw determination slowly giving way to doubt. Kobe said grudgingly, "Very well. If the boy remembers, I'll reopen the investigation. If not, I shall be back for you."

When Kobe had left, Akitada's knees gave way and he sank on his cushion. But he was no longer afraid. Kobe, for all his coldness and lack of imagination, was a fair man and a good officer, and Jiro would remember. They would talk to Sakanoue and to Kenzo and to the other servants. Of course, Koremori's will would be declared invalid, but blood money would not console Yoshiko's family for her death. Akitada would always bear the guilt for that.

And there was still his mother.

But then Akitada thought of the boy Jiro and of the kitten and smiled. In the end the gods were always just.

RAIN AT RASHOMON

The following story shows Akitada's early fascination with the court system and law enforcement in the imperial capital. Readers of Japanese literature may recognize structural similarities to Akutagawa's story "Rashomon," also known from the film, **Rashomon.** *The Akutagawa plot is quite different, of course, and based on a medieval collection of tales.*

Heian-Kyo (Kyoto): 1012; during the Watery Month (July).

Behind the sound of the pattering rain, behind the hiss and gurgle of water sluicing down the tiles, Akitada heard a whisper, ". . . but it's *murder.* Ten bars of silver to kill a woman?"

In this almost casually dramatic fashion began one of the most convoluted cases.

It had been raining most of the day, and the heavens had opened up again just as Akitada reached Rashomon. Grand and two-storied, the southern gate of the capital was the threshold between the civilized urban world of court nobility and artisans and the humble fields and paddies of the peasants who fed them.

Akitada, who had come to welcome back a friend from his tour in the provinces, ducked through the downpour and up the five wide steps to the raised ground floor of Rashomon. Other people were already sheltering from the rain, a sampling of the locals and travelers who daily passed this way.

Sun-browned market farmers and their sturdy wives sat among their baskets, the men naked except for loincloths, the women in faded cotton gowns with scarves tied around their hair. A couple of hunters strolled about, their bows and arrows slung across their backs. Monks from the mountain monasteries, in black robes and silk stoles, kept their distance from their itinerant brethren in brown hemp and huge straw hats. A few government clerks, in the same neat blue gowns and black hats as Akitada, peered anxiously up at the watery skies. In addition to these there were servants, shop boys, and laborers of all descriptions lounging about, glad to have an excuse to dawdle. Even one or two women, heavily veiled upper-class matrons on a pilgrimage or visit, stood about, waiting to continue their journey.

Since the labyrinthine upper story of Rashomon sheltered vagrants and homeless people at night and more recently had become a meeting place for criminals, Akitada saw with satisfaction that the authorities had finally assigned a constable to guard duty. The handsome, red-coated young man stood stiffly near one of the doors, his bow and quiver slung over his shoulder and his hand on the grip of his sword. He was scanning the crowd, letting his eyes move indifferently over Akitada's slim figure in his drenched blue robe and black hat. Just another official, his expression said.

Akitada made his way through the standing and sitting humanity to the other side of the gate and took up a place at one of the thick, lacquered pillars where he could see the eastern highway stretching away through the bluish-grey watery haze toward the distant green mountains.

The scene was quite empty as far as his eye could see. No doubt his friend had sought shelter at one of the roadside inns and would not set out again until the rain let up. Akitada sighed and prepared to be patient. He had looked forward to this meeting. His mind dwelt with pleasure on the preparations at home, and he reviewed plans for the coming days.

Gradually, his surroundings, the low hum of voices behind him, the wind-driven curtains of water outside, and the cascades rushing from the eaves above became a single web of sound and sight, a lulling background to his pleasurable thoughts.

It was reluctantly that he first took note of a discordant sound: the whispering sibilance alternating with a hoarser, grating sound punctuated by a dry cough. Such sounds would have been easily disguised by the rain except for their urgency, the note of excitement.

Akitada guessed there had been a demand and a response, both fraught with meaning. But the first exchanges left Akitada with neither comprehension nor much curiosity. Then, during a lull, came the words: "But that's *murder*! Ten pieces of silver to kill a woman?" The rest was washed away by more splashing of rain and the gusting of wind.

Murder? Akitada thought he must have misheard. Or perhaps he had been dreaming. No one would meet here in broad daylight, in a crowd of people and under the eyes of a constable to discuss, a murder for hire. He tried to recall the precise words, the sound and inflection of the voices. He could not guess the speakers' ages or their profession. Detaching himself quietly from the pillar, he strolled around to see the other side.

There was no one there. At the nearest wall, a mendicant monk, like a bundle of dirty straw, sat asleep, his face sunken onto his chest and his straw hat resting on his shoulders. At the next pillar, two blue-robed officials stood studying a piece of paper. On the other side, a common laborer rummaged in his bundle for something to eat. The red-coated constable was watching a middle-aged man who was teetering on the top step at the far side, peering at the sky before braving the rain, impatient to get home.

Feeling thoroughly foolish, Akitada returned to his position. Soon the driving grey curtains of rain parted briefly, and he saw a group of travelers, with the litter bearers in front, their feet splashing along rapidly. He leaned forward, shading his eyes. Perhaps? Yes! His friend had arrived.

It was not until more than a month later, long after his friend had departed, that the memory of that half-heard conversation returned to haunt him. On the occasion, he was attending a trial of a murderer. All junior clerks of the Ministry of Justice were sent on periodic visits to one of the city's two municipal courts. The minister liked to keep an eye on judicial procedures and current cases to assert the waning powers of the ministry against the police. Akitada usually volunteered and, if that did not work, went without permission.

It had seemed a straightforward case. A robber had entered the property of a minor official, had been discovered in the act by the owner, and had stabbed him to death. The robber had then made his escape, but was apprehended almost immediately trying to sell a costly woman's robe. Due to a bit of very good police work—the minister had called it luck—the robe was identified as belonging to the household of the victim, and the robber had been charged with the murder.

On this occasion, the minister had sent Akitada for two reasons: there had been an abnormally long delay in the trial—the accused had been in custody for a month without confessing his crime—and the judge was Ienaga.

Ienaga had established a reputation as an unemotional and pitiless prosecutor of criminals. For years he had ignored all recommendations of clemency from the government. But he was almost seventy now, and the minister hoped to catch him in a judicial error and have him dismissed for senility.

When Akitada arrived, the trial had already started in the main hall of the municipal police headquarters. Only a handful of people were in attendance—a meager showing, but robbery had become a common occurrence in the capital and it was raining.

Black-robed and black-hatted, Ienaga sat stiffly on the dais, holding the baton of his office before him and glowering at the courtroom. Neither his posture nor his fierce expression could hide his age and frailty.

To either side of the judge, two scribes knelt over low desks, taking notes of the proceedings. Below the dais, to the right and left, stood constables in red coats and white trousers.

The defendant, chained hand and foot, knelt directly below the judge, flanked by two prison guards with whips and prongs. He was a rough-looking man, in his mid-thirties, incredibly hairy and dirty, but with powerful shoulders and muscular thighs and legs. Akitada was always sickened by the defendants in murder cases. Regardless of their crime, he found their abject hopelessness painful to watch. But his revulsion had never been as strong as on this occasion, and he searched for a reason. There was nothing appealing about the man. Neither was his crime negligible or defensible. A creature like this should have seemed no more than a ferocious animal gone on the attack, but this man gave the impression of a patient beast of burden submitting to human abuse.

AKITADA AND THE WAY OF JUSTICE

Ienaga wound up a summation of the charges, rapped his baton sharply on the boards and called for the witnesses. Akitada prepared to listen and watch. Outside the steady rain drummed on the tiles of the roof.

Testimony of the Maid Servant

My name is Sumiko. I work in the house of Ishigake Takanobu. On the morning of the tenth day of the Rice-Sprouting Month I found my master dead in the mistress's room. He was covered with blood on his chest and back and was lying in a puddle of blood. I screamed and ran for help to Otagi, the steward. That is all I know.

Testimony of the House Steward

My name is Otagi. I have been the house steward in the family of Ishigake Takanobu for ten years. When the maid Sumiko came to me, I went immediately to the mistress's quarters and found my master dead. He had been stabbed in the throat and the weapon, my master's own hunting knife, lay beside him. I also saw that a robbery had taken place, because the clothes chests were emptied and a silver mirror and other costly belongings were missing. I immediately reported the murder to the police. That is all I know.

Testimony of the Police Sergeant

My name is Kishida. I am a sergeant of the municipal police. On the tenth day of the Rice-Sprouting

Month I was called to the residence of the assistant secretary of the Bureau of Palace Repairs, Ishigake Takanobu. I found that the assistant secretary had been killed by having his throat cut with a hunting knife and that a robbery had occurred. After interviewing the staff, I prepared a list of stolen articles and determined that Ishigake had surprised the robber and that the criminal had then killed the secretary and made his escape with the goods.

Testimony of the Constable

My name is Constable Yojibei. On the tenth day of the Rice-Sprouting Month, around the time of the noon rice, I observed the defendant Hajimaro offering a woman's robe for sale in the market. When he could not account for the robe, I arrested him on suspicion of theft. My sergeant sent me to the house of the murdered Ishigake Takanobu to show the woman's robe to the maid. The maid identified the robe as one stolen by the murderer. That is all I know.

Testimony of the Defendant

My name is Hajimaro. I am a poor soldier out of work. On the tenth day of the Rice-Sprouting Month early in the morning I was walking down Nishiki Road towards Takakura Street, when I passed an open gate. I had not eaten for two days and decided to beg some rice. I saw no one in the courtyard and entered the house. Inside I found a dead man covered with blood. I was frightened, but my hunger was greater than my fear. In my desperation I stole a woman's robe from a *clothes rack. Then I heard someone coming and left. When I tried to sell the robe the next day, I was arrested. That is all I know.*

Akitada found plenty to criticize in the way Judge Ienaga conducted the hearing. He had heard the witnesses in quick succession and without comment or question. Indeed, their testimony had been so brief and concise that Akitada suspected that they had told their stories several times already. Much time had passed, and the judge should have probed their recollections more thoroughly. Worse, there were some glaring omissions. What had happened to the other stolen articles? Why had the victim carried a hunting knife into his wife's room? And where, for that matter, was that wife's testimony?

But something far more startling had happened during the testimony. The constable had a speech impediment which caused him to lisp. In itself such a thing would not have meant much to Akitada, but the combination of the hissing sounds with the rain on the roof, and the man's red uniform had caused a sharp memory to flash through his mind: the conversation overheard in Rashomon more than six weeks ago. He then recognized the constable as the one who had been standing guard that rainy afternoon, and the man lisped much like one of the speakers Akitada had overheard, the one who was to kill an unknown woman.

But even if this representative of the law was indeed involved in a murder plot, it could not have anything to do with the case on hand. The victim here had been male.

Akitada put the matter from his mind when the judge pronounced sentence. Ienaga found the defendant guilty of robbery and decreed a punishment of one hundred lashes with bamboo whips. Such an ordeal was harsh, but Ienaga did not confine himself to a mere hundred lashes. He ordered additional beatings to be administered until a murder confession could be extracted from the defendant.

Summary justice! Akitada sighed and was making his way out of the courtroom, wondering what he should do about the lisping constable, when a disturbance caused him to turn around. The judge was listening with evident impatience to an elderly couple. He was leaning forward, his hand raised to his ear to hear better.

Could Ienaga be deaf? If so, he should have disqualified himself. Perhaps the preceding hearing had been a carefully rehearsed farce. Akitada drew nearer.

"What? What?" shouted Ienaga, waving his baton. "Speak up! I can't hear you. You say you lost your daughter?"

The elderly man shouted, "Yes, Your Honor! She has not been seen since . . ."

Ienaga interrupted him, "Why are you bothering me with this? I know nothing of the matter. Report it to the police. Court closed!" He rapped his baton and was helped up by his clerks who rushed over to assist him out of the room.

AKITADA AND THE WAY OF JUSTICE

The two elderly people stood helplessly as the hall emptied, keeping close together, and after a while the wife began to cry. Her husband put an arm around her shoulders and murmured something. She nodded and together they turned and walked away slowly.

Akitada was becoming very angry with Ienaga. Even if the case against the robber appeared justified, it had been handled too quickly and too carelessly. And if Ienaga was indeed deaf, he must be dismissed from his office. He decided to follow the old couple.

They were making their way through the rain toward Suzaku Avenue, walking side by side with the slow, dejected gait of people who have given up hope.

Catching up, Akitada pulled them under the eaves of a building and introduced himself.

"You work in the ministry of justice, Sir?" asked the man, bowing deeply, his face suddenly hopeful.

The wife fell to her knees in the mud of the street and cried, "Oh, please, sir, in the name of Holy Amida, tell us what to do? If you have a child, sir, have pity on us."

"Please get up, madam," said Akitada, deeply moved, "and tell me what happened."

She got up, but it was her husband who told him about his daughter—the wife of the murdered secretary—who seemed to have vanished into thin air.

"When we heard of the murder," he said, "I went immediately to offer my condolences to the Ishigake family. To my horror, the son turned me away, saying that my daughter had left the household. When I asked him when and why, he said only that his father had divorced her and sent her away shortly before his death. I don't believe him, because Chiyo did not come home. She did not even send us a message."

A divorce would certainly explain why no reference was made to the widow during the hearing. And if the husband had sent her away in anger, she might well have left her finery behind. But what had he been doing in her empty apartments? With a knife. And, again, Akitada thought of the lisping constable and the meeting at Rashomon. He asked, "Were you close to your daughter?"

Husband and wife exchanged glances. The mother said defensively, "Chiyo did not see us after she married. And we did not visit because we were afraid her new family might take it amiss."

The husband shifted his feet. He looked both ashamed and angry. "I was against it from the start. I am only a poor schoolteacher. We could not even give her a dowry. But Chiyo had her heart set on marrying a rich man and made eyes at the late secretary even though he was almost my age. Chiyo is very beautiful, and he came to me. He offered me money for her."

Akitada could imagine the reaction to such an insult. Poor but respectable, the school teacher would have been deeply offended that the rich man wished to buy his daughter as if she were a common prostitute.

"You refused, I take it." Akitada said.

The man nodded, still angry. "Of course. But my daughter left us. The next day we got a letter, saying she had gone to him to be mistress of his house and heart. I did not respond and forbade my wife to visit.

AKITADA AND THE WAY OF JUSTICE

But now . . ." He broke off, placing a hand over his face in grief. "Where could she be?" he asked dully.

Akitada promised to ask some questions on their behalf, and they were touchingly grateful. As he was by no means sure of success and, in any case, had no time to pursue the matter, he watched with mixed feelings as they walked away into the gray drizzle with lighter steps, convinced that they had found an advocate in him.

The minister received Akitada's report on Judge Ienaga with satisfaction. The story of the missing wife intrigued him, because there was always a chance that it might be connected with the murder, in which case Ienaga could be dismissed. Therefore he permitted Akitada to take the rest of the day off to investigate her disappearance.

Ishigake junior was a pale, fleshy young man who tried to appear sophisticated. Akitada's visit clearly puzzled him, but he dared not question the sudden interest of the Ministry of Justice in his father's divorce.

"I cannot tell you much," he said querulously. "I was not here. But my father's ill-considered . . . er . . . connection with a young female from a totally unacceptable family was naturally of great concern to me."

"Naturally." No doubt about it, thought Akitada, glancing around at the trappings of wealth. If another son had been born to the unsuitable wife, he might have usurped a doting father's affections, and the pudgy young man might have lost his inheritance. He coughed, saying apologetically, "Like everyone else, I seem to have caught a cold. The weather has been so wet. Perhaps you, too, have had that misfortune?"

The young man looked blank. "I never get sick," he said. "In any case, there is little to tell, except that apparently my father came to his senses and sent the person back home to her family."

"Ah," said Akitada, "but that is the problem. She seems not to have arrived there. What with your father's tragic murder, one cannot help wondering if the same man may be responsible for her disappearance."

Young Ishigake frowned. "But the steward told me that my father's . . . that she had been sent away the day before. He said that Father was very angry, and she left the house in tears." He paused. "I'm afraid the steward insinuated that she was very flirtatious and might have been involved in some liaison. Perhaps she has gone to her lover."

It certainly sounded possible. By her parents' testimony, Chiyo was a spoiled and headstrong young woman. And, having defied her strict father, she would hardly have returned to her parents if she had been divorced for adultery. Akitada thanked Ishigake and left.

Otagi, the house steward, was hovering near the entrance. He handed Akitada his boots.

Akitada thought the man looked nervous. "I heard you testify in court this morning," he said, sitting on the wooden platform to slip his boots on.

The servant's thin face was expressionless. "Yes, sir," he said.

Akitada held a boot in his hand and studied the man. He looked about forty years old. His hair was thinning and his face prematurely lined. "I understand from your master that you saw your mistress leaving this house."

Otagi stiffened. "I doubt that my late master's son would refer to a woman of her class as my mistress," he said frostily. "It was regrettable that my late master should have brought someone so unsuitable into this house, but it was no surprise to me that he sent her back to the streets."

"You did see her leave the day before he died?"

Otagi nodded. "And good riddance, too."

Akitada's brows climbed in astonishment. The man's vindictiveness was surprising, and he expressed himself with an astonishing freedom, even for a trusted upper servant. His speech suggested an above-average education, and he might well come from a better class of people than his present status indicated. "Did you not think it strange that she took none of her things with her?" he asked.

"She came here with nothing," Otagi said, pursing his thin lips, "so why should she take anything? It was enough that she lived in luxury here. She did not deserve it. Women are as deceitful as snakes."

Akitada finished putting on his boots thoughtfully, then reached for his straw coat. "By any chance," he asked, "did your master suffer from a cold about a month ago?"

Otagi stared at him. "A cold? Yes, he did. And a bad cough. I was sent to the pharmacist. How did you know?"

"Something someone said." Akitada nodded and left.

Even putting aside the steward's misogyny and the stepson's resentment, it seemed that Chiyo had left the Ishigake house under a cloud. Akitada glanced up at the sky. It was an unrelentingly thick gray color, and the rain was worse. His straw cape was becoming heavy with moisture and cold water trickled unpleasantly down his neck. With a sigh he turned his steps toward police headquarters again. The Ishigake case was puzzling, and he could not get the lisping constable out of his mind.

Sergeant Kishida was an old acquaintance of Akitada's and answered his question readily enough.

"Yojibei? Oh, he's well enough nowadays, a bright lad with a good future. Mind you, I'd not have given you two coppers for his chances when he first came to us. His mind was not on his duties. But he's come along quite well lately since he got married. That'll settle a man down amazingly." The sergeant laughed tolerantly.

"Was he assigned to guard duty at Rashomon about six weeks ago?"

Kishida thought. "Six weeks? Rashomon duty is punitive. Nothing to do but stand around from dawn till dusk." He chuckled. "But six weeks ago Yojibei may have been in trouble. A moment?" He went to a heavy ledger which lay on a stand in the guard room and flicked through the pages. "Yojibei, Yoji . . . ah, yes. Here he is. Ninth day of the Rice-Growing Month. Guard duty at Rashomon from sunrise till sunset. Now I wonder what he got that for?" Kishida muttered, scratched his head, then his face brightened. "Of course, the rascal was reported for gambling. That must have been it. Well, he's toed the line since the captain had a word or two with him."

"I see. By the way, that case you and he testified for this morning, did you ever find the rest of the stolen goods?"

The sergeant's face fell. "Nothing but the robe," he said. "I figure he divided the stuff with his cronies. It'll turn up in time. Good thing he confessed to taking the robe. We knew we had him, when he told us about that."

"He told you? You mean he confessed to the theft immediately?" Akitada asked, astonished.

"He did indeed. Surprised me, too."

For some reason this example of eccentric honesty in a man accused of murder made Akitada extremely uncomfortable. He said, "I am curious about something Constable Yojibei said. Can you tell me where I can find him?"

"He's gone off duty. Let me check." Kishida rummaged among his papers. "Here it is. He lives behind the Yoshida Shrine, in Rokkaku Street."

Akitada sighed. It was a long way in the rain. The chilly wetness had penetrated to his robe which clung unpleasantly to his back and chest.

Yojibei's apartment was in a small street of long houses. In this weather the surroundings looked incredibly dreary. Water poured unchecked from patched roofs, the wooden walls were blackened by moisture, ragged fencing leaned drunkenly, and the rest was an unrelieved expanse of brown mud. Apparently the constable rented space from a noodle maker. Through the open doorway, Akitada could see the drying racks filled with strings of pale buckwheat noodles. Yojibei's quarters had a separate entrance, and when he knocked on the door, a woman's voice called out to come in.

He removed his muddy boots and soaked straw coat, slid back the door, and stepped into a good-sized room which consisted of a large area with *tatami* mats on the floor and a screened off food preparation corner. The tasteful arrangements surprised Akitada in such a humble dwelling.

A pretty young woman in a blue cotton gown knelt on the mats, engaged in stitching lengths of fabric into a man's robe. She stared at Akitada in surprise. "What do you want?"

The tone was peremptory, upper class. Akitada smiled. "My name is Sugawara. I work in the Ministry of Justice and am investigating the murder of Ishigake Takanobu."

The young woman dropped her needle and turned absolutely white. Akitada said gently, "I am addressing his widow, I think?"

She cried out, put both hands over her face, and burst into heart-wrenching sobs.

The door behind Akitada slid back. "What's going on here?" a male voice cried.

Recognizing the lisp, Akitada turned to the handsome young constable and said, "Ah, Constable Yojibei.

AKITADA AND THE WAY OF JUSTICE

I came to see you, but I find that the young lady I have been searching for has been in your care all along."

Yojibei paled. "Who are you?"

"Sugawara, from the Ministry of Justice. Sergeant Kishida gave me your address. It seems there are some aspects of the murder of Ishigake that you neglected to report."

The constable staggered. For a moment Akitada thought he was going to faint, but instead he stepped past him to stand protectively in front of the young woman. "She has done nothing. It is entirely my responsibility."

Akitada raised his brows. "Are you confessing to the murder?"

"No!" They cried out together. The woman reached up to clutch the young man's hand.

"It is not his fault," she cried. "He saved my life and I begged him to take me away from that house. He is a good man." And she burst into an agitated account of her own foolish pursuit of the wealthy Ishigake, her defiance of her father's stern admonitions, and her misery in the home of an abusive husband.

"And how did Yojibei find you?" asked Akitada, who had listened to the story skeptically.

Seeing her sudden fear, the constable squeezed her hand reassuringly and said to Akitada, "I suppose, I'd better make a clean breast of it, sir. I used to keep bad company before . . . that is, I used to gamble and I wasn't very lucky. In fact, I owed a lot of money. The men I played with are a rough lot, and they told me if I didn't pay up, they'd kill me. I'm only a constable and

I knew I couldn't pay what I owed. I told them to go ahead and kill me. That's when they put me in the way of making some money. They said they knew a man who would pay ten bars of silver to have his wife killed. It was wrong of me to go meet that man, but I didn't want to die and I had some idea that I could trick him out of the money somehow. Well, I said I'd do it, and he paid me half the silver."

"Ah," nodded Akitada. "You met Ishigake at Rashomon the day before he died."

Both young people stared at him in shock.

"I believe," Akitada continued, "Ishigake had a cold that day."

"Were you there?" Yojibei gasped.

"My own husband paid to have me murdered," wailed Chiyo.

Akitada looked at her. "Why?"

"He accused me of infidelity. How could I have met men when I had never left my rooms since my arrival? He set his servants to spy on me, especially that odious Otagi."

"Did you give your husband reason to accuse you of faithlessness?"

"Never. But he knew I was sickened by his lovemaking. One day he went into a rage and beat me. I told him I'd run away and find another man, one who was young and treated me properly. He was furious. And that's when he started having me watched." Silent tears coursed down her cheeks. "He need not have bothered. I had no place to go."

"Why not go back to your parents?"

"How could I go back after the scenes I'd made to be allowed to marry him? I was miserable. Then that dirty old Otagi started making suggestive remarks." She blushed. "I was so frightened I thought I'd better tell my husband, but that made it worse. He said I was lying to get rid of Otagi, and he beat me again. I thought he'd kill me if I didn't stop him. That's when I threatened to go to his superiors at court and show them my bruises. He got very quiet then and apologized, saying he was jealous because he loved me so much. I didn't believe him, but I was glad I finally had something I could use against him."

Akitada grimaced. "You made your point so well that he decided to have you killed." He turned to Yojibei. "And why did you not carry out your agreement?"

"I never really intended to." The constable looked down at the young woman and said simply, "Especially not when I saw Chiyo. I think I fell in love with her then."

She smiled through her tears and pressed her cheek against his hand before releasing it. Turning to Akitada, she said earnestly, "I've been foolish . I know that now. How stupid to think that a wealthy husband was more important than one who cares for me! Yojibei saved my life."

"Please believe us, sir," Yojibei pleaded. "I did not kill Ishigake. He was alive when we left together."

Ah, thought Akitada, here it comes. "What happened?"

Again the two lovers exchanged a glance, their hands finding each other again. Yojibei said, "He found us together. I . . . it was not my first visit. I'd gone to his house right away, straight from Rashomon, as soon as my relief came. I was to do it that night, if I could, and I thought, the rain . . . well, there are fewer people about then, and I could take a look. He'd left the gate open for me and I stood in the dark, in the rain, and watched Chiyo through the open shutters, and that's when I knew I could never do it. She was so beautiful, and she looked so sad. I made up my mind that I would warn her."

Chiyo took over. "I was frightened at first when he just appeared out of the rain, but Yojibei was so gentle and kind. He told me to leave that house, because someone had asked him to kill me. I didn't believe him. Besides how could I go? I had no money, nothing. After he left, I couldn't eat or sleep. Then my husband came in the middle of the night, and I could see that Yojibei had told the truth. My husband had expected to find me dead. He looked disappointed, and he was hateful and cold. He asked me if I had heard any noises earlier in the night. I told him I had. That there had been someone in the garden, but I had shouted for the maid and whoever had been out there had left. He was satisfied with that and went away. And I wished I had left with Yojibei."

The constable said, "I didn't sleep either, worrying about her. So I went back again. She was glad to see me, and we talked." He flushed. "She said I had been right and thanked me. And I . . . we made love. When he came in, he found us together."

She gave a little sob and hid her face against Yojibei's thigh. "He was like a madman, screaming terrible things. He had a knife, and . . . I thought he was going to kill us both."

The constable released his hand from her grasp and straightened his shoulders. "I took away the knife and hit him with my bare hands," he said. "I knocked him out. I know he was alive because I checked. Then Chiyo said that he must've brought the knife to kill her himself. That made us angry, and we took some gold from his sash. With what he'd already given me, we had enough to pay off my debt and find a place for us to live. I figured it wasn't stealing. He owed Chiyo that money for what she had to put up with. Anyway, we left that house together before he could come around and shout for help."

Akitada sighed. "I trust you have been with the police long enough to know how weak your story sounds."

The constable's shoulders sagged. "Please, sir," he begged, "at least keep Chiyo out of it. She's suffered enough."

"No. I won't have you lose your life because you saved mine!" She rose and stepped in front of Yojibei. "Help us, sir," she cried. "If they arrest Yojibei, I'll confess to the murder myself. I'll say, I took my husband's knife and ran it through his body."

Akitada raised his brows. "Didn't Yojibei tell you that your husband's throat was slashed?"

Akitada trudged back to police headquarters through the same steady drizzle. His straw raincoat was heavy with rainwater and his boots squelched at every step. He no longer bothered to avoid the puddles.

Sergeant Kishida was looking into one of the cells in the jail, and suppressed a smile when he saw Akitada's sodden figure. "Did you find Yojibei?"

Akitada nodded. His eyes fell on the prisoner in the cell, the robber Hajimaro.

This time Akitada was close enough to see his face. The man was younger than he had thought in court, only about twenty-five or thirty, and under the dirt and straggly hair and beard he had a well-shaped face with large, soft eyes and a mouth which could smile even under these circumstances. Though he was sitting chained to the wall, he bowed a little to Akitada, who nodded in return.

The sergeant said, "Hajimaro took his punishment like a man. I wish we could let him go. Listen, Hajimaro," he pleaded with the prisoner, "if you confess, it'll go easier with you. You can say he came at you with the knife and you defended yourself and cut him by accident."

Akitada looked at the sergeant in astonishment. Rehearsing a prisoner in a lie to get him a lighter sentence was the last thing he would have expected a policeman to do. Especially not Kishida, who was as upright as a young pine.

But the prisoner amazed him even more. He spoke patiently, as if he had explained himself before, "I cannot do that, because it wouldn't be true."

Kishida stamped his foot. "Don't you understand, man? They'll whip you till you confess or die. Do you want that?"

"No." Hajimaro sighed, then smiled again. "You're a kind person, Sergeant, but we all must die some day. For someone like me it's not a bad thing. No more hunger or cold. No getting old and sick. No worries. Just peace."

Akitada shuddered. "When will they begin to question him again?" he asked Kishida.

"As soon as the captain comes back. Any moment."

"Can you ask for a delay? I would like you to come with me to the Ishigake mansion. I think I know who really murdered Ishigake."

The door was opened again by the house steward. Otagi looked with disfavor at their dripping clothes but admitted them.

"The young master is busy with his accounts," he said coldly. "If it's about the stolen things, can you come back some other time?"

Kishida said, "This gentleman is with the Ministry of Justice. He has some questions concerning the murder of your late master."

Otagi protested, "But that is over. I myself heard the judge pronounce sentence."

Akitada said, "You may not be aware of the fact that the prisoner has not confessed. The case is still open and subject to review. Now, if you will lead us to your room, we will not need to bother your master."

Otagi blinked. "My room? It's . . . dirty. We can talk in here." He walked to a sliding door and pushed it open.

"Your room," repeated Akitada, his voice allowing no argument.

"But," stammered Otagi, "it hasn't been cleaned. And it's too small. And cold. You would not like it at all."

"Go!" snapped Kishida, putting his hand on the short sword he carried in his sash.

The reason for Otagi's reluctance became evident when they entered his room. Here was the missing silver mirror. And next to it stood lacquered boxes of cosmetics. Quilted silk bedding was still spread across the floor, with a lady's sheer white under gown lying crumpled on top. And against the wall stood the trunks which were, no doubt, filled with Chiyo's silk robes.

Kishida's jaw sagged. "You stole the stuff yourself?" he said to Otagi, then turned to Akitada. "Is he the killer?"

Akitada nodded. To the steward he said, "So you killed your master when he caught you stealing those things."

The man was as pale as the silk under gown. "No. He didn't catch me," he cried. "I found him dead. It's just . . . well, she was gone. Nobody needed those things anymore. The young master's not married. So I thought . . ." He paused. "I thought I'd store them here."

"You're lying. And you lied to the judge," Kishida accused.

Otagi compressed his lips.

"I found your mistress and had a talk with her," said Akitada. "She says you used to spy on her. It was you, wasn't it, who told your master that his young wife was betraying him? You did it out of spite, because she rejected your advances and complained to her husband about you."

Otagi flared up. "What if I told him? There really was a man with her. I heard them together."

"And you called your master and sent him to her room?"

Otagi avoided Akitada's eyes. "It was my duty."

"I think you did it because you were furious that she had rebuffed your own desire."

Otagi flushed. "She lied about that. The master didn't believe her. He believed me," he cried. "She was nothing to me. I wouldn't look at a woman like that."

Akitada went to pick up the silken under gown. "But you sleep with her clothing and in her quilts," he said. "Look, Sergeant. It is perfectly obvious that he slept here."

The steward sagged to his knees and burst into tears of frustration and pain. "She was so beautiful," he sobbed. "And he beat her. I would've done anything for her. I took her special delicacies from the kitchen, and flowers from the garden. The cosmetics . . . I gave her those . . . and some of the clothes. The master was mean with her, and I thought . . . but she wouldn't . . . she said I disgusted her." He rocked back and forth in his pain.

Akitada asked more gently, "Why did you kill your master when you found him unconscious?"

There was a long silence, and then Otagi said, "I heard him shouting that he would kill them both. It was terrible. He was a man with a violent temper, and I was sorry for what I had done. There was a fight, a lot of noise. Then it got quiet, and I heard a door close. When I went in, I found him unconscious on the floor. Chiyo had left with her lover, and I knew that he would see her dead for what she had done." He sobbed softly. "I could not let him do that to her."

That afternoon the rain finally stopped. Akitada was standing near the gate to the jail, when Hajimaro came out, a free man at last. He watched him amble off aimlessly, his muscular build shortened by the drooping shoulders and hanging head. Would he make his way to Rashomon, to join the hopeless poor there, perhaps to learn to lie and cheat, to rob out of greed rather than hunger?

"Hajimaro," he shouted.

The other man turned.

"Do you need work and a place to stay?"

The robber's face broke into its gentle smile. He nodded.

At that moment, the clouds parted and the sun came out again.

AKITADA AND THE WAY OF JUSTICE

INSTRUMENTS OF MURDER

In 1014, Akitada undertakes his first major official assignment in Kazusa province. These adventures are described in **The Dragon Scroll**. *Back in the capital the following year, he courts and marries his childhood sweetheart, Tamako, daughter of his former professor, whose death is part of Akitada's investigation into the cases described in* **Rashomon Gate**. *The story that follows involves an incident that happened shortly after the events of* **Rashomon Gate**, *but before Akitada left the capital again to take up his duties as provisional governor of Echigo province. It features Tora, his loyal but disrespectful assistant, and the tradesmen and artists of the city.*

Heian-Kyo (Kyoto), 1015; Leaf-changing Month:

Akitada was playing his new flute to the breaking dawn. He was constrained to practice in the far corner of his garden, in a vine-covered shack, well away from the main house, because his efforts grated on the ears of his household. They were too polite to say so but had a habit of scattering every time he pulled out his beloved flute.

Therefore he was surprised to see his secretary Seimei coming quickly toward him along the smooth stones of the old path. He broke off a tender rendition of "The village in the forest" and called out, "What's the matter?"

Seimei stopped breathlessly to wipe beads of perspiration from his wrinkled brow. In spite of the early hour, it was already hot and humid though summer was past. "I'm very sorry, sir," he said, "but there is a constable at the gate. He says that Tora has been arrested for a double murder."

Akitada's mouth fell open. "Tora? A double murder?"

"Yes, sir. It sounds serious. The earth always shakes when we least expect it."

Akitada sighed and tucked his flute into his sleeve. "There is some mistake, of course, but I had better go and see. Bring me my cap and tell my wife that I have been called away."

AKITADA AND THE WAY OF JUSTICE

"I brought your cap, sir." Seimei produced it from his voluminous sleeve, along with a small bronze mirror. Holding up the mirror, he said smugly, "They say 'Have an umbrella ready before it rains!'"

Peering into the mirror, Akitada adjusted the stiff black silk cap on his topknot and tied the black cords under his chin. "Very well. If you haven't done so already, you might send to the ministry and tell them I'll be a little late. It shouldn't take long to clear this up."

But he met with difficulties the moment he arrived at the office of the warden of the East River Village, a pleasure quarter on the left bank of the Kamo. His name meant nothing to the fat warden and red-coated constable, and the colored trim on his hat denoting his rank passed unnoticed. The warden merely stared rudely and said, "No one is admitted. Orders of the Metropolitan Police."

Akitada snapped, "Announce my presence to the person in charge of the case or I shall report your insolence."

The warden opened his mouth, thought better of it, and disappeared. The sound of muffled voices came from the rear of the building. Someone said loudly, "Did you say 'Sugawara'?" The warden's reply was inaudible, but the other voice was still raised in frustration: "Get rid of him—any way you like. That's all I need. The officious meddler from the ministry!"

Nothing further happened. Akitada cast a glance at the impassive face of the constable on duty, sighed, and then went to sit on a grimy mat in the corner. After a moment he drew his flute from his sleeve and began to play the opening notes of "The village in the forest."

The inner door opened abruptly and an official, wearing a red tunic and the insignia of a police inspector on his black cap, burst into the room.

"What's this infernal noise?" he shouted. His eyes fell on Akitada. He took in the silk robe and the blue rank trim on his cap and swallowed. Then he bowed and said, "I beg your pardon, sir. This filthy hovel distorts sound dreadfully."

"Really?" Akitada looked about him vaguely. "I'm Sugawara. You have my servant in custody?"

"Oh." The inspector looked as if he had bitten on a cherry stone with a sore tooth. He waved his hands and said quickly, "It's nothing, sir. Nothing at all to require your attention. Merely a small matter of obstructing the law, sir."

"Not a double murder?" Akitada asked, disappointed.

"No, no. Just a silly mistake of the local authorities. Your man came across two bodies and called the warden who did not like his manner and arrested him. When I arrived and looked into the matter, it all became clear. Your servant is free to go. The case is solved."

"You have already solved both murders?"

"Oh, yes. It was one murder only. A beggar stabbed a drunken wrestler during a robbery, and then succumbed to his evil deed."

"I beg your pardon?"

"He died of natural causes near his victim. It will close the case." The inspector looked complacent.

Akitada raised his eyebrows. "That is very strange indeed. Perhaps I might have a look at the bodies?" He rose and tucked the flute back into his sleeve.

The inspector cleared his throat. "Er . . . ah . . . I'm expecting the coroner."

"No trouble at all, my friend," Akitada said breezily and started toward the corridor. "It's a particular interest of mine, you know. You may not be aware of it, but I have been able to solve a number of puzzling crimes in the past. I should be delighted to offer my views on this case."

The inspector gulped and moved aside. "Er . . . there is really no case . . . down the hall and to the left," he said, but Akitada had already passed him and was stepping into the room in question.

The dead men lay naked on grimy straw mats. One looked to be in his thirties or early forties, a big, handsome man with muscular legs and arms and a belly which showed signs of turning to flab. Several stab wounds to the left chest and side had torn the thick skin, bleeding profusely down the left side of his belly, groin and upper thigh. The cause of death was obvious, but Akitada peered at the wounds, gauging their width and placement, touching the skin and dried blood, and moving fingers and wrists. Then he turned to the other body.

This man was in most respects the opposite. He was elderly—at least sixty, thought Akitada—short, fat and unhealthy looking. His arms and legs were pitifully thin and weak. Akitada inspected every inch of the body, paying particular attention to the scalp and face, but found no wounds, only a trickle of blood from one nostril and ear. For a few moments he stood, pursing his lips and pulling his left earlobe. Then he bent again to check the dead man's palms, fingernails, and the soles of his feet.

The inspector, who had followed him and watched impatiently, offered a comment now. "That's the killer. A common beggar. They hang about the river front begging from drunks returning from parties. When times get bad, they turn to robbery. This one must've found the wrestler sleeping it off—you can still smell the wine on him—and tried to get his money from his belt. No doubt the wrestler caught him at it, and the beggar had no choice but to kill him."

Akitada looked at the policeman. "With what?" he asked.

The inspector pointed to a package wrapped in oiled paper. "A short sword. We found it in a rain barrel near the site."

Akitada unwrapped the parcel, exclaimed in surprise, and raised a short sword, perfectly clean, its slim graceful blade mounted on a grip of black metal heavily inlaid in pure gold with a design of waving grasses. "How did a beggar get a sword like this?" he asked. "For that matter, what makes you think he is a beggar?"

"His clothes, sir." The inspector indicated two bundles in the corner. "As to the sword, we cannot be sure yet, but he either took it from the victim or he stole it someplace earlier."

AKITADA AND THE WAY OF JUSTICE

Akitada grunted. He undid the first bundle and found the beggar's rags, a torn grey robe, its tattered bottom so short it probably barely covered his legs, for there was nothing else except the white loincloth. The robe was horribly stained with blood on the front, the right side, and the right sleeve. The loin cloth was quite clean. Akitada frowned, holding up the garments and looking from them to the corpses and back again. Then he put them down and took up the wrestler's clothes: a loin cloth, a silk under robe, sky blue cotton outer robe with a large white pattern of waves and cranes, and a black and white checked cotton sash. Both robes were slashed and blood-soaked in the chest area, and the sash and loin cloth were deeply stained. He nodded and put them back.

"May I now see my servant?" he asked.

Tora crouched in the corner of a bare cell in the back of the warden's house. His face was bruised, and his hands and feet were chained, and there was blood on his clothes, but he greeted Akitada with a grin.

"Knew you'd come, sir. I told the fools you'd straighten them out in short order. Never saw a warden as stupid as this one. Have you seen the bodies? Any ideas what happened?"

Akitada raised his hand. "Not so fast! I should be the one to ask you what happened."

"Oh. One of the victims is Kiyomura, a fourth-rate wrestler. I've never laid eyes on the other one. I ate supper last night with Kiyomura and some others in the Phoenix Pavilion. That's a restaurant on the river. It was hot, and the Phoenix Pavilion has balconies hanging over the water. There's a cool breeze with a fine view of the city and of pleasure barges with lots of pretty girls in them, and they serve an excellent cheap wine."

Akitada frowned. "Spare me the details of your frivolities. What about the wrestler?"

"Kiyomura used to be a pretty decent wrestler, but this year he didn't place at all. Too much high living, I think."

"How did he support himself?"

Tora shook his head. "It's a mystery. Last night he had plenty of money. Bragged that he'd found his own gold mine and talked about getting gifts from an admirer."

"Sometimes wrestlers enjoy the sexual attentions of male patrons. Could that have been the case here?"

"Not him. He was always going on about women and how his latest lady love is a great beauty. Ando confirmed it."

"Ando?"

"One of the other fellows. A raw youngster, but he's a talented painter and he was nagging Kiyomura about this girlfriend. He wants to paint her as the goddess Kannon." Tora chuckled. "Ando's at an age where every pretty face looks like a goddess, and Kiyomura was his hero, even if he treated the poor kid like a stray dog. Come to think of it, Ando was supposed to take Kiyomura home. Kiyomura was drunk when I left."

"Might Ando have had a reason to kill him?"

"He's just a boy. Still, Kiyomura had a cruel streak, especially when he was drinking. He always made fun of Ando and Ando was getting pretty sensitive." Tora shook his head. "No, I'll never believe it. For that matter, Kiyomura quarreled with just about everybody last night."

"Oh?"

"Well, he made both Saemon and Hiraga angry. Saemon's a pharmacist with a shop near the bridge, but most of his custom comes from the River village. He does a great business in aphrodisiacs, ointments, massages, needle therapy and *moxa*." Tora shuddered. "Never could understand people who like to be stuck with needles or have those herbal pills burned on their backs. Hiraga's a sword smith. What's the matter?"

Akitada's brows had shot up. "A sword smith? A good one?"

"The best! A real craftsman. I've wondered why he spent time with the rest of us. His family's large, and he's more serious and settled. Of course, Saemon's married, but Saemon has a new wife and no children yet. Ugly fellow, Saemon, but his business is good and he saved up to buy out one of the courtesans in the village. Kiyomura never missed a chance to rib Saemon about it."

"So Kiyomura managed to insult the painter Ando and this Saemon last night. What about the sword smith?"

"He did worse than that with Hiraga. He slapped him. I thought Hiraga would kill him then and there." Tora broke off in dismay. "Forget that. Nothing happened. Hiraga calmed down, and Kiyomura apologized."

"I don't suppose Hiraga had one of his swords with him?"

Tora looked uncomfortable. "Well, he always carries a short sword. It used to drive Kiyomura crazy. Kiyomura wanted that sword, but Hiraga wouldn't sell it to him. Told him to stick to wrestling, that swords were for swordsmen."

"Hm." Akitada pulled his earlobe and thought. Then he got up. "Luckily that inspector does not seem to suspect you any longer, but I don't like this case. I'll have you released, and you can take me to talk to your friends."

As the inspector was seeing them out with ill-concealed relief, they met a constable walking in with a slight, sallow-faced man in a plain dark blue robe.

"Saemon," said Tora and stopped. "What are you doing here?"

The pharmacist had a long, lantern-jawed face and sparse ill-kempt hair, but his black eyes were sharp and intelligent and moved instantly from Tora to Akitada. There was a flicker of interest, and then the man bowed very humbly.

Tora made the introductions and added, "Saemon can testify to Kiyomura's temper last night. Is that why you're here, Saemon? To give a statement?"

"No, Tora. I was called to examine the bodies. My place is just across the bridge, and I happened to be home. A terrible thing, but I'm afraid I know nothing about it. I left the restaurant hours before the rest of you." Saemon clutched his bamboo case of medicines and instruments with long, sinewy fingers and looked at the inspector.

"If you'll excuse us?" The inspector pointedly held the door open for Akitada and Tora and bowed them out.

"So the pharmacist lives nearby," Akitada remarked as they were walking away from the warden's office.

"Yes. Look." Tora pointed at a stand of willows on the river bank where a huddle of locals stood talking and staring at a dark-stained patch of weeds. "That's where it happened."

Akitada nodded without much interest, glancing briefly at the rain barrel of the first house they passed. "Let's talk to the young painter first," he said.

Ando lived in the city, not far from the bridge, in a narrow tenement where he shared quarters with other single men and women of modest means. Many of them clearly kept late hours, for the doors were closed and sounds of snoring filled the narrow, dark hallway. A slatternly female, not much more than a child but with smudged rouge staining her lips, blinked sleepily at them from a doorway.

"Ando?" she said vaguely. "Oh, he's down that way. The last room on the right." She called after them, "Why don't you stop by on your way out? I can show you something better than pictures. Two for the price of one."

They found the painter in a frenzy of destruction. He was ripping apart a scroll of ink sketches, balling up the pieces and flinging them violently about a room which was perfectly bare except for a large silk painting of a goddess and a box of paints. The goddess was impressive but faceless.

When he saw his visitors, a look of panic replaced the angry scowl on his face. His attempt at growing a mustache emphasized his boyish looks. "Tora," he said, "what do you want?" He dropped the shredded sketches and kicked the pieces into a corner. Akitada picked one up and smoothed it out.

"Please don't look at it!" cried the painter. "Here, give it to me. They are just old scribbles. I have better stuff, if you're interested."

The sketch showed the face of a young woman, her hair coiled behind her head and a small caste mark between her eyes in the manner of Buddhist deities. Akitada glanced at the painting. "I think this is a charming face for your Kannon," he said. "Most of the paintings of the goddess depict round-faced Chinese matrons. I like this Japanese beauty very much better."

The young painter snatched at the sketch. "No. It's all wrong."

"Relax, Ando," said Tora. "This is my master, and we're not here about the painting. Last night Kiyomura was killed on the other side of the river."

"Kiyomura's dead?" Ando paled and his arms dropped to his sides. "I had nothing to do with it," he said quickly.

"We did not imply that you did," Akitada assured him, putting the sketch into his sleeve. "But you were to accompany your friend home last night. What happened?"

"I didn't. He sent me away. He was quite well when I left. I swear it."

"Don't be a cursed fool, Ando," cried Tora. "He wasn't well when I left. He was drunk and mean, and you know it. How did you expect him to get home in that state?"

Ando's livid features flushed. "Why should I care?" he said. "The bastard's never had a word of thanks for anything I've ever done. Just, 'Hey, boy, fetch me some wine from the wine shop. I'll pay you later,' or 'Stop hanging around like some hungry cur!' or 'When's the last time your mother gave you suck, you baby?'" He broke off, and turned to the painting of the goddess in a fresh fury. Picking up a small knife used to trim brushes, he slashed at the goddess's elegant robes and veils, her dainty hands and feet, and the coiled dark hair on her bejewelled faceless head. "I'm not a child!" he sobbed. "I'm a man. I'll show him. I'll show them all."

"Stop, Ando," cried Tora, trying to take the knife away from him.

"Come," said Akitada, taking Tora's arm. "He needs to be alone."

Outside Tora said, "We should have kept at him. I've never seen Ando so upset. I bet there's a woman behind it. Maybe it's Kiyomura's latest courtesan."

Akitada stopped. "Courtesan," he muttered. "Perhaps . . . the motive is there . . . and it would explain . . . but how to prove it?" He shook his head in puzzlement.

At that moment, two constables ran up, twisted Tora's arms behind his back, and tied them with chains before either of them could protest.

"Sorry, sir," gasped the inspector, panting up behind them, "but we must arrest your servant again. New information."

"What, in the name of the ten judges of hell?" snarled Tora, struggling between the scowling constables and getting viciously prodded with their steel rods.

"You were heard to threaten the victim," said the inspector, catching his breath.

"That cursed Saemon! I might have known he'd make trouble."

The inspector looked at Akitada, shook his head regretfully and said with feeling, "Believe me, sir, I'd do anything to avoid this. But your servant was found on the scene, his robe blood-stained,"—he cast a glance at Tora's sleeve which did show some rust-colored splotches—"and now we have two witnesses who say that he was threatening the victim's life only hours before the murder."

Akitada looked at Tora, who had paled and mumbled, "We had a small disagreement at the Phoenix Pavilion. The waitress must've heard. And I checked Kiyomura's body. That's how I got his blood on me."

"You should have told me. What did you argue about?"

Tora looked away. "He said some things about you, sir."

Akitada bit his lip. The gossip about his interest in crime was not flattering. Looking at the inspector, he pleaded, "Why not wait until you finish your investigation? What about the identity of the second man or the owner of the sword?"

The inspector shook his head. "The investigation is in the hands of the Metropolitan Police, sir," he said in an official tone.

"Inspector, it is essential that a good coroner take a very close look at the second victim . . ."

The inspector's face stiffened, and he cut in, "The coroner has seen both bodies and confirmed earlier findings. That is all I can tell you at this time." He turned his back on Akitada and motioned to his constables to proceed with their prisoner.

"Wait! I must have a word with Tora first."

"Aren't you coming with us, sir?" Tora asked, his voice filled with panic.

"No, Tora. I had better solve this mystery as quickly as possible. How do I find the sword smith's place?"

Tora explained, adding loudly for the benefit of the inspector and the constables, "Don't worry about me, sir. I know you will be back with the name of the real killer in no time at all."

Akitada made one last appeal to the inspector. "The so-called beggar's identity must be verified. . ." he began, but they were already walking away from him.

Neither his certainty that Tora was innocent, nor his virtual certainty about the killer was particularly reassuring at this moment. Knowing a thing was not the same as proving it. Moreover, as Tora was now officially charged with murder, questioning would begin immediately, and this involved vicious beatings until the suspect's resistance was broken and he confessed. The situation had suddenly turned ominous.

Hiraga lived in a street of prosperous craftsmen but his home was modest. Akitada could hear children's voices and the sound of metal striking metal. As soon as he opened the creaking bamboo gate, a small boy appeared and was joined immediately by three others, each slightly bigger than the first. They stood and stared at him.

Akitada saw them and smiled. "Good morning."

The boys blushed furiously and ran away. The smallest took off, shouting for his mother. A short chubby woman appeared, flustered, with a baby strapped to her back and wiping wet hands on her apron.

"Welcome to this humble house." She bowed several times, waking the baby, which blinked at the bright sunlight and set up a wail. Its mother jiggled it and said, "Please come in and forgive my rude children. If you have come to place an order, my husband will soon be free."

"Mrs. Hiraga?" Akitada asked, slipping off his shoes and stepping up to the oiled wooden floor in his white socks. He smiled at the squalling child and tickled it into gurgling laughter.

"Yes." She blushed and touched her apron. The baby set up another wail. "Please forgive the noise and my dirty clothes. There is much work with all the children. We have eight, and they are a constant shame to their parents."

"On the contrary. You are blessed." Akitada took out his flute and blew a few notes for the baby. It fell silent, gulped, and stared with open mouth.

"Ah, your son has a fine ear for music." Akitada exchanged a smile with its mother. "Your husband is a lucky man to have such a fine family."

She blushed with pleasure. "Five unmannerly boys and three useless girls," she sighed. "We are a great burden to him."

The noise in the back of the house had ceased, and the sword smith appeared.

"Welcome," he said with a bow, sliding open a door, and nodding to his wife. Akitada entered a large room that held nothing but two or three cushions and many swords of all sizes on carved wood stands or on hooks on the walls, some in beautifully worked scabbards, others showing their naked blades of bluish steel. Akitada went over to look at them, taking up a few to test their weight and balance. He complimented Hiraga on his superb workmanship.

"I have far to go in my craft," the sword smith said modestly. "Is the gentleman a swordsman?"

"No. My name is Sugawara, and I am here on another matter."

The sword smith's face fell, but he indicated the cushions, and Akitada seated himself. Hiraga joined him, looking politely expectant. Mrs. Hiraga, without baby, brought wine and a plate of pickled vegetables. She served them and then seated herself near the door.

Akitada sipped and praised the wine, then said, "The wrestler Kiyomura was murdered last night. I believe you know him?"

Mrs. Hiraga gasped and her husband started up. "Kiyomura murdered?" He stopped and looked at Akitada more sharply. "Forgive me, sir. How stupid of me. You must be Tora's master. What happened?"

"Tora has been arrested. He found the body, and a man called Saemon told the police that Tora threatened the victim's life."

"Saemon's a fool." Hiraga made a face. "Kiyomura was very drunk and made all of us angry last night. It meant nothing. How did he die?"

"He was stabbed several times on his way home, probably with a short sword found in a rain barrel nearby."

Hiraga stiffened. "A short sword?"

"Yes. I wondered if it might be yours. It is very similar to some of your work. The handle is very dark, almost black, with an inlay of golden reeds on the grip and sword guard."

There was a cry from the door.

Hiraga said nothing but rose and left the room. When Akitada looked after him, he noticed an expression of terror on the wife's face. Hiraga, however, returned in a moment, carrying another short sword. He extended it to Akitada, saying, "This is the one I carried last night."

Akitada received it with a bow. It was beautiful and looked like the murder weapon except that this grip and hilt were ornamented with a silver filigree of leaves and flowers. Its blade, like those on display, had a fine blue sheen that had been lacking in the sword found by the police. Akitada commented on this.

"Water damages the metal. No true swordsman would throw a fine blade into a rain barrel." Hiraga's voice was tight either with anger or nerves. "That is why I do not sell my swords into improper hands. The other sword . . . It may be one of mine, but I did not have it last night." There was a pause during which he glanced at his wife before adding, "However, you said Kiyomura was stabbed. You will notice that the blade of a sword turns slightly upward. The sharp edge is underneath. It is not effective for stabbing, as anyone familiar with swords will tell you."

Akitada nodded. "You are quite right. Still, would it be possible to kill a man using this sword like a knife?"

"Yes. But only someone completely unfamiliar with swords would do such a thing." Hiraga glanced again toward his wife who seemed to have become smaller and shrunk into herself.

"Or a man who wished others to think so," Akitada said.

"True, my lord." The sword smith's face was expressionless. There was a soft sob and then the sound of the door closing. Mrs. Hiraga had left.

"Thank you. You have been very helpful." Akitada got up, followed by his host. In the hallway they passed a hanging calligraphy scroll with a Chinese verse: "Alive, man is a passing traveler—dead, a man come home. One brief journey between earth and heaven." Akitada gestured at the saying. "It is true," he said, "that man's life is short and uncertain, but his greatest blessing is his family."

For a moment Hiraga looked puzzled; then he nodded slowly and bowed.

The pharmacist's house was on the river bank, two doors down river from the bridge. A large sign advertised all sorts of cures and treatments. An older woman with a suspicious manner answered Akitada's knock. "The doctor's been called away and his wife is still abed," she said sharply.

"I shall wait until he returns. Please let your mistress know I am here."

"I am the doctor's sister," she snapped, leading Akitada to a room with dirty mats and a tattered screen decorated with garish flowers and birds. She muttered under her breath, "Mistress! That one? Honest women rise with the dawn and serve their husbands, but not this one. A harlot. Singing lewd songs, gallivanting about till all hours, and then sleeping the day away." She tossed a cushion on the floor for him and flounced out of the room, leaving Akitada to bide his time.

Women's voices, raised in lengthy and angry argument, assaulted his ears as he waited.

Saemon's wife surprised Akitada. She lacked the vulgarity he had expected from a former courtesan. A slender young woman in a pale blue silk gown, she came in quietly, carrying a flask and two cups, and greeted him with the relaxed informality found only in upper class courtesans.

AKITADA AND THE WAY OF JUSTICE

"Forgive the wine, your Honor," she said in a melodious voice, giving him a practiced glance from under long lashes. "I'm afraid it is not what you're used to."

"Your company will more than make up for it," Akitada said with a smile.

"My husband will return soon. I hope your Honor is not in ill health?"

"Not at all. I'm here on a different matter. Tell me, do you know the painter Ando?"

She frowned prettily. "I don't think so."

Akitada pulled the sketch from his sleeve. "He intended this for the head of a painting of Kannon. It looks like you."

She looked, smiled, shook her head. "You flatter me, sir,"—another sidelong glance and smile—"but it is not of me. Only the hairstyle is similar." Her hand touched the coil of glossy hair on her neck with practiced grace.

"My mistake. I stopped at his place to tell him of the death of a friend. It was the reason I came to see your husband."

"A death? How sad."

"Yes. A wrestler by the name of Kiyomura was killed last night."

"Ki—" Her voice failed.

Akitada, pretending not to notice her shock and the sick pallor of her face, said "The police blame vagrants. They are searching for the killer now. Do you mind if I pass the time practicing my flute?" Without waiting for her permission, he took the instrument from his sleeve and blew a few notes. "The weapon was a sword made by the sword smith Hiraga." He blew a few more trills. "I hope you don't mind my playing. I have so little time for it."

"No." Her eyes wandered about the room. Akitada played, watching her restless eyes, her hands twisting the silk of her gown.

"Do you have to play that tune?" she cried suddenly.

Akitada lowered his flute with a look of surprise. "You don't like love songs? Oh. The murder. Forgive me. Yes. Very tragic. An athlete at the beginning of his career. Perhaps you have heard of him?"

"Kiyomura had no honor," she said bitterly. "Why should I care if someone killed him? He used women like paper tissues, soiled them, and threw them away."

"Ah. You were his lover," Akitada said softly. "I think the painter must have seen you two together and made the sketch from memory."

"You must despise me," she said with a shudder. "Once a whore, always a whore. That is what my husband's sister says. But we fell in love a long time ago, before Saemon met me. Back when I was very young and when Kiyomura was different. I would have gone with him to hell itself then, but he was married to his profession." She laughed bitterly. "We both changed." She covered her face with trembling hands. "Kiyomura is nothing to me, nothing!" she cried.

Akitada looked thunderstruck. Then, in his gentlest voice, he lied. "You are wrong. He loved you all his life, you know. That is why he failed at wrestling."

She lowered her hands. Her cheeks were wet with tears. "Truly?"

AKITADA AND THE WAY OF JUSTICE

Before Akitada could confirm his lie with other lies, the sliding door flew back on squeaking tracks, and her husband walked in. "What's this?" he cried, glaring at his wife. "How dare you entertain men in my absence?"

She rose with a quiet restraint Akitada admired, and said, "Lord Sugawara has come to see you, husband."

Saemon recognized Akitada belatedly. He snapped to his wife, "Put on something decent! You look like a slut." Seating himself across from Akitada, he bowed and muttered, "Sorry, my Lord."

Akitada put on his haughtiest manner and let his eyes move over Saemon's shabby blue cotton robe. "Hmm."

Saemon fidgeted. "I hope you will pardon this humble place, sir. I'm a poor man. Is it about Kiyomura?"

"Yes. I am told you laid certain charges against Tora while suppressing other evidence. I wondered why."

Saemon flushed. "I told the truth. It could not be helped."

"All of you quarreled with the wrestler. All of you had cause to kill him."

"Not I."

"On the contrary. You had the best reason of all."

Saemon bared yellow teeth in an attempt at a smile. "Your Honor is joking."

The sliding door opened again, and Saemon's sister came in with more wine and another cup. Noticing Saemon's clothes, she asked, "Why are you wearing that old thing? What happened to your nice gray robe?" Without waiting for an answer, she deposited the tray and grumbled, "If you didn't let that slut spend your hard-earned money on that beggarly Hiraga bunch, you'd have proper clothes for a man of your standing."

Saemon hissed, "Stop your babbling, woman! Your foolish chatter offends our guest."

The woman drew herself up sharply. Angry color suffused her face and the resemblance to her brother was startling. "Foolish am I? All day and all night I work and worry, and that is what I get? I take care of your house, your clothes, your meals like a servant. And I keep an eye on that whore you brought into our home who spends your money like water while we live like paupers. Hah! I hope she bought that sword to slit your throat some night."

"Out!" Saemon was up, pointing a shaking finger at the door. His sister tossed her head and left. He said to Akitada, "I made the mistake of marrying a former courtesan. It has upset my household. I shall return in a moment," and followed her.

The walls were thin, and again Akitada could hear angry shouting from the back of the house. He took his flute from his sleeve and looked at it thoughtfully. There were sounds of a scuffle and then a woman's cries, abruptly stifled. Saemon returned, breathing heavily, and sat back down.

Akitada said, "You performed the examination of the bodies. May I ask what you found?"

AKITADA AND THE WAY OF JUSTICE

Saemon calmed down a little. "Kiyomura was stabbed repeatedly," he said. "At least two thrusts went straight to his heart. The beggar died of an apoplexy, possibly brought on by witnessing the murder."

"Ingenious."

Saemon frowned. "What do you mean? And what did you mean by saying I had the best motive."

"Jealousy is a powerful motive, although in your case envy, pride, and greed entered into it also. You are an ordinary, hard-working man who toiled and saved for many years to buy the love of a beautiful woman. Then Kiyomura, who was by all accounts an obnoxious wastrel and womanizer, arrived on the scene and not only took your new wife, but asked her to support his luxurious life style with your money."

Saemon was on his feet. "That's a lie!"

"Is it? Kiyomura was particularly liberal with money last night, wasn't he? And he enjoyed cruel taunts. He talked about an admirer and bragged that he had found a goldmine, and then he looked at you, and you realized that you had been subsidizing his life style all along."

Saemon cried, "Lies, all lies. Has my wife --?"

Akitada said quickly, "No. Your wife has not betrayed you. You betrayed yourself in your past actions. Perhaps Hiraga's presence last night reminded you of his wife's visit to your house. You knew that Hiraga would think you unworthy of one of his swords. But Hiraga's wife sold your wife a weapon without her husband's permission because a large family of hungry children requires more income than a sword smith with such exacting standards in his customers can supply. When you discovered the sword, I am sure it rankled that your money had gone toward the support of Hiraga's family. In any case, the quarrel between Hiraga and Kiyomura gave you an idea of the perfect revenge. You rushed home for the sword your wife had purchased—out of compassion for Mrs. Hiraga, I suspect, although you assumed it was for her lover—and you ambushed the drunken Kiyomura, intending to cast suspicion on Hiraga."

A slow breath escaped from Saemon's lips. His right hand crept to his sash and his eyes stared fixedly into Akitada's. Then, exploding into sudden movement, he rushed forward. Something flashed in his raised hand. Akitada barely managed to twist out of the way, bringing his flute down sharply on Saemon's wrist. There was a crack, a cry of pain, and then Akitada pinioned the pharmacist to the floor, twisting his arm behind his back.

The door opened abruptly.

"Ah, just in time, Inspector," said Akitada, looking up from Saemon's back. "Here's your killer. I was wondering how to proceed. You must have the power of divination."

The inspector gestured to two constables who quickly tied the dazed Saemon with the thin chains they wore around their waists. Saemon's wife, dishevelled, one eye blackened, and bruises covering her pale face, came in after them. She did not look at her husband. Her eyes were on Akitada.

"Thank heaven you are all right, sir," she said through swollen lips. "I hurried as fast as I could."

The inspector said, "She has accused her husband of Kiyomura's murder and identified the sword as one she purchased recently. Kiyomura was her lover."

Saemon's sister joined them, her eyes flying around the room.

Saemon jerked on his chains and cursed his wife. "Demon!" he cried, his face distorted with fury, "Whore! It's all part of a plot. I'm charging her, Inspector. She killed the wrestler herself because she found a better lover." He jerked his chin towards Akitada. "Yes, a nobleman. I caught them at their filthy game, and this is what they did, trying to get rid of me now."

Akitada was as dumfounded by this accusation as everyone else. Not so Saemon's sister, who cried, "It's the truth. She was a whore before he married her, and she sleeps with every man who will have her still. I knew at once what this . . . this person"—she pointed at Akitada—"had in mind when he came here. He made sure Saemon was gone and then asked for her. But I sent for my brother, and he came at once. They were doing it, right there, on the floor of her husband's house. Slut!"

The inspector's eyes went to Saemon's wife, took in the bruises and the tearful look she gave Akitada, and asked, "Is that why your husband beat you?"

"Of course it is," cried the sister. "Only a saint could have restrained himself."

Saemon's wife did the worst thing she could possibly do. She ran to Akitada, knelt and pressed his hand to her cheek. "Forgive me," she sobbed. "I did not wish to cause you trouble. I would gladly die to undo this evil thing."

Akitada saw suspicion change to certainty in the inspector's eyes. And her husband smiled. The man was as slippery as an eel and about to escape the net. Worse, Akitada's reputation, already damaged in the eyes of his superior, would not survive this tale of sexual misconduct leading to a false murder charge laid against a respectable citizen.

He considered his situation and knew that the inspector was also put to a test. If he threw in his lot with Akitada, his punishment for a miscarriage of justice could be exile. And what about Tora?

After an uncomfortable moment, the inspector walked to Saemon and bent to untie his chains. Saemon's lip twitched in triumph. His wife released Akitada's hand with a small cry of despair and ran from the room.

"You are making a mistake," Akitada said. "This man has killed twice, for the other body you found is his second victim, not a beggar, but an innocent passerby who must have happened upon a murder scene before the killer could wash the bloodstains off himself. That is why I insisted you discover his identity."

Saemon shouted, "Even an idiot could see there were no wounds on the beggar. How was he killed?"

Akitada walked to the wall and bent to pick up a slender steel needle. "This," he said, extending the needle to the inspector, "is the weapon that man tried to use against me before your arrival, and he had used the same method to eliminate the witness to his crime. I suggested a careful examination. Instead you asked the murderer to investigate the cause of death. Even if you do not find a needle in the man's head, you will find blood in the man's ear or nose." He turned to Saemon. "You may not know how to use a sword, but you are a skilled acupuncturist with medical training. Not only are the tools of your trade always with you in that satchel you carry, but you know how to inflict a fatal wound, whether it is a sword cut to the heart, or a needle puncture through an ear or nostril to the brain."

"You will find no needle," cried Saemon, "and bleeding from the nose and ears is common in cases of strokes."

The inspector looked from the needle in his hand to Saemon and the chain which still lay at the pharmacist's feet. Before Saemon could speak again, his sister shouted, "Besides anyone can use those needles. It means nothing. I can testify that my brother returned early last night."

"You cannot," said Saemon's wife from the door. All eyes went to her. She was very pale except for the bruises, and she clutched a brown-striped man's robe to her chest. "My husband left in a grey robe yesterday. I went to look for it and found this instead."

The inspector snatched the robe from her hands and held it up. It was clearly too large for the thin Saemon.

"It's not his," Saemon's wife said unnecessarily. "I've never seen it before. What happened to your grey robe, husband?"

"The police have it," said Akitada. "Your husband traded clothes with his second victim. He tore it to make the dead man look like a vagrant, forgetting that beggars rarely wear clean, white loin cloths.

"Tie him up again," the inspector told his constables.

Saemon cursed, and his sister wailed, "Don't believe them. She's an evil woman. What kind of wife turns on her own husband? Tell me that."

They ignored her. The constables led Saemon away, and the inspector turned to Akitada. "A very strange case. It will depend on identifying the second man, easily done of course, but . . . er . . . my apologies for your inconvenience. Your servant will be released immediately." He bowed and was gone.

Saemon's sister stood uncertainly for a moment, then she looked at the younger woman. "You have no right here anymore," she said venomously. "Get out of my house! If you're here when I return, I'll have you whipped through the streets for the adulteress you are." Then she ran after the police.

Saemon's wife hung her head. "She's right," she said, wringing her hands. "I am a terrible wife. I betrayed my husband, again and again. Now he will die because of me. I know I am worthless. There is nothing to do, but to die."

Akitada said quickly, "No. Life thrusts difficult choices upon us. Your courage and sacrifice have saved my servant's life and given peace to the spirits of the murdered men. You have also averted a good deal of unpleasantness for me and my family. Such acts will not go unrewarded. You may stay in my home until you find another, and you may count on me for money or any other help toward a new life."

She flushed and her eyes moistened. "Your home?" She shook her head with a sad smile. "You are very kind, sir, but your ladies would not welcome someone like me. No, don't insist." She paused. "But if I might borrow travel funds? I would like to see my parents again. They are getting old and I would like to look after them. "

The sun was setting. A refreshing wind blew from the western mountains, and here and there sere leaves drifted from the trees. The willows on the bank of the Kamo had turned yellow, and their dancing branches looked like threads of golden silk against the brown brocade of the river. The heat had finally broken, but Akitada, who was walking across the bridge, had a face full of gloom.

"Sir, sir!" Tora was running toward him, grinning broadly. "I knew you would do it."

Akitada stopped. "I paid a heavy price," he said sadly, reaching into his sleeve and holding out his broken flute.

THE CURIO DEALER'S WIFE

*Akitada serves for four years in the North (**Black Arrow** and **Island of Exiles**) before returning to the Ministry of Justice in the capital. Married and with a young son, he has to deal with the death of his mother and patch up family disasters while a serial killer targets him and his family (**The Hell Screen**). The next three cases happen afterwards, during the happiest years of his marriage. In the first, Akitada's empathy draws him into the lives of the ordinary people around him. In this story, Captain Kobe reappears as the conscientious officer of the law.*

Heian-Kyo (Kyoto), 1020; Frost Month (December).

Akitada was on his way to the curio store when he saw her. The woman was standing on a stone at the corner of the substantial and well-kept Hamada property, peering over the fence into the narrow garden beside the house.

It was not this fact which made him pause. Many hungry beggars checked out the premises of prosperous merchants in search of a friendly servant. This woman, who was no longer young, was dressed poorly for this chilly season. Her clothing was of the cheapest faded cotton, and she wore mended straw sandals on her bare feet. But there was a certain cleanliness about her, and her silver-streaked hair had been pinned up with great care. Also, her thin figure was very straight and her bare arms and hands graceful. None of these things were common among female beggars. Besides, Akitada thought, there was something familiar about her hairstyle and the way she held her shapely head.

He approached and startled her. She stepped down from the stone quickly but then relaxed.

"Forgive me," said Akitada, inclining his head politely. "For a moment I thought I recognized you."

Her face was slender, lined by age or anxiety, the eyes lustrous as if moistened by unshed tears, and her lips were compressed firmly. Akitada thought she looked like someone who held in her pain by sheer force of will.

She averted her face. "Possibly," she said softly and brushed past him.

The voice reminded him. It was deep for a woman and had a lovely resonance.

"Mrs. Hamada!" Akitada exclaimed. "Wait! You are Mrs. Hamada, aren't you?"

She stopped without turning; just stood there, perfectly still and straight, waiting.

He walked around her and bowed again. "My name is Sugawara. I am with the Ministry of Justice and I used to visit your fine store quite often in the past. Once you waited on me. I was buying a flute."

As he spoke, his eyes fell to her clothing, her straw-sandaled feet again. The prosperous merchant's wife he recalled had worn plain but costly silk gowns and silk stockings.

"I am no longer Mrs. Hamada," she said, not raising her head.

Thoughts raced through Akitada's mind. He vaguely remembered hearing that the curio dealer Hamada had left for a business trip to China or Korea. But that had been years ago. Had he died? Had she remarried and fallen on hard times? Who owned the store now? There had been small children, boys who would have inherited.

"I am sorry. You lost your husband then?" he asked.

"In a manner of speaking," she said, and glanced back at the store with a look of anger and longing. "The man who returned from China is not my husband, but he now has my home and my children."

Akitada, taken aback but curious and touched by her distress, invited her to a small restaurant nearby and ordered bowls of noodle soup for both of them. She accepted the invitation with a quiet grace, and ate hungrily but with great neatness. When she was done, she lowered her bowl, laid aside her chopsticks, and bowed deeply to him.

"You are very good," she said, with a little catch in her voice. "I cannot remember when I ate last."

"You have no money?"

"Neither money, nor home. When I realized that he was an impostor, I accused him. The charge was heard in court. I lost. The moment the judge confirmed his identity, he turned to me and pronounced the words of divorce. Right there in court, in front of everyone. When I got home, the doors were barred to me. In a moment, I lost everything—my children, my home, my clothes, everything."

"But how do you live?"

"Oh," she said quickly, "I have been sleeping at the Charity Hospital. I give them a hand sometimes, and they tolerate me. The clothes I wore to the trial I traded for these and used the extra money to pay clerks to draw up petitions to the court to reopen the case. They have been rejected."

"How long have you been without a home?"

"Six months. I have only seen my children twice. When you saw me, I was trying to look for them in the garden. I go every day. Usually his servants chase me away."

Silence fell as Akitada considered her extraordinary tale. It was not plausible. The man who had returned must have been recognized by neighbors, servants, friends, customers. The municipal judge would have investigated and heard witnesses before finding against her. Was she mad? He began to regret having told her his name and occupation.

Mrs. Hamada's hands twitched. He could see now that they were work-worn, the nails chipped and broken. "I must go," she whispered. "Unless . . ." She gave a small gasp. "The Ministry of Justice," she cried. "You work for the Ministry of Justice, sir? Oh, sir, do you know of something else I might try?"

Actually Akitada's predicament was not without humor. His reputation as a solver of mysteries and crimes had gained him a certain reputation among the noble families and government officials, but it clearly had not penetrated to this strange woman. She merely hoped for legal advice.

"Tell me," he asked, "why no one else has suspected the man was not who he claimed to be."

"My husband . . . or . . . this man spent four years traveling and buying goods. On his return journey he was ship-wrecked off the coast of Tsushima island. He caught the smallpox there, and almost died. It was another year before he could hide away on a fishing boat and return to Japan."

"But five years is not very long," said Akitada dubiously.

"The man who claimed to be my husband is very like him, except . . . the smallpox has scarred his face terribly. And he limps on the same leg as my husband did."

"What about his hair? His voice? Height? Mannerisms?"

"They were close enough. And he knew things, I don't know how, but he knew all about the shop and the children, even his mother's favorite story."

"His mother is alive? What does she say?"

"Mother is nearly blind and hard of hearing. She was overjoyed when he returned. Besides even I, at first . . ." She flushed crimson and whispered, "I wanted to believe. But a wife knows."

Akitada made up his mind. He paid for the food and told her, "Be near the store tomorrow at the same time. I must check out some things."

He went back to the curio store first. Hamada's was the largest and best of its kind in the capital and carried not only a variety of fine games and musical instruments, but also children's toys. Today was a special day in Akitada's family. His son, having turned four this year, would be putting on his first pair of trousers on this day. The soothsayer had been consulted, the day pronounced auspicious for the ceremony, the boy's mother, grandmother, and aunts were arranging an elaborate family feast, and Akitada had been on his way to buy his son a present when he had encountered Mrs. Hamada peering over the fence for a glimpse of her own sons.

The store bustled with customers. A loud-voiced, barrel-chested man with a horribly scarred face—no doubt the alleged Hamada—had joined his assistants to wait on clients. Akitada was greeted by a very young salesman with a timid manner and he asked to see some toys suitable for a small boy.

While he waited, he studied the curio dealer surreptitiously. He did not recall Hamada from earlier visits, never having been an important enough customer to get the personal attention of the owner. The smallpox had left thick scar tissue and holes in the man's cheeks and chin and distorted his nose and lips. In every other respect he was of ordinary appearance, middle-sized, broad-shouldered, thickened about the waist, his hair heavy and straight and neatly tied up. His voice, too, though strong, was ordinary, and his speech that of any city merchant. More significantly, he seemed to know his merchandise.

"Are any of these what the gentleman was looking for?" The shy young man was pointing to an assortment of balls, sticks, shuttle-cocks, and kites. "For a boy who is active?" he added with a little smile.

Akitada smiled back. Oh, yes. His boy was very active. A football? He had always enjoyed that himself. But perhaps four was a little young. Stilts? No. Too soon. A painted *giccho* ball with its curved stick? The little fellow could manage that well enough, and it would teach him agility. On second thought, though, the noise of a large wooden ball rolling about the wooden corridors of his home all day long might not be desirable. Kites in winter? Hardly. Akitada sighed. "It is not a good time of year for out-door sports," he said to the young salesman.

"How about a spinning top, then?" boomed a voice behind him.

Akitada turned and almost recoiled. A demon's face was grimacing hideously at him, wide purple lips drawn back to bare crooked yellow teeth. The man who called himself Hamada was taking an interest in a sale. No doubt this ghastly expression was a smile. Akitada controlled a strong sense of revulsion and nodded pleasantly, "Yes, perhaps. Thank you for the suggestion."

"We have a very fine one," continued the curio dealer, "large and painted with dragons in many colors. Children love the way the colors mingle when it spins.

Get it, Noro!" The young assistant bowed, and ran. "Idiot!" growled the dealer.

"What?" asked Akitada, startled.

"That boy who waited on you. He's an idiot and lazy. Don't know why I took him on. His father couldn't pay me enough to put up with such a slow fool. Have to lay into him with the bamboo almost every day."

"I thought he was very helpful."

The apprentice, out of breath and with beads of perspiration on his brow, returned with the magnificent top.

"Well?" thundered the curio dealer, glaring at the unfortunate youngster. "Are you just going to stand there? Show the gentleman how the thing works."

"Yes, sir," the apprentice whispered. With trembling fingers he wound a string about the top and attempted to spin it. But in his nervousness, he let the top scoot off to disappear in the folds of a customer's full trousers.

Hamada's face darkened with fury. He raised a fist.

Akitada said quickly, "It is the perfect gift, Mr. Hamada. Please have the young man wrap it for me." While he waited for the toy to be retrieved, his eye fell on a zither a customer was strumming. "Do you still have your father's Chinese lutes?" he asked the curio dealer.

The man swelled with pride. "Of course. Our family treasure. Would you care to have a look, sir?"

"I am in a hurry today, but I know someone who would be very eager to see them. He is a collector of rare instruments."

AKITADA AND THE WAY OF JUSTICE

Hamada's eyes narrowed greedily. He rubbed his hands. "A collector you say? It so happens I might put them on the market. The expense of a growing family, you understand."

"Then perhaps I might return tomorrow at this time with my friend?"

"Of course, of course. It would give me the greatest pleasure." The dealer bowed Akitada out of the store with many expressions of delight.

From Hamada's, Akitada went directly to the Imperial Office for Court Music and had a chat about Chinese lutes with the retired court musician Tamemori.

Afterward he paid a visit to the Municipal Police Headquarters and asked to speak to Captain Kobe. This meeting was difficult. A number of years ago, Akitada had solved a particularly complicated series of murders on the grounds of the Imperial University, and this embarrassment had not made Kobe very fond of him. In fact, the police captain considered Akitada a mere dilettante, a meddler in things that did not concern him. Therefore, it took all of Akitada's persuasive powers to have him agree to his plan.

The following day, shortly after the noon hour, three very important-looking personages entered Hamada's store. Akitada, in official silk robe and black cap led the way. Behind him came an elderly man, venerable with his white hair and beard, in a gorgeous brocade robe, and a tall, middle-aged gentleman in semi-formal court dress and with a very superior scowl on his stern face.

The young salesman recognized Akitada immediately.

"This way, your Honor," he said, bowing deeply and leading them to the back of the store. "Mr. Hamada expects your Honor and the noble gentlemen."

Hamada awaited them in his private quarters, a small, luxuriously matted room behind the public sales area. He knelt immediately and bowed deeply. On a low table next to him rested three ancient musical instruments resembling zithers. His visitors approached and looked at them.

"Cushions!" hissed Hamada to his apprentice, and cushions appeared immediately.

They seated themselves, and Hamada said, "I understand there is an interest in these rare instruments." He rubbed his large, square hands nervously and looked at Akitada's companions. "My father's Chinese lutes are three of only five authentic ones in this country. The other two are owned by His Majesty. Nothing else in this humble shop approaches them in rarity. How can I be of service to your Excellencies?"

"Thank you for letting us see your treasures, Mr. Hamada," said Akitada. "This is Counsellor Tamemori, and the other gentleman is Captain Kobe, a special friend of mine."

Hamada bowed deeply to both.

Kobe leaned forward and poked one of the lutes with a long finger. "Don't look like any lutes I ever saw," he commented.

Hamada said quickly, "Chinese lutes are different in design from Japanese ones," and turned his attention to the elderly man.

"I assume," said Akitada to the curio dealer, "that your father told you all about the provenance of these instruments."

Hamada smiled. "Certainly. My father was extremely proud of these and made sure that I understood their value and everything about them."

"Can you play them?" asked the white-haired Tamemori, caressing one of the lutes and touching the silk strings lovingly.

"I'm afraid I have no musical talent," said Hamada. "But my ancient mother used to play a little. My father taught her the technique. Excuse me a moment."

Hamada left the room.

"Well?" asked Akitada, looking at Tamemori.

The old man nodded. "I think you are right. The instruments are authentic, but they should have been oiled, and the silk re-strung. These lutes will not play in their present condition, and may already be damaged by the neglect."

Kobe said grimly, "Well, we'll see soon enough. If you're right, I would not want to be in his shoes. He will have to explain a number of very suspicious circumstances."

Akitada raised his brows. "You surprise me. In your office yesterday you acted as if my suggestion were mad."

Kobe flushed. "You have a way of interfering in police investigations. Briefly then: When his wife brought charges, we checked. He carried the real Hamada's travel documents and told a convincing story, but I thought privately that he was vague about the places he had visited. By a coincidence, shortly before this Hamada appeared in town, we caught a bandit who claimed that a gang was operating between here and Naniwa on the coast. The gang specializes in robbing merchants traveling between the capital and the port city. The prisoner claimed that the gang had been selling off Chinese imports, painted scrolls, jade carvings, fine porcelain jars and so forth." He paused, then added heavily, "If they caught the real Hamada on his return from China and if one of the gang members decided to impersonate him, the merchant must be dead." He broke off when the door opened.

Hamada was leading an ancient woman in a black silk gown. She was bent almost double and nearly bald. Guiding her to the table, he said loudly, "Mother, these are three noble gentlemen who wish to hear you play Father's lute."

"What?" she said, peering at the visitors nearsightedly. "Lute, did you say?

My fingers are much too stiff." She lowered herself painfully onto a cushion, and, muttering to herself, handled all three lutes, one after the other.

"Do the lutes have names?" Akitada asked Hamada.

The curio dealer hesitated, then said, "Yes, of course. All famous lutes do."

"Well, what are their names?" snapped Kobe.

"Hmm. This large one here is called Singing Breeze, the one next to it Temple Bells, and the small one Cricket."

"What did you say?" asked Tamemori, leaning his white head forward and putting a hand to his ear.

"They are called Temple Bells, Singing Breeze and Cricket, your Excellency," repeated Hamada loudly.

The old woman raised her head. "What?" she asked sharply. "What is called Cricket?"

"Never mind, Mother. Show these gentlemen how they sound."

"I used to know the song 'Dancing with the Blue Phoenix.'" She stroked the strings of the lute Hamada had called Temple Bells. "Singing Bell needs new strings. Why doesn't it have new strings?"

Hamada looked apologetically at his visitors. "I'm afraid my mother is very old. Her mind wanders. Of course everyone knows that it is wrong to replace any part of an antique. It destroys its value."

Tamemori sighed. "It is very disappointing. I had my heart set on seeing the proper touch demonstrated. It is not necessary to play a tune. Could your mother just show us how she plucks the strings?"

The old woman stared at Tamemori. "You're my age, sir. Did you hear me when I played Singing Bell?" she asked in a quavering voice. "I played for the Crown Prince. Were you there that day?"

"Come, Mother," Hamada said in a peremptory tone. "Time to go back to your room." He tried to lift her to her feet, but she slapped aside his hands.

"Singing Bell," she cried. "Not Temple Bells. You know it is Singing Bell. And the strings are old, and you have not oiled the wood. Your father used to take such care of the lutes." She burst into tears, and Hamada led her out.

The three men looked at each other.

"Well, are you satisfied?" Akitada asked Kobe.

The Police Captain nodded, rose, and went out. When he returned, he was accompanied by the younger Mrs. Hamada who took one look at the lutes and cried out, "Oh, they must be oiled right away. My husband and I always oiled the lutes three times a year."

Hamada, coming in, stopped. "Who let this woman in? She has no right to be here."

"On the contrary," said Akitada. "It is you who have no right here. The real Hamada would have known all about his treasured lutes and cared for them properly. Counsellor Tamemori here oversees the treasures in the Imperial Music Office. He is an expert on the care of Chinese instruments. And Captain Kobe is superintendent of the Municipal Police. He has some questions about the kidnapping and murder of the real Hamada near Naniwa."

The curio dealer's disfigured face blanched a pasty white. He fell to his knees and touched his head to the floor.

"Then my husband is dead?" whispered Mrs. Hamada.

A heavy silence fell.

AKITADA AND THE WAY OF JUSTICE

Suddenly there was the sound of young voices outside the room. She turned toward it, deep joy suffusing a face wet with tears.

THE MASTER OF GO

Go is a board game that involves strategy. It resembles chess (which was also known in Akitada's time) and is widely played by the upper classes where it inspired the sort of devotion Kawabata describes so well in his great novel, **The Master of Go.** *It would have appealed to Akitada, who is by nature a man of thought and discipline. Here, the rivalry between Akitada and Captain Kobe dominates their reluctant friendship.*

"The proper method . . . was to lose all awareness of self while awaiting an adversary's play."
Yasunari Kawabata, *The Master of Go.*

Heian-Kyo (Kyoto): eleventh century; during the Long-Nights month (October):

A pair of ducks bobbed for food among the drifting leaves, taking turns so that one of them could keep a wary eye on the human watching them from the bridge. A cuckoo burst into sudden song in one of the willows: 'Ho-to-to.' 'Ho-to-to.'

Akitada looked up from the ducks and saw the bird swaying on a slender branch. Sun-bright yellow against the pale blue of the morning sky, the willow's leaves seemed to drift as gently on the breeze as their fallen companions bobbed with the ducks in the current of the canal below. Heaving a deep sigh of satisfaction, Akitada decided that he had achieved the proper frame of mind for his *go* lesson and crossed the bridge.

The *go*-master Nakamura was very poor and gave his lessons in the art of the ancient board game in the back room of an old inn because his house had become almost uninhabitable. The inn was near the university, in a pleasant, quiet street within a block of broad Suzaku Avenue. The inn's clientele was quiet and genteel, its service excellent, and the back room had the sort of elegance and peacefulness never found in ordinary inns.

But when Akitada turned the corner from Suzaku Avenue, he saw a small crowd gathered before the inn's gate. A number of red-coated constables with bows and quivers of arrows looped over their shoulders were just disappearing into the courtyard.

His peace of mind gone, Akitada hurried after them. Nobody was about in the reception area, so he removed his boots quickly and followed the sound of raised voices. With more apprehension, Akitada recognized the gruff tone of Captain Kobe, head of the capital police.

The chief would not have been called out for a minor matter. They had met before, though "collided" would be a better term, and always on murder investigations. Kobe was a conscientious and dedicated official but not particularly imaginative or patient, often charging like a bull after the most obvious solutions. Akitada had interceded in more than one of Kobe's cases until the captain had developed an intense aversion to his meddling.

Kobe and his men had not bothered to remove their boots and were making a lot of noise. Akitada, moving silently on stockinged feet, caught up with them at the door to the back room. The short, monkey-faced innkeeper Itto and a middle-aged, tearful maid were talking anxiously, but the captain shoved them aside impatiently and disappeared into the back room, followed by his constables. Akitada slipped in behind them.

The inn's back room had the old-fashioned elegance of old palace rooms. Its floor and beams were dark with age, and the grass mats had turned a deep golden color. When paper-covered screens were pushed open, the occupants had a charming view of an enclosed garden with an ancient stone lantern. At the moment the garden was bright with sunshine and color. Golden chrysanthemums and brilliant red maple leaves spread against the brown bamboo fence like embroidery on a woman's festive gown.

The scene inside was a stark contrast, though it was colorful enough with the red coats of the police. But death has a sobering effect. Nakamura, black-robed and white-haired, lay beside his *go* board. He had died painfully. His body was twisted, the formal gown gaping to reveal thin, age-spotted legs and a glimpse of white loin cloth. He had vomited some green, blood-flecked substance over the front of his dark robe and onto the grass mat. His hands were clenched, and the normally handsome thin face was a mask of agony, a swollen tongue protruding from blue lips.

Akitada stepped forward to pull the master's robe down over the spindly, knotted limbs. A friend, newly-found and irretrievably lost.

"Sugawara!"

Akitada looked up and bowed. "Good morning, Captain. A very sad occasion, but I am glad to see you looking well."

"What are you doing here?" Kobe's manner was stiff.

"I came for my lesson," Akitada said mildly. He bent again to feel Nakamura's hand. It was still faintly warm.

"Don't touch anything." Kobe stepped between him and the body. "What do you mean, you came for a lesson?"

Akitada indicated the *go* board. "Master Nakamura was a teacher of the game of *go*. I am one of his pupils. The practice is very useful for sharpening the mind. What happened?"

Kobe was clearly torn between getting rid of Akitada and finding out what his connection with the dead man was. He gave in with an ill grace. "Very well. Sit down over there, and keep quiet. When we're done, you can answer some questions."

Akitada obeyed meekly. He watched and listened as Kobe worked. One of the red-coated policemen set up a small portable desk and took notes while Kobe walked around the room dictating his observations. He noted location, time of day and date, the identity of the victim, and contents of the room. Then he knelt by the body, commenting on its appearance and presumed time and cause of death.

Apparently Nakamura had died from ingesting poison of some kind, and as recently as an hour ago.

Kobe paused in his dictation to pick up a cup which lay near the dead man's hand, sniffed, and tasted the dregs. Making a face, he went out on the veranda to spit into the shrubbery. He returned to inspect the pot used to heat the water and opened a small container of powdered tea. Then he resumed his dictation. The water was pronounced harmless, but the box appeared suspicious for he ordered it carefully wrapped.

Akitada noted all of this with the intense interest a sudden death always aroused in him. Suicide could be eliminated because the master had clearly not expected to die in the middle of his lessons, and an accident was most unlikely under the circumstances. On the other hand, Akitada reflected, Nakamura was also an unlikely murder victim. Much beloved among his friends and disciples, he was a poor man, without the worldly goods or political influence to appeal to a killer's greed. At his advanced age he would hardly inspire a crime of passion. That left only anger, revenge, or envy as motives, and for any of these, Kobe would have to probe Nakamura's personal life. Akitada waited for Kobe's next move.

Kobe called in the landlord and the maid.

Itto, with his worried frown and nervous manner more than ever like a small monkey, was still wringing his hands. He avoided looking at the body or the policemen. Instead he addressed Akitada. "Oh, sir," he cried. "Who could have done such a dreadful thing to such a fine gentleman?"

Kobe snapped, "Hey! I'm in charge here. Who found the body?"

Itto jumped. "I did, sir, and I immediately sent for you."

"Did you touch anything?"

"No. Only Master Nakamura." Kobe glowered, and Itto added quickly, "Just to make sure he was dead."

Kobe glanced at the kneeling figure of the maid. "Did she make the tea?"

The maid cried, "Oh, no, sir. I would not dare."

Kobe asked Itto, "Well, who did?"

"I don't know, sir."

"What do you mean, you don't know!" roared Kobe. "You must know. This is your inn."

"This maid usually leaves the things in the morning. The master or his visitors make the tea."

Kobe advanced on the cowering maid. "Is that correct? Come on, woman. I don't have all day."

The maid burst into tears again. "Every morning," she sobbed, "I put out the cups and the master's tea caddy. Then I fill the pot. I fill it at the well, letting the water flow a long time. Just as the master said."

Kobe stared at her suspiciously, then asked the innkeeper, "Who were the master's visitors this morning?"

Sweat beaded Itto's brow. "I don't know, sir. We were busy with the preparations for Major Counselor Ishikawa's birthday party tonight."

Kobe glared. "Stop lying to me. Do you expect me to believe that nobody paid any attention to the comings and goings in an inn?"

"Nobody. We were much too busy," Itto wailed, casting a beseeching glance at Akitada. "If I hadn't passed by the open door of this room on my way to the convenience, I wouldn't have found the body."

Kobe's face turned dark with anger, and Akitada cleared his throat.

"What?" snapped Kobe, glowering at him.

"The lessons had become well established," Akitada explained, "and Nakamura disliked interruptions."

"Then give me the names of all his students."

Akitada shook his head regretfully. "I have no idea who they are."

Kobe glanced around the room. "Did Nakamura keep records?"

"Perhaps, but not here." Akitada was becoming irritated with Kobe's manner. "No doubt," he said coldly, "you will discover more in the coming days after searching his home and talking to all his friends."

Kobe frowned at him. "You must know something. Surely Nakamura discussed his other students? Casual comments like, 'That dunce Ishikawa will never learn the simplest moves'?"

Akitada was shocked. "Never. And certainly not in those terms. It would have been most improper to make such a comment about another gentleman."

Kobe, who had worked his way up from the ranks of the military and preferred commoners to the court nobility, snarled, "Well, one of you *proper* gentlemen killed the old man. Frankly, I don't give a rat's turd for what you so-called *good* people consider proper. You think nothing of poisoning each other, but heaven forbid you should criticize someone's game."

Far from feeling insulted, Akitada nodded. "You're quite right. It *is* a curious phenomenon, if you put it that way. On the other hand, I doubt all of the master's pupils belonged to the *good* people."

"Since you seem to have no useful information," Kobe snapped, "you can leave."

"I would like to stay."

"No. You have no business here." Kobe's eyes flashed, and his color rose again.

"As you wish." Akitada sighed and stood. "May I just take a look at the game board?" Without waiting for permission, he went over to the *go* board with its arrangement of black and white stones. "A race," he said, astonished. "And such a brief one! Ten black stones and nine white ones." Peering into the bowl of game pieces next to the master's seat, he asked Kobe, "Did you notice that the master was playing black?"

"What are you dithering about now?" Kobe said.

"I gather you don't play the game?"

"No. I have better things to do."

"You would be surprised how pertinent the game strategy is to your type of work. The object of both endeavors is capture an opponent, and overcoming an opponent requires careful thought and a knowledge of his personality. For example, consider the peculiar fact that the master was playing black on this occasion."

"I have no time for nonsense. This is a criminal investigation, not a game. Are you leaving?"

"Captain, normally the weaker of two players plays the black, because it gives him the advantage of the first move. The master always plays the white against his students."

Kobe looked puzzled, then his eyes widened. "You mean his last visitor was not one of his students?"

"Exactly. He would play black only against someone equal or better. As far as I know there are only two other people who claim to equal his skill. One is Lord Miyoshi, undersecretary of the crown prince's private office, the other Reverend Raishin, the abbot of the Hojo temple."

Kobe's face fell. "You cannot seriously expect me to accuse either of *them* on such flimsy evidence."

Akitada raised his brows. "I thought you had little regard for the *good* people. No, I was not actually suggesting that. We do not know when the poison was introduced into the tea."

Kobe threw up his hands in disgust. "So all that clever deduction was a waste of time. If that is all you have to contribute, Sugawara, we can dispense with your advice. Please leave and let us get on with our work. And, for once, stay out of my case."

"Of course." Akitada drifted toward the door. "It was an easy win for black," he muttered, shaking his head. "Too easy!"

Kobe shook his head, turned, glared at the game board, and gave it a kick. The stones scattered across the mat.

Akitada grieved for the master, but he stayed out of the case, reminding himself to wait for his chance as Nakamura had often told him during their lessons. Soon there would be developments which would lead him to the killer.

He attended the master's funeral, and found Kobe also there. It was on a gray day threatening rain. Most of Nakamura's students and friends had come, their grief tempered by curiosity. They watched the glowering, red-coated Kobe uneasily. Both of Nakamura's closest contenders for the master's title were there as well. The abbot, Raishin, recited a short prayer, and the heavy-set Lord Miyoshi from the crown prince's staff knelt in the front row, his broad, flat features a mask of sorrow.

After the ceremony, Kobe took Akitada aside. Characteristically, he did not refer to their unpleasant parting but plunged directly into his subject. "We got absolutely nothing from searching Nakamura's place and next to nothing from talking to his friends," he said, as if they were merely continuing an earlier chat. "If you listen to them, he was a saint. Only the maid at the inn didn't like him. It seems Nakamura complained about the service. Remember when I asked her about the tea water? She was as skittish as a young horse. But it may be nothing. So, you see, it really comes down to Nakamura's last visitor. I thought about what you said and have a good mind to question Miyoshi."

To his credit and in spite of his earlier qualms, Kobe was unmoved by questions of rank when he suspected someone of murder. In fact, this was one of his qualities that Akitada respected. "I see," he said now, glancing at the rotund undersecretary struggling to climb into his carriage while servants hovered near. "Do you have some new evidence?"

Kobe looked a little uneasy. "Nothing I'd like to share with a judge. Miyoshi seems to be one of those fools who get so obsessed with a game that nothing else matters. People say he hated old man Nakamura because he was the acknowledged master and Miyoshi couldn't beat him. He was always begging Nakamura for a game, but Nakamura's been turning him down. Until now, it seems."

Akitada started to say something, but closed his mouth again. Patience!

"Oh, and the abbot was the same way, but he is out. He was on a pilgrimage. No doubt praying for better luck." Kobe chewed his lip in indecision. "It's got to be Miyoshi. Right. I'm taking him to headquarters. You can come along, Sugawara. I may need you to explain your reasoning."

Before Akitada could protest such high-handed arrangements, Kobe had stalked off toward Miyoshi's carriage, shouting, "Wait!"

His lordship was, of course, outraged to be taken so unceremoniously to police headquarters in front of everybody. He blustered at Kobe about his rank and position at court, waving his arms about and threatening official complaints.

This produced the opposite reaction from the one intended. Kobe made him an exaggerated bow and announced, "I regret to inform the honored Undersecretary that he has been identified as the last person to see Nakamura alive." Changing his tone, he growled, "Under the circumstances I don't care who you are. As far as I'm concerned you're the prime suspect in a murder."

Akitada almost applauded.

Miyoshi's eyes opened wide and went to Akitada in sudden comprehension. "I see," he said. Sitting down, he arranged his fat jowls into an expression of patient suffering. "It is true," he said, "that I may have been the last person to see Nakamura alive, but I certainly did not kill him."

"Aha." His bluff having paid off so handsomely, Kobe's eyes sparkled, and his mustache seemed to bristle with satisfaction. "Why did you not come forward and report your visit?" he snapped.

Miyoshi was cooperation itself. "My dear Captain, allow me to explain what happened," he said. "First, I swear I did not poison Nakamura. What motive would I possibly have to kill our beloved master. I am a devotee myself."

"I don't care how devout you are. I think you were jealous of him. Perhaps you lost one game too many and killed him in a fit of anger," said Kobe.

"Nonsense. I was very upset when he became ill. Then he went into convulsions, and I wanted to go find a doctor, but he died before I could do so. It was very quick. I remembered the tea and looked at his cup. It contained grains of a white powder in the sediment. I am afraid I panicked. A man in my position in the crown prince's household cannot afford to become involved in murder, so I left."

Kobe glared. "Why should I believe you?"

Lord Miyoshi drew himself up. "You need not believe anything I say, but you cannot hold me, for you have no proof that I put poison in his cup."

"You withheld evidence," Kobe pointed out, "and that's enough for an arrest."

"Not for a man in my position. I have explained and I shall cooperate fully in the future."

"Why did you visit Nakamura?"

"Just a friendly call. I was in the neighborhood. He suggested a quick game, and I agreed."

"*He* suggested it?" Akitada asked, surprised. "What sort of game?"

Kobe snapped, "Never mind that!" Turning back to his lordship, he asked, "Tell me about the tea. Did you have some?"

"No. He made it and offered me some, but I refused. So he drank it himself."

"Lucky you," Kobe, sneered, but with less conviction.

"That was entirely uncalled for, Captain," Miyoshi protested.

"Did you see his previous caller?"

There was an almost imperceptible pause, then Miyoshi said, "He was alone when I entered the room."

Akitada asked from his corner, "But perhaps you recognized someone in the corridor or leaving by the gate?"

Miyoshi fidgeted. "A lot of people go to the inn. It means nothing."

Kobe caught Miyoshi's sudden guardedness and leaned forward. "You saw someone. Out with it! Who was it?"

Miyoshi sighed. "Just one of the students from the university. I cannot remember his name."

"Describe him."

Miyoshi supplied a surprisingly detailed description of a thin young man with narrow, pointed features, small mustache, and furtive manner. Somewhat mollified, Kobe let him go.

"Well, it looks like you were wrong after all," the captain pointed out, quite unfairly, when they were alone. "Miyoshi just didn't want to get involved. Still, I got another lead now. And a good description. Reminds me of a ferret. Of course, most of those bookish youngsters look like that. Do you know who it is?"

"No."

"Well, you haven't been much help. Never mind, our crude methods will get results. Miyoshi came apart quite easily."

"Remarkably easily."

"You think he lied?"

"Not about the ferret, I think." Akitada got up. "Since I'm of little use to you, I shall go home. I really wish I knew Miyoshi's version of the game, though. Let me know if you find out about that."

"Don't hold your breath," Kobe said.

Two days later, Kobe sent him a message: "Student found. Please attend questioning in my office."

Akitada noted the 'please.' Kobe must be desperate.

The ferret's name was Daisai Masahira. He was in his twenties and Kobe's epithet fit him perfectly. He looked both sleek and sly. His sharp nose twitched and his small black eyes flitted around the room as if he were looking for a hidden nest egg. He had quickly weighed Akitada's rank and now ignored him.

Kobe was in low spirits. He was surprisingly courteous with Daisai because, as he explained to Akitada, the student had come in of his own free will. Daisai's family lived in the Otokuni district west of the capital, and he had gone home for a brief visit and thus missed the news of the murder.

Daisai shook his head and murmured, "Terrible. I wish I'd known about the poison. I could've warned the master."

"Never mind, son," Kobe said consolingly. "You did the right thing."

"Do I understand," Akitada asked, "that you were one of Master Nakamura's students the morning he died?"

"Yes. I was the first one. In fact, I was waiting for the master, when he arrived."

Kobe cleared his throat pointedly.

"Sorry," mouthed Akitada, meeting Kobe's eyes.

Kobe asked, "And you say you drank some of Nakamura's tea?"

"Hah!" Akitada bit his lip, as soon as he had spoken.

Daisai shot him a glance. "Yes. I took just a sip to be polite. I don't like tea." Daisai lowered his eyes modestly.

"And?" Kobe urged.

"On my way back to the university, I was quite sick and vomited."

Kobe turned to Akitada. "You see the problem?"

"I think so." Akitada was fascinated by Daisai's manner and asked the student, "Had you been taking lessons long?"

Daisai's eyes went around the room again. "Not really," he said vaguely. "A man in my position must make his way in the world. I decided to become proficient at *go*. In polite company one must be able to perform well at a number of skills. I also practice poetry and dancing."

Akitada murmured, "How commendable!"

"Well," said Kobe to Daisai. "I expect that's all. Thank you for coming in right away. You have been very helpful."

"Any time, Captain." Daisai got up, bowed to both of them, and slipped out the door.

Kobe sighed.

"What's the matter?" asked Akitada innocently.

"How can you ask such a foolish question? I have to start all over again, because the poison was already in the tea when Daisai got there. That eliminates both Daisai and Miyoshi. I swear I'll end up arresting that miserable maid after all."

"The maid?"

"Have you forgotten that she prepared the tea things? And I was right about her. She had a motive. The innkeeper's been trying to fire her. He says she's getting old and forgetful and he wants more attractive maids. She is a widow with five children to support and was scared of Nakamura's complaints. I really hate a case like this."

"Hmm," Akitada said. "Daisai seems to be an ambitious young man who takes his future career most seriously."

Kobe growled, "Who cares? I have more important things on my mind."

"Have you found out who Nakamura's heir is?"

"Yes. He had a nephew. Fellow called Yukihito. Why?"

"I wondered if you planned to talk to the nephew."

Kobe hooted derisively. "Go all the way to Nagaoka? You must be out of your mind. What for? Nakamura was as poor as a temple sparrow. I've been to his hovel. A couple of old blankets, some tattered books, and empty cupboards in the kitchen. He had nothing of value that anyone would kill for."

"Isn't Nagaoka in the district Daisai comes from?"

"Forget Daisai. The poor kid almost got killed himself."

"Well, it was just a thought," Akitada said, getting up. "Let me know, if there are any more developments."

"Developments?" Kobe asked. "What developments? There's only that cursed fool of a maid."

"Oh," said Akitada vaguely, "you never know."

The following day, Kobe arrested the maid for Nakamura's murder, and Akitada decided it was time to make his move. He traveled to Nagaoka on horseback, accompanied by the cry of the geese flying south to their winter homes and the rustling of wind in the dry reeds along the highway.

Nagaoka had once served briefly as an imperial city, but its palaces had long since burned to the ground or been dismantled. Only two large temples, barely maintained by the imperial family, still watched over the paddies, fields, and small farms like two mother hens over their chicks.

Akitada visited both temples, left an offering in each, and burnt some incense in memory of Master Nakamura. The monk who sold him the incense informed him proudly that Nagaoka would soon be a place even holier than Nara, because the Buddha had appeared to the crown prince in a dream and told him so.

Shaking his head, Akitada went to the inn for his mid-day meal. It was no more than a dusty barn of a place. At an open hearth, two women were stirring food or pouring wine for the handful of local farmers or travelers who had stopped in.

Akitada ordered and seated himself next to an old man who was carrying on a teasing conversation with the two women.

"From the capital?" the old man asked, glancing at Akitada's green hunting cloak and black hat.

"Yes, honorable grandfather," Akitada said politely. "Perhaps you can tell me how to find Nakamura's farm?"

"Nakamura?" Bright eyes studied him from under grizzled brows. "He's dead, I hear."

"Yes. I was a friend and came to visit his relatives."

"Only that good-for-nothing Yukihito's left."

"Master Nakamura's nephew?"

The old man nodded and fell into a prolonged thoughtful silence, ignoring all further attempts of Akitada to involve him in conversation. Akitada's food, served by a young maid, was an excellent stew and very decent wine. On an impulse, Akitada ordered another small pitcher of wine for the old man.

His companion poured, drank deeply, and said, "That Yuki. Never did a day's work in his life. Drove his mother to an early grave. A bum."

"How does he support himself then?" Akitada asked, extending his empty bowl to the young maid for a refill.

The old man turned his pitcher upside down to show it was empty. After a sidelong glance at Akitada, he said, "Rents out his fields. Borrows. Gambles. Starves. Until now." He flicked the cup with a gnarled finger.

Akitada sighed and bought him another pitcher of wine. "What do you mean 'until now'?"

The old man drank and scowled. "He sold the land and went away a rich man. This morning."

"So fast? Do you know a Daisai Masahira?"

"It's a small town," nodded the man, emptying the last of his second pitcher into his cup.

Watching this maneuver, Akitada decided to speed up the conversation. "What sort of person is he? Perhaps he knows the Nakamura family?"

"Everybody knows everybody here. He's a black-bellied squirrel, that Daisai." The old man spat with accuracy into the fire. "Him and Yuki used to come here to drink whenever Yuki had some money." He paused with his cup halfway to his lips. "Something wrong about the master's death?" he asked suspiciously.

They locked eyes, then Akitada placed some money on the floor and said, "Forgive me for taking up your time with my idle chatter," and left.

Before returning to the capital, Akitada had a look at Master Nakamura's farm. He found it easily. A few tattered buildings huddled in a grove amidst poor and stony fields, but they were surrounded by many ancient trees and the view was magnificent. The site overlooked a lake and the temples. Only five miles to the northeast lay the capital and the towering mountains beyond.

A crew of laborers was already clearing the site. When Akitada rode up to the main house, a short, fat man emerged, making squawking noises and waving his arms about like an angry goose.

Akitada stopped his horse and waited for the man, who wore the robe and hat of a minor official.

"No one is allowed here," scolded the man. "Orders of His Imperial Highness, the crown prince."

Akitada raised his brows. "Really? I didn't know. You should post warnings, you know. I came to speak to the owner."

The man had taken in Akitada's clothes and his speech and made a belated bow. "Please forgive my rudeness, sir. We have not had time for signs. Nakamura Yukihito sold the property. In fact, he just left for the capital."

Akitada thanked the official and turned his horse homeward.

As soon as he reached the capital, and without bothering to change his travel-stained clothing, he went to look for Daisai at the university. The student was not in any of his classes, but one of his professors told him that a farmer from Daisai's village had come for him. "Daisai looked very upset when he saw the man," he volunteered. "I do hope there is no trouble."

"When was this?" asked Akitada, his heart beating faster.

The professor peered dubiously at the sun. "It cannot have been very long. I just finished my class."

"Do you have any idea where I might find them?"

The professor scratched his thinning grey hair. "You might try the Pear Tree Inn outside the university gate. Most of the young people like to go there."

The Pear Tree Inn was a small restaurant selling cheap wine and food. It was well attended by students and locals. Akitada found Daisai seated in a corner with a stocky middle-aged man in coarse, countrified clothing. Daisai's back was toward the entrance, and

Akitada walked up to them without being noticed. With a smile and a slap on Daisai's back, he seated himself between them.

Daisai turned chalk white and attempted to rise.

Akitada pulled him back down, putting his arm around his shoulder. "Well met, young man," he said jovially. "What are you drinking?"

Daisai gulped. "Ah, nothing. Thank you. We were just leaving, sir."

"Come, keep me company," Akitada urged. "I've just returned from a trip, and my throat is parched with the dust of the road. Your friend, too. I did not catch his name."

Daisai's companion returned Akitada's smile, revealing several gaps in his teeth. He said proudly, "Nakamura Yukihito, at your service, sir."

Daisai squirmed, and Akitada put a restraining hand on his arm. "What enormous luck," he said to the grinning Yukihito. "I've just returned from a trip to Nagaoka to see you. If I'd known I'd find you here, I could have saved myself a long, dusty ride. You're a popular man, now that you've come into your inheritance."

The small eyes in Yukihito's broad face gleamed. He clapped his hands in childlike joy. "I know and I bet you've come from Lord Miyoshi."

Daisai hissed, "No, Yuki! Don't waste the gentleman's time with your problems."

But the master's nephew was too intent on Akitada's purpose. "Did you bring the gold?" he asked eagerly. "We were just about to pay a visit to the crown prince.

It's been taking too long, and I don't mind telling you, the little bit on account that Lord Miyoshi sent is long gone."

Akitada shook his head with a smile. "I regret. Gold is too heavy and dangerous to carry about, but I can take you where you will get what you deserve. Perhaps you'll both be so kind as to accompany me there?"

Daisai made another desperate effort to warn Yukihito. "You're making a mistake," he cried. "This person is with the Ministry of Justice. He knows nothing about your money."

The young farmer looked uncertainly at Akitada. "Ministry of Justice?" he asked.

"There is no mistake," Akitada said, suddenly stern. "Let's go! Daisai, we're going to see Kobe. It's in your best interest to cooperate."

Daisai flinched. Then he bowed. "Of course. I meant to speak to the captain sooner or later. I did not learn until today that Yuki has been in contact with Lord Miyoshi. That was very clever of you, sir, the way you got him to admit it."

"What're you talking about?" Yuki asked, looking from Daisai to Akitada. "What's going on?"

"Let's go, Yuki," said Daisai, pulling his friend up. "The gentleman is quite right. We'd better make a clean breast of it."

The way to police headquarters took them past the popular park called the Divine Spring Garden. It looked no less divine in autumn with its trees a brocade pattern of reds, oranges, and golden yellows, but the street was deserted. Akitada walked between the two men to keep them from talking to each other.

Daisai was so cooperative that Akitada was beginning to wonder if he might seriously expect to weasel out of the situation when they passed into the shadow of a grove of crimson maples. Suddenly he felt a hard and painful blow to the back of one of his knees. It buckled and pitched him forward to the ground. Before he could gather his wits, Daisai's foot shot out to deliver a killing kick to his temple. Akitada managed to twist his head aside at the last moment and deflected the impact to his jaw and shoulder. His ears were still ringing and his eyes watering with the pain of the attack when the impact of a body crushed him into the gravel. Daisai had flung himself on his back, and his wiry fingers were reaching for his throat. Akitada responded by tucking in his jaw.

"Find a rock and hit him on the head," Daisai grunted, struggling.

There was no point in waiting for the reinforcements. Akitada was bigger and stronger than his attacker and in good physical condition. With a mighty heave upward, he unseated the scrawny student and struck him with his fist. Daisai went limp.

Akitada stood up, testing his bruised leg gingerly and cursing himself for a fool. Since Daisai had always cultivated a civilized behavior before, he had kept his eye on the sullen Yukihito. But Daisai's self-improvement program evidently included some very low street-fighting tricks.

AKITADA AND THE WAY OF JUSTICE

Feeling his tender jaw, Akitada looked around for Yukihito. The fellow still stood in the middle of the street, a puzzled look on his broad face. Whether Nakamura's nephew was simply slow or had a little of his uncle's goodness in his veins after all, he had not joined in Daisai's attack.

Akitada brushed dirt and leaves off his gown. "Pick Daisai up and put him over your shoulder," he said to Yukihito. "You look strong enough."

The other man looked up and down the street, then approached slowly. "What are you going to do?"

"Take him to police headquarters. He has some explaining to do, and so do you. Pick him up and follow me."

"He kicked you, but I've done nothing."

"Then you have nothing to fear."

After a moment, Yukihito bent, lifted the limp body of his friend, flung him over his shoulder like a bag of rice, and trotted after Akitada.

In this manner they passed through the streets and into courtyard of the police station, stared at by constables and gathering a small retinue of red-coated guardians of the peace who followed them to Kobe's office.

Akitada knocked and walked in. Kobe was seated behind his desk, reading some document. He got up and stared at Akitada's companions. "What happened to Daisai?" he asked.

"He tried to kill me because I was about to turn him and his partner in for Nakamura's murder."

Yukihito made some confused protest, but fell quiet when the constables drew nearer. Akitada told him to put down his burden and sit, then sat down himself.

"This is Nakamura Yukihito, the master's nephew," he said to Kobe.

Kobe's eyes lit up. "You don't say. How very convenient! When I was checking into that inheritance, I turned up a very interesting surprise." Kobe looked at Yukihito with great satisfaction. "We sent for you, but you weren't on your uncle's farm."

"The farm was mine," Yukihito said, "and I haven't done anything."

"Is that so?" Kobe got up and walked around his desk until he could lean over Nakamura's nephew. "So you're the master's heir, are you? And when you heard the prince wished to build a temple, you knew you were about to strike it rich."

Yukihito shrank back. "It's all legal," he protested. "I signed the papers weeks ago."

"Did you indeed?" Kobe straightened up, grinning broadly. Turning to Akitada, he asked, "How did you guess?"

"There had to be something that would make the master's death profitable. You may remember I suggested finding his heir. When you arrested that maid, I decided I had to do it myself."

Kobe looked embarrassed. "I let the poor thing go. She kept crying for her kids." Glancing at the unconscious Daisai, he asked, "What's he got to do with it?"

"I believe that Yukihito was approached by his friend Daisai with interesting news about his uncle's farm. But perhaps you had better let him tell his story."

Seeing their eyes on him, Yukihito stammered, "You think I killed Uncle?"

Akitada said, "We think your friend Daisai killed him because you promised him and Lord Miyoshi a share in the profits from the farm. That makes you guilty also."

Yukihito shook his head as if to clear it. "Daisai killed him?" he asked. Suddenly tears started to roll down his face. "Not Daisai," he sobbed. "He wouldn't do such a thing. Daisai knew I wouldn't want Uncle to get hurt."

"You'd better tell us about it," said Kobe.

The story, haltingly told by a confused Yukihito, was simple. On one of his visits home, Daisai had told him that the poor land he was cursing was worth a great deal of gold in the capital. He had offered to arrange a sale after Master Nakamura's death in return for a share for himself and a court official. Yukihito, penniless and hounded by creditors, agreed eagerly and signed the papers. Then, by a miracle, it had all come true. His uncle had died, he had sold the farm, and the money would be his as soon is this Lord Miyoshi paid. Kobe listened with open enjoyment.

"You don't say," he remarked when Yukihito was done. "How very nice!" He told the constables to take Daisai and Yukihito away and lock them up. "So you were right," he said to Akitada when they were alone. "Miyoshi was a part of it also?"

Akitada nodded. "He had to be. Miyoshi knew of the crown prince's dream and his plan to construct a fabulous temple in Nagaoka. He will not, I believe, readily confess his complicity, but Daisai will talk. His only hope is to show that he was manipulated by Miyoshi. The nephew, I think, truly was an unwitting tool in their hands."

"Yes. He's too stupid." Kobe slapped his hands on his knees and said, "We'll celebrate. You'll take a cup of wine with me?" Akitada nodded. Overflowing with good will and generosity toward Akitada, Kobe remarked, "I must say it is amazing that you deduced all of this from the arrangement of a few stones on a *go* board."

Akitada accepted the peace offering. "The particular contest they engaged in is called a 'race.' It is much quicker than the ordinary game, because it is won by whoever makes the first capture. It is possible that the master proposed the abbreviated game, as Miyoshi claims. It does not really matter. What *is* peculiar is that a superior player like Miyoshi would lose so badly."

"But how did you know that?"

"Did you make a diagram of the game on the board?"

Kobe flushed. "No."

"Well, let me see." Akitada reached across the desk for a sheet of paper and the captain's brush. Dipping the brush into the ink, he sketched the position of the nineteen black and white stones. "I believe, that is the way it was. We know Nakamura played black. He won because black surrounded and thus captured two white stones."

Kobe stared at the paper and shook his head. "I don't understand."

"Nakamura, playing black, started. They each played nine stones. The final turn was Nakamura's and he completed the capture. But it took two turns to surround the stones, and Miyoshi had a chance to block. He did not block. A child could have played better."

Kobe nodded. "Yes, I see it now. But it's such a little thing to hang a murder on. Maybe Miyoshi had a bad day."

Akitada shook his head. "No. I have thought much about this match. There seems to me only one reason why Miyoshi lost: he deliberately ended the game. Given his many attempts to take Nakamura's title, he must have had a powerful reason to end the game so abruptly by losing. Miyoshi knew that Nakamura would die after drinking his tea."

Kobe cried, "But that means Miyoshi poisoned the tea. What about Daisai? Why did he make up a tale about getting sick from Nakamura's tea when there was no poison in the tea yet?"

"Daisai was his accomplice. It was he who poisoned the tea. Think about it. The murder involved a certain amount of risk which Miyoshi and Daisai shared equally for mutual protection. Daisai put the poison in the tea, and Miyoshi visited Nakamura to make sure the master drank it. When you accused Miyoshi, Daisai came forward with his story. Yukihito was carefully kept out of it, because he represented the missing motive and was clearly not very intelligent."

Kobe thought. "It may be hard to prove."

"Remember one of Nakamura's rules," said Akitada. "'Always use your opponent's weakness.' Yukihito with his naiveté is the weakest link and has already broken the case. Of the remaining two, Daisai has the weaker personality. People like him always save their own skin at the cost of others. He is unlikely to suffer the penalty while Miyoshi goes free, reaping the profits from his crime." He paused and smiled sadly. "I have learned much by playing *go* with the master."

Kobe nodded. Raising his cup to Akitada, he said, "I wish I had known the old man. He must have been something."

Outside the latticed window, a bird began to sing.

Akitada's eyes moistened. After a moment, he said, his voice catching a little, "When I was on my way to see the master, I heard a cuckoo singing in a willow. I should have suspected then. The cuckoo is called the guide of the soul across the hills of death. No doubt it was taking Master Nakamura to paradise where he is even now teaching the immortals how to play the game."

The song stopped and, with a flutter of wings, the bird was gone.

Kobe cleared his throat. "I wonder," he said, "if you would honor me with a small lesson?"

THE NEW YEAR'S GIFT

In the following story, Akitada overcomes his personal convictions to do a favor for a former servant. It is one of several instances when Akitada confronts a tendency for prejudging people in the course of solving a crime. Kobe reappears, now promoted to superintendent and a staunch friend to Akitada.

Heian-Kyo (Kyoto): Eleventh century; in the First or Sprouting Month.

The dark figure crossed the street and paused in front of the rice merchant's shop. A sliver of light from inside briefly lit a young man's face before he melted into the shadow of the doorway.

Only a few doors away a middle-aged couple, huddling together against the freezing drizzle under an oil-paper umbrella, stopped on their homeward walk.

Their name was Otogawa, and they were returning from New Year's dinner at their son-in-law's house.

"Did you see that?" the woman hissed. "Wasn't that Kinjiro sneaking into Itto's place?"

"Damn that Itto!" mumbled her husband, swaying on his feet and nearly dropping the lantern. "Hope the fellow kills him. The old miser's got us like rats in a bag, rot him!"

"If you stayed away from wine and dice, we wouldn't be in this shape," she scolded. "And you're drunk again. As if we had anything to celebrate when you're about to lose the shop."

"Shut up!" he muttered and gave her a push that made the umbrella tilt crazily and drench them both with icy water. He cursed and reeled toward the door of his shop.

His wife followed him inside, muttering angrily. He collapsed on the raised flooring and began to snore. She lit an oil lamp from the lantern he had carried, put away the wet umbrella, then took off her outer wrap and her husband's muddy wooden sandals. She did not bother to cover her sleeping husband but scurried to a narrow window high up in the wall. It looked out over the street and was covered with oil paper which was translucent in the daytime. Climbing on a small chest, she peered through a tear in the paper at the rain-glistening street outside.

She was just in time to see the dark figure emerge from the shop next door and the young man rush past her window.

"It was him," she cried triumphantly. Her husband's comment was a loud snore. She climbed down and went to shake him awake. "Get up! Something's happened next door. You must go over there right away."

"Wha . . .?" He sat up drowsily.

"To Itto's! That young hellion Kinjiro just ran out again. He's done something."

"Why should I care? Serves the tight-fisted villain right if the kid robbed him."

"You fool. If you offer your help, the old man may wait for the money." She slipped the sandals back on his feet and gave him a push toward the door.

With a grunt, her husband staggered out into the icy rain.

The festive New Year's season began badly in the Sugawara household. On the first day of the year, the weather was so abysmal that the emperor could not pay homage to the lodestar, a bad omen for the nation, and apparently also for the Sugawara family. Akitada was passed over in the annual promotions. On the second day, the diviner came to cast his divining rods. When he read the resulting hexagrams, he looked glum and shook his head. Young Yori came down with a fever that night. On the third, the so-called "tooth-hardening" day, Akitada's elderly secretary Seimei bit too heartily into one of the "tooth-hardening" and life-prolonging rice cakes and broke a front tooth, throwing the whole family into gloomy anticipation of his death. Then Akitada caught a cold.

By the morning of the seventh day, the day of the seven herbs rice gruel, he woke with a vile headache and sore throat. His misery grew when no gruel appeared. In fact, there was no breakfast at all—not even a soothing cup of hot tea, though Seimei was usually obsessively punctual and reliable.

Shivering, Akitada dressed and went across the chilly courtyard to the kitchen. There he found to his irritation his entire staff—Seimei, the cook, his wife's maid, and the boy Toshi— who swept the courtyard and answered the gate—clustered around a seated beggar woman.

"What is going on? And where is my rice gruel?" Akitada croaked, glaring at everybody accusingly. This was no time to gossip with stray beggars. It was the busiest time of the year, and he had a cold.

Most of the kitchen surfaces were covered with trays and baskets of New Year's delicacies: melons, radishes, and huge platters of round, flat rice cakes, along with salted trout, and roasted venison and boar, all auspicious foods for the coming year. Among the foodstuffs Akitada saw his bowl of seven herbs gruel—so beneficial for all sorts of ailments, sore throats for example—left to grow cold because of the shabby visitor.

They immediately knelt and bowed to their master. Seimei, senior retainer and family friend, performed this obeisance in a perfunctory manner, sitting up quickly to say, "It's Sumiko, sir. She's in trouble."

Sumiko? Akitada blankly eyed the kneeling beggar woman. She was wet and dirty. On second glance, she looked younger than he had thought, but sickly and misshapen.

"You *do* remember Sumiko, sir?" urged Seimei. "Lady Sugawara's maid? She left us last summer to marry Kinjiro."

"Oh!"

Akitada was shocked. This pale, worn, and slatternly looking woman was their Sumiko? His wife's little maid had sparkled with health, prettiness, and laughter. In fact, they had fully expected her to run off with some wealthy merchant's son. Sumiko had certainly had enough admirers and turned down several good offers of marriage, perhaps because she was attached to Akitada's wife. She had even accompanied them to the north country. For eight years Sumiko had been a part of their family, and then, a year ago, out of the blue, she had announced that she wished to marry a penniless good-for-nothing.

The young man was not only poor, eking out a miserable wage as a messenger between post stations, taking and bringing horses as they were needed, but he had been in trouble with the law. Sumiko had defended him, claiming he was a changed man and would be adopted by a generous relative, but Akitada and his wife did not take this seriously; they attempted to talk her out of it. Sumiko had ignored all warnings and married her man.

"The police have arrested her husband for the murder of his adoptive father," said Seimei now, justifying all of Akitada's misgivings about the match.

Sumiko burst into violent sobs.

"She says Kinjiro didn't do it," Seimei continued, "but they have no money, sir, and Sumiko isn't well. She expects her first child any day. Not knowing where to turn, she has come to you."

Akitada looked again and saw that the pitifully creature in her loose faded garment was indeed in the last stages of pregnancy. He was not as a rule a superstitious man, but now he thought of the diviner and wondered what new calamity had just befallen them. This, however, he did not say. Instead he exclaimed with false heartiness, "And quite right, too. Welcome, Sumiko. We'll soon have you smiling again."

The young woman raised herself with difficulty, supporting her grotesquely swollen belly with both hands. Akitada marveled that she could have walked any distance in her condition. Her face had a translucent bluish pallor, and her lips were colorless. As he searched for more soothing words, she gave him a tremulous smile, and for a brief moment he recognized the old Sumiko.

"You're cold and wet," he said. "Have you eaten today?"

She shook her head.

The cook jumped up. "I'll heat some of the seven herbs gruel."

Sumiko waved the offer away. "I only came to beg your help for Kinjiro, sir." She hesitated, then added pathetically, "For old times' sake." Fumbling in her sleeve, she produced a small package wrapped in crimson silk. This she extended to Akitada. "And to wish you and your lady an auspicious year."

Akitada took the gift from her icy fingers and unwrapped a small carved tortoise, symbol of long life and happiness. The tiny creature on the palm of his hand was a lucky charm, not expensive, but clearly treasured for its magic powers. If anyone needed luck, it was Sumiko, but he could not refuse this traditional New Year's present.

"Thank you, Sumiko," he said. "I am very sorry about Kinjiro's trouble and will certainly try to help." He was afraid he sounded as dubious as he felt. To his mind, Kinjiro's reputation made his guilt a virtual certainty. "But you must eat some gruel first." His own stomach growled. "The herbs will be good for you and your child." Casting a hungry glance at his bowl of gruel and a pitying one at Sumiko, Akitada told Seimei to make the young woman comfortable and bring her to him later.

Back in his study, he sat down behind his desk, placed the tortoise in front of him, and drummed his fingers dejectedly. He wished he had snatched one of the rice cakes on his way out of the kitchen. He wished Sumiko had not appeared today of all days, bringing such a gift. With a sigh, he rose and went to a chest where he kept his valuables. Inside lay a small stack of gold coins. He took one and a sheet of decorated paper to wrap it in.

Placing his gift for Sumiko next to the turtle, he waited. Seimei eventually appeared with a steaming bowl of gruel and busied himself making Akitada's morning tea.

"What's the story?" Akitada asked, raising the bowl to sniff the aroma of parsley, borage, garlic, and other pungent green things, before taking a cautious sip. His wife Tamako had gathered the first greens of the year herself. They were added to the usual plain rice pottage in honor of the season and to ward off disease during the coming year. While Akitada doubted such long-range effects, he was very fond of the flavor and thought its medicinal properties soothed his painful throat.

"It appears that Kinjiro was invited for New Year's dinner at his adoptive father's house," Seimei told him, "but they quarrelled and Kinjiro left in anger. The next morning the old man was found stabbed to death." Seimei measured tea into a small cup of Chinese porcelain painted with sprays of pink plum blossoms. This also was a custom of the season. "Itto's neighbors testified that they saw Kinjiro return during the night. He does not deny it, but says he left the old man alive and parted from him on the best of terms and with a gift of silver."

Akitada's face lengthened. "That sounds highly unlikely."

"Yes, it sounds unbelievable, and it's his word against that of the widow. She says they quarreled when her husband told Kinjiro he had cancelled the adoption. Kinjiro became angry and threatened him. The police have searched Kinjiro's room and found the silver but no weapon. With his reputation, they had no choice but to arrest him."

"They found no murder weapon?" Akitada sipped his gruel slowly, savoring it. "What about this adoption?"

Seimei brought the teapot over and placed it on a small wooden brazier, warming his hands over it. "It's quite true, sir. Kinjiro's immediate family is dead, but his grandfather had a cousin called Itto, a rice merchant here in the capital. This Itto was childless and when he reached his eightieth year, he gave up hope and adopted Kinjiro as his heir."

"Great Heaven!" Akitada put down his bowl abruptly. "Not the Itto in the eastern market?"

"The same, sir. The second richest rice merchant in the capital."

Akitada shook his head in amazement. "What an extraordinary stroke of good fortune for that ne'er-do-well. And it is this wealthy and most generous man that Kinjiro is supposed to have killed?"

"It is. Fortune and misfortune are said to be like the twisted strands of rope. But if you have finished your gruel, may I bring Sumiko in? She is waiting outside in the corridor."

"Yes, of course. And inform my wife that she will stay with us for the time being."

Sumiko looked marginally better than before and had stopped crying. He presented her with the gold coin and his good wishes for a happier future. Without unwrapping it, she bowed and expressed her gratitude with a humility totally out of character for the pert young woman Akitada remembered. He sighed inwardly. No point in rubbing in that she should never have put her trust in Kinjiro, adoption or not.

"Sit down, Sumiko," he said in a kindly tone. "Seimei tells me that Kinjiro was adopted by a wealthy man."

She had folded her hands again protectively over her swelling abdomen. "Yes, and we thought ourselves blessed at first. But Kinjiro was unhappy from the beginning. He tried working for Master Itto until they quarreled and he left." She looked at Akitada earnestly. "Kinjiro does have a temper, but he would never hurt the old man. He's like Mount Fuji; he erupts, but there's no harm in him."

Akitada doubted that. "What did they quarrel about?"

She hesitated. "Master Itto wanted him to move into his house and run his business."

"But surely that is not too much to ask of one's heir."

She lowered her head. "Without me, sir."

"Without you? You mean he wished you to keep separate establishments?"

"I mean he wished Kinjiro to divorce me so he could arrange another marriage for him. You see, Kinjiro married me without his approval."

Akitada was appalled and did not know what to say. He began to have more respect for the unlucky Kinjiro. "And this quarrel happened on New Year's Day?" he finally asked.

"Oh, no. It was last autumn. Kinjiro came home drunk one day and refused to go back to the rice shop.

AKITADA AND THE WAY OF JUSTICE

When I asked him what was wrong, he said it was all over. The adoption wasn't working out." She paused and looked down at her hands which were now twisting restlessly in her lap. "I begged him to go back, but he was too proud. I offered to leave him, but I was with child, and he wouldn't hear of it. He lost his job and the allowance Master Itto had paid him. The post house would not take him back, and he could not find other steady work. For a while he did small jobs here and there, but soon we had hardly any food and the landlord threatened to throw us out in the middle of winter. The day before New Year's I thought I would have to go begging in the streets, but Master Itto sent a boy to invite Kinjiro to New Year's dinner." She sighed deeply.

Kinjiro's motive for murder and robbery could hardly be stronger. Akitada suppressed his apprehension and asked, "What happened?"

"Master Itto was pleased to hear that there would be a child and changed his mind about me, but he wanted Kinjiro to give his first son to a monastery. You see, he was afraid of dying. He thought that the Buddha would look kindly on such a sacrifice made on his behalf, and that the boy would be a monk and pray for his soul. When Kinjiro refused, Master Itto accused him of heartlessness and ingratitude. He said he was not his son if he only wanted his money and would give nothing in return. Kinjiro told him to keep his money, and that Itto was certainly no father of his. It must have been a terrible argument, but I made Kinjiro go back that night to apologize. I told him it was a son's duty to obey his father. Besides we were starving and soon would be in the street, and he would have neither a son nor a wife. So Kinjiro went back, and Master Itto was so pleased that he gave him two bars of silver to pay our debts and told him to bring me the very next morning to live with him and his wife so that I and my child would be properly looked after." She sighed again and said forlornly, "We were so relieved."

The misery of this young couple, caught between starvation and selling their unborn child to win a selfish old man's way into paradise, left Akitada speechless. After a pause, he asked, "What can you tell me about the Itto household?"

"There is Master Itto and his wife. And Hayashi who's the shop manager. And a boy for the rough work."

"Not many servants for a wealthy man," commented Akitada.

"Master Itto was careful with his money."

Akitada considered such economies miserly but did not say so. "Did Itto have any enemies that you know of?"

She shook her head helplessly.

There was little more to tell. The police had come the following day and arrested Kinjiro for the murder. Sumiko had spent a week appealing to constables, judges, and prison guards, hardly eating, and sleeping only from exhaustion. This morning she had run out of options and turned to Akitada.

The case against Kinjiro did not appear particularly knotty, but neither was it hopeful. In fact, everything pointed to him: motive, opportunity, personality, and past history. Kinjiro was desperately poor, while Itto had been a wealthy man without heirs; Kinjiro had been seen at Itto's place near the time of the murder; he was known as a man of violent temper, they had quarreled once again on the very day of the murder; and he had a police record.

But apart from being unable to refuse Sumiko's plea after her years of faithful service, Akitada was touched that Kinjiro had stuck by Sumiko even when tempted with a life of comfort and wealth.

"Well," he said in a bracing tone, "let me see what I can do. Meanwhile my wife will make you comfortable here until this matter is resolved."

Sumiko wept with gratitude.

Akitada found Itto's shop in the market quarter. All the shop fronts were festively decorated for the season, and shoppers crowded the roads on either side of a narrow canal. A small Buddhist temple adjoined Itto's property on one side, and an oil seller occupied the other. In front, a bridge spanned the canal, and on the other side stood a small wine shop, the Kingfisher Tavern. Its entrance was also decorated with pine branches, straw ropes, and paper twists in celebration of the New Year.

The chilly wind had caused Akitada's throat to ache again. He decided to have some of the hot spiced wine that was served during the holiday season and plan his strategy.

It was early and there were no customers in the Kingfisher Tavern. The landlord, a morose looking elderly man in a black and white checked cotton robe, stood in the doorway watching the shoppers. His expression turned hopeful when Akitada approached, and he rushed over to welcome his noble guest with smiles and bows. Akitada ordered the wine and sat where he could watch the street. The wine arrived, pleasantly sweet and warm to his raw throat and chilled body.

At the temple across the way, two old beggars sat on the steps in spite of the cold and boys skipped up and down between them. Just inside the gatehouse a monk sold incense to a couple of women who had come to pray for good fortune during the new year. The pervasive spirit of hopefulness was painfully at odds with his errand for Sumiko and her unborn child—and its father, who might not live out the month.

Itto's shop took up the front of a large property which extended far to the back. The rice merchant would not have had much trouble sharing his living quarters with Kinjiro's growing family. No doubt the old man had begun to feel lonely with just an aging wife to keep him company in his large house.

The shop door was covered with a blue curtain bearing in white the symbol of a bale of rice and the characters of Itto's name. It was decorated with the ubiquitous pine branches and led to the business premises, part of which could be seen under the propped-up shutters. A clerk was inside, serving a customer. An agile youngster behind him ground rice kernels into flour by running on a wooden wheel which kept large mallets pounding away and adding to the cheerful noise of the busy street.

Akitada reached for his wine flask and found it empty.

Instantly the landlord appeared at his side with a fresh one. "Good, isn't it?"

"Yes, thank you. You must do an excellent business here."

"So, so. Now and then people grab a bowl of noodles or a plate of vegetables and rice and rush off again. But there's only me, and it's more than a man can handle by himself." He looked wistfully across the street.

"I suppose you get to know your neighbors pretty well," said Akitada, following his eyes.

"Have you heard about the murder?"

Since the landlord seemed eager to chat, Akitada invited him to share a cup of wine. "What happened?" he asked.

The landlord sat and poured. "The old man was killed the night of the first, and the police have arrested his adopted son. He was no good, that boy, always quarrelling with old Itto. Itto's wife was beside herself with worry. She's a great little woman, that Mrs. Itto, handsome and hard-working. The old miser didn't treat her well. She's free of him now and rich to boot." He smiled. "Itto was past seventy when they got married," he went on. "The old fool wanted children. No such luck!" He chuckled.

Akitada raised his brows. "Men have been known to father children in old age," he pointed out. "It's women who become barren. How old is Mrs. Itto?"

"Not yet forty. She'll need a good man to look after her interests." He turned to look across the street.

"There she is now," he said, "talking to that Hayashi. He's the manager, a dry stick, but he knows the business. Fine looking female, wouldn't you say, sir?"

A small, brisk woman had appeared from the back and was speaking to the clerk. She wore a black silk gown belted rather tightly, which emphasized her generous bosom and round hips. Her hair was parted in the center and gathered behind her head. Even at this distance, she appeared overtly feminine. Akitada adjusted his image of a frail old widow.

"An old man with a much younger wife," he mused aloud. "Did the police suspect her of having a hand in the murder?"

His host stared at him. "Heavens, no," he said. "Why should she bother when old Itto had one foot in the other world already and all his wealth coming to her? No, no. The young fool did it all right. The Otogawas saw him."

"Oh?"

"Yes. That's their shop next door." The host leaned a little closer. "Otogawa gambles. There's a rumor that he owed Itto some money and would have to sell his business, but since Itto's died, he's looked as happy as a starving sparrow who found a pot of rice."

"Surely he will have to repay his debt to Itto's widow."

The landlord smiled. "If the widow asks for it."

Akitada watched the animated Mrs. Itto chatting with the customer and remembered that the Otogawas had pointed the finger at Kinjiro.

"It's a strange world," he said, shaking his head. His cup drained, he reached for his string of copper coins and paid. Then he strolled across the bridge and into Itto's shop.

The manager rushed up, bowing deeply. He was a skinny man in his forties, with anxious eyes and an obsequious manner.

"I wish to see the owner," Akitada told him, raising his voice over the noise of the rice mallets.

The man cast a nervous glance over his shoulder. "Might I be of some assistance, sir? I'm the manager and take care of all the business."

"Really?" Akitada raised his brows and eyed him sharply. "And your name?"

"Hayashi. Most humbly at your service, sir." Another bow.

"Well, this does not concern you."

Mrs. Itto joined them. On closer view, she had a round, handsome face with full lips and bright eyes. The eyes took in Akitada's appearance with minute interest. She, too, bowed deeply. "This insignificant person is the Widow Itto. How may I be of service?"

"It's very noisy here. My visit concerns your husband's murder. Is there somewhere we can talk privately?" Akitada glanced pointedly at Hayashi.

She said quickly, "Mr. Hayashi runs my business. I have no secrets from him." She hesitated. "There's only my husband's office."

"That will do very well. Allow me to express my condolences on your loss." Thinking Hayashi's promotion interesting, Akitada made no further objections to the man's presence.

She led the way to a large room behind the shop. Hayashi trailed behind. Itto's office was a gloomy place with rich dark wood furnishings. The carved shutters over the single high window were closed. Mats, lamps, cushions, and chests were all of good quality, proof of the comforts enjoyed by wealthy merchant families.

A corner of the room had been set aside for an ancestral shrine. Wooden plaques bearing the names of the deceased surrounded a small painting of a seated Buddha. Various vessels held food offerings to the spirits of Mr. Itto's ancestors, among them a small pyramid of New Year's rice cakes. The newest of the wood plaques occupied the center.

Akitada approached the altar and bowed respectfully toward the late Itto's plaque. "I see you honor your husband's forbears. An admirable family custom."

Mrs. Itto joined him, lit some incense, and bowed also. Hayashi, clearly a reluctant companion, hung back.

On a shelf behind the altar table rested some family heirlooms: an old ledger with purple silk cover, a finely made lady's fan, and another for a man, a pair of spurs with silver mountings in a pattern of intertwined reeds, an old wooden baton of office with some faded writing on it, the breastplate of a suit of armor, also decorated with reeds, and a quiver of dusty arrows.

"Apparently your husband's family enjoyed an illustrious past," commented Akitada. His eyes watered from the pungent smoke of the incense.

"One of his ancestors was a general who won a big battle. My husband was very proud of his family." She turned away, touching a sleeve to her eyes.

The suffocating scent burned in Akitada's sore throat and made his head hurt. He moved away from the altar. A low desk, littered with papers and documents, stood near one wall, a cushion, slightly askew, in front of it. Two plain wooden chests, the kind used to hold coins and silver, their doors and drawers heavily reinforced with metal and locks, stood on either side. This was where the rice merchant had transacted the financial side of his business, and where he must have been working late when surprised by his attacker.

His widow, following Akitada's glance, shuddered and averted her eyes quickly. "Forgive me for bringing you here," she said. "We're ordinary working people who cannot observe mourning customs. My husband was at his accounts when his relative attacked him and stole the silver from that chest. My husband's spirit has been exorcised, but you may wish to go back to the shop."

"Not at all," Akitada said, wishing his head would stop throbbing. "What a terrible crime! My name is Sugawara." When she did not react to his name, Akitada added, "I'm with the Ministry of Justice and have been asked to look into the case." He did not mention that the request had been made by his former maid. "Did you lose much silver?" The chest looked as though it held a great deal more than the two silver bars found in Kinjiro's room.

She raised a plump hand to her eyes. "I lost my husband. That's enough."

"I suppose one of your servants discovered the crime?"

She nodded. "The boy. I sent him to see if my husband wanted his morning rice."

"You had not missed your husband during the night?"

She flushed a little. "My husband was sleeping here when he was working on the accounts. At year's end people pay their debts and the accounts must be kept carefully. But won't your lordship sit down and take a cup of wine?" She placed some cushions and invited Akitada and a reluctant Hayashi to be seated, then clapped her hands. When no one appeared, she exchanged a glance with the manager, who got up quickly and left.

They sat silently for a minute or so. Akitada's headache made him dizzy, and his throat felt full of thorns. He swallowed painfully, hoping the wine would soon appear. In the shop the noise of the mallets ceased abruptly, a blessed silence, for each thump had raised an echoing throb in Akitada's skull.

Mrs. Itto said, "It is hard for the boy to hear anything over the sound of the mallets."

Akitada nodded. He remembered that there were no other servants.

She twisted her hands nervously. "If only my husband had listened to me, this would not have happened.

I felt it in my bones that the young man would do my husband harm." She fidgeted some more, then got up. "Excuse me please, while I see what's keeping the wine."

The moment she was gone, Akitada went to the merchant's desk. A ledger lay open, the entries making tidy rows, listing sums of money paid to or received from various persons, and the purpose of the payment. The more recent entries were in a different, less precise hand. Akitada turned a few pages. Itto had not only bought and sold rice, but like other rice merchants had lent money against rice and other property, being in effect a sort of pawnbroker. The amounts collected before the New Year were impressive, but a few sums were still unpaid. Akitada found the name of Itto's neighbor Otogawa with a substantial debt of twenty silver bars. It had been crossed out crudely and without Itto's neat notation of date of repayment.

Pursing his lips, Akitada glanced at the two chests. The lower door of the right one stood slightly ajar, and he gently eased it open. Inside were the tools of the merchant's trade, four abacuses, two ink stones, several brushes in their holders, water flasks, a scale for weighing silver and coins, and, at the very back, a peculiar upright lacquer rack with a silver design of grain or grasses. He was bending to look at it more closely, when he heard steps in the corridor and hurriedly resumed his seat.

The widow entered, followed by the boy with a tray. Having set this down on the floor between their cushions, he left. A moment later the mallets started up again.

"Hayashi had to wait on a customer," Mrs. Itto explained as she joined Akitada. "Please allow me to pour you a cup of spiced wine."

"Thank you." He drank, but his throat still ached abominably, and he spoke with difficulty. He wished himself home. Only Sumiko's pallid face and her little tortoise held him back. "I wanted to ask what your plans are for the future," he told the widow.

She stared at him, no doubt surprised because she had never laid eyes on him before this day, but answered readily enough. "I shall carry on my husband's business with the help of Mr. Hayashi."

"How admirable! Most women shy away from the difficulties of worldly affairs. But then it is lucky that you have a man you can trust."

She flushed. "You misunderstand, sir. I am perfectly capable of looking after the business myself. My late husband taught me a little and I used to have my own shop before I married him. I wouldn't think of turning money matters over to someone else, no matter how devoted."

She had spoken quite sharply. Mrs. Itto clearly was a woman who not only could take care of herself but also manage the faithful and accommodating Mr. Hayashi. Akitada said, "Forgive me for prying into your family affairs, but I had wondered what Master Itto's arrangements are for his adopted son's family." Seeing her blank astonishment, he added, "Perhaps I should have mentioned earlier that Kinjiro's wife Sumiko once worked for us. I continue to take an interest in her welfare."

For a moment she looked stunned. Then she cried, "Oh, it is too much! You expect me to support the wife of the man who murdered my husband? Imagine foully killing someone who offered a helping hand." Her face was flushed with anger. "I warned my husband. 'He is nothing but a common criminal,' I said. But my husband worshipped the memory of his family and wanted to continue the line. At the same time he hoped to do a good deed for an unfortunate relative. He wished to present a good account to Emma-o when he appeared before the judge of the dead. So he chose this Kinjiro, a handsome fellow with a bad character. I told him it would do no good, but he said the boy could change. 'Fast ripe, fast rotten,' I said.' In the end he agreed with me and cancelled the adoption." Looking at Akitada with tragic eyes, she cried, "And that is why the young devil killed him. Oh, my poor husband!" and burst into tears.

She appeared genuinely upset, and Akitada questioned his suspicious mind. After all, younger wives could be as devoted to their husbands as old ones. "Believe me," he said apologetically, "I understand your feelings. It must seem shocking to you, but if the adoption papers are still in effect, Kinjiro's wife and her unborn child have some claims on your husband's estate."

She clenched her fists, crying, "I told you, he changed his mind! He tore up the papers."

"Ah," said Akitada, rising, "in that case, of course, there is no more to be said. Please forgive my intrusion on your grief."

Sobbing into her sleeve, she muttered, "I shall not rest until my husband's murderer is punished."

At the shop's door, Hayashi was talking to a balding, red-faced man in a dark cotton robe. Both bowed deeply. Akitada paused to wish them an auspicious year and to comment on the weather. They returned his good wishes and agreed it was a long way from springtime yet.

When Akitada lingered, Hayashi said, "This is Mr. Otogawa, our neighbor."

"Oh," said Akitada, "you are the one who saw the killer."

Otogawa shook his head. "No, your honor. Actually it was my wife. From that window there. She shook me awake, crying 'Get up! Something's happened. You must go check on Mr. Itto."

Akitada put on a look of interest. "And did you?"

The man gulped. "Er, no. No, I didn't really. The fact is . . . too much wine at my son-in-law's house." He grinned sheepishly.

Akitada nodded his understanding. He turned to Hayashi. "And you, of course, had the day off to spend with your family?"

"Yes, of course, sir." The answer was prompt, but Hayashi looked nervous.

Akitada glanced up the street toward the temple. "With a temple right next door, I expect the good monks were a great comfort to Mrs. Itto in her bereavement."

Otogawa gave a sharp, braying laugh. "Not that temple. Old Itto's been feuding with the abbot for years about the property line. No, Mrs. Itto went to the Purple Cloud Temple for the funeral arrangements."

Hayashi cleared his throat. "If you will excuse me, sir, and Mr. Otogawa, I must get back to business."

Akitada looked after him. "A hard-working man."

Another sharp laugh from Otogawa. "Now more than ever." He glanced toward his shop. "But I mustn't gossip. My old woman says I have the big mouth of a fool." He brayed again. "And the big laugh of a fool, too." He turned to go.

Akitada kept step with him to his shop door. A strong smell of cheap lamp oil met them. Inside a sharp-faced woman was measuring oil into small jugs.

"I'm back," announced Otogawa, walking in.

"You've been long enough!" she scolded, intent on her task. "Talking to that henpecked Hayashi again?" Her eyes fell on Akitada in the doorway, and she got up, simpering and bowing. "Sorry! Sorry, sir. I didn't see you."

"The gentleman was visiting the Ittos," explained her husband.

Akitada smiled at her. "I understand you are the one who identified the murderer."

She preened a little. "So I did. He was rushing out of the old man's house as if all the devils of hell were after him. Carrying away Itto's silver."

"You could see that much in the dark? Were you very close to him?"

"I was at that window there." She pointed towards a narrow slit, covered with a wooden grille. "He was this close"— she measured the distance with her hands— "and he was grinning like a fiend."

"No doubt you ran next door to warn the Ittos?"

There was an awkward silence during which husband and wife looked at each other. "No," she said. "I didn't know he'd killed the old man."

He said, "It would've done no good."

"How do you know?" Akitada asked quickly. "Perhaps you might have stopped the bleeding in time."

"No way," cried Otogawa. "He had too many wounds. In the belly, the chest, the throat. You never saw so much blood . . ." He broke off abruptly when his wife jostled him. "Or so they say."

"Go see to the soup or it will be ruined," she snapped.

"Don't let me keep you from your meal." Akitada turned away.

Taking a deep breath of clean winter air to clear the stench of oil from his stuffy head, Akitada considered Otogawa's slip with great satisfaction. So the neighbor had gone to see Itto after Kinjiro left, and they had kept that fact to themselves. Only someone who had been there could describe Itto's wounds so precisely, and to suppress such knowledge argued guilt. Kinjiro had not contradicted their testimony, but it was their testimony which had got Kinjiro arrested. Earlier Akitada had wondered if they had traded favors with the widow, a release from their debt in exchange for turning in Kinjiro, but now he considered another, much darker motive. Had Otogawa gone to see Itto, argued with him about his debt and killed him, knowing he could pin the murder on Kinjiro?

Akitada paused in front of Itto's shop to wipe beads of perspiration from his face. He felt feverish and dizzy and knew he should be in bed. Shivering, he wished once again that Sumiko had chosen a better time to ask his help. If only his head were not so fuzzy, or his limbs so infernally heavy. Still, he was done. All he had really needed to do was to find another suspect, one who could be offered to the police instead of Kinjiro. And Otogawa would serve admirably.

But he stood undecided. Inside the shop Hayashi was busy with a customer. He too had raised certain suspicions in Akitada's mind, but that would take more effort. No. He would go to Police Superintendent Kobe, convince him of Kinjiro's innocence, and then return to his warm and comfortable home to be cared for by his family.

The trouble was he was dissatisfied with the Otogawa solution. Something nagged at his mind, something he had overlooked on his visit to Itto's place.

Shivering in the icy wind, he wracked his muddled brain. It had been in the rice dealer's room. Something had been out of place, or missing.

Missing like the weapon used in the crime.

And then, suddenly, he knew.

The missing weapon was a sword, the sword of Itto's illustrious ancestor. The shrine had held all sorts of mementos of the famous general except the most important one, the sword. And there had been one, for its lacquered stand, decorated with nodding grasses, had been tucked away in the back of Itto's chest.

The question was what had happened to the sword. His eyes fell on the adjoining Temple of the Four Heavenly Kings. Temples relied on the generosity of the community. The New Year's season was a particular blessing in this respect because many people presented gifts on that occasion. Akitada decided to pay one more visit.

The beggars looked at him hopefully. He gave both a few coppers, then climbed slowly to the temple gate. The incense-selling monk in the gateway, seeing the silk robe and stiffened hat of an official, jumped up in hopes of a generous contribution to the temple. "Welcome, welcome, your honor," he cried, bowing with his palms pressed together. "May the Buddha bless you and guide your steps through this dark world."

Akitada dabbed at his face and nodded his thanks. "I was passing and thought I would pay my respects," he said vaguely, looking around. "Perhaps someone can show me around?"

Akitada's rank produced a guide who was a senior monk. Burdened by advanced years and a large belly, he waddled slowly and spoke in a fruity, ponderous voice. He was determined not to leave out the smallest detail, and Akitada, who wished for nothing so much as a dark corner in which to sit and rest his aching body, had to pretend interest and devotion. In desperation he finally interrupted and croaked a question about the temple's treasures.

His guide, flattered by this thirst for knowledge, led him to a small treasure house. "I'm afraid we have little to impress your lordship," he said apologetically. "Just gifts from ordinary people in the quarter, though there are one or two valuable items. A sutra copy commissioned by a wealthy patron is perhaps special enough to show to a person of your discernment."

The treasure was indeed modest, a collection of lacquer boxes inlaid with mother-of-pearl or bone, an old lute with broken strings, and several pieces of porcelain. Akitada admired the sutra scroll, which was indeed fine, written in gold ink on deep blue paper, before he found what he had come for.

Half hidden behind a large brass censer, lay a short sword, the kind called *wakizashi*, worn in the belt and used only for close combat on foot. This particular sword had been made for ceremonial occasions; its ornate grip was decorated with silver inlay, as was its finely lacquered scabbard. The silver decorations depicted swaying reeds, the same reeds which had decorated the breastplate on Itto's altar and the sword stand in the merchant's chest.

Akitada pounced on it. "An instrument of death," he cried, turning it in his hands. "Surely this is a strange gift for a temple."

"A family heirloom, we think," the monk said. "Some of the craftsmen and merchants in the quarter are descendants of military families or have taken wives from noble houses."

The sword was old but well-kept. When Akitada pulled it free of the scabbard, it moved easily, and the blade, ordinary steel, was clean and quite sharp, with a fine edge along both sides and a sharp point.

"You 'think'? Do you mean that this was donated anonymously?"

"Yes indeed. A special present on New Year's Day. It's common for people to leave small gifts of money or food at the gate during the night, but leaving a fine sword like this was a little unusual. Mind you, we were very glad to receive it. Some day it may pay for temple repairs."

Akitada put the sword back. "Thank you," he said. "It has been a most enlightening tour." Fishing a handful of silver coins from his sash and pressing them into the smiling monk's hand, he added, "I feel deeply blessed by my visit and hope that you and your temple will enjoy a prosperous year."

It was strange how much better he felt a little later when he walked into Superintendent Kobe's office and said cheerfully, "The blessings of the New Year to you, my dear Kobe. I have found the sword used in the Itto murder."

Kobe, his old friend and sometime rival, raised his brows. "May you prosper and live a hundred years. How did you know we were looking for a sword?"

Akitada chuckled and sat down. "I didn't." Then he explained about Sumiko and his visit to Itto's shop and the temple. "The sword is Itto's. It has the same pattern of reeds as Itto's military heirlooms, and the sword's stand is hidden in one of his chests. Someone left the sword at the temple gate during the night of the murder." Akitada smiled with satisfaction. "And that means Kinjiro could not possibly be the killer."

"How so?"

"Kinjiro was seen leaving by the nosy Mrs. Otogawa. He was rushing off in the opposite direction."

"True." Kobe frowned. "If you're right, where does that leave us? He was the only one with a motive."

"Not at all. In fact, Kinjiro was the only one without a motive. Old Itto had forgiven him. On the other hand, I chatted with a few neighbors and found at least six of them had reasons to wish Itto dead." Akitada cleared his throat. "Do you happen to have some hot wine?"

Kobe sent for it and poured.

His throat eased, Akitada continued, "For example, there is the Kingfisher Tavern across from Itto's shop. Its landlord has been lusting after Itto's wife and expects his luck to turn, now that she's a widow. And then there are the Otogawas. They owed Itto twenty bars of silver and were about to lose their business. The debt was cancelled in Itto's account book, but not by Itto's hand. Otogawa described the murdered man's wounds to me and commented on the bleeding. That means he entered Itto's house after Kinjiro left, but lied about it to your people. It's possible that he found the old man alive, killed him, altered the books, and threw the blame on Kinjiro. Then there is the widow who seems to have formed a very close relationship with her manager Hayashi. Both had strong motives, for when Itto reconciled with Kinjiro that night, the young man became his principal heir. Itto's widow would have to depend on Kinjiro for support. It is likely that she listened at the door as the two men talked and, when Kinjiro left, she entered, took the sword from the ancestral altar and stabbed her husband to death. She may have been helped by Hayashi. After the murder, someone cleaned the sword and left it at the temple gate—a clever and quick way of disposing of the murder weapon. And that brings us to the monks who had a long-standing feud with Itto over the line between their properties."

Kobe grinned weakly. "Not the monks," he said, "and I don't see any of the neighbors taking the time to carry away the sword. The widow's a possibility."

Akitada nodded. "Of course it was the widow."

"How can you be so certain?"

"Only she would have hidden the sword stand in her husband's chest. A sword stand is a distinctive object. She could not leave it on the altar without the sword. Being only a woman of the common class, she would not have known that the absence of a sword among military heirlooms is a sign of dishonor. Itto would never have prided himself on an ancestor who had lost his sword."

Kobe slapped a hand on his desk. "Why didn't I think of that? The trouble is we'll never prove she did it."

"Oh, I don't know," said Akitada. His head was beginning to throb again and he felt incredibly sleepy. "My task is done," he said, getting to his feet. "I promised Sumiko that I would prove her husband's innocence. But if I were you, I'd confiscate Itto's books. In a business like his, there are bound to be illegalities. I would not be surprised if you find that the Ittos and Hayashi have been lending money illegally. Bring in the widow and her manager, along with the Otogawas, and question them. I think the Otogawas and Hayashi will have plenty to tell you once you put a bit of pressure on them. Hayashi looked brow-beaten and afraid of the widow."

When Sumiko and Kinjiro came to thank Akitada for his help, he was outside with his wife. On that sunny morning Tamako had come to him in great excitement and led him to the far corner of the garden.

"Look!" she had cried, pointing upward at the ancient plum tree which stretched its gnarled and lichen-covered limbs against the limpid blue sky. "It's not dead after all and spring is finally here. The old tree is going to bloom again."

Akitada looked up and saw a touch of rosy red, the color soft yet bright against the black bark. And then he saw another blossom, fragile as porcelain, and another. The twigs were covered thickly with pale buds, their tightly folded petals flushed with pink, each promising to become another perfect flower, the earliest harbinger of spring.

They were both smiling at the auspicious omen when they heard the steps on the gravel path and saw Kinjiro and Sumiko walking towards them. Sumiko, pretty as a flower herself, carried a small bundle tenderly in her arms, and Kinjiro, tall and well-built, had his arm around her shoulders and a broad grin on his handsome face.

"Oh, I can see why Sumiko married him," murmured Tamako, eyeing the young man with admiration.

"Ah, yes," nodded Akitada. The corner of his mouth twitched. "He is a very wealthy man now that Itto's widow has confessed."

"That's not at all what I meant," Tamako reproved him.

"No?" Akitada raised a brow. "Then it must have been due to the auspicious little tortoise." He put an arm around Tamako's shoulder and drew her close.

THE O-BON CAT

In the year 1021, tragedy strikes when Akitada loses his small son Yori in a smallpox epidemic. This loss destroys the happiness he had found in his marriage and family life and leaves him psychologically scarred. The events in the following story happen in Otsu a few months after the child's death as Akitada travels home during the O-bon festival of the dead. (This story forms the foundation of the novel, **The Masuda Affair***.)*

Otsu, Lake Biwa, Japan: the O-bon festival, 1021.

The First Day: Welcoming the Dead

He was on his homeward journey when he found the boy. At the time, caught in the depth of hopelessness and grief, he did not understand the significance of their meeting.

Sugawara Akitada, not yet in the middle of his life, was already sick of it. A man may counter hardship, humiliation, even imminent death, with resources carefully accumulated in his past and draw fresh zest for new obstacles from his achievements, but Akitada, though one of the privileged and moderately successful in the service of the emperor, had found no spiritual anchor in his soul when his young son had died during that spring's smallpox epidemic. He went through the motions of daily life as if he were no part of them, as if the man he once was had departed with the smoke from his son's funeral pyre, leaving behind an empty shell now inhabited by a stranger.

Having completed an assignment in Hikone two days earlier, Akitada rode along the southern shore of Lake Biwa in a steady drizzle. The air was saturated with moisture, his clothes clung uncomfortably, and both rider and horse were sore from the wooden saddle. This was the fifteenth day of the watery month, in the rainy season. The road had long since become a muddy track where puddles hid deep pits in which a horse could break its leg. It became clear that he could not reach his home in the capital but would have to spend the night in Otsu.

Otsu was the legendary place of parting, a symbol of grief and yearning in poetry and prose. In Otsu, wives or parents would bid farewell, perhaps forever, to their husbands or sons when they left the capital to begin their service in distant provinces of the country. Akitada himself had made that journey, not knowing if he would return. But those days seemed in a distant past now. He cared little what lay ahead.

At dusk he entered a dense forest, and darkness closed in about him, falling with the misting rain from the branches above, and creeping from the dank shadows of the woods. When he could no longer see the road clearly, he dismounted. Leading his tired horse, he trudged onward in squelching boots and sodden straw rain cape and thought of death.

He was still in the forest when a child's whimpering roused him from his grief. But when he stopped and called out, there was no answer, and all was still again except for the dripping rain. He was almost certain the sound had been human, but the eeriness of a child's pitiful weeping in this lonely, dark place on his lonely, dark journey seemed too cruel a coincidence. This was the first night of the three day O-bon festival, the night when the spirits of the dead return to their homes to visit before departing for another year.

If his own son's soul was seeking its way home also, Yori would not find his father there. Would he cry for him out of the darkness? Akitada shivered and shook off his sick fancies. Such superstitions were for simpler, more trusting minds. How far was Otsu?

Then he heard it again.

"Who is that? Come out where I can see you!" he bellowed angrily into the darkness. His horse twitched its ears and shook its head.

Something pale detached itself from one of the tree trunks and crept closer. A boy of about five or six. He caught his breath. "Yori?"

Foolishness! This was no ghost. It was a ragged child with huge frightened eyes in a pale face, a boy nothing at all like Yori. Yori had been handsome, well-nourished, and sturdy. This boy in his filthy, torn shirt had sticks for arms and legs. He looked permanently hungry, a living ghost.

"Are you lost, child?" asked Akitada, more gently, wishing he had food in his saddle bags. The boy remained silent and kept his distance.

"What is your name?"

No answer.

"Where do you live?"

Silence.

The child probably knew his way around these woods better than Akitada. With a farewell wave, Akitada resumed his journey. Soon the trees thinned and the darkness receded slightly. Grey dusk filtered through the branches, and ahead lay a paler sliver which was the lake and—thank heaven—many small golden points of light, like a gathering of fireflies, that were the dwellings of Otsu. He glanced back at the dark forest, and there, not ten feet behind, waited the child.

"Do you want to come with me then?" Akitada asked. The boy said nothing, but he edged closer until he stood beside the horse. Akitada saw that his ragged shirt was soaked and clung to the ribs of his small chest.

A deaf-mute? Oh well, perhaps someone in Otsu would know the boy.

Bending down, Akitada lifted him into the saddle. He weighed so little, poor little sprite, that he would hardly trouble the horse. For the rest of their journey, Akitada looked back from time to time to make sure the boy had not fallen off. Now and then he asked him a question or made a comment, but the child did not respond in any way. He sat quietly, almost expectantly in the saddle as they approached Otsu.

AKITADA AND THE WAY OF JUSTICE

Ahead beckoned the bonfires welcoming the spirits of the dead. Most people believed that spirits got lost, like this child, and also that they felt hunger. Otsu's cemetery was filled with tiny lights which marked a trail to town, and in the doorway of every home offerings of food and water awaited the returning souls, those hungry ghosts depicted in temple painting, skeletal creatures with distended bellies, condemned to eat excrement or suffer unending hunger and thirst in punishment for their wasteful lives.

In the market people were still shopping for the three day festival. The doors of houses stood wide open, and inside Akitada could see spirit altars erected before the family shrines, heaped with more fine things to eat and drink. So much good food wasted on ghosts.

They passed a rice cake vendor with his trays of fragrant white cakes. Yori had loved rice cakes filled with sweet bean jam. Akitada dug two coppers from his sash and bought one for the boy. The child received it with solemn dignity and bowed his thanks before gobbling it down. As miserable and hungry as this urchin was, he had not forgotten his manners. Akitada was intrigued and decided to do his best for the child.

He asked if anyone knew the boy or his family, but grew weary of the disclaimers and stopped at an inn. The boy had looked around curiously but given no sign of recognition. Akitada lifted him from the saddle and, with a sigh, took the small hand in his as they entered.

"A room," Akitada told the innkeeper, slipping off the sodden straw cape and his wet boots. "And a bath. Then some hot food and wine."

The man was staring at the ragged child. "Is he with you, sir?"

"Unless you know where he lives, he's with me!" Akitada snapped irritably. "Oh, I suppose you'd better send someone out for new clothes for him. He looks to be about five." He fished silver from his sash, ignoring the stunned look on the man's face.

After inspecting the room, he took the child to the bath.

Helping a small boy with his bath again was unexpectedly painful, and tears filled Akitada's eyes. He blinked them away, blaming such emotion on fatigue and pity for the child. The shirt had done little to conceal his thinness, but naked he was a far more shocking sight. Not only was every bone clearly visible under the sun-darkened skin, but the protruding belly spoke of malnutrition, and there were bruises from beatings.

Judging from the state of his long matted hair and his filthy feet and hands, the bath was a novel experience for him. Akitada borrowed scissors and a comb from the bath attendant and tended to his hair and nails, trying to be as gentle as he could. The boy submitted bravely. Afterwards, soaking in the large tub as he had done so many times with Yori, he fought tears again.

They returned to the room in the cotton robes provided by the inn. Their bedding had been spread out, and a hot meal of rice and vegetables awaited them. At the sight of the food, the boy smiled for the first time. They ate, and when the boy's eyes began to close and the bowl slipped from his hands, Akitada tucked him into the bedding and went to sleep himself.

The Second Day: Ghostly Phenomena

He awoke to the boy's earnest scrutiny. In daylight and after the bath and night's rest, the child looked almost handsome. His hair was soft, he had thick, straight brows, a well-shaped nose and good chin, and his eyes were almost as large and luminous as Yori's. Akitada smiled and said, "Good morning."

Stretching out a small hand, the boy tweaked Akitada's nose gently and gave a little gurgle of laughter.

But there were no miracles. The boy did not find his voice or hearing, and his poor body had not filled out overnight. He still looked more like a hungry ghost than a child.

And he was not Yori.

Yet in that moment of intimacy Akitada decided that, for however long they would have each other's company, he would surrender to emotions he had buried with the ashes of his first-born. He would be a father again.

Someone had brought in Akitada's saddle bags and the boy's new clothes. They dressed and went for a walk about town. Because of the holiday, the vendors were setting out their wares early in the market.

Near the Temple of the War God they breakfasted on a bowl of noodles. Then Akitada had himself shaved by a barber, while the boy sat on the temple steps and watched an old story-teller who regaled a small group of children and their mothers with the tale of how the rabbit got into the moon.

On the hillside behind the temple, a complex of elegantly curving tiled roofs rose above the trees. Akitada idly asked the barber about its owner.

"Oh, that would be the Masudas. Very rich but unlucky."

"Unlucky?"

"All the men have died." The barber finished and wiped Akitada's face with a hot towel. "There's only the old lord now, and he's mad. That family's ruled by women. Pshaw!" He spat in disgust.

There was no shortage of death in the world.

Akitada paid and they strolled on. The way the boy clung to his hand as they passed among the stands and vendors of the market filled Akitada's heart with half-forgotten gentleness. He watched his delight in the sights of the market and wondered where his parents were. Perhaps he had become separated from them while travelling along the highway. Or they had abandoned him in the forest because he was not perfect. The irony that a living child might be discarded, while Yori, so beloved and treasured by his parents, had been snatched away by death was not lost on Akitada, and he spoiled the silent boy with treats—a pair of red slippers for his bare feet, a top to play with, and sweets.

No one recognized the child; neither did the boy show interest in anyone. But one odd thing happened. After having clung to Akitada's hand all day, the boy suddenly tore himself loose and dashed into the crowd. Akitada panicked, afraid he had lost him forever.

But the boy had not gone far. Akitada glimpsed his bright red shoes between the legs of passersby, and there he was, sitting in a doorway, clutching a filthy brown and white cat in his arms. Akitada's relief was as instant as his irritation. The animal was thin, covered with dirt and scars, and looked half wild. When Akitada reached for it, it hissed and jumped from the boy's arms.

The child gave a choking cry, too garbled to be called speech. He struggled wildly in Akitada's arms, sobbing and repeating the same strangled sounds, his hands stretching after the cat. Akitada felt the wild heartbeat in the small chest against his own and soothed the choking sobs by murmuring softly to him. Eventually, the boy calmed down, but even after Akitada bought him a toy drum, he still looked about for the stray cat.

When night fell, they followed the crowd back to the temple where the O-Bon dancers gyrated in the light of colored lanterns. Akitada had to hold the boy so he could see over the heads of people. His eyes were wide with wonder at the sight of the fearful masks and bright silk costumes. Once, when a great lion-headed creature came close to them, its glaring eyes and lolling tongue swinging his way, he gave a small cry and burrowed his face in Akitada's shoulder.

It was shameful for a grown man to weep in public. Akitada brushed the tears away and knew that he could not part with this child.

He lost the boy only moments later.

Someone in the watching crowd shouted, "There he is," and a sharp-faced, poorly-dressed woman pushed to his side. "What are you doing with our boy?" she demanded shrilly. "Give him back!"

Akitada could not answer immediately, because the child's thin arms wrapped around his neck with a stranglehold.

A rough character in the shirt and loincloth of a peasant appeared behind the woman and glared at Akitada. "Hey," he cried, "that's our boy. Let go of him." When Akitada did not, he bellowed at the bystanders, "He's stolen our boy! Call the constables!"

Akitada loosened the boy's grip and saw sheer terror on his face.

But it was over all too quickly. A couple of constables appeared and talked to the couple, whose name was Mimura. The man was a fisherman on the lake about a mile north from Otsu near the forest where Akitada had found the boy. They handed the weeping child over to his parents with a warning to keep a better eye on him in the future.

Though Akitada knew he had been foolish to give his affection to a strange child, his heart ached when the parents dragged the whimpering boy off. He suspected that they had abused him and would do so again, but he had no right to interfere between a parent and his child. This did not stop him from wandering gloomily about town, trying to think of ways to rescue the boy.

Then he saw the cat again.

Perhaps it was due to the festival's peculiar atmosphere or his confused emotions, but he was suddenly convinced that the cat was his link to the boy. This time he knew better than to rush the animal. He kept his distance, waiting as it investigated gutters and alleyways for bits of food. At one point it paused to consume a large fish head, and he hurriedly purchased a lantern. Eventually the animal stopped scavenging and moved on more purposefully. The streets got darker, there were fewer people, and the sound of the market receded until they were alone on a residential street, the cat a pale patch in the distance – until it disappeared with the suddenness of a ghost into a garden wall.

Akitada was still staring at the spot when the soft flapping of straw sandals sounded behind him. An old man approached. A night watchman with his wooden clappers. In the distance sounded a faint temple bell, and the watchman paused to listen, then used his clappers vigorously, calling out the hour in a reedy voice. The middle of the night already.

When the old man had finished, Akitada asked, "Do you happen to know who owns a brown and white cat hereabouts?"

"You mean Patch, sir? She lives in the dead courtesan's house on the lake." He pointed at the wall up the street.

Patch? Of course. The cat was spotted. And that must be what the boy had tried to say. "The dead courtesan's house?" Akitada asked.

"Nobody lives there anymore," the watchman said. "It's a sad ruin. The cat belonged to her."

"Really? Do you happen to know who owns the property now? I might want to buy it."

The watchman shook his head. "Dear me, not that place, sir. She killed herself because her lover left her. Her angry ghost roams about the garden in hopes of catching unwary men to have her revenge on. I always cross to the other side when I pass."

Akitada looked at the watchman doubtfully. It was the middle of the O-bon festival, and the man was superstitious. "How did she die?"

"Drowned herself in the lake."

"Were there any children?"

"If so, they're long gone. The house belongs to the Masudas now."

Akitada thanked the man and watched him make a wide detour up ahead before following more slowly.

When he reached the spot where the cat had disappeared, he saw that a section of the wall had collapsed and he could see into an overgrown garden hiding all but the elegant curved roof of a small villa. The night watchman turned the corner, and Akitada scrambled over the rubble, aware that he was trespassing. He felt foolish but was more than ever convinced that he must find the cat.

A clammy heat rose from the dense vegetation. Everywhere vines, brambles, and creepers covered shrubs and trees. His feeble lantern picked out a stone Buddha, half-hidden beneath a blanket of ivy. Strange rustlings, squeaks, and creaks were everywhere, and clouds of insects hovered in the beam of his lantern. The atmosphere was oppressive and vaguely threatening. When he felt a tug at his sleeve, he swung around, but it was only the branch of a gaunt cedar.

AKITADA AND THE WAY OF JUSTICE

There was no sign of the cat, just dense, towering shrubs and weirdly stirring curtains of leafy vines and wisteria suspended from the trees. He would have turned back, had he not heard a door or shutter slamming somewhere ahead.

When he reached the house, he was covered with scratches, itching from insect bites, and his topknot was askew. But there, on the veranda, sat the cat, waiting.

The small villa was dark and empty, its shutters broken, the paper covering its windows hanging in shreds, and its roof tiles shattered on the ground. The balustrade of the veranda leaned at a crazy angle, and where once there had been doors, black cavernous spaces gaped in the walls. But once it must have been charming, poised just above the lake in its lush gardens, perhaps a nobleman's retreat from official affairs in the capital.

The lake stretched still and black to the distant string of tiny lights on the far shore where people were celebrating the return of their dead. No one had lit candles or set up an altar in this dark place, but Akitada suddenly felt a presence which sent shivers down his back. He looked about carefully, then walked to the villa. The cat watched his approach with unblinking eyes, motionless until he was close enough to touch it; then it slipped away and disappeared into the house. He called to it, the way he had heard young women and children call to their pets, but the animal did not reappear.

The veranda steps were missing, as was most of the floor. The house, vandalized for useful building materials, had become inaccessible to all but cats. He was turning away, when he heard a faint sound, almost a wail and definitely not made by a cat. He swung back and caught a glimpse of movement inside the house.

A tall pale shape—a woman trailing some diaphanous garment?—had moved across the opening to one of the rooms and disappeared. For a moment Akitada blinked, the hair bristling on his head; then he called out, "Who is there?" There was no answer.

He ran around the corner of the house and climbed one of the supports, holding up his lantern to direct its beam into the room where he had seen the woman. The room was empty. Dead leaves lay in the corners and rainwater stood in puddles on the floor. In spite of the warm and humid night, Akitada felt suddenly cold.

When he stepped down from his perch, his foot landed on something which broke with a sharp crack. In the light of the lantern, he saw a shimmer of black lacquer and mother-of-pearl, a wooden toy sword, proof that a small boy had once lived here. He picked up the hilt and saw that it was just like one he had bought Yori during the last winter of his life. It had been an expensive toy, its handle lacquered and ornamented to resemble the weapon of an adult, but Yori's pleasure in it as father and son had practiced their swordplay in the courtyard of their home had been well worth it.

A sudden irrational fear gripped Akitada. He felt as if he had intruded in a strange and forbidden world, and left quickly. When he reached the broken wall again, his heart was pounding and he was out of breath.

Dejected, he returned to the inn. He was no closer to finding the boy or making sense of what was troubling him. A courtesan's ghost, a cat, and an expensive toy? What did it all matter? He was too weary to bother.

The Third Day: The Ghosts Depart

In spite of his exhaustion he slept poorly. The encounter with the child had brought back all of the old grief and added new fears, for he lay awake a long time, thinking that he had abandoned the boy to his fate without lifting a finger to help him. When he finally did fall asleep, his dreams were filled with snarling cats and hungry ghosts. The ghosts all had the face of the boy and followed him about, their thin arms stretched out in entreaty.

Toward dawn he woke drenched in sweat, certain that he had heard Yori cry out for him from the next room. For a single moment of joy he thought his son's death part of the dream, but then the dark and lonely room of the inn closed around him and he plunged back into despair. Waking was always the hardest.

The last day of the O-Bon festival dawned clear and dry. If the weather held, Akitada would reach Heian-Kyo in a few hours' ride, but he decided to chance it and spend the morning trying to find out more about the boy, the cat, and the dead courtesan. He thought, half guiltily and half resentfully, of his wife, but women seemed to draw on inner strengths when it came to losing a child. In the months since Yori's death, Tamako had quietly resumed her daily routines, while he had been sunk into utter despair.

The curving roofs of the Masuda mansion rose behind a high wall, its large gate closed in spite of the festival. Did the Masudas lock in their ghosts? Akitada rapped sharply and gave his name to an ancient male servant, adding, "I am calling on Lord Masuda."

"My master is not well. He sees no one," wheezed the old man.

"Then perhaps one of the ladies?"

The gate opened a little wider, and Akitada was admitted. The elegance of the mansion amazed him. No money had been spared on these halls and galleries. Blue tile gleamed on the roofs, red and black lacquer covered doors and pillars, and everywhere he saw carvings, gilded ornaments, and glazed terra cotta figures. They walked up the wide stairs of the main building and passed through it. Akitada caught glimpses of a painted ceiling supported by ornamented pillars, of thick grass mats and silk cushions, and of large, dim scroll paintings. Then they descended into a private garden. A covered gallery led to a second, slightly smaller hall. Here the old servant asked him to wait while he announced his visit to the ladies.

From the garden came the shouts and laughter of children. An artificial stream babbled softly past the veranda, disappeared behind an artificial hill and reappeared, spanned by an elegant red-lacquered bridge. Its clear, pebble-strewn water was quite deep. A frog, disturbed by Akitada's shadow, jumped in and sent several fat old koi into a mild frenzy.

Suddenly two little girls skipped across the bridge, as colorful as butterflies in their embroidered gowns, their voices as high and clear as birdsong. An old nurse in black followed more slowly.

Lucky children, Akitada thought bitterly, turning away. And lucky parents!

The old man returned and took him into a beautiful room. Two ladies were seated on the pale grass mats near open doors. Both wore expensive silk gowns, one the dark gray of mourning, the other a cheerful deep rose. The lady in grey, slender and elegant, was making entries into a ledger; the other, younger, lady had the half-opened scroll of an illustrated romance before her. The atmosphere was feminine, the air heavily perfumed with incense.

The lady in gray raised her face to him. No longer in her first youth but very handsome, she regarded him for a moment, then made a slight bow from the waist and said, "You are welcome, my lord. Please forgive the informality, but Father is not well and there was no one else to receive you. I am Lady Masuda and this is my late husband's secondary wife, Kohime."

Kohime had the cheerful plain face and robust body of a peasant girl. Akitada decided to address the older woman. "I am deeply distressed to disturb your peace," he said, "and regret extremely the ill health of Lord Masuda. Perhaps you would like me to return when he is better?"

"I am afraid Father will not improve," said Lady Masuda. "He is old and . . . his mind wanders. You may speak freely." She gestured at the account book.

"I have been forced to take on the burdens of running this family."

Akitada expressed his interest in buying a summer place on the lake, within easy reach of the capital, and in a beautiful setting. Lady Masuda listened politely until he asked about the abandoned villa. Then she stiffened with distaste. "The Masudas own half of Otsu. I would not know the house you refer to. Perhaps . . ."

But the cheerful Kohime chimed in. "Oh, Hatsuko, that must be the house where our husband's . . ." She gulped and covered her mouth. "Oh!"

Lady Masuda paled. She gave Kohime a look. "My sister is mistaken. I am sorry that I cannot be of more assistance."

Akitada was too old a hand at dealing with suspects in criminal cases not to know that Lady Masuda was lying. Of the two women, Kohime was the simpler, but he could think of no way to speak to her alone. Thanking the ladies, he left.

Outside the old servant waited. "There's someone hoping to speak to you, my lord. The children's nurse. When I mentioned your name, she begged for a few moments of your time."

Turning, Akitada caught sight of the elderly woman in black peering anxiously over a large shrub and bowing. He returned her bow.

"I don't believe I have met her," he told the old manservant.

"No, my lord. But when her son was a student in the capital, he was accused of murdering his professor. You cleared him and saved his life."

"Good heavens! Don't tell me she is the mother of that . . ." Akitada had been about to call him a rascal, but corrected himself in time, " . . . bright young fellow Ishikawa."

"Yes, Ishikawa." The old man laughed, rubbing his hands, as if Akitada had been very clever to remember. "When the gentleman is ready to leave, I shall be waiting at the gate."

Akitada had no wish to be reminded of Ishikawa. The case had happened a long time ago, in happier years, when Akitada had been courting Yori's mother, but he sighed and stepped down into the garden.

Mrs. Ishikawa was in her sixties and, it seemed, a much respected member of the Masuda household, having raised both the son and the grandchildren of the old lord. Akitada managed to end her long and passionate expressions of gratitude by asking, "How is your son?"

"He is head steward for Middle Counselor Sadanori and has his own family now," she said proudly. "I am sure he would wish to express his deep sense of obligation for your help in his difficulties."

Akitada doubted it. Ishikawa, a thoroughly selfish young man, had been innocent of murder but deeply implicated in a cheating scandal which had rocked the imperial university, and he had held Akitada responsible for his dismissal. But as Akitada gazed into her lined face with the kind eyes smiling up at him, he was glad he had spared someone the pain of losing a son.

"Perhaps you can help me," he said. "There is an abandoned villa on the lake. I was told it belongs to the Masudas, but Lady Masuda denies this."

The old lady looked startled. "Peony's house? Lady Masuda would not wish to be reminded of that."

Peony was a professional name often used by courtesans and entertainers. Akitada guessed, "Lady Masuda's husband kept Peony in the villa on the lake?"

Mrs. Ishikawa squirmed. "We are not to speak of this."

"I see. I will not force you then. But perhaps you can tell me about a cat I saw there. It was white with brown spots."

Her face brightened momentarily. "Oh, Patch. Such a dear little kitten, and the boy doted on it. I used to wonder what became of it." Tears suddenly rose to her eyes and she clamped a hand over her mouth, realizing that she had said too much.

Akitada pounced. "There was a little boy then?"

"Oh, the poor child is dead," she cried. "They're both dead. My lady says Peony killed him and then herself." A stunned silence fell. "Oh, sir," she whimpered, "please don't mention that I told you. It was horrible, but there was nothing we could do. It's best forgotten." She was so distressed that Akitada nearly apologized. But his mind churned with questions and, while he respected her loyalty, he saw again the boy's face as he was dragged away from him.

"Mrs. Ishikawa," he said earnestly, "two days ago I found a deaf-mute boy. He was about five years old, and when he saw the cat, he recognized it. I think he tried to say its name."

She stared at him. "He's the right age, but Peony's boy talked and sang all day long. It couldn't be him."

From the garden came the voice of Lady Masuda calling for the nurse. Mrs. Ishikawa flushed guiltily. "Forgive me, my lord, but I must go. Please, forget what I said." And with a deep bow she was gone.

Akitada stared after her. If she was right about Peony's child being dead, then the boy belonged to someone else, perhaps even to the repulsive couple who had dragged him away. But how did Lady Masuda come to tell such things to the nurse? Surely because Mrs. Ishikawa had known Peony and her son and had been fond of them. The elegant lady who had been bent over the account book knew what was in the interest of the Masudas, and the dubious off-spring of a former courtesan was best assumed dead.

As he walked back to the gate, the glistening roofs of the Masuda mansion testified to the family's substantial wealth, all of it belonging to an ailing old man without an heir. Akitada wondered about the deaths of the courtesan Peony and her child. Perhaps all the years of solving crimes committed by corrupt, greedy, and vengeful people had made him suspicious. Or perhaps his encounter with the wailing ghost had put him in mind of a restless spirit in search of justice. He was neither religious nor superstitious, but there had been nothing reasonable about the events of the past two days. Or about his own state of mind.

And suddenly, there in the Masuda's courtyard, he realized that the bleak and paralyzing hopelessness, which had stifled him like a blanket for many months now, had lifted. He was once again pursuing a mystery.

Turning to the old servant who waited patiently beside the gate, he asked, "When did your young master die?"

"Which one, my lord? The old lord's son died three years ago when his horse threw him, but the first lady's little son drowned last year." He sighed. "Now there are only the two little girls of the second lady, but the old lord cares nothing for them."

Akitada's eyebrows rose. "How did the boy drown?"

"He fell into the stream in the garden. It happened a year ago when Mrs. Ishikawa was away on a pilgrimage and the other servants weren't watching."

So Lady Masuda had also lost a son. And Peony, and possibly her son, had died soon after. Also by drowning. Were all these deaths unrelated accidents?

A picture was beginning to shape in Akitada's mind. To begin with, the story was not unusual. A wealthy young nobleman falls in love with a beautiful courtesan, buys out her contract, and keeps her for his private enjoyment in a place where he can visit her often. Such liaisons could last months or lifetimes. In this case, the death of the younger Masuda had ended his affair, but there had been a child. What if Lady Masuda, who had lost first her husband and then her only son, had, in a grief-maddened state, one night wandered to the lake villa and killed both the rival and her child?

AKITADA AND THE WAY OF JUSTICE

Akitada had much to think about. He thanked the old man and left.

Crowds already filled the main streets of Otsu, most in their holiday best and eager to celebrate the departure of their ancestral ghosts. Akitada contemplated wryly that for most people death loses its more painful attributes as soon as duty has been observed and the souls of those who were once deeply mourned have been duly acknowledged and can, with clear conscience, be sent back to the other world for another year. Tonight people everywhere would gather on the shores of rivers, lakes, and oceans and set afloat tiny straw boats containing a small candle or oil lamp, to carry the spirits of the dear departed out into the open water where, one by one, the lights would grow smaller until they died out completely. But what of those whose lives and families had been taken from them by violence?

Akitada asked for direction to the local warden's office. There he walked into a shouting match between a matron, a poorly-dressed man, and a ragged youngster of about fourteen. The warden was looking from one to the other and scratching his head.

As he waited for the matter to be settled, Akitada pieced together what had happened. Someone had knocked the matron to the ground from behind and snatched a package containing a length of silk from under her arm. When she gathered her wits, she saw the two villains running away through the crowds. Her screams brought one of the local constables who set off after the men and caught them a short distance away.

The package was lying in the street and the two were scuffling with each other.

The trouble was that each blamed the theft on the other and claimed to have been chasing down the culprit.

The ragged boy had tears in his eyes. He kept repeating, "I was only trying to help," and claimed his mother was waiting for some fish he was to have purchased for their holiday meal. The man looked outraged. "Lazy kids! Don't want to work and think they can steal an honest person's goods. Maybe a few good whippings will teach him before it's too late."

The matron, though vocal about her ordeal, was no help at all. "I tell you, I didn't see who did it. He knocked me down and nearly broke my back."

The warden shook his head, apparently at the end of his tether. "You should have brought witnesses," he grumbled to the constable. "Now it's too late, and what'll we do?"

The constable protested, "Oh come, on, Warden. The kid did it. Look at his clothes. Look at his face. Guilt's written all over him. Let's take him out back and question him."

Akitada looked at the boy and saw that he was terrified. Interrogation meant the whip, and even innocent people had been known to confess to crimes when beaten. He decided to step in.

"Look here, Constable," he said in his sternest official tone, "whipping a suspect without good cause is against the law. And you do not have good cause without a witness."

They all turned to stare at him. The warden, seeing a person of authority, cheered up. "Perhaps you have some information in this matter, sir?"

"No. But I have a solution for your problem. Take both men outside and make them run the same distance. The loser will be your thief."

"A truly wise decision, sir," cried the matron, folding her hands and bowing to Akitada. "The Buddha helps the innocent."

"No, madam. The thief got caught because his captor was the better runner."

They all adjourned to a large courtyard, where the constables marked off the proper distance, and then sent the two suspects off on their race. As Akitada had known, the thin boy won easily. He thanked Akitada awkwardly and rushed off to purchase his fish, while the thief was taken away.

"Well, sir," said the delighted warden, "I'm much obliged to you. It might have gone hard with that young fellow otherwise. Now, how can I be of service?"

Having established such unexpectedly friendly relations, Akitada introduced himself and told the story of the mute boy. The warden's face grew serious. When Akitada reached the Masuda family's account of Peony's death, he said, "I went there when she was found. There was no child, dead or alive, though there might have been one. Bodies disappear in the lake. The woman Peony had drowned, but there was a large bruise on her temple. The coroner's report states that the bruise was not fatal and that she must have hit a rock when she jumped into the lake. But there were no rocks where she was found, and the water was too shallow for jumping anyway."

"Then why did you not speak up at the time?"

"I did not attend the hearing. Someone told me about the verdict later. I did go and ask the coroner about that bruise. He said she could have bumped her head earlier." The warden added defensively, "It looked like a suicide. The neighbors said she'd been deserted."

Akitada did not agree. He thought Peony had been struck unconscious and then put into the water to drown, and if the boy was indeed her son, he might have seen her killer. But that boy was mute. Or was he?

"The boy I found," he said, "was terrified of the people who claimed him. I thought at first it was because he expected another beating. Perhaps he did, but I think now that they are not his parents. I believe he has a more than casual connection with the cat and could be Peony's missing son."

"Holy Amida!" breathed the warden. "What a story that would be! They live in a fishing village outside town. I'll ride out now and check into it. If you're right, sir, it may solve the case. But that would really make a person wonder about the Masudas."

"It would indeed. I'll get my horse from the inn and join you."

The weather continued clear. They took the road Akitada had traveled two days before. On the way, the warden told Akitada about the Masuda family.

AKITADA AND THE WAY OF JUSTICE

The old lord had doted on his handsome son and chosen his first wife for her birth and beauty, but the young lord did not care for his bride and started to visit the courtesans of the capital. His worried father sought to keep him home to produce an heir by presenting him next with a sturdy country girl for a second wife. She proved fertile and gave him two daughters before he lost interest again. It was at this time that the young husband had installed Peony, a beautiful courtesan, in the lake villa, where he stayed with her, turning his back on his two wives. The old lord forced him to return temporarily to his family, and the first lady finally conceived and bore a son, but her husband died soon after.

And, mused Akitada, while all of Otsu took an avid interest in the births and deaths in the Masuda mansion, hardly anyone cared about the fate of a courtesan and her child. In fact, he was surprised they had been allowed to continue living in the villa.

When Akitada and the warden reached the fishing village, they found the man Mimura leaning against the wall of a dilapidated shack, watching the boy sweep up a smelly mess of fish entrails, fins, and vegetable peelings. Dressed in rags again, the child now sported a large black eye.

"Hey, Mimura?" shouted the warden. The boy raised his head and stared at them. Then he dropped his broom and ran to Akitada who jumped from his horse and caught him in his arms. The child was filthy and stank of rotten fish and he clung to Akitada for dear life.

Mimura walked up, glowering. "If it's about the boy, we settled all that," he told the warden. "I should've asked for more than the bits and pieces he gave the kid, and that's the truth." He turned with a sneer to Akitada. "You had him a whole day and night. That ought to be worth at least two pieces of silver."

The warden reddened to the roots of his hair, and Akitada realized belatedly that he was being accused of an unnatural fondness for boys. A cold fury took hold of him. "That child is not yours," he thundered. "And stealing children is a crime."

Mimura lost some of his bravado, and the warden quickly added, "Yes. This boy's not registered to you, yet you claimed him as your own. I'm afraid I'll have to arrest you."

Mimura's jaw dropped. "We didn't steal him, Warden. Honest. He's got no family. We took him in, the wife and I."

"Really? Out of the goodness of your heart? Then where are his papers? Where was he born and who were his people?"

"I'm just a poor working man, Warden. This woman gave him to my wife and she paid her a bit of money to look after him." He turned to call his slatternly spouse from the shack.

She approached nervously and confirmed his story. "I was selling fish in the market. It was getting dark when this lady came. She was carrying the boy and said, 'This poor child has just lost his parents. I'll pay you if you'll raise him as your own.' I could see the boy was sickly, but we needed the money, so I said 'yes.'"

"Her name?" the warden growled.

"She didn't say."

"You called her a lady. What did she look like?" Akitada asked.

"I couldn't tell. She had on a veil and it was dark. And she was in a hurry. She just passed over the boy and the money and left."

"How much money?" the warden wanted to know.

"A few pieces of silver. And a poor bargain it was," Mimura grumbled. "He's deaf and dumb as a stone and a weakling. Look at him!"

"Did you give him the black eye?" Akitada asked.

"Me? No. He's a clumsy boy. A cripple."

Akitada lifted the boy on his horse. "Come along, Warden," he said over his shoulder. "You can deal with them later. We need to find this child's family."

On the way back, the small, warm, smelly body in his arm, Akitada was filled with new purpose. He outlined his suspicions to the warden, cautiously, for he was now certain that the child could hear very well.

"So you see," he said, "we must speak to Lord Masuda himself, for the women are covering up the affair."

The warden, who had been admirably cooperative so far, demurred. "Nobody sees the old lord. They say he's lost his mind."

"Nevertheless we must try."

The Masuda mansion opened its gates for a second time. If the ancient servant was surprised to see Akitada with a ragged child in his arms and accompanied by the warden, he was too well-mannered to ask.

But he shook his head stubbornly when Akitada demanded to see the old lord.

"Look," Akitada finally said, "I think that this boy is Lord Masuda's grandson, the child of the courtesan Peony. Would he not wish to know him before he dies?"

"But," stammered the old man, "that boy is dead. Lady Masuda said so herself."

"She was mistaken."

The old man came closer and peered up at the child. "Amida!" he whispered. "Those eyebrows. Can it be?"

He took them then. They found the old lord in his study. He sat sunken into himself, one gnarled hand pulling at the thin white beard which had grown long with neglect, his hooded eyes looking at nothing.

"My lord," said the servant timidly. "You have visitors." There was no reaction from Lord Masuda. "Lord Sugawara is here with the warden." Still no sign that the master had heard. "They have a small boy with them, my lord. They say . . ."

Akitada stopped him with a gesture. Leading the child to the old man, he said, "Go to your grandfather, boy."

For a moment he clung to his hand, but his eyes were wide with curiosity. Then he made a bow and a small noise in the back of his throat.

Lord Masuda's hand paused its stroking, but he gave no other sign that he had noticed.

The boy crept forward until he was close enough to touch the gnarled fingers with his own small ones. The old hand trembled at his touch, and Lord Masuda looked at the child.

"Yori?" he asked, his voice thin as a thread, "is it you?"

The boy nodded, and Akitada's heart contracted. He turned to the servant. "Did he call the boy 'Yori'?"

The servant was wiping his eyes. "The master's confused. He thinks he's his dead son whose name was Tadayori. The child looks like him, you see. We used to call him Yori for short."

It was a common abbreviation—his own Yori had been Yorinaga—but Akitada was shaken. That he should have crossed paths with this child during the O-bon festival when his grief had caused him to mistake the small pale figure for his son's ghost and he had called him "Yori" now seemed like an omen. Fatefully, the child had come to him, and together they had encountered the extraordinary cat which had led him to Peony's villa and the Masudas.

The old lord was still looking searchingly at the child. Finally he turned his head and regarded them. "Who are these men?" he asked his servant. "And why is the boy dressed in these stinking rags?"

Akitada stepped forward and introduced himself and the warden. Lord Masuda looked merely baffled.

"My lord, were you aware of your son's liaison with the courtesan Peony?"

A faint flicker in the filmy eyes. "Peony?"

"They had a child, a boy, born five years ago. Your son continued his visits to the lady and acknowledged the boy as his." There was just a broken sword for proof, but a nobleman buys such a sword only for his own son.

The old lord looked from him to the boy and then back again. "He resembles my son." The gnarled hand stretched out and traced the child's straight eyebrows. "You hurt yourself," he murmured, touching the bruised eye. "What is your name?"

The child struggled to speak, but there was an interruption.

Lady Masuda swept in, followed by Kohime. "What is going on here?" she demanded, her eyes on her father-in-law. "He is not well . . ."

Akitada's eyes flew to the child. He had hoped for a confrontation between the boy and Lady Masuda, and now he prayed for another miracle. The boy turned toward the women and his face became a mask of terror and fury. He catapulted himself forward, his voice bursting into gurgling speech, "I'll kill you, I'll kill you." But he rushed past Lady Masuda and threw himself on Kohime, fists flying.

Kohime shrieked, gave the child a violent push, and ran from the room.

Akitada bent to help the boy up. He had guessed wrong, but his heart was filled with joy. "So you found your voice at last, little one," he said, hugging him. "All will be well now, you'll see."

"She hurt her. She hurt my mother," sobbed the child.

"Ssh," Akitada said. "Your grandfather and the warden will take care of her."

AKITADA AND THE WAY OF JUSTICE

Lady Masuda looked very pale, but her eyes devoured the child. "Oh, I'm so glad he is alive," she cried. "How did you find him? I've been searching everywhere, terrified by what I have done."

The old lord glared at her. "Are you responsible then?" he asked. "He resembles your son, don't you think? Both got their father's eyebrows."

She smiled through tears. "Yes, Father. But he's so thin now, poor child. And I gave that woman all the money we had."

The warden cleared his throat. "Er, what happened just then, sir?" he whispered to Akitada.

"I think Lady Masuda knows," Akitada said. "It would be best if she explained, but the child . . ." He turned to the boy. "What *is* your name?"

"You know. It's Yori. After my father," he said, as if the question were foolish.

Lord Masuda's face softened. "Yes. That was my son's name when he was small. But you were about to suggest something?"

"Yes, but perhaps Yori might be given into the care of your servant for a bath and clean clothes while we discuss this matter."

"Oh, please let me take him," pleaded Lady Masuda.

"No," said Lord Masuda. "You will stay here and make a clean breast of this." She hung her head and nodded. Her father-in-law looked at the old servant. "Send for my other daughter and bring the child back later." When they had left, he sat up a little straighter.

"Now, Daughter. Why was I not informed about this grandson and his mother?"

She knelt before him. "Forgive me, Father. I wished to spare you. You were so ill after my husband died."

"You were not well yourself after you lost your child," he said, his voice a little gentler.

She bowed her head. "I knew where my husband was spending his time. Women always know. I was jealous, especially when I heard she had given him a son when I was still childless. But then my husband returned to me, and after my own son was born, I no longer minded so much that my husband went back to her."

Lord Masuda nodded. "He told me that he wished to live with this woman and her child. As he had given me an heir, I permitted it."

Lady Masuda hung her head a little lower. "But he died. And then my son also passed from this world . . ." Her voice broke, and she whispered, "Losing a child is the most terrible loss of all." For a moment she trembled with grief, then she squared her shoulders and continued. "I became obsessed with my husband's mistress and her boy. I wanted to see them. Kohime was very understanding. She came with me. It was . . . an awkward meeting. Peony was very beautiful. I could see they were poor and I was glad. We watched the boy play with his kitten in the garden, and suddenly I thought if we could buy the child from her, I could raise him. He was my husband's son, and . . ." She hesitated and looked fearfully at Lord Masuda.

He grunted. "I should have taken care of them. If you had brought him to me, no doubt I would have agreed to an adoption."

"I went home and gathered all the gold I could find, and Kohime added what she had saved, and we went back to her. But when we told her what we wanted, she became upset and cried she would rather die than sell her son. She snatched up the boy and ran out into the garden. We were afraid she would do something desperate. Kohime went after her and tried to take the child. They fought..."

Lord Masuda stopped her. "Here is Kohime now. Let her speak for herself."

Kohime had been weeping. Her round face was splotched and her hair disheveled. She threw herself on the floor before her father-in-law. "I didn't mean to kill her," she wailed. "I thought she was going into the lake with the child and grabbed for her. When we fell down, the boy ran away. She bit and kicked me. I don't know how it happened, but suddenly I was bleeding and afraid. My hand found a loose stone on the path and I hit her with it. I didn't mean to kill her." She burst into violent tears.

Lord Masuda sighed deeply.

Lady Masuda moved beside Kohime and stroked her hair. "It was an accident, Father. The boy came back," she said, her voice toneless. "He had a wooden sword and he cut Kohime with it. I saw it all from the veranda of the villa. When Kohime came running back to me, she was covered with blood. I took her into the house to stop the bleeding. She said she had killed the woman." She brushed away tears.

A heavy silence fell. Then Akitada asked gently, "Did you go back to make sure Peony was dead, Lady Masuda?"

She nodded. "We were terrified, but after a while we both crept out. She was still lying there, quite still. The boy was holding her hand and weeping. Kohime said, 'We must hide the body.' But there was the boy. Of course we could not take him back with us after what had happened. We thought perhaps we could make it look as if she had fallen into the water by accident. We decided that I would take away the boy, and Kohime would hide the body because she is the stronger. I tried to talk to the child, but it was as if his spirit had fled. His eyes were open, but that was all. He let me take him, and I carried him away from the house. I did not know what to do, but when I saw a woman in the market packing up to return to her village, I gave her the money and the child."

The warden muttered, "All that gold, and the Mimuras beat and starved him."

"And you, Kohime?" asked Lord Masuda.

Kohime, the plain peasant girl in the fine silks of a noblewoman, said with childlike simplicity, "I put Peony in the lake. It wasn't far, and people thought she'd drowned herself."

"Dear heaven!" muttered the warden and looked sick.

"You have both behaved very badly," said Lord Masuda to his daughters-in-law. "What will happen to you is up to the authorities now."

After a glance at the warden, who shook his head helplessly, Akitada said, "Peony's death was a tragic accident. No good can come from a public disclosure now. It is her son's future we must consider."

The warden was still staring at Kohime. "It was getting dark," he muttered. "You can see how two hysterical women could make such a mistake."

"You are very generous." Lord Masuda bowed. "In that case, I shall decide their punishment. My grandson will be raised as my heir by my son's first lady. It will be her opportunity to atone to him. Kohime and her daughters will leave this house and reside in the lake villa, where she will pray daily for the soul of the poor woman she killed." He looked sternly at his daughters-in-law. "Will you agree to this?"

They bowed. Lady Masuda said, "Yes. Thank you, Father. We are both deeply grateful."

Akitada looked after the women as they left, Lady Masuda with her arm around Kohime, and thought of how she had said, "Losing a child is the most terrible loss of all."

When they were gone, the old lord clapped his hands. "Where is my grandson?"

The boy came, clean and beautifully dressed, and sat beside his grandfather. "Well, Yori," the old man asked, "shall you like it here, do you think?"

The boy looked around and nodded. "Yes, grandfather, but I would like Patch to live here, too."

They put down their offering of fish. The cat was watching them from the broken veranda. It waited until they had withdrawn a good distance before strolling up and sniffing the food. With another disdainful glance in their direction, it settled down to its meal, and Akitada threw the net. But the animal shied away at the last moment and, only partially caught, streaked into the house, dragging the net behind. A gruesome series of yowls followed.

"Patch got hurt," cried the boy. "Please go help her."

Reluctantly, Akitada climbed into the villa. He used the same post from which he had looked for the ghost, but this time, he crossed the broken veranda and stepped into the empty room. Walking gingerly on the broken boards, he found the cat in the next room, rolling about completely entangled in the netting. He carefully scooped up the growling and spitting bundle and returned. He already had one leg over the banister when he heard the mournful sound of the ghost again. Passing the furious cat down to the boy, he looked back over his shoulder.

One of the long strips of oiled paper covering a window had come loose and slid across the opening as a breeze from the lake caught it. Its edge brushed the floor and made the queer wailing sound he had heard.

So much for ghosts.

Outside, Patch, a very real cat, began to purr in Yori's arms.

It was almost dark before Akitada returned to the inn to collect his belongings and pay his bill. He would not reach home until late, but he wanted to be with his wife on this final night of the festival. They would mourn their son together, sharing their grief as they had shared their love.

When he rode out of Otsu, people were lighting the bonfires to guide the dead on their way back to the other world. Soon they would gather on the shore to send off the spirit boats, and the tiny points of light would bob on the waves until it looked as if the stars had fallen into the water.

Some day he would return to visit this Yori, the child who had come into his life to remind him that even in the darkest depth of despair man may find a spark of new hope.

MOON CAKES

*This is another New Year's story. Here, the holiday marks a chance for a new beginning for Akitada, who has become increasingly alienated from his family and friends. Tora turns up, and Bishop Sesshin is an old friend from the novel **Rashomon Gate**. Moon cakes were traditionally served during this season.*

Heian-kyo (Kyoto): the New Year, 1021 to 1022

The old monk leaned heavily on his tall staff. He wore a thin, worn robe, and the drifting snow had dusted his large-brimmed straw hat and the ragged straw cape with white. His straw sandals clung to feet that were blue with cold.

Hossho, who had gate duty at the temple, eyed him suspiciously. The monk looked weak with fatigue as he took the steps one at a time, resting often, making small gasping sounds of effort or pain. Hossho had no patience with wandering beggars who thought they served the Buddha by renouncing the world so completely that they became a burden on others. This one looked like one of those hermits who spend their lives in some primitive hut on a mountaintop, eating bark and acorns, and then decide to seek out a temple because they are sick and need a place to die.

It was sinful, to his way of thinking, to run up new debts when one should be clearing his accounts before the New Year. This old beggar was bringing bad luck—and probably disease—at this auspicious time.

"You, there," he called out from a safe distance. "Best not tarry here. It's getting dark and the snow's getting worse. I'm about to lock up for the night."

The old monk stopped and raised his head so he could look up at Hossho from under the brim of his hat. His face was deeply lined and pale except for some feverish redness under the eyes. "I need to stay overnight," he said in a meek voice. "Just until the New Year."

Hossho shook his head firmly. "Not here, old fellow. We're full up for the celebrations." In fact, room might have been found, but the abbot had invited noble visitors and would not want them offended by the sight and smell of this one—or worse, infected by whatever disease the man carried.

Because of the meekness of the man's plea, Hossho expected him to turn around promptly and retreat under the rock he had crawled from, but the old monk's eyes narrowed, he grasped his staff more firmly and took the last steps with surprising energy.

"You have no business turning people away," he said quite sharply. "Now go to your abbot and tell him that I must stay." He waved Hossho away with an imperious gesture.

Hossho opened his mouth in outraged response, but the strange monk hobbled past him and lowered himself to the ground under the sweeping roof of the temple gate. He clearly was not going to leave, and Hossho did not want to touch him. Biting his lip, he went for reinforcements.

The day after New Year's, the sun reappeared, the snow began to melt, and Akitada took his dog for a walk to check for signs of spring among the many trees along the banks of the Kamo River.

An hour later, they were back, muddy, chilled, and limping. The dog had picked up a thorn in one paw, and Akitada's old leg injury rebelled against the cold and exertion. Akitada sat down in the warm sunshine on the steps to his house to remove the thorn and then brush dirt and twigs out of the dog's coat. After his unfortunate remark about the excessively sweet moon cakes this morning, he had no wish to offend his wife and staff again. His household had been under the impression that he was fond of the sweet confection and had gone to great lengths to procure the ingredients and to prepare the cakes for the New Year. Now an instant coldness had spread through the family, and Akitada had escaped to the less complicated relationship with his dog.

The dog, aptly named Trouble, had been with him for several years now and, because both managed to give offense to the women in the household despite their best intentions, a bond had formed between them. Akitada was brushing, making soothing comments, and getting his face licked when the tall, well-dressed monk arrived.

Young monks of a lofty type were not seen very often at his house, and Akitada suspected this one might be lost.

"Yes?" he asked while Trouble went to investigate the visitor.

"The servant sent me to you." The monk twitched his neat black silk robe away from the dog's inquisitive nose and stared down at Akitada, whose muddy gown was covered with gray dog hairs. "Umm, Lord Sugawara?" he asked dubiously, kicking the persistent dog away. Trouble wrinkled up his nose and growled.

"Yes." Akitada called the dog back and resumed brushing him. He aimed the strokes of his brush vigorously in the monk's direction. "And you are?"

The monk stepped away from the cloud of dog hairs and extended a folded note with two fingers. "Shinnyo, private secretary to His Imperial Highness, the bishop," he said stiffly and cast a disbelieving glance at the semi-ruinous state of the Sugawara residence. It was clear that he thought master, dog, and house well-matched and unworthy of his visit.

But Akitada forgot him. He had laid down the brush and unfolded the note. Only one member of the imperial family was a bishop, and he was an old friend.

AKITADA AND THE WAY OF JUSTICE

A few hours later, he sat, more suitably attired, in Bishop Sesshin's study, sipping hot tea and feeling sorrowful.

Sesshin had grown shockingly old. Once a plump man, filled with lively energy, he had shrunk to a mere shadow of himself. His eyes were still kind, but his hands shook and his skin hung in yellow folds where the flesh had disappeared from the bones. It was all too easy to see the grinning skull beneath the face.

Worse, there was a vagueness in Sesshin's manner that suggested he had little patience for business with the living any longer. Seeing him this way grieved Akitada greatly because he was fond of Sesshin.

"You and your family are well, I trust?" the bishop asked Akitada after a long silence.

"Yes, your Reverence." No point in reminding this unworldly man that they had lost their only child in the recent epidemic and were patching up the pieces of their married life.

"Good," Sesshin murmured, plucking at his sleeve.

Akitada shifted a little to ease his painful leg and wondered if Sesshin had forgotten that he sent for him. "I hope all is well with your Reverence?" he ventured after another long pause.

Sesshin tried to speak and coughed instead, a cough that left him gasping. Shinnyo, the secretary, rushed over to hand him his cup and help him drink. "I'm old and weary and shall die soon," Sesshin said when the fit was over. Akitada opened his mouth to protest, but Sesshin waved the words away. "Don't bother, Akitada.

There is no time." Each sentence was an effort for the prince bishop, who spoke in short gasps, catching his breath in between. "I have sent for you . . . because something has happened that I wish to set right if I can. It involves a member of my family . . . and may affect the imperial succession."

Akitada hid his shock and waited.

Sesshin took a ragged breath and said, "You may leave us now, Shinnyo." He waited until the door had closed behind the secretary, then said, "There's a person, a very highly-placed person . . ." He paused to take another sip of tea with a hand that shook so badly that he spilt some. The fine brocade stole, Akitada saw, was already stained. Sesshin began again. "Never mind. I trust you and hate all this secrecy. The second prince is in trouble."

Prince Atsuhira was Sesshin's nephew and uncle to the reigning emperor who was still very young. The prince had a reputation for great charm and learning and was very well liked by high and low alike.

"I hope it's nothing serious," Akitada said, aware that it probably was.

"It may cost him his life," Sesshin said bleakly. "He wrote a letter to a young woman. A letter from a man in love is from a man not in his right mind." He took another sip of tea. "It expresses a wish that he were emperor . . . so that he could make her his empress."

"Oh!" That was indeed serious. Wishing to remove an emperor in order to ascend the throne oneself was a matter of high treason. Akitada asked, "Who has the letter now?"

Sesshin was racked by another cough and reached for his cup again. "You get right to the point as always," he said after a moment. "I do not know. And, yes, in the wrong hands, that letter is his end. It will be interpreted . . . as calling on the gods to strike His Majesty dead. The prince has a poetic temperament. He doesn't always mean what he writes. In any case . . . I was offered the letter . . . for a very large amount of gold. A friend was to make the payment and bring the letter to me." Sesshin's breath rattled alarmingly after this effort.

Akitada thought. "There may not have been a letter, your Reverence," he suggested. "A daring criminal may merely have pretended to have it in order to collect the gold."

Sesshin shook his head. "I'm not in my dotage, Akitada. He provided a copy and I showed it to the second prince. The prince admitted to writing it. No, an evil man has got hold of the letter. And my friend has disappeared. Along with the gold."

More puzzling information. The prince-bishop's friend must be a person of high rank, and those who "live above the clouds" did not disappear unless they wished to do so. "Do you want me to find him?"

Sesshin looked bleak. "He may be dead. I want you to find the letter. Since nothing has happened, there may still be time. Do you know Kiyomizu-dera?"

"The Pure Water Temple? Yes, of course."

"I know the abbot and though it was not easy at my age, I paid him a visit the night before the New Year. That accounts for my illness. My friend was to bring the letter to me there. He never came." The bishop gave Akitada a pleading look. "Since he would not betray me, he must be dead. Will you help? Perhaps I'm sending you on a dangerous journey, but I may not live long." He broke off to cough again.

Akitada said quickly, "I am honored by your trust and shall do my utmost." He tried to sound optimistic but was more at sea than ever. "Who is this friend, your Reverence?"

"A hermit. His name used to be Ueda. Please find out what happened. Quietly. We can trust no one."

The name meant nothing to Akitada. He felt completely inadequate to the request but said, "Of course, your Reverence. Where does this Ueda live?"

"I believe he travels among the temples near the capital. But you must not ask for him by name. Thank you, Akitada." Sesshin sighed and closed his eyes.

When the secretary saw Akitada out, he said, "He is very ill. I have to lift him. He can no longer stand or walk without support. Please be sure to do whatever he asks. The worry is very bad for him."

Akitada revised his first impression. He still did not like Shinnyo very much, but the young monk clearly cared for the ailing bishop.

It was an impossible case. Akitada was to find a hermit he had never met and who must remain nameless. Moreover, he could not let anyone know he was looking for him. And somewhere someone had collected a great deal of gold for a letter that had disappeared along with the hermit.

AKITADA AND THE WAY OF JUSTICE

If indeed the exchange had taken place.

If it had not, or if the hermit had been killed and the murderer had found it, then the letter might already be on offer to the prince's enemies.

Akitada decided to begin at Kiyomizu-dera. On the way into the snowy hills on the outskirts of the capital, he thought about Sesshin dying. Such thoughts always brought back his own grief for his son. This time he felt doubly bereft for he would lose a good and loyal friend who had often interceded on his behalf in the past.

He forced his mind to consider the situation. Sesshin had said that the missing letter affected the succession. The young emperor had put on a man's trousers a year ago but had not yet produced a son. There were some nasty rumors that he enjoyed himself with pages. The appointment of a crown prince would assure the succession, should the emperor die childless. And Sesshin's candidate surely was the second prince of whom he was quite fond. Equally surely, the chancellor was opposed to such an arrangement.

Someone was playing a very dangerous game, and Akitada was about to step into the middle of it.

At the temple gate, he tied up his horse and went to sign the visitors' book. An eager young monk appeared at his side.

"Abbot Genshin will be delighted to receive you, my lord," the chatty young man informed him after a glance at his name. "Just now he has some troublesome visitors, but I doubt they'll stay long. Can you imagine? They think we are hiding their senile father. It's nonsense, of course, but the Reverend Father decided to speak to them. May I show you around meanwhile?"

The young monk seemed tolerant of eccentric questions, so Akitada asked, "Do you ever lose any of your visitors up here?" He gestured around at the steep, densely wooded mountain site and haphazard disposition of halls, paths, and stone steps.

The young monk laughed heartily. "'In the great Void,'" he quoted, "'nothing is lost because nothing exists'. Here, if worshippers lose their way, they start shouting and we go to get them."

Akitada saw that his guide was certainly nimble enough to rescue lost souls. He, on the other hand, had a painful leg and was quickly out of breath.

Beyond the Gate of the Benevolent Kings stood an ancient bell tower. Akitada took the opportunity to sit down on a rocky outcropping to admire it. The bell tower was a small building, stone below and wood above, but the gracefully curving roof was missing tiles, and stones and plaster had fallen from the foundation. A mangy cat sniffed nearby.

The young monk decided to urge a donation. "We lack the funds for a proper rebuilding program," he explained, clapping his hands at the cat which gave him a baleful look.

Akitada's own home needed repairs even more urgently than the bell tower.

"The bell is quite large and has a particularly fine tone," the monk continued. "We rang it the night before the New Year. One hundred and eight times, one stroke for every human weakness that must be discarded before the New Year can be faced with a pure mind." He frowned and picked up a rock to throw at the cat. The cat hissed and departed.

Akitada considered human weaknesses, including those that made young monks throw rocks at harmless cats. "Did you have many visitors that night?"

"Oh, no. The abbot had a guest, that's all. Just as well. It wasn't Hossho's best performance, I'm afraid. The ringing was very ragged."

"Hmm. What about travelers seeking shelter?"

"Oh, we get beggars sometimes, but Hossho is quite firm with them."

"Ah, yes," muttered Akitada. "One must be firm with beggars." He rose and they walked through another gate, past a three-storied pagoda with handsome red lacquer trim, and then climbed up and down a number of steep flights of stone steps.

Akitada's guide returned to the subject of the institution's many services and needs, while Akitada wished himself elsewhere. Shivering in the chill air, he interrupted the lecture to ask the monk if greeting visitors was among his regular duties.

"Oh, no. I'm helping out today, because our regular gatekeeper isn't here. Just like Hossho to go off on his own business."

"This Hossho must be a very busy monk," Akitada observed, suppressing a sneeze and wondering if he would pay with a cold for this excursion.

"Ha ha!" laughed the young monk. "You don't know Hossho. He's always trying to get out of work."

When they reached the great hall with its enormous sweeping roofs, Akitada limped inside with a sigh. He made his bow to the eleven-faced and thousand-armed Kannon, briefly admired the gilded divinities, and then stepped onto the great veranda. This jutted out six stories above a wooded gorge and offered a famous view of the capital below.

His guide pointed out more attractions. "Over there is the Shrine of the Eight Hills. It's well attended by ladies because the god who is enshrined there helps lovers."

"Why is that only attractive to ladies?" Akitada asked, thinking of the prince's secret love and the dangerous letter.

"Ha ha. Gentlemen know their hearts but they don't always tell, do they? That's very frustrating to women so they come to ask the god if there is hope." The young monk chuckled. "There are two sacred rocks there. If they can walk blind-folded from one to the other, it means happiness. The shrine priest makes a very good income by offering his arm. We only have the waterfall and the lucky jump. It's not nearly as profitable."

"A lucky jump?"

"Oh, yes." The monk leaned over the balustrade and pointed downward. "If you make it down without getting hurt, you will have a wish fulfilled."

Akitada peered into a ravine. "That looks dangerous." Somewhere below he heard the faint sound of water, but the cliff was so thickly overgrown with scrub and evergreens that he could not see the bottom. A large number of crows sat on the branches of a crippled pine tree.

The monk pointed a little to the left. "The waterfall is over there. People call it the Sound of Feathers Fall. Its water cures diseases. We have had many miraculous cures."

"Surely that's more useful than the two rocks," Akitada said. "Or do you have to jump to get down there?"

The monk laughed heartily again. "Not quite, but the path is a little steep. Not too many sick people manage it."

Akitada eyed the crows again and sighed. "I would not mind getting rid of this pain in my leg," he said.

The path was precipitous and slippery, especially this time of year. Akitada gritted his teeth. The waterfall, when they reached it, was quite small and pooled into a basin. A bamboo dipper awaited the afflicted believers, and Akitada dipped out a measure of the icy water and drank. He shivered and sneezed.

The young monk clapped his hands. "There! The pain is leaving your body already."

Akitada thought it more likely that he had caught a cold but did not say so. Instead he limped into the dense shrubbery, heading toward the pine with the crows.

"Where are you going, sir?" his guide cried after him.

"Call of nature."

The crows gave raucous warning cries at his approach and reluctantly rose with a clatter of wings to find a safer perch. On the ground near the pine's trunk, Akitada found what had attracted them. The broken body of a monk lay in a small patch of snow. The dead man might have been sleeping under the tree except for the season and the odd angle of his head and the blood on his face. His limbs lay relaxed, one arm under his body, the other folded across his middle. One foot lacked its sandal.

Akitada looked up. The cliff rose sharply to the scaffolding of beams that supported the veranda. It was impossible to see much, for shrubs and trees grew all around him and in the crevices of the cliff. He saw some broken branches, suggesting that the dead man had indeed jumped or fallen from above. In another month or two, the leaves would make even a partial view impossible. If it had not been for the crows, the body might never have been found.

This then was surely Sesshin's missing messenger—dead, to add to Akitada's sense of hopelessness. He bent to search the body. There was no letter. He straightened up, frowned, and made a systematic search of the whole area. He found the other sandal hanging in a shrub quite a distance from the body. In the process, he tore his trousers in several places, knocked his hat askew, scratched his face, and got a large thorn in his right hand. He also sneezed again.

His guide called out to him. Akitada did not bother to answer. He eyed the side of the cliff, then shook his head. How did that sandal get into the shrub? He returned to the body and examined it carefully.

AKITADA AND THE WAY OF JUSTICE

His guide made his way noisily through the underbrush and found him. "There you are, sir. I was getting—" He gave a loud gasp. "Amida. It's Hossho. What's he doing here?"

Hossho, the gatekeeper and bell ringer, had a bruised and broken neck. He also had badly bruised shins. Akitada's guide proposed that Hossho must have taken the jump from the veranda because he wished to be reborn in paradise.

"But," protested Akitada, "doesn't the Buddha forbid taking your own life? I would have thought Hossho committed a grievous offense by jumping and lost salvation."

"Not at all, sir," said the young monk, looking quite cheerful. "Hossho's faith in the powers of Kannon was so great that I'm sure he had his wish granted. Besides, all he had to do was to utter the Buddha's name as he was falling. That's sufficient to gain entrance to the Western Paradise."

Akitada thought it was a wonder that all of the monks had not long since vaulted over the balustrade. Aloud he said, "I believe Hossho was murdered. You must report his death to the police."

This upset his guide who insisted on reporting to the abbot first. Akitada was cold, sore, and depressed. His case had just become more complicated. Instead of finding a missing hermit, he had the body of a murdered monk on his hands. With a sigh, he climbed back to the top.

The abbot's assistant, a cadaverous individual with a disconcerting way of watching Akitada from the corner of his eyes, let them in. Akitada's guide reported Hossho's death with great excitement, not omitting his belief in the miraculous powers of the jump and Hossho's desire to find a shortcut to Nirvana. Akitada had to cut him off with a demand to see the abbot.

The Venerable Genshin, a handsome middle-aged cleric, was seated in a comfortable study overlooking the mountains. He was surrounded by warming braziers, books and pictures, elegant writing utensils, and an exquisite small altar with carved figures of the Amida Buddha and two bodhisattvas.

"Lord Sugawara," his assistant announced and left, softly closing the door behind him.

"Please be seated," said the abbot, clearly unimpressed by Akitada's rank. His speech and manner were those of a high court noble, and he made no attempt to be either courteous or friendly. "My assistant tells me you found the body of one of the monks. I regret extremely that you should have been troubled by this unfortunate affair." He did not quite *tsk*, but the effect was much the same.

Akitada sat near one of the braziers with a sigh of relief. Rubbing his chilled hands over its pleasant warmth, he said, "The monk was murdered, Venerable Father. It will be necessary to call the authorities."

The abbot raised thin eyebrows. "Murdered? Come, we must not judge too quickly. It may be that he has allowed his depth of devotion to tempt him, or it may merely have been an accident in the dark."

AKITADA AND THE WAY OF JUSTICE

Genshin was related to powerful men with ties to the imperial household. It would not do to offend him, but Akitada did not like his reaction to the death. "I regret, Venerable Father," he said firmly, "but the indications are that he was murdered. Do you know if someone had a reason to wish him dead?"

The abbot refolded his hands and looked at them. "I hope you're wrong, but it is true that Hossho could be—how shall I put it?—a little irritating. There have been complaints."

"Are you suggesting that one of his fellow monks murdered him because he was irritating?"

Genshin compressed his lips. "Murder is much too strong a word. It could have been mere mischief."

"Mischief?"

"Well, have you considered that perhaps Hossho was leaning over the railing and, in the heat of an argument, someone gave him a little push, never thinking that he would be seriously hurt?"

Akitada slowly shook his head. "No, Father. I saw his neck. He was not killed by the fall. Someone strangled him, breaking his neck, and then pushed him over the railing." He did not mention that he must have lost a sandal in the struggle, and that the murderer had flung that after him.

The abbot opened his eyes wide. "Ridiculous!" he said. "And sacrilegious."

Akitada was at the end of his patience. If only one could be sure not to step on sensitive toes. The prince-bishop had liked the abbot well enough to pay him a visit, but this man was uncomfortably haughty and uncooperative. Akitada had no wish to spend the rest of his life in exile on some godforsaken island because he had interfered in someone's power play. He took a deep breath and said, "I'm told two visitors came to you because they think their father disappeared from this temple. Surely the police will come anyway."

The abbot sat up stiffly. "We cannot afford to have ugly rumors spread. They are mistaken. Their father was never here. Really, you must not imagine that this temple is a den of murderers. That is quite outrageous."

"Surely it wouldn't hurt to make a thorough search of the grounds and buildings and ask some questions. Someone may have seen the old man."

But it was too late. The abbot had become angry and defiant. Tucking his hands into his deep sleeves, he glowered at Akitada. "I cannot imagine why you would doubt my word. If you persist in mentioning this false story to people and spread tales about poor Hossho's death, I shall be forced to report the matter to His Majesty."

Time to depart, but the ache in Akitada's leg had only just begun to subside. "I beg your pardon, Venerable Father. Finding a body and then hearing that an elderly person got lost at this time of year caused me to imagine some connection between the two. No doubt, his sons will find him soon. What was their name again?"

The abbot huffed. "I do not know. They are in some sort of trade. Such men are very grasping. Possibly they want the temple to reimburse them for the loss of their father."

Akitada nodded. "Ah, you believe him dead then. There is great evil in this world. Thank you very much for explaining the matter." The abbot glared, and reluctantly Akitada staggered to his feet. "Perhaps you should mention their attempt at extortion to the police," he suggested.

The abbot snapped, "The police have no jurisdiction here. As for Hossho's accident, we will deal with it ourselves. I trust you will respect the sanctity of this temple."

It sounded like an order, perhaps even a threat. Akitada bit his lip, bowed again, and left.

His young guide had disappeared, and the abbot's assistant slammed the door behind him. Favoring his sore leg, Akitada limped back toward the main gate. As he passed the bell tower, he saw that the cat had returned to its investigations. At the main gate, Akitada found the new gatekeeper and asked if he had heard about his predecessor's death.

The monk shivered. "Yes, they told me."

"I understand he was not well liked?"

The monk looked uncomfortable. "Hossho got others to do his work, that's all. I didn't know he was so unhappy. I would have been nicer to him."

So the monk thought the death a suicide. Akitada asked, "Could Hossho have admitted the old man who disappeared?"

"Oh, no. His name would be in the visitors' book. I checked."

Akitada accompanied the monk to his cubicle to look for himself. He found his own name, and just above it the names of Yutaka and Hikaru Miyahara. Then he ran his finger up the list of visitors for the week before the New Year. According to the gatekeeper, their names belonged to a merchant family, a group of young monks from another temple, two women, several farmers and tradesmen who had come to collect payment for goods or services before the New Year, and two of the temple's debtors who had discharged their debts.

"What about private guests?" Akitada asked, thinking of Sesshin.

"Private visitors don't sign in."

It seemed Sesshin's messenger had never reached the temple.

Akitada thanked the monk and got on his horse. On the road home, he caught up with two men who were walking. He guessed they were the Miyahara brothers.

For brothers, they were dissimilar. The taller and older one wore a simple dark robe and looked glum, while his companion was a short and fleshy man in cheap, colorful pants and quilted jacket. When Akitada stopped, he saw that he had a black eye and cut lip.

He introduced himself and found that they were indeed the Miyaharas. He said, "I heard about your problem. What made you think your father came to this temple?"

The older brother took a folded note from his sleeve and handed it to Akitada. It was a short letter, addressed to "My elder son." In it, the father explained that he would not arrive until New Year's Day because he was making a stop at the Pure Water Temple. When Akitada looked up, the older brother said, "He never arrived. It isn't like him, sir. We always celebrate the New Year at my house."

Akitada returned the letter. "Could he have forgotten and made other plans?"

The younger brother offered, "Father is never forgetful. His mind is very sharp. He used to be a teacher." His brother tugged his sleeve, and the younger blushed and hung his head.

Something about that exchange made Akitada take a chance. "Does the name Ueda mean anything to either of you?"

They looked at each other. "How did you know, sir?" the older brother asked. "It's a family secret. After my father left the palace, he went into trade and changed his name."

Akitada hid his surprise, saying only, "Ah, that explains it. In that case, I too would like to speak to him. Will you let me know as soon as he turns up?"

They bowed, looking puzzled, and he left them.

At home he soaked his sore leg in a hot bath, and considered the problem. He let his mind move freely and in no particular order among the bits of information he had gathered. What had happened all those years ago to force a well-born and learned man to change his name and take up a trade? It must have been a serious offense. Why then had Sesshin put his trust in such a man? He next thought about the prince and his young woman and what would make them so careless with their correspondence. And he pondered the abbot's behavior. The man had been too quick to reject the possibility of murder and had refused to call in the authorities. Why?

Finally he considered the missing letter that had started this whole business. Since it had been offered for sale to the prince bishop, the motive for the theft had been greed. Greed was a very common motive for all sorts of things. The temple was in need of funds. And the Miyahara brothers might well be desperate for money.

Remembering the younger brother's black eye, Akitada decided that Tora, his trusty servant and assistant, could make inquiries about the brothers. Satisfied with this decision, he closed his eyes and dozed. Images of crows and cats flitted in and out of his semiconscious state, leaving him with an oddly unpleasant feeling. He cut his bath short.

Tora accepted his assignment with pleasure and was gone all night. The next morning, Akitada was in his study, frowning at a tray of moon cakes left by his wife, a reminder that neither food nor human effort should go unappreciated, when Tora strolled in to make his report.

Yutaka, the older brother appeared to be a well-liked and respected merchant who traded in paper and writing utensils. The younger, Hikaru, was a penniless artist. People thought him a harmless idler who drank too much, gambled, and periodically had to be bailed out of jail by his older brother. This year for the first time, the older brother had not been able to discharge all his debts and his suppliers refused him credit. The shop was on the point of closing. The younger brother's injuries seemed to be due to a drunken brawl.

Akitada pursed his lips. "So he's a wastrel and criminal, that younger brother. He is ruining the older one, and that means both have a motive for killing their father and taking the letter."

Tora shook his head. "Don't think so, sir. I liked the fellow. He's full of good cheer and likes women, wine shops, and good conversation." Tora grinned. "It was like old times, chatting him up. You owe me five pieces of silver, by the way."

Akitada glowered. "Five pieces of silver for a night of debauchery with a good-for-nothing? And you a married man and father? How could you? I will not support such a shocking lifestyle."

Tora looked hurt. "An investigation involves certain expenses," he pointed out. "This brother wouldn't have jabbered so freely if I hadn't put him in the right frame of mind. He had got a lecture from his older brother and was pretty glum when I found him in his rented room."

Akitada relented a little. "Well, what did you get for my money?"

Tora helped himself to one of the sweet cakes. Chewing, he said, "Years ago, the old man ran afoul of the chancellor when he walloped one of the imperial princes. Seems the little bastard set a cat on fire."

Akitada sat up. "Ueda laid hands on an imperial child? It's a wonder he was not executed."

Tora nodded and eyed another cake. "These are delicious. Your lady is a treasure. Anyway, it was touch and go. Your friend, the bishop, put in a good word."

"I see." Before his ill-chosen remark about the moon cakes, Tora had said something that jogged a memory, but Akitada could not now recall what it had been. He said peevishly, "Stop stuffing yourself. In any case, none of it explains why the old man should have disappeared now. I think I'd better speak to the bishop again."

The bishop's secretary admitted him and asked eagerly, "Any news?" When Akitada shook his head, Shinnyo said, "A pity. He is worse today. Good news would have cheered him." Akitada felt guilty as, no doubt, was intended.

Sesshin's eyes were dull and his voice weaker. "Well?" he asked, while the secretary fussed around him with tea and an extra stole.

Akitada felt uncomfortable discussing the case with Shinnyo there but decided that the ailing bishop needed him. He reported all that had happened and what he and Tora had managed to learn. The bishop closed his eyes and compressed his lips when Akitada spoke of Hossho's death.

A silence fell. Akitada grieved for the old prince and felt ashamed that he had failed. He offered somewhat desperately, "Reverence, I could speak to the young lady if it is permitted."

AKITADA AND THE WAY OF JUSTICE

Sesshin did not reply for a long while, then nodded. "Yes. I shall arrange it. You may call on her father tomorrow morning."

The home of the second prince's beloved stood among the residences of minor officials. Like Akitada's home, it had fallen on hard times. The overgrown garden looked tangled, and parts of the compound were in ruins. Akitada did not know what to expect of the family. The prince's relationship with the young woman was very unclear to him. Was she a mere kept mistress or an innocent girl who had caught the eye of an heir to the throne? Perhaps her father's manner would explain the situation.

Lord Yoshida served as assistant director in the Bureau of Statistics and looked suited to his duties. A dull and proper man, he did not smile and behaved so correctly and spoke so properly that Akitada felt slovenly by comparison.

He had been informed of the reason for the visit and reluctantly permitted Akitada to speak to his daughter in his presence. It was impossible to guess what his feelings were about the affair between the girl and the imperial heir, but he was clearly upset that the letter should have disappeared from his house. He seemed to look at its loss as a personal failure.

After Yoshida sent for his daughter, Akitada had another surprise. The young woman came quickly. She was alone and carried a fan which she used gracefully, but without the pretense of shyness that causes great ladies to hide behind screens. Perhaps it was her youth or her father's lack of position, but Akitada found her forthright manner charming and unaffected. No wonder the second prince had lost his heart.

Her father said, "Lord Sugawara has come to help us. Please answer his questions, my dear."

The young woman bowed and gave Akitada a tiny smile over her fan. "I am honored, sir," she said in a pretty voice. "It concerns His Highness's letter, doesn't it?"

"Yes." Akitada, grateful for such directness, decided to be equally direct. "Its loss is causing some awkwardness for him. I wondered if you or your father could help me find the thief who took it, for it must have been taken from this house."

She looked at her father. "But it cannot have happened that way. Nobody but His Highness ever comes to my room."

Akitada blushed, embarrassed by such artless candor. The young woman's father cleared his throat. "It was no thief," he said stiffly. "The house is very well protected by guards. My daughter's letter must have been misplaced, and a copy must have fallen into the wrong hands elsewhere."

The daughter added quickly, "We have turned my rooms upside down."

Akitada assumed that the guards had been provided by the second prince and accepted the fact that no outsider could have entered the compound to steal the letter. The possibility had been remote from the start. He asked, "Where did you keep your letters?"

"In a small box in a trunk with my gowns. At first, I took it out and slept with it beside me, but there have been other letters since."

Akitada's heart melted. Oh, to be so young and in love again! He thought of his own troubled marriage and grieved the loss of such happiness. Turning to her father, he asked, "Have any of your servants left the household recently?"

The other man looked taken aback. "Not recently, no. My daughter's nurse got married last year and now lives with her husband who is a brush maker. But that was months ago."

"Was it before or after this particular letter arrived?"

Father and daughter looked at each other. She said after a moment, "It was shortly after, I think, but Kogimi would never—" She broke off, looking upset.

It was what Akitada had hoped to hear. He left with directions to the nurse's house.

The former nurse lived with her husband in a quarter of small shops, but her modest house was getting an addition and had new shutters across the front. Noting this, Akitada knocked on the door. A young maid opened and informed him that the master was away.

"Your mistress, then," Akitada said firmly, causing the little maid to open the door wider so he could step inside. Instead of waiting, he followed her down a stone-flagged hallway, passing a kitchen on one side and a work room on the other. The main living area was on a raised section in the back. Seeing the shiny boards and new *tatami* mats, Akitada slipped off his boots before stepping up.

The nurse sat beside a warming brazier, sewing some garment. She was hardly a blushing bride. Well past her first youth and broad-faced, she had a sturdy body that would soon go to fat.

She looked at him with shrewd eyes and bowed. "My husband's away," she said. "Can I give him a message, sir?"

Having taken in the signs of recent affluence, Akitada was satisfied that he had found his blackmailer. "No," he said. "My business is with you. It concerns the letter you stole and sold to His Reverence."

She dropped her sewing and gasped. "Wh . . .what can you mean, sir?"

"Come, come!" Akitada glowered down at her. "You know the letter was properly paid for—or do you deny that?"

In an agony of indecision, she looked about the room. "N . . . no. I mean . . . what is this about?"

"Don't play games with me," Akitada thundered. "You took the gold but did not turn over the goods. You are a thief and will be arrested."

That shocked her. She wailed, "But I gave it to the old monk. A very old one in a straw cape. He took the letter away with him. I swear by the merciful Kannon." Getting on her knees, she knocked her head on the new *tatami* mat. "Dear heaven, how could I know he was a thief? He had the gold and asked for the letter. I'm just a simple woman. How could I know that there are such cheats in the world?"

AKITADA AND THE WAY OF JUSTICE

Akitada poked her round figure with his foot. "Stop that wailing and tell me when this monk came here."

"It was the last day of the year. Before dusk. It was snowing."

"Can your husband confirm your story?"

She nodded eagerly. "Yes, yes, he can. We were both home the whole day, waiting for him. That old villain of a monk read the letter, then he tucked it in his robe and walked off without so much as a thank you."

Giving her a hard look, Akitada did the same. He was angry at her duplicity and wracked his brain how the couple might be punished without involving the second prince. Preoccupied with his anger, he did not see the cat that suddenly streaked out of the kitchen and into his path. It collided with his boot, hissed and spat, then climbed to a shelf high on the wall, looking balefully down at him.

At that moment, Akitada knew what had niggled at his mind.

Cats.

The cat the imperial child had set on fire and the cat at the bell tower. The cat at the bell tower had had that same baleful expression and had taken an altogether too persistent interest in the broken masonry.

Compressing his lips, Akitada hurried home for his horse.

At Kiyomizu-dera, the young monk was again helping the gatekeeper, but today he greeted Akitada with reserve.

"I want another look at your bell tower," Akitada said, heading off in that direction.

The young monk ran after him. "Why?"

Akitada hurried up the steps, ignoring the warning twinge in his bad leg. "The cat," he said.

"The cat?"

"Yes. The cat was hanging about there. I want to know why."

"Mice, probably," said the monk. "We're in the forest here. The cat is wild, just like all the other animals. The abbot won't let us trap them."

"Quite right, too," muttered Akitada. He was cold and miserable, and very uneasy about what he would find. "You're forbidden to take another creature's life."

He halted before the bell tower's damaged masonry and saw that it was as he had remembered. A part of the foundation had collapsed and someone had stacked the loose stones up again without mortar. He bent to peer more closely at the rubble. Here, under the protection of the wide eaves, the ground was dry and dusty. The tracks of tiny feet passed in and out through small openings between the stones. Nearby were the larger tracks of the cat.

"You see? It's just mice," said the young monk with a smirk.

Akitada sniffed. "What about the smell?"

The monk made a face. "Some of the mice must be dead."

But Akitada had begun to kick at the loose stones. Two large chunks rolled free and the smell got stronger.

His companion pulled his sleeve. "Sir, please don't damage the bell tower."

Akitada shook him off. "Go, fetch the abbot." He returned to his demolition of the foundation.

The poorly covered section of the foundation soon collapsed, revealing a hole. And in the hole were a pair of human feet shod in worn straw sandals. Holding his breath, Akitada seized them by the ankles and pulled.

The corpse of an elderly man in monk's robes slid out. He was dreadfully bruised about the face and head. Thin lines of blood had seeped from his nostrils and the swollen lips. In spite of this, the old man's expression was astonishingly peaceful and content.

As he bent over the body, Akitada got an uncomfortable feeling that he was not alone, but when he turned to look, he saw only the cat watching him from a distance. No doubt the animal felt he was trespassing on its territory. He quickly searched the body. No letter! He peered into the hole but found nothing there except mouse droppings.

This time, he was positive that he had unearthed the missing Ueda. Had the murderer beaten him to death for the letter and taken it away? If so, he had not made any use of it—yet. And that promised a very bad situation. By now the letter might be in the hands of men of such power that neither Akitada nor the ailing bishop could stop the fate that hung over the second prince.

And the killer was under the protection of men of such power that solving the crime would put Akitada and his family in danger.

The sound of footsteps woke him from his gloomy thoughts. The abbot hurried up and stared at the corpse. He gave Akitada a bitter look and groaned,

"Not again. How is it that you keep coming here, bringing dead people with you?"

It would have been funny under different circumstances, but Akitada only said, "You don't know him?"

"I never saw him in my life." The abbot looked again and said, "Great Heaven. Can this be the father of those two fellows?"

"I believe so."

"Nothing to do with us," the abbot said quickly. "He's elderly and must have died naturally."

Akitada bit back an angry remark. Elderly men did not inflict such injuries on themselves and crawl under bell towers to die.

The abbot attempted an alternate explanation. "Or it was a family matter, as I suggested. In that case, I trust you will bring the deed home to the guilty. As for Hossho, his accident has nothing whatsoever to do with this."

Akitada sighed. The condition of the bodies made it likely that both men had died the same night. That meant that Hossho was killed because he had known something about Ueda's murder and posed a danger to the killer. But who was the killer? He cringed inwardly at the prospect of reporting another failure to Sesshin.

But as he thought of the ailing bishop, a startling possibility crossed his mind.

The abbot waited a moment, but when Akitada made no comment, he left, muttering to himself and taking the young monk with him.

Akitada stood beside the corpse, thinking about the probable events of that night. After a while, he nodded unhappily and knelt beside the body. He touched the wrinkled hands and begged forgiveness. Ueda had been a courageous man, a man who had taken great risks in his life to do the right thing. In the matter of the court cat, it had cost him his rank and profession, and now his determination to save the second prince had cost him his life. Akitada wished he could measure up to such an example, but even though he knew who had murdered Ueda, he could not bring the man to justice.

As he looked at the poor battered face, Akitada wondered again at the dead man's peaceful expression. He glanced around. The murder must have happened here, near the bell tower, or perhaps inside it. He got up and walked around the building to the small door used by the monks who rang the great bell.

Someone had rung the bell for the New Year, but that night the ringing had been unusually ragged. And Hossho had had a reputation of getting out of his chores. Yes, that explained it. Ueda had arrived, asking for lodging, and Hossho, the lazy gatekeeper and designated bell ringer, had installed the visitor in the bell tower on condition that he ring the New Year's bell.

The door was unlocked. A narrow set of steps led to the ringing platform. The heavy wooden beam that was used to strike the great bell hung from the rafters. Akitada searched all the nooks and crannies of the interior, then turned his attention to the bell. It was very large, taking up most of the rest of the space. Its bottom rim was so close to the platform surface that a man would have to lie down to look inside. Ignoring the dust on the wooden boards, Akitada stretched himself out and peered up inside the bell.

He saw it immediately: a rectangular patch on the interior surface of the bell. Wriggling around to reach up, he touched paper and something sticky. He pulled back his fingers and smelled, then licked them. It was sweet bean paste like the filling in his wife's moon cakes. Someone had used bean paste to stick the paper to the metal. He reached up and peeled it off carefully, unfolding the paper in the dim light that fell through the openings. And saw that he had found the prince's letter.

His relief was almost dizzying. Smiling, he tucked the precious love note away and left the bell tower.

Outside, he brushed the dust off his clothes and remembered Ueda. His happiness faded. His assignment was complete and national disaster had been averted, but there would be no justice unless he could prove the murderer's guilt. And even then, there was little he could do. He returned to the body of the old man.

The cat was back also, peering cautiously into the opening. When it saw Akitada, it twitched its tail in irritation and stalked off. Akitada was well inclined toward the animal. It had helped him find Ueda and the letter.

In the dry dust under the tower were the tracks of many mice. They were what had brought the cat. But what had brought the mice?

He recalled the bean paste and quickly searched the dead man's robe again. In the folds near his thin waist, he found a few sticky crumbs. Of course. Hossho must have given a New Year's cake to Ueda who had later used the paste to hide the letter, tucking the rest of the cake in his sleeve. That meant Ueda had suspected the killer. When the killer had demanded the letter, the old man had refused. In the ensuing struggle, Ueda had died. When his killer had not found the letter on him, he had hidden the body under the bell tower, hoping to delay the discovery until he was safely elsewhere. There the hungry mice had found the cake.

Yes, it must have happened that way, but there was no proof.

And what about Hossho?

Impossible to know the details of that encounter, but the gatekeeper had probably surprised the murderer before or after the deed. More likely after, when the killer would have been searching for the precious letter. Having been seen and recognized by Hossho, he had lured the monk to the veranda of the great hall and attacked him there. Hossho had fought harder than the aged Ueda, but the killer had broken his neck and pitched him into the ravine.

A terrible night's work for the killer—who had ultimately failed to get what he wanted.

Akitada stayed only long enough to see Ueda laid out in one of the prayer halls and to leave silver for prayers to be said for his soul. Then he returned to the city, stopping first at the home of Ueda's older son to give him the sad news. The son had expected it but wept anyway.

Then he went to see Sesshin. The door was opened with a jerk by Shinnyo, who looked hollow-eyed and jittery.

"Did you bring it?" he demanded.

Akitada did not answer but brushed past him and went in to Sesshin. The bishop looked a little stronger today, but his face was filled with anxiety.

"Any news?" he asked, putting down his string of beads.

In answer, Akitada handed him the letter.

Shinnyo joined them, his eyes on the small sheet of paper.

Sesshin opened the letter and looked at it. He said, "Oh, my dear Akitada, you have done it!" Heaving a sigh of deep satisfaction, he placed the sheet of paper on the glowing coals of his brazier. A flame shot up and it was gone.

Shinnyo made a choking sound. He was staring at the smoking ashes, his hand half extended until he dropped it. "Where was it?" he asked dully.

Sesshin was too happy to notice his secretary's strange behavior. "Yes, where did you find it?"

Akitada's eyes did not leave the secretary. "Ueda brought the letter to Kiyomizu-dera, but he hid it inside the temple bell because he expected trouble."

Sesshin looked startled. "Trouble? Has something happened to him?"

"He was killed. Like the monk Hossho."

"Oh, my poor friend. What have I done?" The bishop closed his eyes and reached for his beads.

Shinnyo still looked at Akitada, his expression unreadable. Sesshin prayed, his words a gentle murmur, the beads clicking softly between his fingers. It was so quiet in the room that Akitada could hear the secretary's labored breathing. At some point, Shinnyo's stare faltered and his eyes roamed about the room—like those of a cornered rat.

Eventually Sesshin raised his head. "But how could such dreadful things have happened?" he asked. "Nobody knew about the meeting at the temple but Ueda and myself."

Shinnyo said harshly, "Any number of people might have known. His Highness, the prince, for example. Ueda's family. The blackmailer. Even the abbot. And the gatekeeper."

"Quite true," Akitada agreed. "But there was one other. And of all of them, only he knew enough, and only he was in the right place to kill for the letter."

Sesshin looked from Akitada to Shinnyo and back. "Who, Akitada? There is no one else."

Akitada let the silence lengthen, then asked, "Are you certain, Reverence, that you can trust your secretary?"

Shinnyo sucked in his breath. The bishop looked at him. His face became set and his eyes flashed. Good, thought Akitada, his old spirit is back.

Sesshin asked in a dangerously calm voice, "Did you do this, Shinnyo?"

"No, Reverence," the secretary said. "Of course not. How can you think so? I knew nothing about the letter. You never told me --"

"You lie," the bishop said, his voice suddenly sharp. "You knew quite a lot. Simply by being around me you found out about the blackmail. You admitted Ueda the night I asked him to buy the letter back. And that night at Kiyomizu-dera, I told you that I expected an important caller and to be on the look-out for him."

Shinnyo blustered, "You have no proof, and neither does Lord Sugawara."

It was true enough. Akitada and Sesshin looked at each other. "Heaven will not forget your deeds," Sesshin said angrily.

Shinnyo relaxed. He almost smiled. "What deeds? Two old men died accidentally. That is all anyone will ever know about it."

"Not quite, Shinnyo," Akitada said. "Since there is no letter and since his reverence won't protect you, your other master—and we can guess who that is—will find ways to silence you. You have become a danger to him."

When the truth of that sank in, Shinnyo cursed. "You meddling fool," he shouted. "I'll pay you back for this." He turned to the bishop. "And you! I cared for your miserable body. I wrote your long, rambling letters. I ran your errands. I put up with your dull conversation all these months for nothing. How dare you judge me?"

Akitada quickly stepped between them. The young monk was tall and strongly built and shaking with fury. Akitada thought for a moment that they were about to fight to the death, but the other stepped away, turned, and ran from the room. Doors slammed, then silence.

"Do you want me to go after him, Reverence?" Akitada asked, taking a deep breath.

"No." Sesshin sounded tired. "Thanks to you, he failed to get the letter. And you are quite right about the chancellor. He does not tolerate such liabilities. Shinnyo will disappear. What matters is that you have saved the second prince. That is all I asked of you, my friend."

Sometime later, as Akitada walked homeward, he thought how praiseworthy were men like Ueda—and how estimable in their own way were cats and moon cakes. Yes, even moon cakes. Fate had a way of balancing things, and his wife's moon cakes, so lovingly prepared for him, deserved his appreciation. It was time to beg pardon and celebrate the season with his family.

THE TANABATA MAGPIE

By 1023, fifteen years after his inauspicious start in the Ministry of Justice, and after several dangerous provincial assignments and almost continuous battles with his superiors, Akitada finally begins to climb the career ladder. The turn in his fortunes dates back to the same smallpox epidemic which took the life of his son along with that of his archenemy, Minister Soga. After years of trying to patch up his private and professional lives, Akitada is finally comfortable in both. The case of another young clerk in the Ministry reminds him how fragile human happiness is.

Heian-Kyo (Kyoto); 1123; the Tanabata Festival:

The day before the festival did not start auspiciously. Akitada's green cap ribbon with the diamond pattern, mandatory when on duty in the Greater Palace, had disappeared, and he tore a hole in one of his white silk socks.

Next, while crossing the courtyard in the dew-sparkling beauty of a summer morning filled with the scent of roses and birdsong, he stepped into dog feces and had to return to the house to change his slippers. When he set out again, the dog, aptly named Trouble, attempted to re-insinuate himself into Akitada's good graces by shoving a drooling muzzle against his good green robe, leaving stains on it.

And now, seated behind the low desk in his office in the Ministry of Justice, he was about to confront a junior clerk with the news that he would be dismissed. Akitada, as senior secretary, intensely disliked such chores, but the minister was out of town and had left instructions that Akitada was to inform young Shigeyori of his deplorable performance evaluation.

To make matters worse, the minister had given Akitada this assignment to make a point about careless recommendations. Shigeyori was taken on against everyone's advice because Akitada spoke up for him. Since then, he had lost track of the young man who was a mere presence in the archives which tended to be cluttered with eager young legal clerks trying to look busy whenever a senior staff member entered the room. He dimly recalled him as a rather good-looking youth who had lately adopted a mustache.

Remembering his own years at the bottom of the career ladder and the many times he had been glared at, threatened, reprimanded, mocked, and called to account, Akitada made an effort to verify the facts first. Shigeyori had a fine university record and had seemed very eager. It was incomprehensible and embarrassing for Akitada that he should have proved unsatisfactory after all.

The facts were dismal and disturbing. The senior scribe and others had complained repeatedly about absences and a lack of diligence in completing tasks in a timely fashion. Worse, a stack of legal documents which had passed through Shigeyori's hands now lay on Akitada's desk. Each and every one of them contained startling errors, omissions, mistakes in Chinese characters, and illegible entries. Since the performance of the entire ministry rested on accurate record-keeping and reliable archives, Akitada was appalled and angry when he sent for the young man whom he had sponsored and who had so signally disappointed his expectations.

Shigeyori sidled in, bowed nervously, and sat. He eyed the stack of documents and looked away quickly. A slow flush crept up his face.

"Um," said Akitada, very ill at ease.

"Yes, sir?" The junior clerk's voice trembled a little.

"You, ah, have been with us almost a year now, Shigeyori."

"Yes, sir." Shigeyori clenched his hands together. He looked young and vulnerable, his face still childishly rounded. The mustache was a mistake, Akitada decided and felt a pang of pity.

"As you know," he started again, forcing his mind back to the long list of offenses committed by this young man and the embarrassment to himself, "we have to submit annual performance reports by the end of the seventh month."

Shigeyori swallowed and nodded. The fear in his large, liquid eyes was almost palpable.

Akitada sighed. "This is a very good and proper rule and affects all of us, from the lowliest scribe to the highest minister of the realm. It assures that the people are served with virtue, duty, honesty, and conscientiousness. We must all demonstrate diligent service and devotion to the public good." He meant to let the young man know that he was not being singled out unfairly, but for some reason Shigeyori's eyes blazed with anger.

"I know all that," he snapped.

Akitada frowned at his tone. He tapped an accusing finger on the documents and said sternly, "I have had a look at your work. And I have spoken to your co-workers. It was an embarrassing task, since I'm the one who spoke on your behalf when you applied for your position. To say that I am disappointed would be an understatement. I'm very much afraid that I cannot recommend any merits, and you know that means dismissal."

Shigeyori went deathly pale. He gulped, then cried, "Everybody here hates me. It's lies, nothing but lies, whatever they've said. As for the documents, I've been given so much work I couldn't do it properly." His voice broke.

Akitada opened his mouth to ask about this possibly extenuating circumstance, when Shigeyori jumped up and shouted, "I should have known that you're just like the rest. There's no pleasing any of you. There never was. I must have been mad to hope. What, a fellow with my background? It's ridiculous. I bet you're all going to have a good laugh about it after I'm gone." He shook a fist at the unoffending door, then turned back to Akitada, tears in his eyes, to say stiffly, "I'll save you the trouble of writing your report and resign now. Good bye, sir!"

His bow was spoiled when his cap fell off. He scooped it back up before slamming out of Akitada's office.

Akitada's jaw sagged. He was still staring at the door when he heard muffled laughter followed by a cry of pain.

He rose and opened the door to look out into the corridor. One of the other young clerks sat on the floor, holding a bleeding nose. His friends stood about him, looking after Shigeyori who was running out of the building.

Akitada was forced to issue another reprimand, this time to the troublemakers who had waylaid Shigeyori after eaves-dropping on his interview. He knew their type from experience. The strong always picked on the weak, and Shigeyori came from a poor provincial family, while they were the sons of court nobles.

That afternoon, Akitada's bad day got immeasurably worse. Superintendent Kobe, Akitada's friend and sometime rival, stopped by. After initial hostilities many years ago when the young law clerk Akitada had put his nose into police matters, Kobe had mellowed enough to ask his advice occasionally. The Superintendent was at least ten years older than Akitada, his hair and beard already gray, yet over time they had become close.

But this was no casual visit. After a greeting, Kobe said, "You have a clerk called Shigeyori?"

The young hot-head must have caused more trouble. Akitada felt vaguely responsible as he nodded.

"He's under arrest for murder."

"*Murder?*" stammered Akitada, aghast.

"Yes. I thought I'd come myself. Anything you can tell me about him?"

Akitada's first reaction was disbelief. "Are you sure? I saw him earlier today. He left here a little overwrought because his performance report was poor, but I cannot imagine . . ." His voice trailed off.

Kobe raised his brows. "You dismissed him?"

"I was getting around to it when he saved me the trouble. Burst into an angry speech that ended with a resignation, then stormed out—after knocking one of his colleagues to the floor for sniggering."

"A violent temper, in other words."

Akitada became cautious. "I don't know . . . it seemed that way, but . . . what exactly happened?"

"He killed Masayoshi. The director of the wardrobe office."

"I don't think I know him. But why? And when?"

Kobe spread his hands. "A few hours ago, around the time of the noon rice. And why do such things happen? His temper explains it well enough. The young have little restraint. In this case, Masayoshi had forbidden visits to his daughter."

AKITADA AND THE WAY OF JUSTICE

"Shigeyori seduced the daughter of a ranking official?" For someone of Shigeyori's low social standing, that was the height of audacity. Akitada had liked his spirit when he had applied for the clerkship, but this was most improper. Still, the boy was very young, and the young make foolish mistakes when they think they are in love. "You are quite sure he's guilty?"

"Reasonably. We have ruled out robbery. Too many servants about and nothing was taken. One of the servants saw him running from Masayoshi's house as if devils were after him. Who can say what sets a violent person off? It does not take much."

Silence fell while Akitada wondered if he had any responsibility for Shigeyori's actions. Perhaps he could have handled the interview more gently. Then it occurred to him that Kobe must have something else on his mind with this personal visit. "Do you have doubts about his guilt?" he asked hopefully.

"Well, he denies doing it. Very firmly. And Masayoshi had enemies. I wondered if you . . ." Kobe hesitated.

"Yes?"

"Shigeyori gave you as a character reference and asked that we talk to you. He thought you might act on his behalf."

Akitada was appalled. What had possessed Shigeyori? And after their unpleasant talk this morning? But perhaps the clerk had been clever, thinking that such an appeal to Akitada's fairness would cause him to feel guilty. It did.

Worse, taking on Shigeyori's case would ruin tomorrow's holiday with his family. They were to take a boat ride on the Katsura River. He had disappointed his wife too often already, and the excursion had been planned for months. Tamako and her maid had been busy cutting and sewing new summer robes for the occasion. This very morning, Tamako had been in the kitchen, humming with happiness as she prepared delicious foods for the outing. No, he would not crush her hopes again.

He was about to refuse outright, when it occurred to him that he might at least use the rest of the day to ask some questions. Possibly something might turn up to help Shigeyori. It would go a long way to ease his conscience and let him enjoy his holiday.

"I don't have much time," he said to Kobe, explaining their plans, "but tell me what happened and I will talk to some people today."

Kobe nodded. "Briefly then: Shigeyori was seen running from the main house where Masayoshi's room is. The servant who saw him said he looked as if he had seen a ghost or something—his words. A short while later, another servant took the midday rice to his master and found Masayoshi slumped over his desk. He had been stabbed in the back. Masayoshi's known visitors that morning all insist that the man was alive and in good spirits when they left."

"And Shigeyori?"

"He claims he never saw Masayoshi. Most likely a lie."

"What did he say he was doing there?"

"Secretly visiting the daughter."

"In broad daylight? When the father had forbidden the relationship?"

"Exactly."

"You have the weapon?"

"No. It was either a large knife or a short sword. We searched Shigeyori's rooms, but he could have thrown it away."

Akitada pursed his lips. "Hmm. Tell me about the other visitors."

"Two of Masayoshi's colleagues, Kajiwara Heizo and Kiso Yasuhira, stopped by on business matters. Neither stayed long. Nothing suspicious about it, but they came separately."

"Did they explain?"

"They said it was routine. Something to do with the wardrobe office."

Akitada raised his brows at this. Few senior officials enjoyed being troubled at home. If Kajiwara and Kiso found it necessary to call on Masayoshi, it was more likely that it was anything but routine.

Kobe apparently agreed. "Office gossip has it that neither was on good terms with Masayoshi."

"They are the enemies you mentioned?"

"Well, they may have motives, though there are others."

"Then he was not well liked?"

Kobe grinned. "He was not a likeable man, forever criticizing others. But there is only one other person with a strong motive. Lord Inage. He was a secretary in the Council of State until recently. He and Masayoshi were both mentioned for a lucrative appointment to the governorship of Omi province next year. Masayoshi made some ugly accusations, and Inage was dismissed. And Inage called there today, very angry. He was not admitted, but he could have slipped in the back way—or sent in an assassin."

An assassin? Akitada frowned. It did not seem likely for someone like Masayoshi, who was of minor importance in the administration. "What about his family? Wives? Children?"

"Masayoshi was a widower with a grown daughter, Lady Otoku."

"Only one child? The one Shigeyori was courting?" Akitada, who had lost a child himself and was now raising a little daughter, felt a sudden sympathy for the dead man. Shigeyori was not his idea of a charming son-in-law. He sighed. "The body has been removed?"

"Yes. It looked like a straightforward stabbing." Seeing Akitada's surprise, he amplified, "Two wounds to the back. Close together. More than likely both fatal."

From across the Greater Palace grounds came the sound of the gong that marked the time. Akitada glanced out through the open doors at the tile-topped walls and curving roofs of the ministries and government buildings. Beyond, in the haze of cooking fires, the city spread southward toward the confluence of the Kamo and Katsura Rivers. Tomorrow he would be there, on a boat, sailing away from his problems.

"The hour of the rooster already," he said. "It will be sunset in another two hours. I'd better start now, if I am to find out anything useful today."

When they rose, Kobe said, "I assume you'll want to speak to the prisoner first?"

"No." The thought of seeing Shigeyori again was so unpleasant that Akitada almost snapped at Kobe. At best, Shigeyori had an unstable character; at worst he was a cunning criminal who planned to gain Masayoshi's wealth by marrying his daughter. Kobe gave him a curious look. "No," Akitada repeated, more calmly. "I'll have a talk with Masayoshi's people. Perhaps there is another explanation."

As he walked through the eastern quarter of the city, he took pleasure in the clear skies, the pleasant breeze, a patch of orange daylilies nodding over a humble bamboo fence, and a pair of sparrows feeding their fluffy youngster. It would be fine weather for their outing tomorrow. Sailing on the river on a summer day was sheer bliss. He pictured tying off the boat at a pretty bank and spreading mats on the grass for the cold picnic his wife Tamako was busily assembling at home. He imagined playing with his little daughter and teaching her how to fish. Perhaps there would be rice cakes filled with sweet chestnuts or sesame seeds, or cold steamed dumplings with shrimp, or quail eggs wrapped in seaweed.

He arrived at the dead man's residence with an unsuitably happy expression on his face. The gatekeeper stared at him in surprise until Akitada rearranged his face and gave his name and Kobe's, adding that he was assisting the superintendent in his inquiries. The man bowed him in, closed the gate, and left.

Akitada paused in the neatly raked entrance courtyard and looked about. He was impressed. The compound was large and well-maintained, its walls newly white-washed and the double gate massive. The main house and adjoining pavilions had expensive tile roofs, and broad stairways led up to deep verandas with red-lacquered balustrades. In spite of the fact that the family consisted only of the master and his daughter, Akitada saw many well-dressed servants—far more than he could maintain on his own salary. Masayoshi's private income must be considerably larger than his stipend from the wardrobe office.

A man's wealth figured prominently among possible reasons for his murder.

He was about to approach one of the servants to begin his questioning, when the gatekeeper reappeared at a run and bowed. "My lady will see you now, sir."

This astonished Akitada. First, no unmarried woman of good family received strange males. Secondly, her father had been murdered only hours before and her lover arrested for the crime.

Intrigued, he followed the servant past the main house to the rear of the compound. They passed a small courtyard garden with a dry landscape behind the main hall and approached a charming pavilion. At the foot of its stairs stood two large Chinese planters with small, neatly trimmed orange trees, in imitation of similar ones in the imperial palace. A few white pebbles had fallen from one of the planters, perhaps disturbed by a bird. So far it was the only place that had not been carefully raked or swept. Masayoshi evidently insisted on good service.

Lady Otoku received him quite informally. She was at her weaving frame, busily moving a bewildering number of wooden shuttles with brilliant silk threads through the weft of what looked like an exquisite piece of brocade.

Many women of noble families were adept at weaving, but none received callers without hiding behind a screen, or at least covering her face with a fan.

Two maids were with her, both busy sewing the simple hempen garments that would be worn by the household in mourning for its master. One of the maids was very young and looked tearful and agitated, but her mistress turned a calm face to Akitada. Lady Otoku was quite pretty, with a round face and even features, but she was older than he had expected, and that perhaps explained her composure.

He bowed. "Forgive my rude intrusion at this time, Lady Otoku. I hope to be of some help."

She nodded. On her gesture, the older maid dropped her sewing, placed a cushion for him, and then went to pour him a cup of wine.

"I am weaving," Lady Otoku said in a soft voice, "because I find that keeping my hands busy calms my mind. The police have arrested a young man, I believe?"

Akitada was not sure he had heard correctly. Perhaps she was signaling that she wished to keep her relationship with Shigeyori quiet. He glanced at the maids.

The older woman was bent over her work again, but the young girl stared at him with wide, frightened eyes. He wondered if Shigeyori had lied about the relationship. The weaving loom produced soft clicks as Masayoshi's daughter worked. He said cautiously, "His name is Shigeyori. I have been told that you know him."

"Yes." She paused to look up from her weaving. "Did Shigeyori do it?"

Her voice was as serene as her eyes. Akitada felt out of his depth at such self-control. "He has denied it, but your servants saw him leaving the main hall shortly before the murder was discovered."

She sighed. "He was here this morning. I do not know if he saw my father also."

Well, she was honest to a fault. Akitada asked, "Who had reason to wish your father dead?"

She frowned at this. "You mean other than Shigeyori?"

Startled, Akitada made sure he had understood her. "Are you saying that Shigeyori had a motive to kill your father?"

"Oh, I thought you knew. He asked to marry me and my father refused. I understand that unpleasant words passed between them."

Akitada digested this. Perhaps her loyalties had shifted to her father after the murder. "This happened today?"

"Oh, no. A few weeks ago. Shigeyori and I hoped my father would change his mind."

"But he continued his visits to you? I take it you welcomed his attentions then. Are you still planning to marry the young man?"

If he had hoped to embarrass her, he was disappointed. She looked sadly at him. "I don't know what to do. I wish to honor my father's wishes, but I cannot think that he fully appreciated Shigeyori." She paused. "I suppose I would like you to find my father's murderer and prove Shigeyori innocent."

Akitada looked at her calm face, her proper gown, the way her hair was tied back so neatly, her air of domesticity at her loom, and wondered how she had inspired passion in the younger Shigeyori. Of course, Shigeyori was ambitious and she would have her father's money. The more he thought about the law clerk, the less he liked his courtship of Lady Otoku.

"The police will do that," he said firmly. "I take it that you don't really suspect Shigeyori. What about others then?"

"My father had many enemies. He said it was a matter of envy. Men wanted his position, or he threatened theirs." She paused to eye him speculatively. "I will pay you well to bring his murderer to justice."

"Thank you, but I won't have the time. I am told some other people called here today. Of course, you may not know about all the comings and goings in the compound."

"On the contrary, I know precisely what goes on. I have run my father's household for a number of years now. The servants keep me informed. My father had several visitors today, but only three of interest. Lord

Inage stopped by briefly. The two clerks from the wardrobe office also reported. Their names are Kiso and Kajiwara and they came separately, Kiso first and then Kajiwara."

She was truly an astonishing female. A sudden suspicion crossed Akitada's mind. "I assume you've already given Superintendent Kobe these facts?"

"Of course."

He bit his lip. "Is there anything you have not told him?"

There was not. Akitada departed after repeating his condolences while she repeated her offer to pay him. He then went to speak to the house servants. Here, however, he got no further. The man who had seen Shigeyori running away was positive the young man had come from the main house and not from Lady Otoku's quarters. He said again that Shigeyori had looked as if he had seen a demon. This might be an imaginative touch on his part, but so far nothing absolved Shigeyori, and Akitada knew he had a temper. They also confirmed that the two clerks had called earlier and that there had been nothing unusual about such visits. Finally, Akitada asked to see where Masayoshi had died.

Masayoshi had conducted his business in a pleasant room in the rear of the main building. One of Kobe's constables lounged on the veranda overlooking the small courtyard, no doubt hoping for a glimpse of one of the maids. Akitada gave his name and briefly peered into the room. The body had been removed and fresh grass mats covered the floor. A neat stack of account books was carefully lined up with a box of writing tools on the desk. The household was nothing if not well-run. Akitada almost wished for slovenly servants.

It was well past sunset by then, but in the scented dusk, Akitada returned to the Greater Palace to visit the wardrobe office, a large cluster of buildings directly north of the imperial residence. The gorgeous outfits and fabrics for the court and for state occasions were commissioned and stored here, but Masayoshi's duties as director would have been light. Kiso and Kajiwara carried out the day-to-day chores. Akitada hoped to find at least one of them still in.

They both were. The festival had kept things bustling in the wardrobe office because the ladies of the imperial household vied with each other in their festive costumes. He found the two clerks together, bent over order books and stacks of precious fabrics. They became guarded when he identified himself and his errand.

Kiso was about thirty—a short, round-faced man with a dark complexion, his button eyes as restless as his movements. Kajiwara reminded Akitada of an emaciated rat. He was much older, with thin grey hair and closely set, narrow eyes. The small goatee and mustache disguised a receding chin.

Fear can rarely be hidden completely, and Akitada had seen it in many forms. These two had the panicked look of small animals cornered in their hole and desperately trying to find some escape.

Of course, many lower-ranking officials lived in constant fear of their superiors, and their nervousness might mean nothing. He countered their apprehension with urbanity. A frightened man might blurt out something, but he might just as well freeze into protective paralysis.

They relaxed a little when questioned about the workings of the office and their co-workers and began to make the obligatory remarks about what a loss Masayoshi's death was to the government.

"Who will take his place?" Akitada asked.

They glanced at each other. Kiso said quickly, "Kajiwara here has the experience and seniority..."

Kajiwara cried, "No, no. Kiso is much the better man. Youthful vigor is needed."

Apparently both hoped for promotion. A motive, albeit weak. Akitada asked, "Do you have an idea who might want Masayoshi dead?"

That brought back some of the earlier fear. Kiso said anxiously, "We heard the police already caught someone."

"They are not entirely satisfied they have the right person."

Kajiwara pursed thin lips. "The young lady was much troubled by unwanted attentions from this young man. The director was very angry about it."

"As I said, the police are looking into it, but there are certain unexplained facts." In truth, Akitada was nearly convinced of Shigeyori's guilt, but he wanted to make sure that these two had nothing to hide. He became aware that Kajiwara was staring at his court hat and remembered the missing rank ribbon. Touching the hat lightly, he said with a smile, "I must have lost the ribbon—or perhaps one of our cats stole it."

AKITADA AND THE WAY OF JUSTICE

Kajiwara rose instantly. "But that's quite easily taken care of. After all you are in the wardrobe office, my dear sir." He bowed. "Allow me. We have all the rank ribbons here. Sixth, is it?"

"Yes. Junior, upper grade. You're very kind."

Kajiwara bustled out, and Kiso looked after him. When the door had closed, he said, "Poor man. He has aged greatly since the affair with his son."

"How so?"

"Oh, it was quite a tragedy. The son fought with a senior noble and inflicted a minor wound. An affair of the heart, they say. It could have been suppressed, you know, but someone insisted on punishment. Kajiwara's son was exiled and died shortly after."

"I'm very sorry to hear it." Tragic love affairs seemed the order of the day. Akitada made a note of the information and of the fact that Kiso had intended him to. He eyed the smooth-faced Kiso thoughtfully and asked, "Perhaps you can tell me why you went to see Masayoshi today?"

That wiped the complacent look off the bland face. Kiso stammered and came out with a feeble, "Oh, it was nothing." He realized that that did not answer the question and added, "Some new weaving technique the director had heard about. He thought he'd found someone to do the work for us." He smiled nervously. "The director liked sending for us."

That certainly sounded like Masayoshi.

Kajiwara returned holding a green ribbon with a very nice diamond pattern. "This is it, I think?"

"Yes. Beautiful work. Thank you." Akitada offered to pay, but Kajiwara would not hear of it.

"Allow me." As he fastened the ribbon to Akitada's hat, Kiso said, "Certain papers belonging to this office are still at the director's house. When may we go to pick them up?"

Akitada said, "I have no idea. Not until after the funeral, I should think. You must ask Superintendent Kobe about that." He thanked both for their time. When Kajiwara made a move to walk out with him, Kiso caught his sleeve and said, "Sorry, Kajiwara, but work presses."

Akitada returned to the ministry to make sure all urgent business was completed before the holiday. It was dark before he was done. His last chore of the day was to dispatch a short message to Kobe about his unproductive interviews. Nothing he had learned had helped Shigeyori, but he felt he had done all he could and went home.

Contrary to most wished-for events, the river excursion turned out to be all Akitada had hoped it would be. The sky was clear, it was warm but no longer as humid as earlier in the season, the boat was ably poled down the river by smiling men, and as the capital receded into a hazy blue distance against the mountains, Akitada left his troubles behind. Here he existed in a different world of laughter and song and the delightful sense of floating gently into an earthly paradise. Yasuko, Akitada's little daughter, toddled about in a bright red dress, red ribbons fluttering from the hair loops above her ears, and her mother looked positively enchanting in the rosy colors that flattered her skin.

They stopped at a shrine to present offerings of fruit and a length of new silk to the gods. They fished from the boat and ate their rice cakes and dumplings on a willow-shaded bank. They fed the ducks with the crumbs and played with their daughter. When dusk came, Akitada and Tamako spread a white cloth between them and, feeling quite silly and young again, each wrote a love poem on a colored slip of paper and tied it to a branch of fresh bamboo. It was, after all, what you did on the one night of the year when the cowherd star was permitted to meet the weaver star by crossing the milky way— a magical night when lovers joined.

Akitada did not think at all about Shigeyori until their journey homeward when Tamako, who was leaning against him, looked up at the starry sky and suddenly said, "You know, the Tanabata tale reminds me of your clerk Shigeyori."

Akitada reached out to pull his daughter back from the side of the boat where she was stretching short arms toward dancing fireflies. "How so?"

"Lady Otoku is the weaver maid and Shigeyori the cowherd. Will the real lovers get together now, do you think?"

He had mentioned Otoku's weaving skills to Tamako. Of course, Shigeyori was hardly a cowherd but, like the weaver maid's immortal father, Masayoshi had objected to his lowly status. Akitada doubted that either felt strongly about the other, but he thought

Shigeyori would pursue the wealthy heiress if there were not the matter of her father's murder.

"I doubt it," he said, then smiled. "The celestial lover crosses on a bridge made by magpies. I don't see how such a thing is possible in this case."

Tamako chuckled. "You're much too literal. I thought you might play the magpie in this instance and bring them together."

Hardly. Akitada snorted, but he pulled his wife a little closer.

The next morning, his new rank ribbon had also vanished. Irritated, Akitada blamed his daughter, the cat, a light-fingered servant, and general carelessness. The pleasant feelings lingering from their outing changed to ill humor. He left the house quickly.

He was still going through the daily assignments with the head scribe in his office at the ministry, when Kobe was announced. He was not alone. A neatly-dressed elderly man accompanied him. The elderly man looked distraught, and Kobe himself seemed a little upset.

To Akitada's intense embarrassment, Kobe announced, "This is Mr. Hakata, Shigeyori's father."

Then, before Akitada could find words to explain why Shigeyori had been dismissed, Kobe added, "Shigeyori killed himself yesterday."

"What?" Akitada searched Kobe's face, hoping he had not heard correctly. "Why? What happened?"

Kobe spread his hands without answering.

Mr. Hakata said, "Before he died, my son told the guard he had brought shame on himself and on his family." Then he sat down abruptly and burst into tears.

Akitada swallowed a wave of nausea. Kobe sat down also and said, "Shigeyori found a piece of wood, sharpened it, and cut his neck. When he was found, he was barely alive. He told the guards he could not face his parents."

Shigeyori's father whimpered. They avoided looking at him.

"Dear Heaven," muttered Akitada. He pictured Shigeyori in his prison cell, scraping away at a sliver of wood, intent on putting an end to his misery, while he and his family were drifting down the Katsura river. It was ironic that Shigeyori had pursued death with greater persistence and care than he had shown in his work at the ministry.

The father still wept quietly.

Kobe sighed.

Unspoken was the thought that the suicide had been a confession of sorts.

The father found a paper tissue in his sleeve and blew his nose. Settling himself a little more properly, he turned red-rimmed eyes on Akitada. "My son always spoke of you with the utmost admiration, sir," he said. "Always. He was so proud to be working under you. Nothing mattered more in his life than to excel in your eyes."

Akitada felt sick. He glanced at Kobe who grimaced.

"I mention this for two reasons," Mr. Hakata explained earnestly. "First, Shigeyori would never have done anything criminal because he could not have looked you in the eye. Secondly, I have come to ask you to clear my son's name. He told me how brilliant you are at solving crimes. He would have wanted you to find the real killer."

Akitada took a deep breath. He could hardly feel worse. Never mind that there was no good reason why Shigeyori should have killed himself if he were innocent. As long as his father believed him innocent, he would think that Akitada had a responsibility, no, a duty, to clear his son's name.

Yet, in spite of all the evidence against Shigeyori, Akitada felt the faint stirrings of doubt, and with them came terror that he had failed another human being and was responsible for his death. What if Shigeyori had killed himself because he could not prove his innocence and Akitada had refused to help him? The thought was monstrous.

Shigeyori's father reached into his sleeve and withdrew a small package wrapped in bright green silk and tied with red silk braid. He unwrapped it and placed two shiny gold bars on Akitada's desk. "This much I could collect," he said, his eyes pleading. "If it isn't enough, I shall go home and see what else can be sold."

Akitada's hand shot out to push the gold away but he stopped himself when he saw the fear in the older man's eyes. Tucking his hands back into his sleeves, he heard himself say, "It is enough. I shall do my best, Mr.

AKITADA AND THE WAY OF JUSTICE

Hakata." Seeing the father's relief, he added, "Your son showed great promise."

Hakata smiled and nodded. "Yes, he was a good boy, a remarkable son in every way. I wonder what happened to make him do such a terrible thing."

For a moment, Akitada thought he meant the murder, but then he realized it was his son's suicide that weighed on Hakata's mind.

"Did he mention the Lady Otoku to you?" he asked.

"No. I think he was afraid to tell me. He should not have reached for the clouds when he knew that I hoped he would marry his cousin. But Shigeyori has not been home in many months, and for the past month he has not written. It must have been because of her." Hakata frowned. "It wasn't like him. We were always close."

Perhaps it had been love after all. Love could cause all sorts of trouble. Akitada wondered if Shigeyori's work at the ministry had declined because of this. Why had he not paid more attention to the young clerk? The young were vulnerable, and their despair often ran deeper than that of more mature men.

Akitada glanced at Kobe. They could not discuss the case in front of Hakata, but Akitada guessed that Kobe also felt responsible.

Hakata and Kobe left soon afterwards, and Akitada mulled over the situation. He had no intention of keeping the gold. Somehow he would find a way of returning it. He had been all but certain that Shigeyori was guilty. How was it that a brief meeting with his father, a meeting which had produced no new information, had changed his mind? He did not trust emotions—neither his sick fear of having misjudged Shigeyori and caused his death, nor his pity for the father who had lost a son—and he sat long, brooding over the situation. In the end, he rose with a sigh.

He went over Shigeyori's records again and talked to his associates. The young men who had mocked Shigeyori only two days ago looked subdued today. They confirmed that Shigeyori had started acting strangely about a month ago. He had spent hours staring distractedly into space. He had been late for work or absent. Once they had teased him that he had fallen for a woman, and he had rushed off angrily. He had started drinking.

A month ago, according to Lady Otoku, Masayoshi had forbidden the relationship.

Kobe returned briefly in the afternoon. He was still upset.

Akitada confessed that he had developed doubts about Shigeyori's guilt, saying, "I've wondered if Shigeyori found Masayoshi dead and was afraid he would be blamed. It would explain his behavior as he rushed away."

Kobe nodded glumly. "I blame myself," he said. "It never occurred to me that he might be unstable enough to do away with himself. I should have posted a guard."

"And if I hadn't been so angry with him, I would have gone to see him in jail. In any case, I should have checked into his problems at the ministry much sooner. But self-recrimination is pointless. I'm going to investigate the murder properly this time. What about Masayoshi's feud with Inage?"

"Oh." Kobe ran a hand over his neatly tied hair. "That happened recently. Both Masayoshi and Inage were being considered for the governorship of Omi province. Masayoshi apparently set out to ruin Inage with a string of malicious allegations ranging from public drunkenness to treason."

Akitada raised his brows. "Treason?"

"It isn't likely from what I know of the man, but Inage's daughter is married to the assistant governor of Mutsu, and he was once suspected of dealings with the enemy in the North. That connection, along with Masayoshi's lies, was enough to remove Inage's name from the list of candidates. Worse, people don't forget that sort of thing and the rumor will be dangerous to his future and that of his family."

Akitada shook his head. "Very nasty. I assume Inage learned the source of the gossip and came to speak to Masayoshi?"

"Yes. They say he was livid with anger. Masayoshi refused to see him, and Inage claims he went home and calmed down. He was not seen again at the Masayoshi residence, but there is so much coming and going there all day that he could have slipped back unnoticed."

"A strong motive. And we know both Kajiwara and Kiso were there that morning."

"Yes, I thought of that. They are the most likely suspects after Shigeyori. Kiso is ambitious and may have wanted Masayoshi's job. But Kajiwara has a much stronger motive. Masayoshi is responsible for his son's exile and death."

Akitada sat up. "Ah. I wondered what Kiso was hinting at. The sly toad! Masayoshi seems to have made a habit of causing trouble for others. Why didn't you question Kajiwara?"

Kobe looked unhappy. "Well, he could have done it. He was the last visitor before Shigeyori, but he claims he left Masayoshi alive and they had a normal business discussion concerning the wardrobe office. I hoped you would get to the bottom of that."

Akitada bit his lip. "Did you believe him?"

"He was very nervous, but I really didn't see him suddenly taking his revenge after all this time."

"True. I can't say I like Kiso much. What if Kajiwara also found Masayoshi dead and was afraid to admit it, knowing that he would be suspected? That would bring us to Kiso. I think Masayoshi sent for him that day. Curious."

Kobe looked interested. "He seemed innocent enough. He says Masayoshi had come to some decision concerning the weaving and dying orders."

"It's all very frustrating." Akitada rose to pace the room. "I wish we had the weapon."

"We looked in all the likely places, but we cannot search the suspects' houses without good reason. Besides, the killer could have tossed the knife into the nearest river or canal." He paused, then said, "Speaking of canals, would you go to see Lord Inage? I think he might speak to you more freely."

Akitada stopped pacing. "If you like. Why canals?"

AKITADA AND THE WAY OF JUSTICE

"No reason. Inage lives on the Muromachi Canal."

On his way to Lord Inage's home, Akitada was conscious of the weight of Mr. Hakata's gold in his sleeve, but Shigehiro's death rested far more heavily on his conscience. Umajiro Road was in a part of the capital that had seen better days but, being near the Greater Palace, the area bounded by the Muromachi Canal still contained substantial older estates and large gardens.

Inage's property was one of these. It was large and heavily wooded. A servant directed Akitada into a landscape planted by a master and lovingly maintained. An elderly man in grubby short pants and a jacket of rough hemp was digging a hole next to three large rocks. When he straightened up to wipe the sweat from his face, Akitada saw that he was tall and his frailty was deceptive. At that moment, the man noticed Akitada and smiled.

"A beautiful day," he cried, waving a hand. "And now I'm also blessed with company. Welcome to my garden."

Akitada was startled by this unorthodox greeting from a gardener, but the man looked so happy to see him that he approached.

"Come, come," the odd character urged. "Would you mind giving me a hand with this rock?" He was about to man-handle the tallest rock toward the hole he had dug. Akitada helped him push the rock in and then stood aside while the gardener took up a thick bamboo pole and tamped down the earth around it. "The roots of a stone must be set deeply," he explained. He gestured to the two smaller rocks. "And it must be balanced with a fore-stone or two. Mine will be a trinity."

"I see," said Akitada, not seeing at all.

"This is an old garden," said the other. "Look at that stone over there, to the north-east. That's a phantom stone. It has been here for generations and is responsible for untold misfortune to my family. Luckily I came across a book—a heaven-sent find— that explains it all. So now I'm setting a Buddhist trinity to face it from the south-west. That will stop the evil." He finished with the stone and gave Akitada a happy smile. "Thank you. All will be well soon, you'll see." He stepped behind the new stone and squinted past it. "Perfect. Now the smaller ones will go here and there. Do you mind?" He bent to lift one of them, and Akitada reached for the other. A suspicion had begun to form in his mind.

"I hope I find you well . . . sir," he said tentatively.

With a soft laugh, the other said, "Yes, it's the master of the house you're talking to. I like to work in my garden. Physical work empties the heart wonderfully of its troubles. And who might you be?"

"I'm Sugawara." Akitada brushed the dirt from his hands and made Lord Inage a small bow.

The smile on the other man's face faded. "Ah. I've heard of you. Are you on a case? Is this about Masayoshi?"

"Yes. One of my clerks was accused of his murder. He may be innocent."

AKITADA AND THE WAY OF JUSTICE

Inage sighed. Wiping his hands on his jacket, he gestured toward the house. "If you don't mind my appearance, we can talk on the veranda."

When they were seated—Akitada on a cushion brought out by his host, Inage on the top step to the garden—Inage said bluntly, "You're casting about for another murderer and have come to me. But you're wasting your time. I did not kill Masayoshi." He waited. When Akitada said nothing, he said, "Oh, I see. No, I didn't hire an assassin either. You really must look elsewhere."

"Yes. Forgive the intrusion, but I had to come and see for myself."

Inage raised thin brows. "And are you so easily convinced? I had every reason to wish the man dead. He was a menace to me and my family. Worse, to our society and nation."

Akitada gestured at the lush landscape. "It was your contentment here, in your beautiful garden, that convinced me. A man does not find peace so easily after shedding blood. Can you tell me where else I might look?"

But the atmosphere had changed. Inage was hostile now. "No," he snapped. "Whoever killed Masayoshi did the correct thing. I know you lawyers wish to see crimes solved and the guilty brought to justice, but too often you have a very wrong idea of what justice is. I shall not help you. At my age, a man has to consider his karma."

Akitada thought of Shigeyori's grieving father. "In that case," he said sharply, "beware that you do not add another sin. The young man who was arrested for the murder killed himself in despair, and his father bows his head in shame. If you know of anything that might ease that father's pain, it is your duty to speak."

Inage stared at him, then lowered his eyes and was silent for a long time. When he looked up again, he glanced across to the trinity rocks and sighed. "We try to avert misfortune but life itself is a misfortune. You speak of one father's grief over the loss of a son. When I was turned away from Masayoshi's gate, another visitor arrived. I knew him, poor man. Masayoshi destroyed his son by demanding he be sent into exile for a minor squabble in which the youngster had been provoked." He turned bleak eyes on Akitada. "How do you decide between two evils, Sugawara? That poor man has already suffered so much and so patiently. What shall I do?"

Akitada said gently, "I know about Kajiwara."

Inage's shoulders sagged. "Oh. Then you think he . . .?"

"I don't know." Akitada got to his feet. "As you say, justice is not an easy master. I shall seek more answers and think." He bowed and left.

He was running out of options. If not Shigeyori, then surely Kajiwara. But Akitada did not like that choice any better than Inage had. If only it could be Kiso! Why had Masayoshi sent for Kiso?

Kiso and Kajiwara were together again, but they seemed calmer today—perhaps because the festival was over, or because they thought Shigeyori's death had closed the investigation. At any rate, they looked relaxed and cheerful until they saw Akitada.

Akitada said, "Don't disturb yourselves, gentlemen. I have just one or two questions. You heard that the young man arrested for your chief's murder has committed suicide?"

Kajiwara glanced at Kiso. "Yes. How sad! I can imagine what his poor parents must be feeling."

Kiso nodded. "So difficult nowadays to raise sons properly. At least this one accepted his punishment like a man. Sometimes suicide is very proper, don't you think?" When Kajiwara made an inarticulate sound, Kiso cried, "Oh, forgive me, Kajiwara. I didn't mean . . ."

But Kajiwara had already jumped up. His hands shook so badly that he clenched them. "You *did* mean it," he shouted. "You never let me forget my poor boy for a moment. You do it on purpose, Kiso. It is very cruel of you." With a sob, he fled the room.

Kiso opened his mouth to explain, but Akitada interrupted coldly. "Don't bother. Your colleague's story is known to the police. Your own, however, is another matter. I think you lied about what you were doing at Masayoshi's that morning."

"What?" The color drained from Kiso's face.

While satisfied with the reaction, Akitada still wondered what Kiso was hiding. He suddenly remembered the neat stack of account books on Masayoshi's desk. It was worth a try. "Come," he said, "you may as well admit it. Masayoshi had questions about the accounts."

"The accounts?" Beads of sweat appeared on Kiso's face.

Akitada smiled unpleasantly. "And I am even more curious to know what you did about it."

"Nothing. I did n-nothing," stammered Kiso. "I mean, he did nothing. That is . . ." He was hopelessly entangled.

"Masayoshi was not the sort of man to overlook improprieties. You killed him and hoped to pin the crime on Kajiwari, didn't you? You knew Kajiwari had an appointment after you."

"N-no, no! I didn't. You made a mistake. He didn't . . . I wasn't . . . I'm innocent." Kiso sweated and wrung his hands. "Please, you must believe me, I'm innocent." He burst into tears.

A very satisfactory reaction. But Akitada had just realized something else: if the wardrobe accounts were the reason for Kiso's panic, it was not likely that he had stabbed his superior and left them behind. He decided to go back and make sure.

This time the imposing gates of the Masayoshi residence were closed, and a taboo sign warned of the recent death. He was admitted by the gatekeeper who was dressed in the drab mourning Lady Otoku's maids had been sewing. The funeral was over and silence hung over the compound.

Lady Otoku was behind a screen, dressed in the dark silks of mourning. Her voice was faint. Akitada thought cynically that screens made it easy for women to pretend emotions they did not feel but realized that he had transferred his disapproval from Shigeyori to the woman he had loved—or at least courted.

After expressing condolences on Shigeyori's death—she listened with deep sighs—he asked for her help in clearing Shigeyori's name.

"Oh," she murmured, "I thought . . . you mean Shigeyori did not do it? But why then . . . oh, how terrible!" She burst into violent sobbing, and the elderly maid hurried to her assistance.

After her self-control on his last visit, Akitada was surprised. It seemed odd that she should collapse now, but perhaps she, too, felt responsible for Shigeyori's death. Embarrassed and concerned for her distress, he rose to withdraw.

"What is it that I can do?" she asked suddenly, her voice thick with weeping.

He paused. "I was curious what brought your father's colleague Kiso here that morning, but it can wait."

"Kiso," she corrected him, "is not my father's colleague. He is a clerk, and he may be a thief. My father summoned him because he had questions about the accounts. Even though Father conducted some of the affairs of the wardrobe office from here, he was very conscientious."

That at least confirmed his guess. "I don't doubt it," Akitada said politely. "What was the outcome of the interview?"

"I never saw my father alive again. Do you suspect Kiso?"

Before Akitada could answer, the door opened. A servant knelt in the opening and bowed. "A thief has been arrested, Mistress," he announced in an excited voice. "By the constable in the main hall."

Lady Otoku gave no sign of surprise at the news. She said, "I see. Is that all?"

But the servant was bursting with more news. "It's Mr. Kiso, Mistress. He was trying to take away the master's books. Now he's off to jail." The servant looked pleased.

"Thank you, Hiko," she said. When the door had closed again, she told Akitada, "How clever of you, sir. So my father's murder is solved. I am deeply in your debt. How very sad that Shigeyori had so little faith in justice."

She had regained her control. Akitada found her complacency tasteless and quickly departed for Kobe's office.

Kobe looked pleased. "The victim identified his killer," he announced and pointed to Masayoshi's accounts on his desk. "Kiso tried to steal them. Have a look."

Akitada took the books up one by one and leafed through. They were the wardrobe office accounts. A loose note tumbled from one. Masayoshi had been angry enough to jot down some figures and the words, "Let that rascal Kiso weasel out of this!"

"It's my fault," Akitada said with a sigh, replacing the books. "I talked to Kiso earlier and frightened him into making this foolish attempt. Apparently he's guilty of falsifying the books, but that is all." He explained his reasoning and saw Kobe's face fall.

"Well," Kobe said, shaking his head, "I had hoped we wouldn't have to start all over again, but it seems we must. There may be another suspect. Masayoshi was involved in an affair with a married woman, and the lady's husband recently returned from four years of provincial service."

Akitada frowned. "An affair?" This sort of thing happened often enough and explained why many officials dragged along their families when assigned to distant places, though some wives flatly refused to leave the comforts and pleasures of life in the capital, while some husbands preferred the freedom of new liaisons at a distance from their homes. "Wasn't Masayoshi getting a little too old for that sort of fling?"

"He was only forty-five."

Akitada grimaced. He was rapidly approaching forty himself. "How did you find out?"

"My wife heard about it. Women know such things first. It seems the husband found her pregnant and sent her home to her family."

Akitada sat up. "She was pregnant?"

"Yes. And an injured husband is a murder suspect."

"But the husband wasn't there that morning, or was he?"

"He wasn't seen, but I'm afraid we have to consider him. It seems strange Masayoshi and his paramour didn't prepare better. They must have expected the husband's return."

Akitada's eyes widened. Then he smiled. "Oh, but I think they did! Of course, they did. There's someone who had a much stronger motive than all of our suspects. Come, we have to go back to Masayoshi's house."

Kobe looked startled. "Why?"

"Sorry. I have been wrong so often in this case that I'd rather make sure first."

Kobe grumbled, but accompanied Akitada to the Masayoshi house. When they crossed the entrance courtyard, Akitada halted. "Shigeyori was seen running from the main hall to this gate?"

Kobe nodded.

"And both Kajiwara and Kiso arrived and left this way?"

"Yes. What difference does it make?"

Akitada started for the main hall. "I don't know yet, but I take it you had their routes searched for the murder weapon?"

"Of course, and the entire neighborhood, including the nearest canal."

Akitada nodded absent-mindedly. They took the stairs and went inside and to Masayoshi's study.

Akitada threw open the doors to the rear veranda and stepped outside. The constable jerked to attention and was ignored. They looked down into a small courtyard with gravel and river pebbles. A memory stirred and Akitada glanced across to Lady Otoku's pavilion.

Kobe said unnecessarily, "The women's quarters."

"Yes." Akitada looked at it fixedly for a moment, then went down the stairs and across the courtyard. Two planters with matching orange trees flanked the stairs to the women's quarters. He looked at the pebbles in the right planter, then thrust his hand among them. Feeling around a moment, he pulled out a short ornamental dagger.

Kobe joined him. "The murder weapon?" he asked. "How did you know it was here?"

"I guessed. I noticed earlier the pebbles had been disturbed and thought a bird had scratched around." Akitada looked at the dagger with satisfaction. The handle was black lacquered wood with a fine silver overlay, but the blade was wickedly sharp. A crust of dirt and a brown substance clung to its top. "If I'm not mistaken, this belongs to Lady Otoku. It is the sort that is given by a father to a new-born daughter," he said. "I'm afraid this one still has her father's blood on it."

"Shigeyori after all?" Kobe looked stunned. "He's the only one who could have taken it from Lady Otoku. Unless you think it was one of her maids?"

"Not a maid," Akitada said, "and the fact that Shigeyori was Lady Otoku's lover doesn't mean he took it."

"But . . . you don't mean she gave it to him? To murder her own father!" Kobe sounded shocked. "What a very nasty thought!"

"I agree. I think she suggested the murder to him weeks ago. That was why he could not keep his mind on his work." He looked up at the pavilion. "Shall we go arrest the lady?"

"Are you sure she knew Shigeyori took her dagger?"

"We arrest her for the murder. I think Shigeyori refused, and she did it herself."

"You mean she killed her own father?"

"Yes. Shigeyori found Masayoshi dead and ran out the front in a panic. The dagger was hidden here—between Masayoshi's study and his daughter's quarters—where she had hidden it after the murder. Then she did her best to pin the crime on Shigeyori by sending him to talk to her father. She expected him to come running back to her with the news, but Shigeyori was too horrified and fled. A good thing you posted a constable or she would have disposed of the dagger by now."

Kobe shook his head in disbelief. "I don't understand it. I don't care how unpleasant the man was to others, he clearly doted on her."

"Sometimes fatherly love is too constricting. And she was about to lose everything. She was her father's sole heiress—until Masayoshi acknowledged another child. If that child was a son, Lady Otoku, as a female, would have to submit to her half-brother's wishes."

"You think she found out about that?" Kobe was thunder-struck.

"I think Masayoshi informed her. They were much alike, you know. Lady Otoku is a strong-willed female, and he had very firm notions about her future. Her own wishes did not matter to him."

Kobe looked at Akitada curiously. "Aren't you shocked?"

"No. I didn't much like her because of her remarkable self-control. She is a clever woman, though, and perfectly capable of pretending grief when it suits her."

AKITADA AND THE WAY OF JUSTICE

Kobe looked unhappy. "This will be difficult to prosecute. A young woman of her class? And such a crime."

"I know." Akitada walked up the steps and called out. A servant came and was sent to announce them.

Lady Otoku was behind her screen again and in the company of the same elderly maid.

They accepted the cushions waiting for them, refused the offered wine, and went straight to business.

"We found the murder weapon," Akitada said.

She gave a small gasp.

Akitada pushed the dagger under her screen. "I believe this is yours."

Lady Otoku gave a high-pitched cry and scooted back. "Take it away," she squealed. Her maid rose, uncertain what to do.

Akitada retrieved the dagger. "Your father's blood is on it," he said coldly. "On the dagger he gave you himself, never suspecting that you would use it against him."

"How dare you? I loved my father. Perhaps one of the servants . . ."

Her maid gasped and turned pale.

Her mistress tried again. "No. If this is really the murder weapon, then Shigeyori must have taken it without my knowledge. Oh, how horrible." She whimpered.

Akitada was suddenly very angry. He rose and moved the screen, so he could look at her. She hid her face with her sleeve. He snapped, "Don't waste our time. We know what happened. You tried to get

Shigeyori to do it, but he could not bring himself to kill another human being, and so you had to do it yourself. Shigeyori committed suicide in jail so he would not have to tell the police about you. He loved you, but you only saw him as a convenient tool to rid yourself of your father."

She had become very still, but when she lowered her arm, her eyes flashed. "Shigeyori was a coward and a weakling. I suspected it, but he was handsome and he was the only man who ever came close to me. My father denied me a normal life because he liked the way I ran his household for him. Far from my using Shigeyori, he used me. He killed my father to get his hands on my wealth."

"I'm afraid Shigeyori could not have done it. As angry as your father was with him, he would never have turned his back on him." Akitada turned to the elderly maid, who was weeping. "You're Lady Otoku's nurse, aren't you?" The woman nodded, brushing away tears. "What happened to the young maid who was here the first time I called?"

Her mistress answered—too quickly. "She went to visit her family."

"In a time of mourning?" Akitada shook his head. "I think you sent her away." He read the answer in the nurse's face and drove the point home, "She knew you had paid your father a visit that morning, didn't she? Or did you get his blood on your gown when you stood behind him and drove your dagger into his back?"

"No!" Lady Otoku jumped up and stamped her foot. "How dare you talk to me like this in a house of death? Leave us this instant."

Kobe was beginning to look uneasy, but Akitada remained firm. "It's over, Lady Otoku. That maid will be brought back, and she will testify. And so will your father's mistress. I have no doubt your father discussed his plans for his unborn child and for your future with her."

He saw her eyes widen. Before he could stop her, she darted forward to snatch up the dagger. Placing its tip to her throat, she cried, "Don't come near me."

The purpose of the dagger was known to all highborn women. They would use it to end their lives when dishonor threatened. And a woman with the determination of Lady Otoku did not hesitate for a moment.

The following morning, Akitada went to his study to get Mr. Hakata's gold. He intended to return it with the explanation that the police had solved the case.

When he opened the door, he disturbed a bird that had flown in from the garden. For a moment, it fluttered wildly about the room with a clatter of wings, then it escaped through the open doors. Akitada only caught an indistinct glimpse of its dark shape and of something red flitting through the air before it was gone. On the desk lay the package with the gold, but the red silk braid was gone.

Bemused, Akitada walked out on his veranda and looked up into the trees. There was a slight movement on one of the branches. A feathered thief, he thought and remembered his lost rank ribbons. It was so easy to misplace blame. Up there, no doubt, a magpie nest was luxuriously lined in red and green silk brocade.

The trouble was that human beings were neither as infallible nor as fortunate as the immortals. There had not been a magic bridge for Shigeyori and Lady Otoku.

WELCOMING THE PADDY GOD

In this final story, Akitada is fifty—older but not necessarily wiser. Now it is his former rival, Kobe, who doubts a prisoner's guilt, while Akitada pursues the case more out of boredom than concern for a fellow human being. Over the years, he has become set in his ways and is less inclined to self-examination. But in the end, his understanding of human nature and his innate desire to get to the bottom of a puzzle save him from making a bad mistake.

Heian-Kyo (Kyoto), 1039; the Ever-Growing Month (April).

The two gentlemen met by accident as they crossed Nijo Avenue on a sunny morning of the third month of the year. They bowed, eyeing each other with cautious smiles.

"Kobe?" murmured the tall thin man. He wore costly court attire and had a touch of gray at the temples. "What an unexpected pleasure! I hope you are in good health?"

"Thank you, Excellency," boomed the white-bearded official, "and you and your family also, I hope?"

They moved aside to let traffic pass. Polite preliminaries allowed them to test the waters, before flinging themselves into the more dangerous currents of discussing crime.

The thin nobleman, Sugawara Akitada, had risen from obscurity in the Ministry of Justice to high office in the imperial administration because he had a knack for solving difficult criminal cases and smoothing over politically explosive incidents. Superintendent Kobe of the Metropolitan Police had moved up quickly and held his post by patient and stubborn plodding.

Their paths had crossed often, usually to their mutual frustration, though they had eventually surprised each other into cooperation and friendship.

Friendly relations established, Akitada asked, "Any interesting cases?"

Kobe hesitated only briefly. "One. A monk in the Western Prison. A particularly repulsive crime—robbery and murder. The man has confessed, but the evidence has disappeared into thin air."

Akitada raised his brows. "If he confessed, surely your job is done."

"Yes, but . . ." Kobe fidgeted, looking uncomfortable. "You know I like things neat. It's not just that we cannot account for the silver. Something else is not quite right. Something about that confession and the man himself."

Akitada was intrigued by Kobe's uncharacteristic diffidence. "Do you suspect an accomplice? What does the prisoner say?"

Kobe threw up his hands in disgust. "Just that he's guilty. No details. He doesn't know what happened." Pause. "Would you have time to talk to the man? I would like your opinion."

Time hung heavy on Akitada's hands at the moment. He was between assignments and bored with the enforced leisure. Besides, there was the novelty of being asked by Kobe. "Well . . ." he said, pretending hesitation.

"I was just on my way to the prison," Kobe urged. "Would you care to come along? As a favor?"

Akitada accepted.

The capital had an eastern and western half, each with its own administrative system. The western half had begun to decline a century earlier until large parts of it were inhabited mostly by the poor, the outcasts, and criminal gangs. Being jailed in the Western Prison usually meant that the prisoner and his crime were of the lowest type. Most officials in Kobe's position would have washed their hands of a confessed killer of no standing, glad to rid the capital of one of its vermin. But Kobe had always had a conscience.

"Tell me about the case," Akitada said as they walked along Nijo under the pale new leaves of the willows in front of the Imperial Palace.

The crime, or crimes, it appeared, had taken place in Higa, a village near the capital. A peasant had returned late one night from a trip to the market and found both his daughter and his money box gone. He shouted for his daughter and searched the property for his silver. Finally a noise alerted him to an abandoned well. He saw a large, bloodied monk climbing out of it. The monk seemed shaken and claimed to have fallen into the well. After he left, the farmer inspected the well and discovered at its bottom his young daughter's corpse. She lay covered with blood and with her clothes disarranged. Next to her was the empty money box. The horrified farmer called for his neighbors. Together they brought up the dead girl whose neck was bruised and broken. It looked as though she had been raped and strangled. A short time later, the local constables found the monk down by the river, washing the blood off himself. Although he was a very large man, they overcame him and threw him in a cell.

"Hmm," said Akitada. "It wouldn't be the first time a monk forgot his vows. Theirs is an unnatural life. The crime sounds straightforward enough."

Kobe scowled. "Oh, he confessed to all charges, even rape, but wait till you hear."

The prisoner was the most repulsive creature Akitada had ever seen. A huge man, he squatted toadlike on some stinking straw in the corner of the cell, shackled at the ankles and wrists. He looked perfectly capable of the most heinous crimes. His fleshy face was swollen and a sickly yellow color where it was not covered with purple bruises and brown scabs; his body seemed bloated rather than fat, and he was dressed in filthy rags. When they entered, he raised bulging, bloodshot eyes to them. His thick lower lip drooped dejectedly, letting a thin line of saliva seep down his stubble-covered chin.

He looked like a dangerous half-wit, Akitada thought and wondered if Kobe's trouble was that his prisoner was mentally deficient. The government was reluctant to counter-sign execution orders for such people.

But the monk disabused him of this notion immediately. "Good day to you, Superintendent," he greeted Kobe, his voice hoarse but educated. "Please forgive my rudeness, but it's difficult to bow. I seem to be unable to move very much, and I'm afraid I can't invite you to sit on this floor."

"Never mind that, Ennin," Kobe said. "His lordship here would like to hear your story."

The ugly creature rolled its eyes to Akitada and nodded a greeting. "If you wish, but there's little to tell," he said apologetically.

Missing teeth, a split lip, and assorted scabs and bruises suggested that he had been beaten severely. His dirty rags were actually a very old, stained, and faded monk's robe which had once been black, and the stubble-covered skull had been shaven.

Even to someone with Akitada's cynical views on Buddhism, it seemed extraordinary that a monk should be accused of such a collection of crimes. On this occasion, he had broken the monastic vows of poverty, of celibacy, and of nonviolence. The man must be an animal.

The blood-shot eyes studied Akitada also, and the monk smiled. The smile lit up the grotesque, animalistic features and superimposed an emotion so incongruously human that Akitada drew in his breath.

"The problem is," the monk said, "that I don't remember what I did precisely, though, of course, I can see now that I must have done it. I'm quite horrified. She was such a pretty young girl, and so kind. I don't remember touching her, but I could see that I had." To Akitada's astonishment, the man blushed and lowered his eyes. "She was partially . . . nude, and there was blood on her. Though perhaps that was mine. I seemed to have cut my head. But what was much worse, I must have strangled her afterwards. I suppose she fought me, but I have very strong hands."

He held them out for Akitada to see: huge, dirty paws with long, broken fingernails. "There was a lot of blood on my hands and robe when I woke. The farmer said I robbed him of some silver, but I don't remember that either, though I must have done it, for his money box was right there in the well beside me." He paused, waiting for Akitada to comment.

Akitada had listened in astonishment. "What were you doing at the farm? Did you know the farmer and his daughter?"

The monk averted his eyes again. "Not to say 'know.' I had spoken to them when I stopped for alms. The young woman was always very kind and generous, but her father's a tightwad. He caught her giving me food and was so angry he tried to beat her with a broom. I stopped him, but he called me names. I'm afraid I shouted also. It was not pleasant."

"What's wrong with your memory?" Akitada asked.

The monk hung his head. "It's the wine," he confessed. "I'm not supposed to drink, but I'm weak. Sometimes people give me a few coins instead of food and I buy wine."

"Yes," put in Kobe, "he was still half drunk when they brought him in. Stank of wine, in fact. No doubt he celebrated with the stolen silver."

"I'm very sorry," murmured the big monk. "I cannot seem to help myself. I wish I could be more precise about what happened. It's such a dreadful thing to have done. She was kind to me, and so pretty I . . ." He colored to his ears and looked down at his huge hands. "Most women don't like me," he said sadly. Akitada and Kobe exchanged a glance.

Kobe said, "So you went back later, when she was alone, to have your way with her and found she didn't like you either. That made you angry again, didn't it, and you attacked and killed her. Then you stole their silver for good measure."

The monk nodded. "I don't remember, but yes, it must be so."

Kobe snapped, "You keep saying 'It must be so.' It *was* so, wasn't it?"

The monk raised tired eyes to him. "If you say so."

"Heavens, man," shouted Kobe, "either admit it or defend yourself. This is a capital charge."

The monk smiled sadly. "Dying is easy, Superintendent," he said. "Living is hard."

Later, in Kobe's office, Akitada remarked, "Perhaps he confessed so readily because he was beaten. The marks are still all over his body, and from the way he sat and moved, I think your men must have broken some ribs."

Kobe was frustrated and his temper flared. "Don't accuse me of using torture. We found him this way after the local men got through with him. Seems one of them had been fond of the girl."

"Oh. Sorry." Akitada sighed. "Well, perhaps he expects more of the same if he changes his story. Strange, he practically admitted lusting after her. You would expect him to deny raping her, especially when confronted by the victim's bloodthirsty boyfriend."

"Didn't I tell you? The coroner said she wasn't raped, though someone tried to. I expect she fought him off. She had some bruises, and he had a lot of cuts and scratches on his face and scalp."

"I see. It's possible that he was too drunk to remember. When will he be brought before a judge?"

"In a day or so."

"So soon? But there's no time to do anything. He will be found guilty and condemned to death before we've had time to cast about for additional evidence."

"I know. I suppose I had hoped that you would have one of your brilliant flashes of insight."

Akitada looked for sarcasm in Kobe's face but failed. "You do me too much honor, my friend," he said and sat down. "Well, let's see what we have. This

Ennin had been in the habit of begging food at the farm. The pretty farmer's daughter gave readily enough, but shortly before the murder the farmer discovered this and abused both verbally and physically. Ennin admits he got angry. Perhaps he was angry enough for revenge."

"Perhaps."

"We can assume that Ennin knew the farmer was going to market and would not return until late. He got drunk, then went back to the farm, tried to rape the girl, killed her instead, and took the money box with enough silver to keep him in wine for the foreseeable future. Is that the way you see it?"

This time Kobe looked uncertain. "Yes, I suppose it could have happened that way. But what did he do with the twenty pieces of silver that were in the box? The farmer caught him trying to climb out of the well. And there was no silver on him when they found him by the river."

"He had time to hide it or pass it to a friend. Has it occurred to you that his claim of sudden memory loss is a little too convenient? He may be protecting someone."

"We searched everywhere and questioned everyone in the village. There was no accomplice. They know Ennin well and say he's a loner. He's a mendicant monk who moved into the village a month ago, sleeping in stables or storehouses at night and begging his food during the day. He doesn't have any friends or associates. He's not a likable man." Kobe paused. "That's why I want to be certain. Do you understand?"

Akitada nodded. He, too, felt guilty about his aversion to the man. "There's another possibility. He could have committed the theft earlier in the day when the girl was at work in the paddies, then tossed the box into the well and hid the silver somewhere. Later he got drunk to celebrate his wealth and went back for the girl. Drunkenness would explain his having tumbled into the well with the girl and also account for his sudden memory loss."

Kobe nodded slowly. "Yes. That makes sense. We have only his word for when he went to the farm. And he was quick enough to wash her blood off himself after the farmer saw him."

Akitada rose. "Right. That must be it, then." He added, almost regretfully, "The simplest explanation is usually the right one."

The following morning was particularly warm and pleasant. There was the scent of fresh leaves on the gentle breeze, and birds sang in all the trees. Akitada decided his horse needed exercise.

The road to Higa village was not particularly scenic, but yellow kerria blossomed in the hedges, and bluebells nodded in the grass. Higa was in a valley where a small river provided water for rice paddies. In its center a handful of modest buildings gathered like a flock of brown sparrows about a few grains of millet. On the hillside, among the pale springtime green of trees, rose the pagoda of a temple. Akitada rode along the river into the village and found that a small hostel and a Shinto shrine were the principal buildings. All around, to the foot of the forested hills on either side, stretched the rice paddies like a flowered quilt, fallow now, but covered with blossoming weeds. Already farmers were busy mending dikes and turning over the rich black earth. Soon river water would be diverted into the trenches and flood the fields in time for planting the new rice.

Stopping at the hostel, Akitada tied up his horse and ducked under the lintel of the low door. It was very dark inside. The smell of fermented rice wine met his nose. An elderly woman greeted him with many bows and led him to a wooden platform. Not bothering to remove his riding boots, he sat on its edge and ordered some wine and pickled radish.

The woman was a cheerful creature, small and quick, though her wrinkled skin looked like the leather of an old boot.

"Your Honor comes from the capital, no doubt?" she asked, bright black eyes scanning his plain clothes with interest as she poured his wine.

Akitada smiled. "You have sharp eyes."

This encouraged her. "I make a sort of game out of guessing what people do, you know. Now, your Honor, for example, came to take a look around Higa, isn't that right?"

Akitada smiled and nodded.

"Ah! So. It must be about the monk then. Let's see. The big fool confessed, so it's not about Tsume. If it's not about the murder, it must be about Katahachi's silver, right?"

She was quite good at her game. Akitada said, "I won't say yes or no. Why do you call the murderer a fool?"

She shook her head impatiently. "Because he is. I knew it the first time I saw him. He acts like a baby for all he talks like a learned fellow. Mind you, he's as ugly as a toad, and people don't like him, but that's no reason to aggravate them. A monk's supposed to be modest and humble when he asks for alms. And he's supposed to say some holy things to make you feel blessed. This fellow was always reprimanding and arguing. I can't imagine how he managed to get food as long as he did. What's more, he's been buying wine—which he isn't supposed to drink in the first place, is he?"

"Do you think he was a thief?"

"Maybe. How else would he get the coppers for the wine?"

Akitada peered into his cup. The wine was thick, grainy, and dull in color. But it was sweet to the tongue, burning his throat but leaving a pleasant glow in his belly. It had been quite cheap for its quality. The monk would not have needed much of this to get drunk.

Complimenting his hostess on her wine, Akitada asked, "Do you know the farmer he robbed?"

"Katahachi? Of course. One of my best customers this time of year, even if he claims poverty every time the tax man comes."

"He's been drinking a lot?" Akitada asked in surprise, wondering how reliable a witness the farmer was.

A drunken farmer catching a drunken monk climbing out of a well stretched his imagination.

"Oh, no. Katahachi buys the wine for the god. Some farmers do. To welcome the paddy god. Katahachi buys only the best, and fresh every day." She shook her head. "Katahachi really believed the god was in his paddies until Tsume's murder. Now he says he's ruined. The god has left because death has polluted his farm. He's one unhappy man, is Katahachi."

Akitada knew all about welcoming the paddy god. During the first months of the year, each farmer set up an altar to the paddy god in his home or near his paddies, and served up refreshments of boiled rice, nuts, and wine, thus tempting the god to take up his abode there during the crucial time of the new planting.

"You can't blame him," he commented. "Misfortune has struck his house twice already. He lost both his daughter and his savings."

"And the paddy god, too."

The door curtain flew back and two young men ducked in. The shorter one was muscular, with a pugnacious jaw, and wore the red tunic of a local constable; the other one looked frail and had a face scarred by smallpox. He wore a bright blue quilted jacket and patterned trousers like a city dandy. They were laughing at some joke.

The thin fellow tossed a silver coin on the platform. "Some of your best, Mrs. Endo," he called out in a reedy voice. "None of that rot-gut you sell to strangers." He glanced at Akitada. Akitada's plain dark robe and worn boots must have looked shabby compared to his own colorful outfit.

"Back from the capital early, Hanzo?" asked the hostess sourly. "And with money to spare? What happened? Are all the dancing girls taken?"

The thin fellow glowered. "Never mind what I do with my money. Bring the wine."

She served them, returning the change in coppers which he pushed carelessly into his sash.

His stocky companion had been staring at Akitada. Now he asked, "You're not from here? Just passing through?"

Akitada raised his brows. "Don't you have something more interesting to do in Higa than to question visitors?"

The young man flushed with anger. "I'm a police constable. It's my duty to keep an eye on strangers. We've had a murder here."

The hostess glared at him. "Mind your manners, Gombei. The gentleman is from the capital, come to check into the missing silver." She told Akitada, "Gombei was fond of the dead girl, so he's a bit jumpy, sir."

Gombei apologized, "Sorry if I was out of line, sir." But he added insult to injury. "Didn't mean to be rude, but a man in my profession's got to be on his toes. There's a lot of riffraff on the roads nowadays."

The thin young man now pushed himself forward. "I'm Hanzo, at your service, sir. We all hope poor Katahachi gets his few coins back. And so will the tax collector, I know." He smirked.

AKITADA AND THE WAY OF JUSTICE

"I see." Akitada silently cursed the woman for giving him away. So Gombei was the constable who had beaten the monk. Akitada disapproved of unnecessary cruelty, but there appeared to be extenuating circumstances in this case. He added more mildly, "You take your responsibilities seriously, Constable. That's commendable. Have you made any progress finding the missing silver?"

The two young men exchanged a glance, then Gombei said, "No, sir. We looked, of course, but I figured the police in the capital would have it out of the monk by now."

"He's been questioned but remembers nothing."

Gombei shook his head. "That's what he says. I bet we could've made him sing."

"The law forbids the beating of prisoners without authorization," Akitada said severely.

"Er, yes, sir. Of course. Well, we must be going. Good luck, sir, and feel free to call on me any time." Taking his companion by the arm, Gombei left hurriedly.

Mrs. Endo muttered, "Young good-for-nothings, both of them. Think only of their pleasure. At least Gombei's working, but that Hanzo just squanders his poor, doting mother's money in the city." She filled Akitada's cup again.

He asked, "Did the monk buy his wine here?"

"Yes. I was sorry for him, poor ugly thing. The children mocked him and hardly anyone would give him anything. Some days he didn't eat. After he first came, I'd feed him leftovers after hours sometimes.

One day he had some coppers and asked for sake. Well, I stared at him and he turned as red as a maple leaf in autumn. 'It's so cold,' he says and can't look me in the eye. Well, he *was* shivering, so I gave him the wine and he thanked me with such nice words, like a poem a gentleman might recite for some fine lady. After that he came every night for wine." She sighed. "Until that rascal Gombei arrested him."

So she had a soft heart. Somehow that unprepossessing lump of helpless humanity in the Western Jail had touched some tenderness in the old woman. "Did you ever find out where he got the money?" Akitada asked.

She shook her head. "I asked him, but he clammed up. Acted ashamed somehow. It was never more than a few coppers, though."

As he paid for his wine and asked directions to Katahachi's farm, Akitada recalled the monk's peculiarly guilty manner about buying the wine. He had thought it due to shame for drinking, but now he wondered.

Katahachi's farm was the usual huddle of dwelling and outbuildings gathered under a grove of pines and surrounded by paddies in various stages of preparation. Katahachi must be a hard-working peasant, Akitada thought, for his dikes and ditches were in good repair, as were the roofs of his house and sheds. A few chickens and sparrows searched for millet in the courtyard, but Katahachi was not home.

AKITADA AND THE WAY OF JUSTICE

Akitada tied his horse to one of the pines and went to look for him. He passed a new well and peered at the water below. Then he stuck his head into every shed, calling out each time without getting an answer. One of the sheds was filled with low trays of rice seedlings, faint green wisps in black soil. The soil looked cracked and dry, and several trays of seedlings had already succumbed to neglect. Akitada shook his head. If Katahachi had given up, he would lose his farm and starve. Every man, woman, and child depended on a plentiful rice harvest. The nation's welfare hung on the labors of even its humblest peasant.

The other sheds contained farming implements and a small stock of supplies. In one, a pile of dirty rice straw in a corner was covered with some rags; perhaps a bed for a dog. The rice barrels held just enough grain to see Katahachi through until harvest time. Akitada wondered if the peasant had already paid for his seed or had meant to use some of his silver to do so. Few peasants had enough seed rice by this time of year, having paid four tenths of the harvest as tax.

Near the last shed, Akitada found the old well, now only a low ring of stones surrounding the opening. The peasant, or someone else, had placed some boards over the opening—rather belatedly. Akitada moved these aside. The well was not very deep, having been filled to within a man's height with stones and dirt. The dirt was scuffed up, as were the stone walls of the well shaft, marked by the monk and the policemen scrambling in and out. There was a darker area in the dirt which might be blood.

Covering the opening again, Akitada thought about the box which had contained the silver. Twenty pieces, was it? If the monk had hidden the silver, why had it not been found by now? And the landlady had said that Ennin always paid with copper coins.

If someone else was the thief, who was it? And why had none of the silver shown up? In a small village, everyone knew everyone else's business. Sudden spending would raise instant questions. But the landlady at the hostel, for all her inquisitiveness, had known nothing.

Musing in this manner, Akitada reached the rear of the farm, and here he found its owner.

Katahachi was kneeling at the edge of the first rice paddy. He had built a makeshift shrine there to the god who blessed the rice harvest. A young pine tree was placed upright into the ground and decorated with chains made from braided straw and twisted slips of papers inscribed with prayers for a good harvest. Before it, Katahachi had set small dishes filled with gifts for the god. Akitada had seen many such humble arrangements throughout the country.

The peasant, a small, lean man with a skin burned dark from work in the sun, wore a clean white cotton jacket and pants. He must have heard Akitada's approach, but did not turn. His head bowed, he muttered prayers to the divinity.

Akitada bowed to the god and voiced his own request for a plentiful rice crop.

Without turning, Katahachi said bitterly, "It won't do any good. He's gone. It's the pollution."

No need to ask what pollution. Katahachi's daughter had died on the property, and the Shinto divinities abhorred death. Akitada asked, "Then why do you pray?"

The peasant just shook his head in misery.

The man's misfortune must seem overwhelming. Akitada looked out over the waiting fields, shimmering with their new growth of flowering weeds and buzzing with bees, a testimony to the rich soil awaiting cultivation and the young rice plants. But who would do the planting for him as he worked the paddle pumps which would keep the fields irrigated? He had lost his daughter—a pair of skillful hands and a strong young back, and hope for future generations. As if that were not enough, he had also lost all his savings. Twenty pieces of silver were a substantial testimony to a lifetime of working hard and saving even harder. And now he believed he had also lost the blessings of the god.

"Perhaps," Akitada suggested, "the god had already bestowed his blessing and moved on before your misfortune."

Katahachi pondered this and his shoulders straightened a little. He turned to look up at his visitor. His face fell and he immediately bowed, touching his forehead to the ground. "Please forgive this poor old man, your Honor. I've lost everything. No use asking me to pay. It's all gone."

Evidently he mistook Akitada for a tax collector. And the silver, or part of it, must have been ear-marked to pay off rice loans. Akitada said soothingly, "Never mind. I'm not here for money. Please get up. You're Katahachi?"

The peasant scrambled up. "Yes, your Honor. How may I serve you?"

"I heard of your daughter's death. You have my sincere condolence."

"Yes. Terrible! The murderer took all my silver also," he said disconsolately, as if this were the greater disaster. "Twenty-five pieces. And who will plant my fields now? Already the young plants are wilting. Tsume always took care of them. Ever since her mother died."

"I'm very sorry," said Akitada. "I heard your daughter had a soft heart and befriended the monk, but that you disapproved."

Katahachi turned a shade darker. "That one! That vicious devil! I knew he was after my silver the first time I laid eyes on him. He's as ugly as a demon, a devil from hell disguised as a monk. Look at what he did! And that foolish girl kept feeding him while he was waiting to have her and steal my silver. I thank the Buddha I won't have a devil for a grandson." He bowed three times in the direction of the monastery and murmured, "Amida, Amida, Amida."

Clearly Katahachi was a simple-minded man with a strong attachment to superstitions. To distract him from his tirade against the monk, Akitada nodded toward the small shrine and said, "I see you made the paddy god welcome with special gifts."

Katahachi looked at the little pine and the many small bowls, each filled with food, wine, or coins. "The god hasn't been back since it happened. Do you truly think that he's already blessed my paddies?"

"No doubt about it," said Akitada firmly. "You had better hurry up to tend to your plants and weed the paddies. I expect your neighbors' wives and daughters will plant for you."

Katahachi brightened. "Yes. They'll help. Thank you for your sage counsel, your Honor." He looked longingly toward the shed with the trays of plants. Akitada walked back with him.

"How did you happen to have so much silver in the house?" he asked.

"Twenty-seven pieces." Katahachi announced it with a mixture of pride and outrage. "Nearly thirty years I've been putting a silver coin in there whenever the harvest was good. Five of them my father left me. I was going to give those to Tsume's husband."

"You had picked her husband then?"

The peasant nodded. They had reached the seedling shed, and he peered in. "Look at that. Half of them dead as straw. Tsume always took care of them. Oh, it's no use. I'll never pay the next tax, even if the authorities forgive the loan." He sagged to the ground in the doorway, squatting on his heels and shaking his head.

"Nonsense," Akitada said briskly. "Up with you and fetch some water. Most of the seedlings will revive. Hurry."

Katahachi muttered but he shuffled off, returning with a pail of water from the well. Akitada watched as he moved among the trays, moistening the parched soil.

"You say your daughter was to be married soon? To a local man?"

Katahachi jerked his head in the direction of a neighboring farm. "Masazaemon's son. His widow sent a go-between. A good marriage for my girl even if the son doesn't take to farming. Tsume was very pretty and a good worker, but they were greedy. He and his mother told the go-between they wouldn't settle for less than fifteen silver pieces and my farm when I die." Katahachi left for another bucket of water.

When he reappeared, he said, "I might've done it, but then I heard that he's visiting the whores in the capital, spending the last harvest's money on women and wine there. I told the go-between that such a son-in-law is more trouble than he's worth."

"What about the constable? Wasn't he interested?

Katachachi spat. "Gombei? He's got nothing. No farm. No family. Besides Tsume couldn't stand him."

"How do you know?"

Katahachi gave a rasping laugh. "He kept bothering her till Tsume tossed him in the irrigation ditch."

Akitada rode back to the capital in a thoughtful mood. His visit to the crime scene had left him more confused than ever. The biggest hole in the case against the monk, the question where the missing silver was, remained unanswered. In addition, he now had several new facts which teased his mind. The girl had almost married a wealthy farmer's son, not the constable who had been in love with her and been rejected. And her father seemed more grieved over the loss of his silver than the death of his daughter. Had he loved her so little? The monk claimed that Katahachi had tried to beat the girl. And he had a reputation for being a tightwad. What if he had returned to find his silver gone and had taken out his fury on his daughter for allowing the theft to happen? Perhaps, having strangled Tsume, he had put the body and the empty box in the well, trying to pin her death on some robber. Katahachi was a liar, for the amount of his loss had grown even as he had told Akitada about it. Clearly he expected to be forgiven any debts because of the tragedy. Katahachi's tale of woe took on a more sinister significance.

And what about Ennin? If the monk had taken the silver, where had he obtained the coppers he had paid for the wine?

Immersed in such disturbing thoughts, Akitada almost passed another humble shrine to the paddy god. This one was near the road, perhaps so that passing travelers could offer their prayers.

Akitada dismounted to repeat his requests for a plentiful harvest. When he reached the decorated pine, he saw that the offerings, a small bowl of rice and another of nuts, were much more modest than Katahachi's. But then Katahachi had been at pains to counteract the pollution of his daughter's murder. He had heaped several bowls with the best rice, added a large flask of rice wine, plus assorted nuts and fruits and, for good measure, a plate of copper coins.

Akitada clapped his hands to announce his presence to the god and then bowed deeply. As he murmured his prayer, a strange idea entered his mind. He straightened, stared at the bowls, then bowed again more deeply, giving his thanks to the god.

The rest of the journey to the capital he accomplished at a brisk canter. He went directly to the Western Jail and demanded to see the prisoner right away. The sergeant of the guard hedged, but then compromised by having Akitada admitted while sending a message to Kobe.

The monk looked, if anything, more repulsive than before. He had been snoring until the rattling of the cell door woke him and he started up, his mouth sagging open and his bulbous eyes peering up nearsightedly. He made an unpleasant snorting sound in the back of his throat and wiped some spittle from his chin. "Arhem," he rasped, making a move to rise and subsiding with a groan. "Is it you again, sir? You catch me at a disadvantage. Day and night are no longer distinct, and so I sleep whenever I can. It's one of the benefits of being incarcerated."

The guard snapped, "We'll see about that. Criminals of your kind shouldn't be allowed to sleep. Next you'll kill and rape people just so you can get in jail and lie about all day snoring your head off, you lazy beast."

Akitada told the guard, "You may lock me in and leave. I'll call you when I'm done."

The man gave Akitada's slender figure a dubious glance and went to check the prisoner's chains. "I suppose you're safe enough if you stay away from him, sir."

"I've just returned from Higa," Akitada told the monk when they were alone. "Tell me, Ennin, why did you not stay at the temple while you were in the village?"

The ugly face flushed, and the protruding eyes became moist. "They threw me out," he muttered, hanging his head. "It's my drinking. You know that I get into mischief when I drink."

There it was again, the sense that this ugly, unloved human being had somehow become convinced he was responsible for all sorts of misdeeds while drunk. "Were you already fond of wine when you became a monk?" Akitada asked curiously.

"Oh, no. It was due to my work. And it came upon me so gradually, so very pleasantly, that I considered myself especially blessed. You see, I was put in charge of brewing the sake."

"You were brewing sake in a monastery?"

"Oh, yes. By imperial order. We made the finest sake you could wish to taste. And I made sure of it by tasting every batch. I have a very fine tongue for good sake, sir."

Akitada leaned against the cell wall and marveled at the contradictions of the Buddhist faith, which forbade the consumption of sake but most practically turned its hand to providing the rest of the nation with it. And so Ennin, tasting his brew industriously, had become too fond of it and got into "mischief." Whereupon his monastery had, no doubt regretfully, decided to do without his superior brewing skills.

"The rice must be polished most thoroughly, you see, to aid in the fermentation," Ennin was telling him, and then it's boiled in the finest spring water. Fushimi has especially good water. Then yeast is added and it's steamed again, and more water and rice are added, altogether three times . . . but you will not wish to hear all that, I'm sure. Toward the end I made a few mistakes. The tasting—sometimes you cannot be certain and must make adjustments, and the sake was of the sweetest, most potent kind—everyone said so—and I made some miscalculations, fell asleep at a crucial time, overturned a barrel or two, and spoiled a few batches." He sagged in dejection. "They were quite right to send me away."

"You must have missed your daily ration of sake," commented Akitada dryly.

Ennin gave a rueful nod. "People are very good, but they don't offer wine to a monk."

"But you bought wine from the woman at the hostel in Higa, didn't you?"

Ennin cringed, but nodded again.

"Where did you get the copper coins?"

The monk shrank further into himself. "Some people give money to poor monks," he whispered.

"Who gave you those coins?"

No answer.

"Did you steal them?"

Ennin raised both hands to his face and began to sob.

"I saw where you slept in one of Katahachi's sheds. Did you steal the coins from his shrine to the paddy god?"

The fat monk wailed and moaned, making snuffling gulping noises.

AKITADA AND THE WAY OF JUSTICE

Akitada waited until he became calmer, then said more gently, "You know, you should have told the police about this. They think you bought the wine with the silver in Katahachi's box."

Ennin raised a blubbery face from his hands and gaped at Akitada. "But I must have done so. The box was in the well when they arrested me. Along with poor Tsume."

"I think the day of Tsume's death you went to get Katahachi's offerings as usual, eating the food, drinking the wine, and taking the coins. Then you bought more wine and got drunk. On your way back to Katahachi's shed, you stumbled into the old well and passed out. Someone else later threw the dead girl and the box down there."

For a long time Ennin said nothing. Then he whispered, "Thank you. Amida is good," and bowed his head in prayer.

Heavy steps approached outside and the cell door clanked open again. Kobe strode in with a broad smile. "I was told you were here," he said genially, "and came right away. The trial is to start tomorrow. If there's anything new, I would be grateful for the information. We like to give the judge a sound case."

Akitada explained how Ennin had been helping himself to Katahachi's offerings to the paddy god.

Kobe frowned. "What paddy god? You don't mean that farmer's been leaving money lying about for anyone to steal?"

The prisoner put his head in his hands again and gave a low moan.

"Katahachi is such a miser that his generosity to the paddy god is the talk of the village," said Akitada. "Of course, in a rice-growing community nobody would dare touch what is the god's. They fear a bad harvest too much. Katahachi was convinced the god was accepting his gifts until the day Tsume died."

"The fool." Kobe glared at Ennin. "And nobody but a Buddhist monk would steal from the paddy god. You probably thought a bad harvest would bring more worshippers to Buddha."

"Oh no," wailed the prisoner. "I would never do such a thing. My own monastery had a shrine right in its grounds. We respect the ancient gods as deeply as you. I don't know what came over me. At first it was the food. I had not eaten in more than a day, and I thought the god wouldn't mind if we shared. But there was also a flask of wine there and . . . I took just a tiny taste, for memory's sake. It was delicious, but I could not quite make out how it differed from our own wine and took another sip. I'm afraid, Superintendent, after that I couldn't control myself, and my old weakness was upon me again. It got worse, and one day I couldn't resist taking a few coppers to buy more wine. And after that . . ." His voice trailed off miserably.

"You should be ashamed of yourself!" snapped Kobe. "Where's your self-control? Anyway, you're by no means in the clear. It only explains where you got the money for the wine."

The monk nodded. "I know. But the gentleman thinks I'm innocent. And I've been thinking and thinking these many days, and I really never believed I could have done what they accused me of. Tsume was very kind to me. I used to think how lovely she was. Just like a beautiful flower. Beauty is very precious to me because I'm so ugly myself, you see. So I really don't think I would have done anything to harm Tsume."

Kobe stared at him. "And I suppose that means you're retracting your confession," he snapped and turned abruptly to leave.

Akitada nodded to Ennin and followed Kobe back to the prison supervisor's office.

There Kobe faced him. "Do you by chance have another suspect to offer in his place?" he demanded.

Akitada hesitated. "No. But . . ."

"Yes, yes. I had my doubts. But what now?" When Akitada said nothing, Kobe sighed deeply. "Well, it's not your problem after all. I'll think of something." And when Akitada still did not speak, he bowed with formal politeness. "Since our paths will hardly cross after you take up your high office in Kyushu, allow me to express my gratitude for your sage counsel in this trifling matter."

There was a time when Kobe's quick mood changes had angered Akitada, but with success had come understanding. His new assignment was not announced yet, so he did not comment on it and merely said mildly, "You didn't let me finish. As I indicated, I have visited Higa village. I think you must find the silver. When you do, you'll also discover who killed the girl, for she gave her life for Katahachi's silver."

Kobe snorted. "Do you expect me to search every farm, stable, hostel, shrine, hut, or temple there?

Where am I to start? What if the silver is gone? It doesn't take long to get rid of money in the capital. It's only a few hours from the village."

"So it is," said Akitada quickly. "So it is. How clever of you! I had not thought of that. Then all you have to do is to ask who has visited the capital since the murder."

"Well, we know Katahachi did. You don't suppose he lost the money gambling and only pretended someone stole it?"

"Ah! Entirely possible. But would he kill his daughter?"

Kobe chewed on his mustache. "No, I suppose not. He might have beaten her, but he needed her to tend his fields. What about that constable who had his eye on her?"

"Another good possibility. She was promised to another man and rejected his attentions. He may have become angry enough to attack her. Perhaps he didn't mean to kill her, but once she was dead, he could have taken the silver."

"And then the bastard tried to pin it on the monk."

"Yes, he did beat him and got a confession. But did he leave for the capital during the crucial time? Of course you can always search his place for the silver."

"I'll do that."

"Good. And you might ask a few questions of a certain Hanzo who seems to be his friend. The owner of the hostel, Mrs. Endo, made some comment that he'been unusually flush with money—I saw him pay with silver coin—after returning from the pleasure quarter of the capital."

Kobe's chin sagged. "What? Nobody mentioned him to us."

Akitada smiled. "Village people don't volunteer gossip to strange policemen but talk quite readily to each other. I suggest we go back. If you invite the whole village to a hearing, you may discover other secrets."

Kobe considered, then smiled broadly. "Did you say 'we'?"

When Akitada and Kobe entered the hostel the next day, the villagers and local police had already assembled. Gombei stood stiffly at attention in front of the other constables. Toward the back, the reedy youth Hanzo waited next to a tall, stiff-backed elderly female with the sturdy, sun-burned features of a farmer's wife. She held a bamboo fan and stretched to stare at Kobe and Akitada. Katahachi, looking expectant, waited in front of a group of farmers.

Akitada nodded a greeting to Mrs. Endo, who hovered, bright-eyed with curiosity, near the wine barrels. He and Kobe removed their boots and seated themselves on the wooden platform. Everyone bowed, and Kobe told Gombei and Katahachi to approach. The old man and the young one knelt and bowed again.

"I have assembled the village here, because there are more questions concerning Tsume's death and the theft of Katahachi's silver," Kobe announced. "Suspicions have been raised about police procedure in the investigation. Corporal Gombei has been accused of beating a false confession out of the monk Ennin."

He gestured and two burly guards from the capital moved to the front and turned to face the villagers, chains and metal rods clanking at their leather belts, their leather whips at the ready. Gombei began to tremble. "Take a good look, Corporal," Kobe growled. "That's the equipment we use in the capital when prisoners won't tell the truth during official interrogations. These men are specially trained and hate corrupt policemen, but they won't use their fists and boots on you while nobody is looking. Oh, no, they only use their whips openly and only in the service of justice. Now, what do you know about this silver?"

Gombei shuddered and cried, "I didn't touch the silver."

"Hah!" Kobe smiled unpleasantly. "But you know who did."

Gombei looked around desperately. "No . . . I didn't mean . . ." He broke off when one of the guards began to unwind the leather thongs of his whip.

"You were saying?" Kobe asked in a silky voice.

"Wait," a woman's voice interrupted.

The elderly female at Hanzo's side pushed forward through the crowd and knelt.

"This insignificant person humbly begs to be heard," she said. When Kobe nodded, she turned to point her fan at Gombei. "That person has long been a bad influence in this village. Everybody knows that he drinks and fights and chases after women, and that he's been bothering Tsume for months. If the monk didn't do it then Gombei's the guilty one. But my son and I have nothing to do with any of this. Please allow us to return to our planting."

"If you have no information, why do you interfere in this hearing?" Kobe barked. "State your name!"

She bowed. "This humble person is the widow of Masazaemon."

Akitada said to Kobe, "She must be the mother of the man who had intended to marry the dead girl."

Mrs. Masazaemon bridled. "No. That's not true. We turned down an offer because the girl was quite unsuitable."

Katahachi immediately called her a liar. As soon as he had been admonished and fallen silent, Kobe told the widow, "It seems you're a material witness and will remain."

The woman bowed and returned to her place beside her son. The two whispered together.

Kobe turned back to Gombei. "You were about to tell us who took the silver," he reminded him.

Gombei was sweating. "Your Honor misunderstood. What I said has nothing to do with this crime. A friend offered me the loan of two silver pieces when I complained that my uniform was getting shabby." He added virtuously, "Of course I had to refuse. A policeman cannot afford to be indebted to someone in his village."

This was so patently lame that Kobe merely snapped, "This friend's name?"

Gombei flushed and muttered something.

"Speak up!" snarled a guard, tapping him sharply on the head with his whip handle.

"It was Hanzo," Gombei admitted sullenly. "He always has money to spare. His mother gives it to him."

Hanzo's mother cried, "Gombei's a liar. Hanzo has no silver. We're very poor."

One of the farmers shouted, "You're poor because you let him spend all the harvest money in the capital. He even sold your seed rice. That's why you have no rice seedlings to plant this spring. I told you so when you came asking for some of mine."

Furiously, Hanzo's mother turned on him. "You talk too much. It's not Hanzo's fault that his father died and left him nothing. The boy's not strong enough to be a farmer. He goes to the capital to study to become a teacher."

There was subdued mirth at this among the farmers. Akitada remembered the young man's flashy clothes and the carelessly tossed silver coin. "I think," he said aloud, "that a parent may not always know what a grown son does. You didn't see him pay for wine with a silver coin as I did yesterday."

Kobe pointed at Hanzo. "You," he growled. "Come up here!"

The reedy youth sidled up to his mother, who demanded, "Did you help yourself to my seed money again, rascal?"

One of the farmers cried, "What seed money?"

Hanzo flushed. "Don't make a scene, Mother! It was nothing. Just one piece I'd saved."

Mrs. Endo suddenly piped up, "Oh, you had more than one piece. You've been paying with silver ever since the night you and Gombei got drunk. I saw you pull several pieces from your sleeve and wondered if your mother had sold that rice paddy to Katahachi."

Katahachi said quickly, "She offered to sell it, but I said 'no.' It's bad land, hard to get to and the water disappears as quick as in a rice pot."

"It's perfectly good land," snapped the mother, glaring around her. "Katahachi's an old skinflint, and his daughter was a sharp-tongued harpy. Because we turned down the girl, they spread scandal about us."

Katahachi, Mrs. Endo, Gombei, and several farmers all started speaking at once. Kobe roared for silence and then asked Mrs. Endo, "Which night was it that Hanzo and Gombei got drunk and paid with silver?"

She thought. "I remember the monk came that night and bought his wine."

"Could it have been the night of the murder?"

She looked startled, then nodded. "Yes. It must've been. It was the last time the monk came, and when they told me about him being drunk when he killed Tsume, I remember thinking that it must've been on my wine." She looked a bit guilty. "Gombei didn't ask me if the monk got the wine here."

Kobe grunted. "Gombei didn't care. Too busy beating a confession out of him." He turned to Hanzo. "Did you take Katahachi's silver?"

"No," cried Hanzo. "Why blame me, when the place is full of vagrants and thieves?"

Some farmers murmured in agreement, but Katahachi stared fixedly at Hanzo and suddenly shouted, "You. It was you! You took my silver because I turned you down. I wouldn't buy your barren paddy nor give you Tsume with a fat dowry. I want my silver back, every piece. And if you've spent it, you piece of dung, I'll have your land. I should've known it was you, always snooping about and bothering Tsume at her work. You lazy dog, you just wanted my silver and my hard-working Tsume so you could waste my money on your pleasure while she worked your fields for you."

"My son's no thief," cried his mother.

Ignoring them, Kobe turned to Gombei. "Pay attention now, for your life may depend on it. While we're talking, my men are searching both your place and Hanzo's farm. They're very thorough."

Gombei paled, and Hanzo clutched his mother's arm.

Kobe continued, "We know you were together that night. Did you and Hanzo go to Katahachi's farm?"

Sweat pearled on Gombei's face. "I m-may have done," he stammered. "I mean, I was pretty drunk already that day. Hanzo came to the police station and told me that Tsume was sorry about throwing me in the ditch and wanted to talk to me."

"That's a lie," cried Hanzo.

The door of the taproom opened, and one of the metropolitan police constables came in. He carried a clinking bag in one hand and dangled a wooden amulet on a string of small shells in the other.

AKITADA AND THE WAY OF JUSTICE

Katahachi rushed forward, grabbing for the amulet. "My wife's amulet," he cried. "I kept it with the silver." His eyes went to the bundle, and his face lit up. "You found it. You found my silver. Amida be praised!" Falling to his knees, he embraced the constable's legs.

"Good work," boomed Kobe. "Where was it?"

"Where you said to look, sir. In the young man's clothes chest. Five pieces."

Hanzo's mother cried, "Then that Gombei put it there!"

"Five pieces?" wailed Katahachi. "I had thirty!"

But Kobe was looking at Hanzo's mother. "So," he said. "The constable used no names, but you knew all along your son had the silver. You're both under arrest."

Mrs. Masazaemon turned white. Her son fell to his knees and started weeping. "I didn't kill her," he whimpered. "I swear it. Gombei's trying to pin the murder on me when all I did was take the silver. And there were only fifteen pieces," he wailed with a look at Katahachi, who called him a liar and demanded the other twenty-five.

Gombei was stunned at this betrayal by his erstwhile friend. "He m-must've killed her, because I d-didn't," he stammered, then burst into speech. "He was talking about how easy it would be. He knew where Katahachi kept the silver, and said a penny-pinching fool like him didn't deserve it. I told him I was sworn to uphold the law, but he laughed, saying he'd only been joking, but that it was a good time to visit Tsume because Katahachi was going to the capital and wouldn't be back till late. So we went. Hanzo stayed in the main room, while I went to look for Tsume. She was sleeping in the back of the house, but when I embraced her, she got angry. She called me names, and threw things at me. I was so upset, I ran out the backdoor and home. She must've caught Hanzo stealing the silver, and he killed her."

Hanzo screamed, "He lies! He told me himself that he tried to rape her but she fought him off. He was afraid she'd talk, so he strangled her. When I heard all the shouting, I ran off with the box of silver."

This caused another burst of excitement, and Kobe shouted again for silence. Turning to Akitada, he said softly, "Your idea worked, but one of them is lying."

Akitada shook his head. "No. They're both telling the truth, at least as they see it. I think there's more to come. Why not charge all three and see what happens?"

The guards had established order with their whip handles, and Gombei was rubbing his head, while Hanzo sobbed piteously in the arms of his mother.

Kobe regarded the group in disgust. "All right. The men are charged with attempted rape, murder, and robbery, and the woman with being an accessory. We'll get at the truth with some floggings." He nodded toward Hanzo. "Start with him."

Hanzo screamed when the guards ripped his robe down to his waist.

"No," cried his mother, wrapping her arms around her son. "He didn't kill her. I did."

Shocked silence fell.

The widow released her son and stepped forward. Her voice was flat but firm. "Hanzo told the truth. The girl came to my house and accused him of the theft. She was very disrespectful. My son denied taking the silver, but after she left, I searched his room and found the box. My son is weak, and that Gombei must've put the idea in his head. I took the box with the silver back to Tsume and begged her not to ruin my son. I even offered to give them the rice field to forget the matter, but she wouldn't hear of it. Suddenly something seized hold of me then, some evil demon. I didn't mean to kill her, but my hands went round her neck and I shook her. When I saw that she was dead, I carried her to the well, along with the empty box, to make it look like she'd been killed by robbers. The silver I hid under Hanzo's clothes."

Kobe rose. He seemed to tower over the woman. "You killed the girl?" he roared. "Your obsession with your worthless son caused you to murder an innocent person, and you would've let the monk die for it? And here today you put the blame on Gombei, a disgraceful wretch but neither a thief nor a murderer. Be careful what you say, woman, for your punishment will be severe. The law does not tolerate false accusations."

She threw back her head. "Do with me what you want. I'm a mother. I did it for my son." She turned to embrace Hanzo.

But Hanzo flinched away with a look of horror. "How could you, Mother?" he said. "You've ruined my life."

I. J. Parker

Ennin was walking out of the gate to the Western Prison when Akitada walked in. He looked cleaner and healthier, his hair and beard were trimmed, his eyes were clear, and there was a spring in his step.

"Ah," said Akitada, pausing to admire the clean cotton pants and jacket which had replaced the filthy monk's robe, "You're a changed man, Ennin."

"Yes. And I've taken back my old name. It's Higeyoshi, sir." The ugly man looked down at himself with a grin. "I find the religious life is not for me. In any case, a drunken monk gets in too much trouble, while a drunken brewer of sake, or a poet, or even a high official like you enjoys the respect of all his friends. I'm a master at brewing sake, and not bad at making poems either." He blinked up at the flowering cherry tree above them and recited, "Come cherry flowers! Now's the time for us to go. If we hang about too long, we'll weary our company."

Bowing to Akitada, he smiled sweetly, and walked through the gate in a gust of white petals.

About the Author

I.J. Parker was born and educated in Europe and turned to mystery writing after an academic career in the United States. She published her Akitada stories in *Alfred Hitchcock's Mystery Magazine,* winning the Shamus award in 2000. Several stories have also appeared in collections (*Fifty Years of Crime and Suspense* and *Shaken).* The award-winning "Akitada's First Case" is available as a podcast. Many of the stories are collected in *Akitada and the Way of Justice.*

The Akitada series of crime novels features the same protagonist, an eleventh-century Japanese nobleman/detective. It now consists of ten titles. *The Emperor's Woman* is the latest. Most of the books are available in audio format and have been translated into twelve languages.

Her historical novels are set in twelfth-century Japan during the Heike Wars. The two-volume *The Hollow Reed* tells the story of Toshiko and Sadahira. *The Sword Master* follows the adventures of the swordsman Hachiro.

The Akitada series in chronological order

The Dragon Scroll

Rashomon Gate

Black Arrow

Island of Exiles

The Hell Screen

The Convict's Sword

The Masuda Affair

The Fires of the Gods

Death on an Autumn River

The Emperor's Woman

The Collected Stories

Akitada and the Way of Justice

The Historical Novels

The Hollow Reed I: Dream of a Spring Night

The Hollow Reed II: Dust before the Wind

The Sword Master

I. J. Parker

For more information, please visit I. J. Parker's web site at http:www.ijparker.com. You may write the author at heianmys@aol.com.

Books may be ordered from Amazon and Barnes&Noble. Electronic versions of the novels are available for Kindle and PC. The short stories are on Kindle and Nook. Please do post Amazon reviews. They help sell books and keep Akitada novels coming.

Thank you for your support.

Printed in Great
by Amazon.co.u
Marston Ga